The BLACK STALLION
and the LOST CITY

THE BLACK STALLION SERIES

By Walter Farley

The Black Stallion

The Black Stallion Returns

Son of the Black Stallion

The Island Stallion

The Black Stallion and Satan

The Black Stallion's Blood Bay Colt

The Island Stallion's Fury

The Black Stallion's Filly

The Black Stallion Revolts

The Black Stallion's Sulky Colt

The Island Stallion Races

The Black Stallion's Courage

The Black Stallion Mystery

The Horse-Tamer

The Black Stallion and Flame

Man o' War

The Black Stallion Challenged!

The Black Stallion's Ghost

The Black Stallion and the Girl

The Black Stallion Legend

By Walter Farley and Steven Farley

The Young Black Stallion

By Steven Farley

The Black Stallion's Shadow

The Black Stallion's Steeplechaser

The Black Stallion and the Shape-shifter

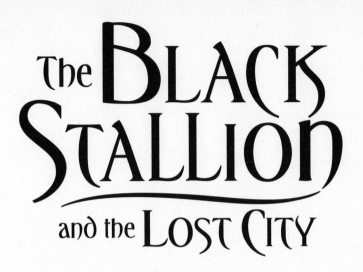

The BLACK STALLION

and the LOST CITY

Steven Farley

Random House 🏠 New York

Published in the United States by Random House Children's Books,
a division of Random House, Inc., New York.

Random House and the colophon are registered trademarks
of Random House, Inc.

Visit us on the Web! www.randomhouse.com/kids

Educators and librarians, for a variety of teaching tools, visit us at
www.randomhouse.com/teachers

Library of Congress Cataloging-in-Publication Data is available upon request.

ISBN 978-0-375-86837-5 (trade) — ISBN 978-0-375-96837-2 (lib. bdg.) —
ISBN 978-0-375-89887-7 (ebook)

Printed in the United States of America

10 9 8 7 6 5 4 3 2 1

First Edition

*To my family
and my animals*

Contents

1

The Race Scene

Hollywood had come to the Balkans. Fresh off his latest sensational blockbuster, acclaimed director Stiv Bateman had set his sights on ancient Greece, Thrace and the story of the young king Alexander the Great. It was an extravagant picture with an extravagant budget, a cast of thousands and big-name stars. It also included the participation of Alec Ramsay—who many horse-racing fans considered to be a real-life young Alexander—and his horse, a real-life Bucephalus, a stallion known only as the Black.

Anyone who followed horse racing had heard about the mysterious Black, a horse as notorious for his personal history as for winning races. The Black's hatred of the whip was legendary in track lore. Rumors hinted the midnight-black stallion had even killed his previous owner, an Arabian tribal sheik, in revenge for mistreating him with a whip. And, as was fabled of the legendary Greek king Alexander and his black stallion

Bucephalus, it was said that no one but Alec Ramsay could ride the Black.

From his hilltop vantage point, Alec looked out over a wide valley crowded with horses, men and machines. They were high in the Rhodope Mountains of Bulgaria in a location that had been chosen just for this scene. It was in a seldom-visited part of Thrace, almost a day's drive from the production headquarters in the city of Xanthi, across the border in Greece. Before them, a thousand actors were taking their places on a prepared battlefield. The small army that was the film crew hung back along the sidelines among towers of lights and camera cranes.

Alec kept an eye on the Black, who nibbled at some grass as they waited together outside the wardrobe and makeup trailers. The stallion was carefully groomed and tacked up in a specially designed saddle, bridle and light armor. Flashes of sunlight danced off a polished copper breastplate lying against his coal-black chest. His ebony mane fringed the contours of his fine head and long, powerful neck, and his silky tail rose and fell behind him like the crest of a black wave.

Alec tried to hold the stallion steady as Leigh, a production assistant from the film's wardrobe department, crouched beside Alec's leg. She fiddled with the hem of his costume, a plain toga of fine linen.

"Keep still, please," she said through a mouthful of safety pins.

Alec did his best not to move, then closed his eyes as Harv, the makeup guy, dusted his face with powder. Through the lead line, he could feel the Black move his head beside him.

"Guess this has been pretty crazy for you," Harv said.

Alec popped open his eyes and blinked. "I'm not used to it," he said, "but it's been fun, really exciting. Who wouldn't want to be part of something like this?"

That was certainly true enough, Alec thought. How often do you get a chance to be in the movies? Even his parents and Henry Dailey had thought it was a great idea. "Take the money and run." Wasn't that what everyone had said he should do? It still amazed Alec that the film's publicity people had asked him to stand in as Alexander in a few scenes and had been willing to spend so much money to make it happen. Just for starters, his airfare over here with the Black must have cost thousands of dollars. Certainly it was the Black they really wanted, more than Alec himself. Few horses in the world could project his strength and beauty. It made Alec proud to think other people recognized this fact too.

Harv chuckled and gave Alec another swipe with the powder brush. Alec closed his eyes again and took a deep breath. No matter how well he and the Black were being treated, somehow he still couldn't help but ask himself what he was doing there—though it was a little late to be wondering about that now. He knew before he took this job that it wouldn't be as simple as everyone made it out to be.

Sure, he thought, everyone was nice, and the food and accommodations were first-rate, but all the waiting around was driving him crazy. As the producer had promised, Alec didn't really have to do much acting; he just had to show up for some riding scenes and a few stand-in shots like this one. So far, all Alec and the Black had done was some close-up work with the Black and an interview with Alec for a supplemental behind-the-scenes feature.

This time Alec and the Black were doubling for Alexander and Bucephalus in a shot that would lead up to one of the battle scenes. Bateman said he wanted a look that only the Black could give him.

A young woman carrying a clipboard walked toward them. "They want you on the set, Alec, whenever you're ready."

Harv handed Alec his bronze helmet and helped him get it centered and adjusted on his head and around his face.

Five minutes later, Alec and the Black were down on the set. Spread out before them were many, many actors and extras costumed as ancient Greek soldiers and armed with shields and spears. Some were assembled into blocks of infantry so tightly grouped together that they functioned as a single weapon, like a human tank bristling with spears. Behind the porcupine-like phalanxes of warriors stood hundreds of horses and riders, everyone waiting for the fanfare that was the signal to begin.

Marshals in golf carts shuttled between the different groups of infantry and riders, doing crowd control. Muscle-bound actors with long hair roping out from under their helmets argued and laughed. Sour-faced old guys watched the clock. Photographers' lights flashed as the actors and extras posed in the warrior outfits, everyone standing around, everyone passing time, waiting, waiting, waiting, everyone finding it almost impossible to stay busy. These were moments of patience for some, moments of nervousness for newcomers and a traffic jam of anticipation for everyone.

Alec's attention gravitated to the horses. He marveled at how many breeds were represented here. There were Arabians with flowing manes and tails, compact Andalusians and statuesque white Lipizzans. All were decked out in plumes, skirts of armor and breast and head plates, some with unicorn spikes, all meant to recall warhorses from ancient times.

Positioned along the edges of the battlefield, technicians were making last-minute adjustments. Some wore headphones and fiddled with soundboards. Others were hunched over consoles lined with blinking meters and dials. To one side, crane trucks with hydraulic lifts hoisted camera operators in baskets up into the air.

Alec took it all in, scanning the crowd for familiar faces. He recognized the producer Freddy Roth in his sport jacket and jeans, arms folded across his chest, eyes focused, apparently deep in thought. On the other side of the field, he saw Karst Balastritis standing with his sixteen-year-old son, Matt, and thirteen-year-old daughter, Xeena. The three were working for the production team, Karst as a top trainer and Matt and Xeena as wranglers and assistants. Matt and Xeena were doubling as extras and stunt riders too.

Karst was one of the first people Alec had met when he arrived in Xanthi almost a week ago. He was a proud native of this land, a big, gregarious man with dark hair and olive skin. Karst and his kids reminded Alec of a close-knit circus family—athletic, hardworking and full of energy.

Someone called his name, and Alec turned to see Jeff, the assistant to Freddy Roth. The skinny, young Australian wore aviator sunglasses and a New York Yankees baseball cap turned backwards. A jumble of laminated ID cards hung like medallions around his neck.

"There's been some rethinking about the schedule and the next scene," Jeff told Alec. "We just got the latest weather report, and they're calling for a chance of rain tomorrow. Stiv wants to stage the race in front of the assembled troops before the big battle scene now, when the weather is good, rather than risking a washout tomorrow. The course is all marked out down by the river. You know where I'm talking about?"

Alec nodded. "I walked it with Karst yesterday."

"Great," Jeff said as he started to hurry off. "See you there."

The last-minute change in plans was a pleasant surprise for Alec. He'd been looking forward to the race scene. Alec and the Black were to play the parts of Alexander and Bucephalus for the riding sequence and were to win the race. It would be a natural for the Black, Alec thought, and probably their biggest scene in the entire film. They wouldn't even have to act. If nothing else, it would be more exciting than the beauty-pageant posing he had been doing up to now.

A few minutes later, the horses picked for the race were grouped down by the river. Karst and the other trainers had done a good job in selecting the runners, and it was plain to see that these were some of the best-looking horses of the hundreds assembled there for the battle scene. Some were long-limbed and lean. Others were compact and solid. All looked fit, capable and ready to race.

Just off the riverbank in an idling speedboat, Stiv Bateman and a camera crew waited to film the race. The director, a burly man with a heavy beard, military boots and camouflage pants, sat in a raised chair near the bow of the boat. Two other camera boats were floating farther upstream. Radio static from walkie-talkies crackled in the air.

The horses lined up for the start at a spot marked by a strip of white tape on the ground. A short distance from where the tape ended, a heavy-duty pickup truck idled, ready to track the race from onshore. Mounted on the back of the truck was a small cherry picker. From his roost in a basket atop the crane's arm, a camera operator fiddled with his equipment, then leaned forward to frame up the shot in his viewfinder. Another team of photographers stood behind a camera on a tripod positioned in the grass. Next to them, the assistant director paced back and forth like a football coach on the sidelines of a big game. A guy holding a clapboard slate stood ready to identify the scene and take number.

Alec sat up and tested the spring in his stirrups. It didn't matter now that he was dressed in some silly costume of an ancient Greek king. This was a race, even if it was just a staged one, and Alec and the Black were in their element. Alec rested his face against the Black's neck, his eyes focused ahead, his knees pressed against the stallion's shoulders.

Once the horses were more or less in position, Bateman called out, "Okay, people. Get into character now, but wait for my signal to go. Ready. Speed!"

"Speed!" echoed the soundman from his position offscreen. The assistant with the clapboard stepped in front of the camera. "*Young Alexander,* scene seventeen-B, take—"

Suddenly there was a squeal from one of the horses. The assistant standing in front of the camera jumped back to get out of the way as two runners broke from their positions in line and charged ahead in a false start.

"I said to wait for my signal!" Bateman cried out impatiently.

Outriders caught up to the horses before they could get too far and helped steer them back to the starting line. Meanwhile, Alec and the other riders did their best steadying their mounts and keeping the line intact.

Finally the two runaways were back in place, and the sound and cameras started to roll once again.

"Action!" Bateman called from his perch on the bow.

There was an instant of relative stability and then they were off. The camera-laden speedboats in the river wound up their engines and moved out in pursuit.

Voices filled the air as the riders urged on their horses. A colt on the outside bounced out and half reared before his rider could set him on his way. The rest bolted off in a mad panic. In a split second, Alec had the Black after them.

The Black gathered himself and settled into stride. Alec coaxed the stallion along and guided him closer to the river's edge on his right. The Black felt good and was anxious to run after so much standing around over the past few days. The horses swerved and started to bunch up as they approached a bend in the river.

Alec did his best to hold the Black back. Bateman's instructions were for a come-from-behind win to the race, with a close finish. But, as always, once he got going, the stallion wanted to run all out. This was just another race to the Black, and he would do whatever he could to get out in front. Alec could feel the pull in the reins all the way to his shoulders.

As the horses swung into the right-hand turn, Alec switched modes and went from restraining the Black to encouraging him. The Black responded and they galloped into the middle of the pack, slowly gaining ground on the others.

Alec moved with the stallion as they came out of the turn. Edging farther to the inside, he pulled the Black just to the left of a big gray colt running hard a length off the water's edge. The Black paced the horse a moment, then started to pull away. Alec saw a lead runner directly in front of the Black was losing steam and coming back fast. He guided the Black to the right and started to drop in, just in front of the gray, moving to the inside slot along the river where there was a clear path to the lead.

Suddenly the gray's rider shouted a warning. There was someone running up the inside that Alec couldn't see! Even worse, with the gray blocking the view, the oncoming rider hadn't seen Alec make his move for the inside path either.

On a professional racetrack it might have been different. There the gray's rider would have known that it was his responsibility to give a heads-up to the other riders in such a situation, especially when two horses running hard on either side of him were making for the same spot and couldn't see each other. But this wasn't a racetrack and these riders weren't jockeys. By the time Alec heard the gray's rider call out, it was too late. The Black was already on a collision course with the inside runner, a big bay who was sprinting ahead like a mad demon and trying to squeeze his way between the gray and the riverbank.

Once he realized what was happening, Alec had no choice but to check the Black with a hard pull on the reins. It kept him from dropping in on the bay, but it was too late for the bay and the gray running next to him. Blocked to the left by the fading leader, and in front by the Black, the gray was trapped. He spooked and broke hard to the right, careening off course and taking the approaching bay with him. Instantly the two horses went flying over the riverbank, hitting the water six feet below with a mighty splash.

Over the clamor of grunting horses and shouting riders, Alec could hear Bateman calling out orders from one of the camera-laden speedboats that had been tracking the runners from the river.

"Keep the camera on them!" Bateman squawked over his bullhorn from his position on the bow.

Alec pulled the Black up and circled around to see if he could help the riders who had gone into the river. Down in the water the horses were shrilling. A minute later, they and their riders scrambled up a low spot in the embankment. Alec recognized one of them as Karst's daughter Xeena and suddenly realized she was the rider who had been caught on the inside when the gray spooked and charged the river. Thankfully no one seemed to have been injured in the spill beyond a few scratches and getting wet. Xeena and the gray's rider were already laughing it off. What a relief, Alec thought. He knew there was no way he could have prevented the accident, though he and the Black certainly had been a factor in causing it. In the end, there was no one to blame.

"That was terrific," Alec could hear Bateman call out to the riders from the water as they turned their horses back to the staging area. "Bonuses all around for you people. Now let's go back and do it again. Just try to stay out of the drink this time."

2

Acracia

The Rhodope Lodge, where Alec was staying, housed a cavernous dining room, and that night it was packed with cast and crew. Everyone was eating at different tables, more or less self-segregated according to job description—actors with actors, carpenters with carpenters, camera people with camera people. Alec took a plate of food from the buffet and found a place with some of the horse folk, Karst Balastritis, Xeena and Matt. It was easy to see that the three were related. All had the same curly black hair, broad shoulders, sharp eyes and high cheekbones. And there was something else, too, Alec thought, something in their bearing that set them apart from the rest of the people here.

The Balastritises were speaking in Greek, but when Alec joined them, they switched to English, a language they all spoke quite well, especially Xeena and Matt. Alec appreciated the courtesy, as he knew only a few words of Greek. Karst watched him with warm, friendly eyes and a smile that made people feel good every time he turned it on.

Matt was talking excitedly about how he had landed the job of wrangler for a scene Bateman was shooting the next day. It would mean an extra bonus for him. Karst was saying it was a lot of money for someone his age and that he shouldn't let the bonus go to his head. Karst's voice was stern, but Alec could see pride in the trainer's face as well.

"Go to his head?" Xeena teased. "Not Matt. He already thinks this film is really about him."

Her brother gave her a smile and laughed. "Please, little sister," he said. "I am just doing my job here. You should do yours and try to keep from riding your horses into the river."

Xeena's eyes flashed. "You know that wasn't my fault," she said. "You saw it, Alec. Could I have helped what happened during the race? What choice did I have? It was either go into the river or get run over."

Alec nodded his head in agreement. "It looked that way to me."

"Let's just say I'm not surprised that if somebody had to go off course, it would be you," Matt teased.

Karst held up his hands. "Enough, you two," he said in his thick Greek accent. "Everyone doing fine and no one blaming anyone for anything. Now quit fighting and eat your dinner."

Halfway through the meal, Jeff, the producer Roth's assistant, came over to their table. Jeff congratulated Alec on his ride that day. He said the scene looked great, and the footage of the accident was a real bonus. Bateman was saying that the horses flying off the riverbank and splashing into the river had turned out to look spectacular.

"And tomorrow?" Karst asked Jeff. "I hear there is big schedule change."

Jeff laughed. "Yes, well, big changes at the last minute seem to be par for the course with Stiv."

"Hokay," Karst said. "You the boss."

Jeff smiled and shook his head. "I'm just a link in the chain on this job, like you. Anyhow, the word is that now the weatherman says it's not going to rain tomorrow after all. That means the crew will be splitting up into three different units—red, blue and black. Matt, you are staying here to work on the battle scene with the red and blue units, like we talked about earlier."

Matt nodded eagerly.

"Alec, you and the Black are with the black unit and will be heading up into the mountains. The trip will probably take most of the day, depending on the road conditions. Once you reach the location site, you'll spend the night there. The following day, after the scene is set up, Stiv will helicopter in and supervise the shot."

Jeff asked Karst and Matt to go over to Bateman's table and meet with some of the camera and lighting guys. They wanted to talk over some particulars about the different shots they were planning for tomorrow.

"So, what is the place we're going to?" Alec asked Jeff after Karst and Matt left to meet with Bateman.

Jeff sat down at the table with Alec and Xeena. He took a roll from the bread basket. "Some monastic refuge in a place called Acracia," he said between bites. "It's supposed to be beautiful there. Lots of wildlife, some small forest reserve up in the mountains, no roads, no houses or towns the cameras would have to work around. Just unobstructed views, trees and wide mountain vistas, much like what the area might have looked like back in Alexander's day."

"Sounds great," Alec said. "Where is it?"

"Up on Mt. Atnos," Jeff said. "It's in an area that is usually closed to the public. It took months to get the okay to film there, and we had to pay a hefty fee. The permission just came through, which is another reason for the last-minute change in plans. The monks don't allow cars on the premises, so we have to stay at a compound outside the monastery. There is no electricity either. We'll manage with our generators, though."

A moment later, Karst and Matt came back to their table.

"Alec and the Black are going up to Mt. Atnos tomorrow," Xeena said excitedly, "to the monastery in Acracia."

"Boss say I go with them," Karst said. "You come too." From the way the family exchanged glances, it was obvious the names meant more to them than just spots on the map.

"I still can't believe it," Matt said. "I didn't think the monks let anyone up there anymore."

"Me neither," Xeena said.

Karst shook his head. "I no believe it too. Boss must have pay much, much money."

"I wish I was going with you," Matt said, "especially after all the stories Popi used to tell about those woods when we were little."

"You have'a your hands full right here," Karst said. "You do good job, make family proud." His eyes shifted to the exit. "Now we go for sleeping. We wake up early tomorrow."

Shortly after daybreak, crews worked to get the convoy of horse vans, camera cars and equipment trucks in the black unit ready to set off for Mt. Atnos. There were about a dozen vehicles in all, including a truck carrying a cargo of snakes that were to play a part in a scene planned for the black-unit shoot. As the cages were being loaded onto the truck, Conrad, one of the snake wranglers, showed Alec his favorite one, a four-foot-long leopard snake he called Litzy. Conrad draped her around his neck and cooed gently to the snake as if she were a beloved pet. Like her breed's namesake, Litzy had spotted markings, and Conrad maintained that her species was the most beautiful of all European snakes.

"Looks like a viper but she ain't," Conrad said in his heavy British accent. "You can tell because she don't have the vertical pupils. See? Most all vipers have vertical pupils." He held the snake's head up so Alec could see the shining black stones of her eyes. "Want to hold her?" Conrad asked.

Snakes didn't bother Alec as they did some people, but he wasn't interested in having one crawl around his neck just then. "No thanks," Alec said. "The Black is sensitive about snakes. If the smell gets on me, it might startle him. I love her leopard spots, though. Very stylish."

Conrad chuckled. "She's a beauty, all right," he said, then gently returned Litzy to her cage.

Alec turned and started to where the Black was stabled. Jeff was sitting in a golf cart parked beside the line of trucks and vans and waved Alec over. He looked at Alec and smiled. "Don't tell me—Conrad was showing off his pets again?"

Alec laughed and asked Jeff about the snakes and

what they had to do with the story of Alexander. Jeff explained that the snakes were part of the film's dream sequence they would be shooting the next day.

"In the dream, Alexander's mother has a vision of her yet-to-be-born son as a two-year-old," Jeff said. "The child is alone, lost in the mountain wilderness and threatened by snakes." Jeff shook his head. "Stiv loves snakes," he explained, "and always tries to work them into his films if he can."

Alec soon saw that, aside from the snakes, there were a number of other animals the black-unit crew was bringing to the mountain shoot with them. There were a few stable ponies for riding horses, a pair of big bay geldings and a beautiful dark-brown, almost black Andalusian mare named Tina that was standing in for Bucephalus in some scenes, like the Black. In addition, there were a couple of goats for background scenery, four or five ducks and a pair of trained weasels.

Finally all was ready and the convoy started off. Alec and the Black rode in Karst's van. Xeena sat on the bench seat between Alec and her dad. Every so often, Alec checked on the Black by peering over the partition into the stallion's stall in the back of the van.

Soon they came to the switchback road that led

up the mountain. Karst expertly navigated the van over the narrow, winding road while Alec looked out the window at the unspoiled forest below. With Xeena's help, Karst passed the time by explaining to Alec that this area was renowned as the homeland of the mythological singer Orpheus. Even now it was fabled that there were enchanted woods here in which whole cities could hide and never be found. There were other tall tales about places that had no deer, squirrels or birds, places shunned by humans and forest animals alike, places where a stream of poisoned water would madden or kill any animal that drank from it.

Karst laughed. "All crazy talk, stories for children. No reason be afraid. Water good here. Best in Thrace. Plenty animals."

The road wound along the edge of a steep valley and then led to a site of broken columns, a long-forgotten ruin from ancient times. "Look at the kites," Xeena said, pointing out a pair of large black birds perched like shadowy sentries atop the remains of a stone wall.

Alec watched the scenery sleepily and was starting to drift off when the convoy stopped to get coffee and fuel and to check their gear. As Karst mingled with the rest of the crew, Alec tended to the Black. The stallion was a good traveler when he wanted to be and dozed quietly in the back of the van. Alec adjusted the stable blanket, which was slipping off on one side.

Xeena came around to the rear of the van and peeked over the open half doors.

"Everything okay?" she asked.

"Shhh," Alec said, pressing a finger to his lips. He quietly slipped out of the Black's stall.

"He's sleeping?" she asked. Alec nodded. Xeena handed him a can of soda. "I thought you might be thirsty," she said.

Over by the cafeteria truck, the voices of the crew rose and fell, laughing, arguing, English mixed with Greek, German, Italian and languages Alec didn't recognize at all. Alec and Xeena sat on a picnic table at the edge of the parking lot.

"So tell me your story, Xeena," Alec said. "I really don't know much about your family except that you come from Xanthi. That and you are all pretty good riders."

"Thanks," Xeena said. "That means a lot coming from you."

"Xanthi seems like a nice place," Alec said. "Has your family always lived there?"

"For a long time. Why?"

"You just seem different than the others."

"What do you mean?"

Alec fumbled for an explanation. "I don't know. There is just something in the way you all carry yourselves, your expressions. It is as if nothing could surprise you."

"We are Thracian," Xeena said. "This land is our home. Our ancestors came from Acracia. Only full-blooded Thracians lived there."

"Acracia?" Alec asked. "Isn't that where we're going now?"

"We're going to the monastery," Xeena said. "The village of Acracia no longer exists. Even when it did, it was small and hard to find, or so the old folks say. It wasn't even on most maps."

"What happened to it?" Alec asked.

Xeena shrugged. "Mom's family left a long time ago. My grandfather Popi was born there, but his family left soon after."

"Why?"

"The goats weren't giving milk. The sheep were dying. Some said it had to do with the water, something about a small, illegal mine that polluted the river upstream. No one really knows the truth. I don't think there is anything wrong with the water anymore, though. The last I heard, the place had been turned into some super-exclusive health resort."

"Have you ever been there?" Alec asked.

"To the resort?" Xeena said. "No."

"You live this close and you have never been there? Why not?"

"Access to the resort is even more restrictive than to the monastery," she said. "The monastery is in the forest reserve on the other side of the mountain. No one I know, or ever heard of, has been to the resort part of the mountain where my grandfather's village used to be."

"Sounds mysterious," Alec said.

"It is," Xeena said. "My cousin tried to get a job there once, but it turned out that all the workers at the resort come from faraway places in Asia. They live on the premises and don't go to town. All supplies are delivered by their own trucks. Someone else said the resort isn't even in business anymore, but no one seems to know for sure. As for my grandfather's village, all that is left are stories."

Karst came around the side of the van and called Xeena over. He spoke to his daughter in rapid Greek. Xeena hurried over to one of the horse vans parked beside them.

"Hokay, Alec," he said, "We go now. Xeena go with other van. You go with me."

Alec did another quick check on the Black and made sure everything in the back of the van was secure and in order. Then he closed the rear half doors and swung up into his seat in the van with Karst.

"Xeena ride with Thomas," the trainer said. "Some his horses, uh . . . not quiet. She help."

The convoy started off again, and soon they were crawling up the switchback road. Alec saw that there was more light in the sky now, the sun bringing warmth into the day.

A tour bus pulled beside them on a straightaway, honking its horn and barreling ahead. Karst made a hand gesture out the window and grumbled an oath in Greek. The bus sent a cloud of dust pouring over them as it roared by. Other than that, there was little traffic, though at one point a line of shiny black Mercedeses with darkened windows flew by in the other direction. "Government cars," Karst said with a laugh. "Big bosses."

In a few minutes, they were surrounded by woods once more. Vast trees on either side interlocked their leafy, moss-covered branches above them. Alec gazed through the windshield at the tunnel of trees and the darker shadows of the woods beyond. Ghostly vapors and traces of mist hung low to the ground in small clearings. Spears of sunlight streaked down through the swaying treetops and flickered on the road ahead. He could hear birdsongs, and the wind coming through the open window carried the scent of forest flowers.

Karst leaned his head out the window and drew in a great breath of air and let it out. "Air nice here," he said. "Mountains make clean. Clear. All the time nice, a' clear."

For many miles, the convoy passed in and out of tree tunnels and through more forest groves and rock gardens. The road divided and a sign, written in Greek, German, English and French, indicated the way to the scenic overlook in the forest reserve. Pointing the other way was another sign, lettered in a language that Alec couldn't read, perhaps Greek or Bulgarian. This was the direction they followed.

The twisting road rose and fell as the convoy made its way up the mountain. The curves were sharp, and in some places the van was forced to slow to a crawl to safely get around them. Alec looked at his watch and realized they had already been traveling for more than five hours.

Soon the road dipped again, running down to a fifty-foot-long wooden bridge that spanned a roiling white-water river. The convoy eased carefully over the bridge and after another mile came to a narrow lane leading off to the south. They turned onto the lane. It was a rougher ride, and the road was splotched in places with dried mud. After about a quarter mile, just over the crest of a hill, they saw the high walls of the monastery.

Two monks, with beards and clean-shaven heads

and wearing heavy robes belted by thick white ropes, were waiting for them at a gate barricading the driveway. After opening the gate, the taller of the two set off up the driveway on foot and gestured for the trucks to follow him.

The monk led them toward a compound of low stone buildings just outside the twenty-foot-high monastery walls. Alongside the outbuildings were rows of white tents set up around a spacious brick courtyard. Karst told Alec the tents had been prepared by a crew that came up last night and had been working all day to get everything ready for their arrival. Each tent served a different purpose. Some were stables for the animals, while others were wardrobe, makeup and dressing rooms for the actors.

The vans and equipment trucks crept ahead and then pulled over to the side of the drive. Alec looked over at the monastery, where he could see the castlelike tops of towers inside the fortified building. "Not bad for summer house," Karst joked. "We stay outside. Monks no like visitors."

Daylight hours were short here in the mountains, even in the summer. The sun was already dipping below the mountaintops by the time Alec had finished unloading the Black from the van and making the stallion comfortable in his tent.

The Black's tent was almost the size of a two-car garage, plenty big enough to accommodate the stallion and its other occupants, the pair of scruffy-looking white goats Alec had seen loading up earlier. The portable stalls inside the tent were made of iron bars, wood and plastic, and it amazed Alec how quickly the carpenters had been able to snap them together. The Black's box stall was large and roomy, with straw bedding covering the ground. There was a wide aisle that contained an area for Alec to keep the gear and supplies he'd brought with him: tack trunks, a couple sacks of feed, blankets, saddles and fold-up stable cots. The tent walls were pegged tight and weighted down with sandbags. Stabled in the next tent were the wranglers' riding ponies, including Cleo, Xeena's favorite. There was another tent for Tina and the other picture horses, and smaller tents for the weasels, snakes and ducks.

Beyond the row of animal tents, in a corner of the compound about forty yards away, the camera crew and other technicians were already busy blocking out a shot and setting up for the director's arrival by chopper the next day. Alec helped tend the other horses but mostly just kept an eye on the Black.

A production assistant showed Alec to his lodgings, a small corner room located in one of the larger outbuildings that surrounded the courtyard. There was a bed, a chair and a table on which sat a large empty

bowl and a pitcher of water. The bathroom was down
at the end of the hall.

Alec washed up and changed his shirt. There was
no mirror in the bathroom, or in his room for that
matter, and he wondered if maybe the monks didn't
believe in them.

When it was time for dinner, Alec set off across
the courtyard and past the outbuildings that were
being used as housing for the production staff, actors
and crew. The buildings appeared so similar that Alec
wondered how he was ever going to find his way back
to his own room again.

Soon he saw a group of people filing through the
high, arched doorway of the building that was apparently serving as the crew's dining room. It didn't take
long for him to realize that the building had been a
large stable at one time, probably more than a century
ago. Alec got a kick out of the thought that the crew
had brought portable stables for the horses and other
animals, and they were now going to be eating in the
original stable.

The room was spacious enough for the fifty or
sixty men and women gathered there. Tables and chairs
were set up in rows to accommodate everyone. The
food was tasty—meat, vegetables and soup, simple but
plentiful—all supplied courtesy of the film producers
and excellently prepared by the location catering staff.

Neither Karst nor Xeena were in the dining area, and Alec figured they must have eaten earlier. He found a place at a table with a pair of young women who turned out to be set carpenters from California. They talked about the ride up through the woods and the quality of the food, and they wondered about the mysterious inhabitants of the monastery. Alec looked around the room once again and could see no sign of the monks who lived in this place.

After dinner, he grabbed his flashlight and walked out to the stable area to check on the Black. He had already given the stallion his supper an hour earlier, a light meal of barley, hay and oats. Alec had brought feed with him all the way from Hopeful Farm, just to be safe.

Alec broke out a pair of soft brushes from the tack trunk and gave the Black a quick grooming for the fun of it. The stallion leaned into the brush strokes with pleasure, then grew impatient and stepped away.

"Had enough, eh?" Alec said. The Black tossed his head affirmatively. Alec smiled. "I know, I know. You want to get outside and do a little exploring. Well, you just have to wait until morning for that."

Alec shuffled his feet through the straw spread out on the floor of the Black's stall. "Look," he said. "It's not so bad here. All the nice bedding we brought in for

you. Why, you're living like a king's horse. Like old
Mister Bucephalus himself."

The Black turned to look out the tent entrance at
the forest beyond. He pricked his ears and raised his
head as if scenting something in the draft of wind leaking through the tent flaps, perhaps something not so
far away. But soon the draft died and the stallion lost
interest, switching his attention to the hay net hanging
in the corner of his stall.

A few minutes later, Alec pocketed his flashlight
and walked out to drink in the night and enjoy the
great, sweet silence of the mountains. A light wind
came from the direction of the monastery. It carried an
odd scent with it, a smell he quickly realized must be
incense burning in the monastery temple.

Above him, the stars sprinkled in the sky mixed
easily with the few isolated specks of light coming
from houses on a distant mountain. Against the cold,
dark backdrop of trees, it was almost impossible to tell
the difference between the house lights and the lower
stars. His gaze shifted along the deep vista, back to
Acracia and the mist-shrouded peaks of Mt. Atnos,
where he could see no lights at all.

3

Diomedes

Alec didn't feel tired, so he decided to take a stroll and enjoy the night. Outside the tent, a few oil lamps hung from tree branches and cast a soft glow over the courtyard grounds. He followed a walkway through the yard to a grass path veering off into the woods. Wondering where it led, he flicked on his flashlight and angled the beam up the path. Suddenly the light blinked off. Alec gave the flashlight a shake, and it came back on again. He made a mental note to put in new batteries when he got back to his room. Without a dependable flashlight, it was hardly wise to go trailblazing. On the other hand, he was still feeling restless after the long ride here and figured the walk might do him some good. He followed the path a little farther as it wound through the woods.

After a minute, he noticed someone with a lantern standing in a clearing up ahead. He drew closer and saw it was Xeena. She seemed to be gazing wistfully up at the mountains and the site of her lost ancestral home, now sealed off from the rest of the world inside the confines of the exclusive Acracian resort.

Alec didn't want to startle her out here in the dark, so to make some noise, he began whistling. He also switched his flashlight on and off.

Xeena turned and waved. "Hey there," she called.

"Lovely night," Alec said. "Not too cold."

Soon they were both gazing up at the stars, trying to identify the different constellations.

"Do you believe in astrology, Alec?" Xeena said after a minute.

Alec shrugged. "There might be something to it, but personally, no, not really. I don't know much about it. Do you?"

"My grandfather used to say our destiny is written in the stars. Popi believed some people could read omens and see prophecy in the night sky. He told me that there is a long history of fortune-telling in these mountains—at least there used to be."

Alec was about to say something but Xeena cut him off. "And he wasn't some superstitious old fool either, just because he believed in astrology," Xeena said defensively.

"I wasn't going to say that," Alec said.

"Popi was smart. He had a gift with languages— learned to speak English on his own. He was the one who taught me. He was also a successful businessman, even though his family was poor when they came to the city. He worked hard, bought a restaurant, then another, then a house and an apartment building. When he disappeared, he was quite wealthy."

"He disappeared?"

Xeena nodded. "One day he just sold everything, emptied his bank account and vanished. The police don't know what happened to him. My father thinks some criminals may have tricked him out of his money and killed him."

"That's awful," Alec said.

"I like to think he just wanted to run off and live by himself, maybe on an island somewhere. He was that type of person. In some ways he never really liked the city, and after my grandmother died . . ." Her voice trailed off.

Alec gestured to the dark side of the mountain. "So nobody lives up there now, aside from the people in the resort?"

Xeena nodded. "It's always been sort of a touchy subject for our families," she said. "No one even talks about the village we came from anymore. What I've learned, I had to find out for myself. Popi used to tell stories about his village that he'd heard as a little boy, stories about a secret horse cult that lived in the forest since ancient times, a cult that worshiped the Thracian god king Diomedes at a secret temple hidden in the woods. Popi said they even claimed to guard the bloodline of a fabled breed of horse that counted Alexander's stallion Bucephalus among its own."

"I thought Diomedes was a hero in the *Iliad*," Alec said. "Or was it the *Odyssey*?"

Xeena shook her head. "That was another Diomedes," she said. "This Diomedes was anything but a hero."

Alec nodded. "I've heard about some of those horse cults living in other parts of Europe in olden times, horrible stories about horses being killed in ritual sacrifices to warriors and kings."

"It was the other way around here," Xeena said. "Here people weren't sacrificing horses to people. Here it was the people who were sacrificed to the horses."

"People being sacrificed to horses?" Alec said. "That's a new one on me."

"These weren't ordinary horses," she said. "You should brush up on your history, Alec. Haven't you ever heard of the labors of Hercules?"

"Sure," Alec said, "at least the one about Hercules cleaning out some king's stables."

Xeena laughed. "I guess that makes sense," she said. "Well, one of his other tasks was to rid the Thracian Bistones of four man-killing mares owned by the king there, horses so fierce they had to be tethered with chains because they could eat right through leather and rope."

"Sounds like a horse I knew once," Alec said.

"The king Diomedes who ruled the Bistones was a cruel demigod, a tyrant descended from Ares—the Greek god of war—and a mortal woman. Hercules captured the king's mares but not before they killed Hercules's friend Abderus, and Diomedes too. According to the myth, Hercules drove the four mares all the way back to Eurystheus, where they were reformed of their bad habits."

"All's well that ends well," Alec said lightly.

"But there is another version of the story," Xeena said, "in which the mares escaped and fled up Mt. Atnos where they were adopted by a tribe of Acracians who lived there."

"Amazing story," Alec said. "And a bit creepy too."

"This is Thrace," Xeena said. "The Greek gods who ruled here weren't all pious and perfect like in some other places. Ours were more like a big, squabbling family, with all the good and bad. They could be noble and kind, but also vain and jealous. They were always fighting among each other and always falling in love with mortals or tormenting them."

A thread of silver light streaked through the sky

and vanished a second later. "Look," Alec said, "there's a falling star. Make a wish."

Xeena stiffened. "I am almost fourteen, Alec," she said. "Wishes are for children."

Alec shook his head. "No, they're not," he said. "It's okay to dream."

"Not if it's an impossible dream." Her gaze returned to the dark side of the mountain.

"Sometimes we don't know what is possible and what isn't," Alec said. "Look at me and the Black. He's desert born, from Arabia. I'm from New York City. Who would have ever guessed that we would have found each other or that we would have lived the lives we have lived together? Things happen. Last month I never would have believed that tonight I would be on some far-off mountain staring up into a Thracian sky."

"To tell you the truth," Xeena said, "neither did I. I am just a kid from Xanthi who happens to know how to ride a little. And that is only because my dad had a job at the mayor's horse farm, and I had an opportunity the other kids didn't. The only people I've known in my life up to now are my family, some of the neighbors and the people I met in school. Now I am hanging out with famous guys like you, and getting paid to do it."

"You have skills, Xeena," Alec said. "You can ride well, and that's why you are here."

The girl's gaze returned to the dark side of the mountain. "That's kind of you to say," she said, and sighed. "It just feels funny to be this close to a place I've wondered about all my life and not be able to go there."

"Maybe you'll get there someday."

Xeena tried to laugh. "Sure. Maybe I'll win the lottery too."

Alec didn't understand Xeena's pessimism, especially at her age. "You never know," he said. "Somebody has to win. Anyhow, you can always dream."

Xeena shrugged. "My dad says you should always hope for the best but prepare for the worst. Maybe that's the difference between Thracians and Americans. Maybe we know a little more about how hard life can be than you Americans do."

"I wouldn't say that," Alec said with a smile. "Life can be hard anywhere."

They stood there a minute more and then walked back toward the monastery in a comfortable silence. "So you ready for tomorrow?" Alec asked.

"Sure. I am going to be in one of the riding scenes, dressed as a warrior."

"Sounds good," Alec said.

"Jeff told me that they will need every person here

who can sit a horse," Xeena said. They talked a little more about the plan for tomorrow and then said their good-nights.

Alec turned down the walkway leading to the Black's tent. He checked on his horse one last time and then, with a yawn, started toward his room and a well-deserved rest. The beam from his flashlight swept up and down the path as he walked along, trying to keep from stumbling over the uneven brick paving.

Finding his way to his quarters, Alec stepped inside the arched doorway and down a short hallway. The door to his corner room wasn't locked, and he stepped inside the dark, shadowy interior.

At that exact moment, his flashlight blinked off again. Alec slapped it against his thigh a couple times to get it working again. As he did, he noticed an odd, musty odor in the air, a smell that hadn't been there when he left the room before.

The light snapped on again, and Alec quickly realized that this wasn't his room at all. He must have gotten turned around somehow and come to the wrong place. This looked like some sort of exhibit room. There were framed black-and-white photographs on the walls and broken pieces of statuary standing in the corners. Curiosity made him direct the beam of light to a pair of long, low glass and wooden display cases lining the walls on one side of the room.

Inside the cabinets were what looked at first like vases and broken pots. As he looked closer through the glass front of one of the cases, he realized that the shelves were laden not with relics but with human skulls and bones.

At first the sight of the old bones startled him, but then curiosity once again got the best of him, and he pointed the flashlight at the framed photographs on the wall. One showed a pair of monks holding shovels and standing in a garden. In a hole in the ground beside them were uncovered pieces of an ancient Greek statue.

Alec stepped over to a wooden bookcase, its top shelf lined with old hardcover volumes, all written in Bulgarian, Greek and German. On a lower shelf was a stack of dusty pamphlets. The paper was brown and brittle with age, probably dating to the mid-twentieth century. Like the books, most of the pamphlets were written in languages Alec couldn't read. Only one was in English. Glancing through it, he realized that at one time there must have been regular visitors to this monastery and that this room must have been some sort of historical archive for the place. Apparently the bones and other artifacts were relics the monks had discovered while gardening or digging foundations for new buildings.

The flashlight started flickering on and off again,

and he quickly left the room. He took the pamphlet with him, hoping no one would mind and figuring he could return it in the morning after he'd had a chance to read it.

Retracing his steps through the courtyard, Alec reached the place where the path divided and he had made a wrong turn, arriving at last at his own room. He lit the lamp and checked all around the room just to make sure that he was in the right place this time and that there weren't any skulls rolling around on the floor. The sight of those old bones in the glass cases still lingered in his mind, and he couldn't help but feel a little uneasy about it now. He doused his face with water from the pitcher on the table. Taking a chair, he picked up the pamphlet he'd borrowed from the visitors' room and began to read.

As he thumbed through the pages, much of them detailing the long history of the monastery and the austere life the monks led there, he found one section that caught his eye. It was a chapter on Diomedes, the Greek demigod Xeena had told him about earlier, and the significance he had to this region. According to one legend, the pamphlet said, the demigod had chosen the forests of Mt. Atnos as a sanctuary to rebuild his kingdom after his defeat at the hands of Hercules. Alec leaned back in his chair and read more about the mysterious Diomedes:

The true history of the tyrant Diomedes is lost in time, but there are many fanciful tales to be told of the horse master of Thrace that are little known to the world outside of Acracia. The accepted view of Diomedes is that this demigod was the caretaker of four flesh-eating mares bequeathed to him by his father, Ares, the Greek god of war. The mares lived a privileged life, sequestered in green pastures forbidden to all save the sacred mares themselves. Diomedes's neighbors avoided his kingdom entirely. If by chance a foolish wanderer trespassed onto his fields, drank the water from his wells, or ate the fruit of his orchards, the unfortunate traveler was quickly reduced to fodder for the tyrant's man-killing mares.

In those days, word of the infamous horrors to be found in the kingdom of Diomedes had spread far and wide, but so had tales of the tyrant's superior horsemanship. According to one Acracian legend dating back several millennia, a spy managed to steal training secrets from Diomedes and return with them to his home in the distant land of Sybaris, in what is now southern Italy. Diomedes soon learned of the spy's treachery, and the score was settled when he dispatched a messenger to the Crotons, neighbors and mortal enemies of the Sybaris, and told them how their foes could be defeated. The next time the two armies met in battle, the Croton soldiers prepared by plugging their horses' ears with wax. Then they sounded their charge by playing a tune Diomedes bade his messenger teach them, a melody that the king had stolen from Orpheus, god of music and poetry. Upon hearing the enchanted melody, the horses of the enemy cavalry threw off their riders and began to dance to a music they could not resist. The battle ended in slaughter and the downfall of Sybaris.

Diomedes's reign of terror finally came to an end at the hands of Hercules, the renowned hero of ancient Greek myth. Hercules fought and overpowered the demigod, casting him to the floor of an arena where he was taken down and devoured by his own mares. Some scholars count this legend, the eighth labor of Hercules, as one of the earliest examples of

an adage that lives on to this day: The evil
you create will one day come back to
destroy you.

That is the story that is told in books
and accepted by the modern world. But
some of the villagers who lived in the region
surrounding Mt. Atnos told another version
of the story. They believed a demigod such
as Diomedes could never be killed, and local
legend had it that Diomedes feigned his
death and that he and his mares live on to
this day, hidden in a secret city among the
wandering trees of a magical forest. Today's
scholars accept that these tall tales about
Diomedes were concocted by the locals as a
means to scare off neighboring villagers
who might have been tempted to expand
their territories into the lush woods and
pastures of Acracia. The same could be said
for the folklore about poisonous rivers and
spring-fed pools that drove mad any animal
that drank from it, including humans.

In more recent times, Acracia has
remained a fairly autonomous region. Due
to its remote location, it escaped much of
the hardship inflicted on the rest of Thrace
by a series of foreign invaders. The last of

those invaders were the Turks, who took all
of Thrace in the fourteenth century and held
it until 1920 when . . .

Alec read a little farther and then turned to the back pages. There he found an illustration of a bearded man with heavy-browed, scowling eyes. The caption below it read, "Diomedes—horse master of Thrace." Alec looked at the illustration a minute and then put the pamphlet away. As macabre as it all sounded, there was something fascinating about the story of Diomedes. It was always helpful to learn something of a place's local history, Alec thought, especially when you had never been there before.

Taking off his clothes, Alec lay down and crawled under the blankets. But sleep would not come, so he got up again, put his clothes back on and returned to the Black's tent stable to sleep on a cot outside the stallion's stall. He wasn't frightened, really, just a little unsettled by the bones in the exhibit room. When he felt like that, it always made sense to stay close to the Black.

4

On the Set

The golden light of dawn was already filling the tent as Alec sat up on his stable cot and threw off his blanket. Molded by years of farm and track routine, he usually slept well and awakened easily, confident and ready to face another day. But this morning he felt a bit anxious as he looked around at the unfamiliar surroundings.

Alec rubbed the sleep from his eyes and stood up. Outside he heard a thumping sound that he assumed was Bateman's helicopter flying in somewhere outside the compound. A minute later, the *chop-chop-chop* faded away as the craft took off and flew back down the mountain. What a way to travel, Alec thought.

The Black was awake, and Alec went to his horse and gave him his feed and some fresh water. The smell of brewing coffee drew him to a table in the courtyard. He had a cup and said good morning to the cast and crew gathered there.

After the Black finished eating, it was time for a light grooming before they headed over to the wardrobe tent. The Black needed to get outfitted for the scene they were shooting that morning.

Alec spent the next hour trying to get the Black to submit to wearing the costume for his Bucephalus stand-in scene. Though the breastplate, feathered headpiece and other armor was lightweight, it was still cumbersome, and the stallion plainly didn't understand why Alec was asking him to wear it. He wasn't a trained movie horse and had never been schooled in the particular skills necessary to play a part in a film.

The Black bucked and pawed and was generally uncooperative, but finally Alec managed to get his horse suited up and more or less ready for the shot. Or rather, ready to wait for the shot. Once again, Alec realized that in the world of movies, everything was about waiting. You always had to be ready when they said you had to be ready, but it also seemed you always had to wait because someone else wasn't ready, or because a light stand fell over, or because a cloud was blocking the sun or because of a million other mishaps that could delay the plans for the day. All the waiting around didn't really bother Alec that much. If his life at the racetrack had taught him anything, it was that it never paid to be in a hurry. At the track, winners waited and watched and didn't get impatient about circumstances beyond their control. Sometimes it just meant finding a relaxing way to fill up the time between races. It seemed much the same here, and Alec was thankful he had a good book to read.

Finally he got the word that the cameras were almost ready, and they wanted Alec and the Black on the set in ten minutes. Alec was already wearing his costume but ducked into the wardrobe tent for last-minute adjustments. Xeena waited outside with the Black. Two costume assistants helped Alec get his helmet on and double-checked the rest of his armor.

"You ready?" Xeena asked when Alec emerged.

Alec nodded. "As ready as I'll ever be."

They started off for the set. Alec gave his horse a pat on the neck. "I wish I could explain all of this to the Black," he said. "He must think I've gone crazy, asking him to wear this stuff."

Xeena laughed. "He looks great anyway. He'll look terrific with the mountains in the background."

The scene was being filmed only a couple minutes' walk away, on a low hill flanked by looming peaks just beyond the compound. Jeff met them there and ran over the setup with Alec one last time. "Alexander and Bucephalus are reuniting after being separated during a battle," Jeff said. "Your job is to stand on top of the hill and call the Black to you when Bateman gives the cue."

"Sounds simple enough," Alec said. "I just hope the Black will cooperate. Anyway, we'll do the best we can."

The set was crowded with clusters of camera people, electricians, lighting people and assistants directing sunlight with reflector boards. Soon the cameras were in position and the crew was ready.

Karst was waiting for them at the mark where the Black was to start from. Alec had decided the best way to ensure the stallion came to him when he was turned loose was to tempt him with food. For this Alec was using a fresh carrot and a Jonathan apple, a tangy-sweet variety that the Black usually couldn't resist. Alec held out his hand and let the Black sniff the apple and then backed away from the stallion, showing him the apple and calling to him. The Black pulled at his lead, but Karst, with a little help from Xeena, held the stallion still. Alec took his position about twenty yards away on top of the low hill.

"Action," Bateman commanded over the bullhorn.

Alec called to his horse again, and this time Karst turned the Black loose. The stallion started for Alec but then gave a shrill neigh and took off in another direction.

"Cut," called the director. "Do it again." Wranglers on horseback and assistants on foot waved down the stallion and turned him back.

"I better get him," Alec said. He jogged out to collect the Black and lead him to his start marker.

"Easy, fella," Alec said. This time he gave the Black a taste of apple and a piece of carrot. But after the cameras were readied and Alec again called to the stallion, once more the Black bolted for the sidelines and out of the shot. They tried again and again. It took five attempts before Alec could finally get the Black to come to him as the director wanted.

Xeena walked with Alec as he led the stallion back to his stall. "That was so embarrassing," Alec said. "It looked like I had zero control over my horse out there."

Xeena nodded. "All the animals have been acting up this morning," she said. "Even Cleo, and she never gets worked up about anything. Maybe there is something in the woods around here. There could be forest predators, a pack of wolves or mountain lions."

"Are there animals like that living here?" Alec asked.

"I didn't think so, but you never know."

Alec shook his head. "Let's not worry about that unless we have to."

"You're right," Xeena said. "Anyway, we have Conrad's snakes to protect us. They are starring in their big scene later today. It should be interesting."

◆　◆　◆

After lunch that afternoon, Alec was sitting with his horse when Xeena popped her head into the tent. "Hey there," she said. "What's up?"

"Just reading my book," Alec said. "How is it going on the set?"

"Pretty good. The snakes seem to be feeling a bit lazy, though. How's the Black?"

"He's okay now. I don't know what got into him before."

Xeena smiled and took a seat on a bale of hay. "It's been that sort of a day for everyone."

"You should have heard the goats in the next stall a few minutes ago, bleating like murder. Something sure had them stirred up." Alec shook his head. "So what's going on with Conrad's snakes?"

"Right now they think the reason the snakes are so sleepy is because the ground is too cold," Xeena said. "Conrad says they need to heat up the sand to get the snakes moving again. Everything is stopped until the crew can bury a sheet of metal in the ground underneath where the snakes will be filmed. Then they will use electricity to heat up the metal and the layer of sand above it, making it hot enough so the snakes will do something more than curl up and fall asleep. You should go check it out."

"Sure," Alec said. He glanced over his shoulder

to where the Black had his nose buried in his hay net. "And what about him?"

"I'll watch him. Don't worry."

"I don't know," Alec said. "He's quiet now but earlier he was really acting peculiar."

"He'll be all right," Xeena said.

Alec thought about it a minute. "Seriously?" he said. "You'll keep an eye on him? I would sort of like to see this."

"Sure," Xeena said. "Go ahead. They are set up just outside the compound. It's not far."

Alec walked to a table and picked up a small black two-way radio. "I'll take the walkie-talkie," he said. "Let me know if he starts acting up."

Xeena nodded. "We'll be fine. No matter what happens, the set is only a minute's walk. Don't worry."

Alec jogged to the gate and out to the set where the crew was shooting the snake scene. The cameras were set up to one side of a Plexiglas barrier. It looked like a clear windowpane and was about six feet high and twelve feet wide. Alec figured the crew had already installed the underground heating pad, because Conrad and one of the other snake wranglers were now raking smooth the ground on the other side of the glass. The rest of the crew waited behind the camera, milling around or checking their equipment. Alec spotted Karst and Jeff sitting on folding chairs beside stacks of black camera cases. They waved to Alec, and he jogged over to join them.

Karst glanced at the set and shook his head. "Snakes," he said. "Train horses is hard. Train snakes and a two-year-old boy? I think we stay here all day."

Jeff laughed. "Whatever else he is, Conrad is a good snake wrangler. If anyone can pull this off, he can."

"Who is in this scene besides the snakes?" Alec asked. "Before, you said it was a dream scene, right?"

Jeff pointed out Carla, the sixteen-year-old actress playing Alexander's mom in the scene. "Freddy Roth has an eye for talent and picked her up in Xanthi," Jeff said. "Never worked in films before. That's her mom, Veronica, standing next to her. The other woman is Helen, from wardrobe." The three women were riding herd on a two-year-old boy who was having the time of his life playing with a toy sword someone had given him and kicking the air with his feet.

"Mr. Kung Fu over there is Otto," Jeff said. "He'll be playing the Alexander-as-a-kid character in the snake scene. Helen is Otto's real mom. They are German expats, living in Xanthi. Helen works in the wardrobe department, and when Bateman saw Otto on the set one day, he thought the kid would be perfect for the dream scene and Helen agreed. I don't think she knew her son's costars were going to be a pair of snakes, though."

Jeff gestured to where the assistants were just finishing smoothing out the dirt in front of the glass. "It
looks like they have the hot pad in place and are about
ready." He glanced at Karst and they both stood up.
"We better stick close in case we can help in some way.
Come with us if you want, Alec," Jeff said. "Just remember to stay well behind the cameras when we get
ready to roll."

A few minutes later, cameras, sound equipment
and actors were all in their places. Conrad stood back
to one side, holding his snake-wrangling tool—a four-
foot-long wooden stick with a hooklike tip. Alec
briefly stepped behind Bateman and the camera crew
framing the shot. He could see that from this angle,
the glass was nearly invisible.

Helen brought Otto to his mark only a foot or
two away from the glass and less than three feet from
the snakes curled up quietly on the other side of the
barrier. Otto barely seemed to notice them and occupied himself with digging a hole in the dirt and letting
the earth crumble beneath his fingers.

"That's perfect," Bateman said. "Terrific. Conrad,
you ready?"

"More heat," Conrad called to his assistant working the controls of the hot pad. Soon the leopard
snakes seemed to wake up from their nap. One slith-
ered to the glass and tried to climb it. Conrad moved

his wrangling tool and pulled the snake off the glass. Then he gave the other snake a prod with the stick to get him motivated.

The snakes turned their attention on each other, facing off, winding up in coils, one twitching the tip of his tail threateningly. "Ready, boss," Conrad called out. "Better go now."

"Action."

Helen called a signal to her son from where she was standing just offscreen. Otto reached up and touched the glass and, for what looked like the first time, noticed the snakes. His reaction was more curiosity than fear as he watched the two snakes getting riled up on the other side of the glass. Suddenly one of the snakes darted off and the other chased it, both streaking for the edge of the glass as if trying to slip around to the other side where Otto was still lolling about in the dirt.

"Stop," Helen called in English as she dashed onto the set and scooped up her son. Conrad and another wrangler chased after the two runaway snakes.

"Cut," called the director.

"No worries, folks. They're not poisonous," Conrad called out. "Just give me a minute here . . ."

Karst nudged Alec with his elbow. "What I tell you," he said with a laugh. "Train snakes? I hope boss knows what he's doing."

The snake wranglers corralled the snakes while Helen listened to Bateman telling her she had nothing to worry about and that her child was in no danger. In the end, Helen apologized for spoiling the shot.

As the crew set up for the next take, Alec began to wonder how the Black was doing. He looked at his watch and decided he'd better get back to the stable. This was a job for all of them, and Xeena probably had other things to do than babysit the Black while Alec hung around the set like a tourist.

That night at dinner, Alec heard the snake scene was finally completed successfully, and after the rest of the day's shooting for the black unit was finished, Bateman helicoptered back to the film's base camp farther down the mountain. The director was scheduled back the next morning to finish up the last few scenes of the monastery shoot with the black unit.

Alec spoke with Conrad and some of the other wranglers. Once again, all anyone could talk about was the trouble they had getting their animals to perform. If they weren't fast asleep and unwilling to wake up, they were trying to bust out of their cages and stalls and run off. Alec wondered about this. In a way it was a relief that the Black wasn't the only one that had acted up today. Conrad said he would be glad when this shoot was over and they could get back home.

5

The Falls

Alec slept on a stable cot in the Black's tent again that night. The next morning he woke late. The first thing he noticed was how unusually quiet it was outside. He hadn't heard a helicopter or even the sounds of the generators powering up at the location site. Alec wondered if Bateman was even here yet.

The Black was awake when Alec stepped into his stall to bring him his breakfast. Alec spoke to his horse as the Black paced around his stall, the stallion feigning indifference to him at first. After a few more turns around the stall, the Black finally allowed Alec to touch his neck, then dipped his head into the feed trough to sniff at the special mix of oats and bran mash Alec had prepared for him. "Good morning to you too," Alec said. He watched the Black another minute and then went outside to the craft-services table to get himself a cup of coffee and a banana.

"There you are," a voice called behind him as

Alec made a beeline for the coffee. He turned and saw it was Jeff. "I checked your room and you weren't there."

"I slept out here. It was nice."

Jeff nodded and smiled. "I wanted to tell you there's been a little change in plans. Bateman's chopper broke down, and they are waiting on a part. It will probably take the rest of the day to fix it. The word is that we should sit tight and wait."

Alec laughed. "Fine with me."

"If you want to join us, some of the guys will be playing a game of cards in the dining room after break-fast to kill some time."

"Thanks," Alec said, and followed Jeff toward the dining area, where an American-style breakfast buffet was set up.

When the meal was over, Alec bowed out of the card game and told Jeff he was going to take the Black for a walk.

"Just remember, the other side of the river is off-limits," Jeff said as Alec got up from the table. "The government guy made that really clear. It's some club or resort or something over there. Plenty to see on this side of the river, I imagine."

"We'll be careful," Alec said.

Alec wanted to give his horse a break today, so when he led the Black from his stall, the stallion wore no saddle or bridle, only a loose halter with a short lead shank attached. A horse like the Black would not tolerate too much tack strapped to his body day after day, just as there were times he would not tolerate too much attention from people, even Alec. One of the important lessons he had learned from his horse, and it was true of all free-thinking animals, including people, was that no matter how much you loved them, or they loved you, the trick to getting along was to know when to leave them alone.

Alec spoke gently to his horse while knotting his fingers in two fistfuls of black mane. "Okay, big guy," he said. "Easy now."

With two quick, springy steps, Alec swung his legs up, rolling through the air to land astride a full seventeen hands of horse. His legs closed about the Black, and everything instantly fell into place, like the start of a familiar conversation.

Alec rested his hands easily on his horse's neck. "Let's go," he said softly, touching a heel to the stallion's side. The Black responded willingly and they set off. Alec saw Xeena, Karst and one of the grooms talking together at the far end of the compound. Xeena noticed Alec and the Black and waved. He waved back.

Passing through the courtyard, Alec turned the Black onto a path through the woods. He settled back to enjoy the ride, listening to the steady rhythm of the Black's hooves on the ground.

The path they were following, really little more than a woodcutter's trail, led to the top of a low cliff above a rushing white-water river. It edged along between the trees and the rim of the cliff and quickly became rough going, even dangerous, with little more than a network of slippery roots for footing.

Alec looked out over the roiling water running fifteen feet below. He dismounted and thought about turning around but decided against it. The path had become so narrow that doing so would likely be even more dangerous. The Black pulled ahead on his lead line, curious about what was beyond the next bend in the trail.

The path turned away from the river and continued upward around masses of jagged rocks until finally arriving at a clearing on the top of a hill. Alec stopped to catch his breath and take in the view. Overhead the sun had fallen beneath the clouds.

Suddenly Alec heard someone calling his name from the direction he had just come. It was Xeena. She was riding Cleo, the laid-back stable pony that she'd brought from Xanthi.

The pony jogged into the clearing, and Xeena pulled her up a short distance away. She swung out of the saddle and landed lightly on the ground. The Black eyed the pony and gave a snort. Cleo bobbed her head lazily.

"Hey there," Alec called to Xeena. "What's up?"

"We came for a walk, like you," Xeena said. "We've been on your trail since you left the monastery."

The Black stamped the ground and tossed his head impatiently. His pricked ears tilted toward the path on the other side of the clearing.

"Easy, fella," Alec said softly. The Black stretched out his neck, pulling on the lead line. Alec moved closer to him and gave the stallion's neck a gentle pat.

"Jeff was saying parts of the forest are off-limits," Alec said after a minute.

"Just on the other side of river," Xeena said. "The resort owns that part."

Alec shrugged. "I guess we're okay here, then. Let's see what we can see."

They both mounted up. Alec nudged the Black ahead. Xeena and Cleo followed close behind. After a minute, they reached another overgrown path that obviously hadn't been traveled in years. "I wonder what's up this way?" Xeena said.

"I guess we'll have to find out," Alec replied.

Grass grew tall on this new trail, and towering trees quivered all around. The trilling of birds filled the air. The Black heard the songs, too, his head held high, ears pitching this way and that, nostrils scenting the wind.

Though still rough going, the path ahead became wide enough that they didn't need to walk in single file any longer. Xeena pulled Cleo up beside the Black as they came to a grove of cedars. Beyond the trees to the east they saw a waterfall pouring from a high cliff on the resort side of the swirling river. For some reason, the sound of the falling waters did not roar but hung almost softly in the air.

"I didn't know there was a waterfall here," Xeena said.

Alec nodded. "No one mentioned it to me either."

Accentuated by the misty vapor rising off the falls, there was a feeling of great age in the tranquil atmosphere, Alec thought, maybe even outside of time. Somehow it was almost frightening to think about the history of a place like this, and how old it really was.

"It is certainly beautiful," Alec said. He wondered aloud to Xeena about the ancients who had surely stood in this very spot and viewed this same misty scene before them now. "Do you ever think about things like that?" Alec asked her. "Here we are looking at the same scenery they did, in a place that probably hasn't changed much in thousands of years. I wonder if the ancient Greeks were like us or if they'd even recognize us as being like them."

"What do you mean?" Xeena said.

"Everything must have been so different back then," Alec said. "Could their world bear any resemblance to the world of today? Did they see as we see, feel as we feel, think as we think?"

Xeena shrugged. "Why wouldn't they?"

"I don't know," Alec said. "People are different wherever you go, I guess, even today. Back then it must have been . . . really different. You can almost feel it in the air here."

"Maybe we should tell Jeff about this place," Xeena said. "Maybe Bateman could shoot a scene up here."

Alec laughed. "Hard to imagine a camera crew following the route we just took," he said.

The stallion led them out of the grove and down to the river's edge. There the trail followed along the riverbank in the direction of the falls. A steep, rocky slope rose up beside the path to their left, and the river ran swift and narrow to their right. Across the river, only about fifty yards away, Alec could see nothing but thick woods.

He looked out at the water cascading down and exploding in the river below. For a moment he thought he saw something moving there, a flash of white against the black rocks and silver spray. "Hey," he said to Xeena. "What's that?"

"What?"

"I thought I saw something over there," Alec said. "Something big."

"Where?"

Alec pointed ahead. "There . . . across the river . . . in those rocks, right beside the falls."

"Where?" Xeena asked again.

"There it is again," Alec said, all his attention focused at the spot across the river.

Just then, the Black lowered his head, sniffing the ground. When he straightened up, he jerked his neck so suddenly that Alec was caught unprepared. The lead shank slipped from his fingers and ran through his left hand.

Alec immediately moved to his horse, but it was too late. The stallion whirled and ran, gaining full stride almost immediately, his mane and tail streaming in the wind he created, the shank trailing at his side. In a matter of seconds, the stallion was fifty yards away.

"Black!" Alec called after his horse, chiding himself for being caught napping and losing his grip on the shank. Thankfully the stallion wouldn't get too far. The trail before him edged the bottom of the steep, rocky slope on one side with the river on the other. It came to a sudden stop about a hundred yards ahead where the path had been washed out by the river.

"Want me and Cleo to go get him?" Xeena asked.

"I better do it," Alec said. "He must be in one of his moods." Alec shook his head and broke into a slow jog. "Crazy horse," he muttered to himself as he trotted along.

The stallion reached the washed-out section of the trail and stopped. "Black," Alec called to him, again not too worried that the Black was doing anything more than playing around.

Then suddenly, with a wild cry, the Black reared, standing straight up on his hind legs, a coal-black silhouette against the swirling waters of the river behind him. Alec heard the longing in the Black's cry and instantly knew there was only one thing that could cause his horse to act this way. And there she was, a fantastic-looking white mare standing to one side of the falls on the opposite bank. Her snow-white coat was so brilliant and pale it appeared almost pink. Strangest of all, her eyes were a dazzling red, almost like rubies. Alec had never seen an albino horse before, but obviously he was looking at one now. She was one of the most strikingly beautiful creatures he had ever seen—and the most unusual.

Alec burst into a sprint, his eyes fixed on the two

horses. The Black slammed his forehooves to the ground and repeated his fierce cry, hoping to attract the mare's attention. Across the river, the albino beauty ignored him, paying the giant black stallion no more attention than she would a braying mule.

In his frustration, the Black stomped and pawed the ground, dragging up great clods of grass and sending them flying out behind him. His cries instantly became more demanding, more a threat than a request. She finally raised her head to listen, and then, with a defiant scream and a flash of snow-white coat, she was gone, lost in the silver mist rising from the falls.

Running as fast as he could, Alec closed to within a few yards of his horse. He called out again, but he knew it was no use. The stallion was beyond listening to anyone now, even Alec. Pawing the ground and uttering one last cry, the Black plunged headlong over the embankment and splashed down into the river. Alec reached the river's edge just behind the stallion and, without even stopping to think, ran in after him.

The Black squealed wildly as he jumped through the shallows. Heedless of Alec's cries, the stallion thrashed his way toward the middle of the river, determined to cross it and reach the mare he'd seen on the opposite side.

"Black," Alec called again, scrambling through

the hip-deep water. The tug of the current rushing downstream from the falls pulled on his legs. The river was little more than twenty feet from one side to the other, but it looked to be deep in the middle. Alec watched as the Black was swept into the deeper water and began to swim.

Alec waded out into the river, making for a shallow place he thought might be easier to cross. Suddenly his foot slipped and he lost his balance, sprawling face-first into the water. Instantly he was moving, caught in a rushing channel that was so deep he could no longer touch bottom. "Black," he cried, thrusting his head out of the water and twisting his neck around, looking for his horse but not seeing him.

Suddenly Alec felt himself reeling and rolling. The current pulled him below the surface. He came up for air and struggled in the whirling streams of water. His cold, wet clothes weighed him down, making every kick and stroke a double effort.

Battling the current was futile, so Alec let it pull him along, trying to keep his head out of the chilly water. He could hear Xeena calling and spun around to look behind him. She had followed him into the river and was standing in the shallows at the water's edge, waving her arms and pointing to the opposite side. Alec looked to where she was gesturing and saw the Black had already reached the other shore and was climbing up the riverbank. The stallion collected himself, clearing his nostrils and snorting explosively.

Floundering in midstream, Alec tried to call out to his horse but only managed to swallow a mouthful of river water. The water closed over him again as invisible hands seemed to drag him down to the bottom. His strong arms flayed the water as he tried to gain traction against the onslaught pulling him this way and that. Even his legs suddenly felt weak and useless as he beat lamely at the water. Finally he found the surface, gasping for air and coughing up water.

How could this be happening? Alec thought. Less than a moment ago, everything had been tranquil here. But now his heart throbbed wildly in his chest, and he felt consumed with a fear and desperation that came from something more than being separated from his horse and the beating he was receiving in the river.

Finally his feet touched bottom, and he clawed his way up the bank on the opposite side of the river, his body shaking with cold and fear and relief. He blinked his eyes, but the very air around him seemed clouded over by a great gray spiderweb.

Alec shook his head to try clearing his eyes and ears again. He heard the stallion's whistle, followed by a wild clamor of birds. Suddenly all sounds died away, everything becoming absolutely motionless and still, everything except the grinding of tree limbs whipped by a sudden wind and the soft murmuring of falling water. He could hear his own panting breath and could feel the thundering of his heart. Then there was something else, a girl's voice calling his name.

He blinked again and turned to see Xeena crawling out of the water and up onto the riverbank. She was soaked, her eyes large with fear and excitement.

"Xeena!" Alec said. "Are you okay? What are you doing here?"

"I wanted to help," she said.

"You could have drowned."

"You could have too."

"Yes, but . . ." Alec coughed and spat up some water. He shook his head once more to try to clear the water from his ears. "That river didn't look like much more than a gentle stream from the other side," he said, coughing again. "I feel like I just swam across the ocean. I must have swallowed a gallon of water."

"Me too," Xeena said.

Again Alec noticed the creaking of the windblown branches in the woods around them. All else was still. The silence seemed heavy, almost oppressive. "There's something really strange about this side of the river," he said. "I feel like I just landed on Mars. Do you notice it too?"

"I don't know," Xeena said. "My skin feels sort of tingly."

"Didn't you say there were old mines around here that polluted the water? Maybe that has something to do with it."

"Maybe," Xeena said. "Did you see that mare? Where did she come from?"

Alec shook his head. "Who knows? If we find her, I bet we'll find the Black, though. Let's go see if we can track them down before they get too far."

"He went that way," she said, pointing in the direction of the waterfall.

There was no path here, and after a few paces, Alec and Xeena had to stop to fight their way through head-high bushes and low-hanging branches. The wind whipped up again, turning the light greens to dark as it traveled through the treetops.

Finally there was space enough between the leaves that Alec could see where he was going. He slowed to a walk and wiped the sweat and water from his eyes. "Black," he called, his voice sounding hollow with exhaustion. The air around him was filled with a loud booming. What had once been the muffled sound of the falls had grown to a deafening howl on this side of the river.

"There he is," Xeena said.

Then Alec saw him too. The Black was storming toward the curtain of falling water pouring from the cliffs a hundred feet above. Alec could see some shadowy spaces between the rocks behind the falls, and it was there the stallion was headed. It looked to be the same spot where he had last seen the mare from across the river. Alec watched as his horse reached the falls and stepped into the shadows among the rocks. Then the Black seemed to disappear behind the curtain of falling water just as the mare had done earlier.

As the path cleared before him, Alec raced down to the edge of the falls. The mighty roar filled his ears and spray fogged his eyes. Wiping the water from his face, he ducked under a jutting shelf of granite.

Here was where the horses had gone, he realized. It was the dark mouth of a cave behind the falls, backlit by bluish sunlight shining in through the sheet of falling water.

Xeena came up fast behind him. "It's a cave," she said. "They went in here. Let's see where it goes."

Alec turned to the girl and shook his head. "I'll do it," he said. "You should stay here. I have enough to worry about right now without worrying about you on top of everything else."

"No way," Xeena said. "I haven't had this much fun in ages."

Alec looked at her and realized she was determined to stick by his side no matter what happened. There was no point in arguing.

"Okay then, but stay close," he said.

A three-foot-wide path rimmed the base of the cliff behind the falls, so smooth and flat it could have been man-made. Alec and Xeena edged their way forward, flattening their backs against the algae-slick rock wall as a rush of water flooded the path and lapped at their ankles. They reached the cave opening, and the noise from the falls howled through the air. Then they heard something else, a horse's scream, the scorching cry of the Black.

Alec stepped into the cave behind the curtain of falling water. He followed the sound of the Black's scream until he saw the stallion clambering across a streambed that ran behind the falls, water rushing high up around his legs.

The stallion whinnied again, and now Alec saw the albino mare standing like a statue, watching them from a ledge beside the far wall of the cave. She was gazing down upon them from the safety of the ledge, playfully tossing her head, her red eyes flashing like scarlet pinwheels. Alec called to his horse, but it was no use. The stallion was intent on reaching the ghostly vision of the white mare, and nothing was going to stop him.

The fast-flowing stream rushed by their feet as Alec and Xeena scrambled into the streambed and began wading through the water after the Black. The stream deepened, and too late Alec realized that the water churning around his legs here behind the falls was split into two opposing streams. The first was shallow and only reached his knees. It swept into the falls and down into the river outside. But the second stream looked deeper and ran in a different direction, inexplicably flowing back in the other direction, *back into the mountain*. Still Alec stumbled along, not knowing which he should fear more—being pulled into the falls or getting sucked deeper into the cave.

Swirling ribbons of roiling water tugged heavily at his legs. Trying to keep his balance was like trying to find footing on a slippery conveyer belt. Ahead he could see and hear the statuesque mare taunting the Black from her perch atop the far ledge.

The Black passed into the second stream and sank, the water covering his back. He gave a furious cry and half reared. Then Alec watched in horror as the stallion slipped and splashed down into the whirling water. "Black!" he screamed, his cry echoing down into the darkness that funneled back into the mountain. The stallion rolled in the water, then raised his head and whinnied again, a cry now filled with terror more than rage. His legs thrashed the water, but it was clear his hooves were no longer touching bottom.

Alec fought his way through the foaming stream, desperate to reach his horse.

"Be careful, Alec," Xeena cried out close behind him.

"Go get help," he called back over his shoulder.

The water deepened, rising past his waist to his chest. The current became stronger, like whirling chains tightening on his legs. Fierce and unstoppable the water ran, not toward the falls and the sun outside, but deeper into the darkness of the mountain. And it was taking the Black with it.

"Black!" Alec cried out again. Straining his eyes in the shadows, he could see his horse struggling against the current of dark, bubbling water that was dragging him downstream and toward the back of the cave.

For a moment, the stallion found enough footing to stop his thrashing and begin fighting the current. Alec splashed closer, coming almost near enough to touch the stallion. All at once, the Black slipped again and rolled into the water. Alec leaped through the air to make one last desperate attempt to reach his horse. His body flattened and was swept up in the turbulence, his hands stretched out.

The fingers of his right hand felt something and closed around the lead shank that trailed in the water at the stallion's side. With the touch of the rope came a feeling of intense relief. Whatever happened to them now, Alec thought, he wasn't letting go. Whatever happened now would happen to them together.

Alec clenched his fist around the shank as the current dragged them deeper into the tunnel. All around him was cold, wet darkness and black water. He saw nothing and heard only the slap of water on the walls of the cave. Alec quickly realized that fighting the rip current was harder now than before. Tied together with the Black, their speed was only increasing, their combined weight making it all the more impossible to battle the current. To make matters even worse, the water was deeper here, and when Alec tried to find the bottom, it was no longer there.

The rushing stream overwhelmed them, running ever faster as it hurried them through the lightless void. Alec fought to keep his head out of the water. All his channels of sense and reason seemed blocked, his brain racked by an overpowering fear. He felt more than heard a roar in the blackness ahead and around him, like the sound of an oncoming train inside a tunnel. The Black's lead shank suddenly jerked wildly and was torn from his hand. Alec grabbed desperately after it but felt nothing but empty space. The water beneath him fell away, and he was in a free fall, tumbling through a hole in the darkest night imaginable.

Alec had taken plenty of spills in his life, but never anything like this. "I am alive," he told himself, thinking of nothing else but those three words and repeating them over and over in his mind as he fell through the air. To black out now would mean to die. His only chance of survival was to stay awake and hope for a soft landing.

After a long drop, he hit the water again, water that felt like concrete as he slammed into it. Dark, cold wetness swallowed him as he was driven deep under the surface. Alec held his breath, hanging on to the three-word chant in his mind telling him he was alive, awake and conscious. He tried to roll himself into a ball and felt his body tossing head over heels until one leg struck bottom. It was a hard hit but not as hard as it might have been in shallower water. Pushing off the bottom, Alec swam for the surface, gasping for air as he finally reached it. Opening his eyes, he saw nothing. Everything around him remained pitch-black.

"Black," Alec screamed as he beat his arms against the current, groping the darkness, listening for any sign of his horse. He knew that if he had survived the fall, chances were the Black had too. And though he could see nothing in the darkness, he knew his horse must be close. He called again but still no answer came.

Alec realized he was now caught in still another underground river running somewhere deep inside the mountain. The current spun him around and dragged him along as he struggled to catch his breath. He commanded his mind to stay conscious. It was his choice to live or die, and he knew he must live.

For many moments, time seemed to stand still. At last he could see the tunnel ahead was no longer quite so dark. He began to make out the contours of the cave walls, twenty feet on either side of him, and the ceiling hanging less than six feet above.

The dark waters of the river funneled around a curve. Alec's legs bumped into rocks. His feet touched bottom, but he couldn't have stopped if he had wanted to. The current quickened as it approached a vertical slit in the dark rock wall.

The opening was a six-foot-wide gash in the rock and through it beamed brilliant shafts of sunlight. The current grew faster still, funneling water through the passageway and spilling Alec out into the blinding daylight. His eyes tried to adjust to the light as he was swept along in the ripping current.

At last he saw that he was now caught midstream in a river little more than thirty feet across, narrow and deep, almost like a canal. Bordering the riverbanks, tall, thick trees stood shoulder to shoulder.

As Alec gathered his wits, again his thoughts were for his horse. Was he still alive? Surely he must be, but where? And what about Xeena? Had she gone back for help, or had she been swept into the underground river too? He could only hope she had been smart enough not to follow him across the stream and was able to get to safety when she had the chance.

But there was no question about the Black, Alec thought. He must be around here somewhere, unless he had been swept down a different tunnel. Alec couldn't believe it. They had been only an arm's length apart when they dropped down into that hole or whatever it had been. Surely the current would have carried them to the same place. But where was that? Again his gaze searched the shore on either side, and again he saw wall-to-wall trees with no sign of anything familiar, or even man-made.

Alec raised his head out of the water. "Black," he called, his voice garbled and weak. He looked around him but could see no sign of his horse, only the monstrous tree trunks and the canopy of leaves above. He leaned back into the water and sidestroked along, edging toward the riverbank. Jolts of pain shot up his left leg as he kicked his feet. For the first time, Alec realized that he must have hit the bottom harder than he had thought.

The river hurried Alec downstream, curving around a bend. Using his good leg and cold, weary arms, he let the current carry him along until he reached the embankment at last. He caught hold of a tangled network of exposed roots beneath a tree trunk leaning over the river. With what seemed like all the strength he had left, Alec dragged himself out of the water and onto the bank. The ground here was all roots, thick and thin, layered on top of each other like a nest of snakes.

He coughed, gasped and cleared his mouth. He tried to speak, just to hear his own voice and confirm that he was indeed alive, but no words would come. He took a couple deep breaths and tried again, finally managing a low, guttural groan. Breathe, he told himself, just breathe. His eyes scanned the roiling water for the Black, but again he found no sign of his horse.

"Black," Alec called out, but he was so weakened by the ordeal that the sound of his cry did not travel far. If he could just find a path through the woods, Alec thought. If he could just . . . He tried to get up and then collapsed out of exhaustion, falling unconscious to the ground.

6

The Far Side
of the Mountain

Two hundred yards upstream, the Black scrambled out of the water and onto a pocket of grass tucked into the dense wall of trees lining the riverbank. The stallion dropped his head and stood still, thankful to feel the earth beneath his hooves once again, his breath coming hard and fast from his battle for life inside the mountain. Maddened by the hellish experience, he screamed an explosive neigh. His body was cut up, bruised and beaten by river rocks, and chilled to the bone by the cold water. And yet he was unafraid and did not feel tired or weakened. Sharpened by his fight for survival, his senses felt more acute than ever. He wanted to run, but, hemmed in by trees, he was unsure where to go. Of one thing the stallion was certain: He was in a strange new land, and instinct told him to beware.

His pains were quickly forgotten as he stared out to the woods and the peaks beyond, his small, fine head raised high, sniffing the air, his nostrils quivering, his ears pointed and alert. Warmed by the sun, his body began to tremble, not from cold but from excitement and curiosity. The unknown woods, the strange path, the liberty to go where and when he pleased, all spoke to him of freedom. The sweet call to liberty was tempered only by one other thought— where was his friend, the boy who shared his life? He searched the air for some scent of him but could find none.

The stallion gazed out into the forest green and waited. Soon the breeze told him someone was there, or had been there not long ago. It was his own kind, of that he was certain, though there was something off about the scent, something unhealthy, the smell of fear and blood. The Black picked up the other horse's trail and before long found hoofprints and a mound of fresh manure. He kept going, wary but confident that whatever lay ahead, his speed, endurance and cunning would keep him safe.

The scent in the wind led to a narrow tree-lined path running away from the river. Soon the Black began climbing higher through the dense forest. The breeze softened, and as it did, the scent of horse became fainter and then vanished completely.

The stallion pawed the ground in frustration as it became clear he had lost the trail and was heading in the wrong direction. He listened and looked about him at the silent woods. Then, with a quick step back, he turned around and returned the way he had come, trusting his senses to lead him where he needed to go.

As the Black retraced his steps down the trail, he was again struck by something very strange. The tall, gnarled trees and piles of rocks that marked the path only minutes before seemed to have moved from one side of the trail to the other. His sense of direction seldom failed him, and the feeling of being disoriented now startled him. Other signs told him he had lost his way, signs he would have noticed had he passed along this path before. He sniffed the air, wary of this place where scents were so easily cleansed from the wind and landmarks seemed to shift and move around of their own accord.

Suddenly the trail opened to a clearing, one that hadn't been there on his way up the mountain path. His eyes remained sharp, his ears and nostrils alert, ready to catch the slightest noise or faintest scent. The sun shone brightly on a patch of inviting green grass. He waited until he was certain there was no sign of danger, then dropped his head to graze.

The sweet, clean grass gave the stallion new energy. Soon he felt enough at ease to lie down. He rolled on the warm ground and kicked his legs in the air. Climbing to his feet, he again whiffed a light gust of wind funneling through the trees. There was no sign of the mare, but once more the breeze carried with it the perfume of other horses.

He stood quietly, watchful and ready. The only thing about him that moved was his mane, stirred by the wind. Once more he felt the excitement of his new-found freedom in this untraveled land. Long-sleeping memories of life in the wild spoke to him as he looked around, memories of his birthplace in the high mountains of the great desert. Now he was free again, free to follow whatever path he chose.

After a minute, the Black struck out to chase the scent of horse, once again smelling the breeze. He found another trail and trotted easily through the woods, his hooves falling softly on the pine needles scattered over the ground. Winding his way through the trees, he lost the scent once more and was again unsure where to go. He stopped and waited to collect himself, listening for the slightest sound and puzzling over how to read the signs his senses told him were here. His powerful gaze searched through the woods. There was something out there, of that he was certain, but what?

The breeze stirred again and brought new information. He veered off the path and zigzagged through clusters of pines until he reached a place where the branches hung low, forming a tunnel of trees. The familiar scent of his kind became stronger here, and there were clear marks on the ground that others had passed this way not long ago.

The stallion moved slowly into the darker shadow of the passageway. Inside, the sound of the wind ceased. Strands of sunlight filtered through the leaves above and cast shifting patterns of light and shadows on the ground before him. After a few moments, the path opened upon a grassy pasture. The Black followed the scent upwind to a small stream. He stood still beside it, his nostrils flared, his ears cocked. There was a faint sound of splashing ahead, beyond a stand of trees.

Following the course of the stream through the trees, the stallion came upon a small pool. His eyes widened as he finally beheld what the signs in the wind had told him were there. It was four mares. Three were splashing about and playing in the water along the streambed. And grazing on the bank of the pool was the magnificent albino beauty he had first seen at the waterfall. She was big, lean but muscular, with a long, arched neck. Her head was small, her eyes large and wide-set. The Black stood silent and watched as the breeze riffled her high-set tail and the snow-white mane fringing her slender neck.

The albino sensed him well before the other mares. She suddenly became alert and raised her head a notch. Then she froze, blades of grass still stuck between her lips, her thick forelock falling down to her eyebrows. In the pool, the other mares were still unaware of the stallion's presence downwind. The albino stared straight at the Black, but she did not cry out or make any effort to warn her sisters of the stallion's arrival.

The Black announced himself with a loud snort. The mares in the pool stopped their playing and turned to him. He remained still and watched them, dazzled by their extreme loveliness. The band of mares looked back at him, then at each other in amazement at the sudden appearance of the stranger. With frightened cries, the three ran from the pool into the woods, but the albino remained.

The stallion waited, but she did not make a move to follow the others. She was plainly unafraid of the Black. Her tail swished angrily as she stared back at this unwelcome intruder who had spoiled her afternoon.

The Black stayed where he was. He knew that in the wild, where there was a band of mares, there would also be a stallion nearby. Moments later, the band returned, but this time they were led by a young stallion with a pale gray coat.

The Black whistled a warning and waited for the inevitable. He felt no fear. His body began to tremble in anticipation of the battle that was to come. It was not his first, and he knew what to expect. His courage and cunning would see him through this fight as they had many times before.

The young gray stallion screamed his challenge, throwing his head and tossing his mane. Then he broke into a run and charged to the pool, making a show of his speed and strength. The Black watched him, content to let the other stallion make the first move. The gray shrilled again, yet there was something uncertain in the sound of his cries. His long-limbed stride fell unsteady. The anxious gray broke his charge, slamming to a stop beside the mare on the far side of the stream leading to the pool. His red-rimmed eyes flashed and bulged in their sockets as he glared at the black stranger silently waiting for him.

All at once, the gray turned his attention to the albino mare, warning her of their danger with squeals and snorts. When she did not heed his commands, he swung his hindquarters around, lashing the air with his hooves. She sidestepped the blow, then with a savage cry, lifted her forefeet to trample the ground between them.

The enraged gray stallion whirled toward the Black and stood battle ready, his nostrils flared, his ears pinned against his head. There was no turning back for him now. Behind him, the band of mares clustered together for protection, watching and waiting for the fight to come.

The gray rocked back on his haunches and sprang forward. This time he leaped over the stream and made a headlong charge at the invader to his realm. The Black stepped forward to meet him, his fury mounting as he rose up on his hind legs, lashing the air with his hooves, then bringing them crashing to the ground. The lead shank dangling from his halter whipped snakelike around his head.

The two horses faced off for a brief moment, and the mountain air rang with their war cries. Then the young gray bravely reared and lunged at the larger, older stallion, his teeth seeking the Black's neck. But the gray was not quick enough, and one of the Black's forehooves caught him squarely in the shoulder. The blow staggered the young stallion. Moving steadily closer, the giant black horse took the offensive and rose up again, his ears pinned, his mane waving about his fine, small head like a black flag.

There were more squeals and the sounds of hooves battering flesh. Overpowering his attacker with cunning and experience, the black stallion landed blow after blow. And then the fight was decided, over almost as quickly as it started. The gray cried out in defeat and wheeled to get away. The Black chased him, but his intention was not to kill but only to frighten.

To kill one so young and inexperienced would prove nothing.

The gray scampered off across the pasture on the far side of the pool, calling for the mares to follow him as he fled. Frightened by the battle, the band had scattered but now regrouped to follow after their defeated leader. All but one.

The black stallion watched the mares run off and knew he could have taken them, but he let them go. He turned his attention to the one who remained. The one who had so captivated his imagination since he first saw her. The whitest of the white would now reckon with the blackest of the black. Surely she would accept him, even praise him in his triumph.

The mare stood in the streambed watching him approach, still unafraid, her ruby-tinted eyes holding him in their powerful gaze. Never had the stallion beheld such a horse. She was beautiful but somehow repulsive at the same time, unimaginably different from the rest of his kind. Almost imperceptible in the scent around her was something frightening, something that spoke of wolf or some other predator.

The Black slowed to stop and then stepped forward to meet her. She whinnied and tossed her head, as if to welcome him. Then, like a great white bird that had been driven from its perch, the mare spun around and bounded away. For a moment it looked as if she might turn back, but then she kept going. The stallion broke after her, but his hesitation had cost him. It would have been easy to catch her in the open, but the stallion knew that once she reached the trees, it would be different. This was her turf, not his. There among the unknown trails of this strange mountain forest, he would be at a disadvantage.

The mare reached the trees and slipped into the shadows. The Black raced in behind her. He had to slow almost to a stop to let his eyes adjust to the dark forest again. Even as he waited, the sound of the mare's hooves ahead told him where to go. Soon he was plunging through the mottled tunnel as fast as he dared.

He broke into a clearing again and searched for some sign of the mare. It was as if she had vanished completely. He frantically scented the wind for some hint as to where she had gone. Her scent was there, but his nostrils caught fresh smells, too, and his pricked ears could hear the sounds of voices, the sounds of people. The wind filled his nostrils again, and then, very clearly, he scented one person in particular, his partner, the boy who was his friend. With a fierce snort, he wheeled around to follow the trail upwind.

7

Acropolis

It was the sound of his horse's cry that brought Alec Ramsay back to consciousness. He lay on the muddy ground, trying to remember where he was and how he got there. Then came the whistle again, loud and clear, a sound unlike any other—the war cry of a stallion. It was the Black. Pulling himself to his feet, Alec followed the sound. The stallion was no more than fifty yards away, not in the water but already up on the riverbank. And he was not alone. A group of men were there, calling back and forth in excited cries and whoops. They wore white robed uniforms and carried pitchforks and spears. They were trying to surround the Black. The men closed in on the stallion like a pack of hungry wolves, threatening him with their weapons.

Who are these men? Alec thought. A hunting party from some mountain tribe? What were they trying to do to his horse?

Alec cried out but could produce only a strangled

gag from his water-tortured lungs. And, even though he was only a short distance away, the hooting men did not see him. All their attention was focused on the Black. Desperate to reach his horse, Alec took a step, only to fall as his injured left leg collapsed beneath him. He got up again and hopped ahead on his good leg. Each painful bounce shot an arrow of pain through his injured left ankle.

Calling out in words of some language Alec did not recognize, the robed men were attempting to maneuver the Black back against the stream. They formed a semicircle in front of the stallion, waving their spears and closing in tighter around him, blocking his escape.

The Black was standing his ground before his tormentors, rearing high, his forelegs striking out into the air. White lather ran in streaks across the glistening black satin of his shoulders. His mouth was open, his teeth bared. Lightning flashed from his eyes.

The men scattered out of the way as the stallion plunged his forelegs to the ground again and again, his body contorted, his eyes filled with hate. Thunder rolled from his hooves with each crash of his pounding legs. Then, with another wild, high-pitched whistle, he reared again.

One man strode forward, braver than the rest. He held a club like a baseball bat. When the stallion's hooves met the ground, the man lunged closer, fiercely swinging his bat.

With a quick side step, the Black avoided the blow. Reversing direction, he turned on his attacker. The man cried out as the stallion stuck him on the shoulder, butting him to the ground. The other men recoiled and then quickly regrouped. Brave in their anger now, they moved in to protect their fallen comrade, pushing the Black back against the stream. The stallion was trapped, magnificent in his savage fury, but also alone and frustrated.

Alec found his voice at last and called out, but the hunters were so caught up in the frenzy of their battle with the Black that they still didn't hear him. Or perhaps they did hear him but were simply ignoring him. Clearly the Black was giving them plenty to think about. Alec hobbled closer as one of the hunters pulled his wounded friend back.

Another hunter raised his spear, and at the same instant that Alec shouted "No," a cry cut through the air, an urgent voice calling out one of the few Greek words Alec actually understood.

"*Oh-hee!* No!"

It was a young woman's voice, and it startled all of them. The men turned in the direction of the shouts, and Alec saw the water-soaked figure of Xeena rush in to step between them and the Black.

More shouts filled the air as the Black noticed his friend. The men could not stop the Black as he broke away and ran to Alec.

Alec raised his arms to the stallion as his horse came to him. With the touch of his horse, Alec felt new strength pulse through his body. He rubbed his face against the wet warmth of the dark coat. The shaking and trembling of his body stopped.

They may not be safe, Alec thought, but they were together and alive.

Between the stallion and the sudden presence of the two waterlogged strangers, the men in the hunting party seemed unsure of what to do. One roared madly, another laughed, and yet another raised his spear and jabbed at the sky. Then, as one, they regrouped and turned their attention to the Black and the young man.

Xeena's voice rose louder. She was not pleading now. Alec did not understand the words, but the meaning was clear: stay away!

The men stopped. But then one stepped forward to confront the girl. Another shouted angrily to Alec in Greek, then in German and finally in English. "Papers!" he demanded.

The Black snorted and pulled back as the men gathered in front of them. Alec held on to the stallion's halter, feeling better for the first time in hours. After what had happened inside the mountain, this was nothing. Certainly the men would help them once they knew what he, Xeena and the Black had just been through. Up close, Alec saw that they all looked to be no more than teenagers. Their spears and white togas made him think of boys dressing up for a school play. But they weren't acting like boys. They were acting like police, and quite unfriendly police at that.

"American," Alec said, raising his hands. "Everything okay. No problemo."

The closest young man's face contorted with disdain at the sound of Alec's casual American voice. "Papers!" he repeated. It was an absurd request, considering the circumstances, like pulling a shipwrecked sailor from the sea and asking him for ID before giving him a cup of water to drink.

Alec patted the pockets of his soggy jeans and shrugged. "Sorry," he said coolly. "I must have left them in my other bathing suit." He wasn't used to being ordered about by a guy wearing a toga. He ignored the man and turned to Xeena. "Are you okay?"

She nodded.

"Tell these psychos that we need help, would you?"

"Papers!" the man barked again, shaking his spear for effect.

Alec was about to tell the man what he could do

with his papers when Xeena said something, and the man turned to glare at her, then pointed his spear off to the right toward the woods.

"Just do what they say, Alec," she said. "They must be the security force for the Acracia resort. They want us to come with them."

Two men walked in front of Xeena, Alec and the Black while the rest took up positions behind. The guards ushered Alec and Xeena to the head of a path leading into the forest. Alec kept a short hold on the Black's lead shank. The stallion had scratches and scrapes along his right side, but otherwise he seemed to have survived their ordeal in the underground river without serious injury. Of course, Alec would not know for certain until he had a chance to stop and examine his horse, and the guards didn't seem likely to agree to that. Alec could see they were still frightened of the Black, and they were dangerous in their fear. The one who had been knocked to the ground staggered along at the rear of the procession, his friends now leaving him to fend for himself.

The guards hurried them up the path, goading them along as if they were criminals. Alec limped ahead, shivering with cold. He was angry about the way they were being treated but smart enough to know that arguing was pointless. Sooner or later they would have to report to someone in authority. When they did, Alec planned on giving whoever it was an earful.

Xeena picked up a stick and handed it to Alec to use as a crutch. Alec started to say something, but she put a finger to her lips and made a sign to him to be quiet. Alec tried to read her expression. Somehow he wanted to laugh, just to break the tension. After all they'd just been through inside the mountain, now they were being hustled along by these spear-happy juvenile delinquents to who knew where? Alec shook his head. Whatever happened, he thought, at least he and the Black were on dry land.

Xeena marched along stoically beside him, her face a mask. What had happened to her in the underground river? Alec wondered. There would be time to talk about it later.

The men led them on, and soon the path opened up to a clearing bordered on one side by a stream and by woods on the other. This stream was narrower and slower moving than the one that had swept them through the mountain. The water was darker, too, almost black, even in the sunlight. Across the stream and beyond a narrow strip of carefully tended grass was a thirty-foot-high stone wall. The wall ran along in a straight line for what seemed a hundred yards or more in either direction before vanishing back into the forest shadows. Alec saw movement atop the wall, someone waving them all toward a heavy wooden gate. Above and beyond the walls were the tops of towers and temples. Some of the high roofs were curved like quarter moons.

What sort of place was this? Alec thought. If this was Acracia, it was supposed to be some sort of upscale resort. But the young men surrounding him didn't look like security guards to Alec. And why all the security, anyway? he wondered. Why the hostility? Didn't anyone see they were hurt and needed help?

The security guards drove Alec, Xeena and the Black forward. There was a small cabin next to the gate, a sentry post. A helmeted guard emerged, dressed in the same white toga-type costume as the others. He looked at them with suspicion. Suddenly everyone began speaking at once.

Again words flew back and forth between Xeena and the guards. Alec wished he knew more than half a dozen words of Greek; at least, he thought Greek was what they were speaking. Perhaps it was Bulgarian or Russian, but whatever it was, Xeena seemed to be holding her own in the conversation, her tone respectful but determined.

All at once, there was the sound of a horn trumpeting through the air. The guards instantly stopped their shouting. Standing at attention, they cast their eyes straight ahead. The sound from the horn faded, and a commanding voice called down from atop the ramparts. Alec looked to where the voice was coming from but couldn't see a thing.

Some guards remained at attention while three others ran to push open the heavy wooden doors. Here we go, Alec thought. At last they'd reached someone in charge. The guards backed off and gestured for them to pass through the gate.

The Black stood still, his head held high, his eyes peering beyond the giant, swinging doors, ready and alert for whatever might come. The stallion swished his tail lightly. Alec waited, knowing that his own frail, human senses could never match those of his horse. If there was danger ahead, the Black would be the first to warn them of it. Alec wondered what time it was. By the position of the sun overhead, he could tell they were already well into the afternoon.

Beyond the open gate were voices, but Alec could see no one. They started over a small wooden bridge, crossing above the stream and the embankment that edged the wall's foundation stones. The dark entrance through the gate yawned at them as they cautiously made their way past the towering wooden doors. The passageway led through thick stone blocks for at least twenty feet. Could these walls really be that thick? Alec wondered.

The passageway opened onto a path of hard-packed red dirt. Alec looked around him. At first he thought the place was a fortress, or perhaps a castle with a moat around it, the sort of place a medieval king might live in. But now he saw that the interior was much larger, a complete city surrounded by walls.

The dirt path ended at a stone block building. Atop the windowless structure was a balcony and beyond that a distant line of columns. A man wearing a sleeveless white tunic was descending steps from the balcony. A blue cloak was draped over his shoulder.

The man came toward them and called out in words Alec didn't understand. He was about Alec's size and young-looking, but his face was framed by a wispy beard. His hair was cut short, unlike the longer-haired security force from the forest and the helmeted guards at the gate.

Xeena returned the greeting, and they spoke a moment. The man kept his eyes fixed on the Black. The stallion threw back his head, and Alec spoke to him and held him still.

"What's he saying?" Alec asked Xeena.

"He says we must come in and that we are lucky to have found our way here."

Alec managed a laugh, gesturing to the troop of guards who had captured them. "I'd say we didn't have much choice in that."

The young man gave a small bow and spoke to Xeena, though clearly his words were meant for Alec as well. Xeena listened and then nodded. "He says we should follow him. He says we are just in time for dinner."

"Dinner?" Alec said. "Tell him we need a telephone."

Xeena relayed Alec's words, and the young man replied with a smile and gestured farther up the path. "He says he apologizes for the way we have been treated and that we should get some dry clothes and a moment's rest."

The robed man bowed again and then started up a path leading away from the balcony steps. Alec didn't have the energy to argue, even if he'd known what language to do it in. Alec, Xeena and the Black followed a path up into the walled city.

They came to a courtyard in front of what looked like a replica of a classic Greek temple, complete with high Ionic columns that rose to support a great gabled roof of carved stone. In the center of the courtyard was a small marble altar. A stone figure rose up behind the altar, a life-size statue of a rearing white horse.

It was an awesome sight, but Alec could hardly appreciate it. He staggered ahead, leaning on his tree-branch crutch for support with one hand and holding tight to the Black's lead with the other. Pain shot through his leg as he tried to keep up with his horse. He would have liked to mount up, just to take the pressure off his ankle, but he didn't dare risk it until he was certain the stallion was sound enough to handle his weight. After all they'd just been through, it seemed a miracle that any of them were still standing at all.

They crossed the courtyard, and their guide led them to a narrow ramp that ran up to the temple, a wide, empty pavilion with a stone floor and high ceiling supported by rows of columns. Passing outside again, they came to a plaza lush with grass and flowering trees.

Under one of the trees, they surprised three girls playing dominos around a stone table. All were wearing white tunics much like their guide's outfit. The girls had been laughing and talking but became quiet and stared as the strangers passed by. The guide greeted them, and the girls politely answered, then returned their attention to their game.

Alec looked around and was surprised to see so few people outside. The buildings bordering the plaza seemed almost empty, though he thought he could see figures moving within the shadows of the doors. But no one stood in their doorways or looked out their windows.

The Black nudged Alec's shoulder as their guide led them to a garden at the far end of the plaza. In the center of the garden, among the flowers and sculpted trees, was a circular fountain of marble and rough stone. On an island pedestal inside the fountain stood another statue of a rearing white horse, its forelegs striking out into the air. Like the statue in the gateway entrance, its neck was long and slender and arched to a small, refined head.

Someone was waiting for them beside the fountain, a short, bald man with a long, wispy beard. Despite the bald head and beard, he looked to be no more than thirty years old with a young face and sharp, deep-set eyes so bright and animal-like they were almost inhuman. He spoke to them in English with a heavy German accent.

"Welcome to the acropolis of Acracia and the palace of Governor Medio, a refuge from the modern world," the man said. "We have been expecting you, young Alex."

"Expecting me?" Alec said. "How's that? And . . . how did you know my name?"

"Could it be any other?" The man smiled and nodded knowingly, as if he and Alec shared some dark secret.

"Actually it's Alec, not Alex, but how . . ."

"Of course it is," he said, cutting off Alec's words. "Myself, I go by the name Spiro. There are few English speakers here, so the governor asked me to carry his blessings and bid you welcome. Acracia is honored to have you, young lord. Her cups are brimming over. May I offer you a drink?" He dipped a large clay cup into the water of the pool and held it out to Alec. "Drink deeply, and of your own free will," he said.

It was an almost ceremonial gesture. Even the cup seemed more like a chalice than a cup. It was hand-painted pottery decorated with horses, moons and stars.

Alec didn't want to be rude, so he accepted the cup and drank. The water tasted cool and clean, incredibly fresh. A tingling sensation warmed his insides. The man then refilled the cup and passed it to Xeena, who glanced at Alec and then drank from the cup as well. The Black sniffed at the water in the pool at the base of the fountain. He snorted, bobbed his head and back-stepped a few paces. "Easy boy," Alec said.

"What magnificence," Spiro exclaimed. "Is he of the red road or the white road?"

"Road?" Alec asked.

"Yes, by what path did he bring you here, the red or the white?"

Alec didn't know what to make of that question. He was cold and wet and had had just about enough of these toga-wearing fools for one afternoon.

"Path? We didn't take any path. We . . . But does it really matter now how we got here? We are tired. We are hurt. I need a telephone. We need—"

"All in good time, Herr Alex," Spiro said. "First you must get out of those wet clothes, have some food and be made comfortable." With a small bow, Spiro backed away and then gestured to the man who had guided them here. "Darius will show you to your quarters."

"Telephone," Alec said. "We need a telephone. Can't you find us a . . ."

Spiro gave no answer. He merely kept his head down in polite deference and continued backing away, then turned and walked off.

"What is it with these people?" Alec wondered aloud.

Xeena looked at him and shook her head. Her wet hair was plastered around her face and shoulders, her skin and clothes splashed with mud. Alec could only imagine how he looked to her.

He took a breath and shrugged. He'd been through so much in the past few hours that he didn't know what to think anymore. There didn't seem to be much else he could do but go along, at least for the moment.

Their guide gestured for them to follow. Alec turned to Xeena. "Tell him we need to get word back to the others about what happened. Surely they are missing us by now and wondering where we went."

Xeena spoke to the guide, and he replied in words

that the girl translated. "He says they will get a message back to the monastery for us. He says we need to come with him and that they have food for us."

"We need to get some food for my horse first," Alec said. "Ask him where the stable is."

Xeena translated Alec's question. The guide gestured to a grand-looking complex of buildings and replied. Alec could see Xeena was surprised at the answer. "He says the Black is coming into the citadel with us."

"Is there a stable there?"

Xeena nodded. "He says they have quarters for horses as well as guests inside. He says the Black is an honored guest, as are we, and deserves the finest accommodations they can provide."

"Guests?" Alec said. "But where in the heck are we, Xeena? Who are these people?"

"I do not have a clue," Xeena said. "The guide is speaking in Greek, but it's a dialect I never heard before. The one called Spiro who spoke English sounded German."

"But why the period clothes?" Alec said. "And these buildings . . . the temple columns, the statues and gardens. Who built them? It's like we just stepped back in time a couple thousand years. Is this a resort or some kind of theme park?"

Xeena shrugged, though her eyes were wide with

curiosity. "If it is the resort, I had no idea it looked anything like this."

Alec sighed. He was in a strange land, and his instincts told him to keep his head and wait and see what happened next before doing anything stupid that he might later regret. Maybe there was a phone in the citadel or wherever it was they were going.

Some food would be nice, Alec thought, again noticing the tingling sensation warming his insides. It was as if the water he'd just drank had been a super-fortified energy drink instead of spring water. He had to admit it was a good feeling, like a second wind, and he found new energy pulsing through his veins as they climbed another ramp. Even his injured ankle seemed to feel better now. Only minutes before, the aching pain had been bad enough to make his skin hurt. Now he felt as if someone were rubbing his leg with a silk cloth and soothing the pain away.

With the renewed strength of his second wind, Alec followed their guide toward a complex of simple, elegant buildings made of finely carved stone.

"That must be it," Xeena said. "The citadel."

Soon they were crossing the marble floor of a gallery. Two rows of columns, seven on each side, supported a double-vaulted ceiling. Stairways and ramps led up to the second story on each end. The ceiling was covered with glyphs and inscriptions written in a language Alec didn't recognize. A faint smell of incense tinged the air.

They turned down a hallway and came to a suite of apartments. Inside were spacious quarters that Darius indicated were accommodations for Alec, Xeena and the Black. There were three main rooms in all, one for Xeena, the middle room for the Black and the third for Alec. There were connecting doors between all the rooms and separate doors leading out to the hallway on one side and half doors to a shared balcony overlooking a plaza on the other side.

The Black's room was unlike any stable Alec had ever seen, more akin to the private sitting room of a wealthy English lord than a stable for a horse. Rich tapestries hung on the wall. The bedding covering the floor was not common straw but some kind of impossibly soft, gold-colored grass, like extra fine wheat or oats, with sweet-smelling white flower petals mixed in.

The Black whiffed at the bedding and then moved to a feed trough, which seemed to be made of ivory. The water pail hanging on the wall beside it was plated with gold.

Alec heard soft voices outside. A moment later, attendants appeared at the door like ghosts bearing gifts for the Black, soft wool blankets, fine brushes, a sponge, pails of fresh grain, almonds and raisins. Then, as quickly as they appeared, the attendants were gone again.

Alec sampled the Black's food before he gave it to his horse. The grain smelled and tasted a little sweet, but otherwise he couldn't detect anything wrong with it. The nuts and raisins seemed fine as well. This was something Alec would have done for his horse in any strange place they found themselves. There was always the possibility of the food being tainted or doped up. It only made sense to be especially cautious in a place like this, where he still felt more like a prisoner than a guest. The feed seemed safe enough, though, and Alec decided to give it a chance.

The Black set upon his food, and the guide beckoned to one of the rooms adjacent to the Black's quarters. Plates were spread out on a table along with bowls of grapes, bread, cheese and yogurt. There were towels and dry clothes folded neatly on an ornately framed bed. A steaming bath waited in a marble tub.

"You okay?" Alec asked Xeena.

"This place," she said. "I've never seen anything like it."

Darius gestured to the tub and spoke. "He says this is my room," Xeena said. "Yours is on the other side of the Black's."

"Sounds great," Alec said.

The girl nodded and gave Alec a soggy smile. They

hadn't had much to smile about in the last few hours, so it was nice to see. Darius spoke some words to Xeena, then bowed and began backing slowly toward the door. Xeena called a question after him, and he answered her in a soft, humble voice. Alec saw that she didn't seem satisfied with the answer and asked it again. Darius only repeated his answer, even more quiet this time. Then he bowed again, stepped out into the hallway and was gone.

Alec looked at Xeena. "What was that about?"

"I asked for a telephone," she said.

"What did he say?"

"It was hard to tell. The dialect he is speaking is very unusual, like I said; at least I've never heard it before. From what I can tell, he just keeps saying they will get the message out."

Alec shook his head. "Let's hope so." He looked down at the serving bowls and suddenly felt his appetite returning. "Come on," he said, picking up a piece of flat bread. "Let's eat."

After they finished a light meal, Alec stepped through the connecting door to the Black's stable, where he spent the next few minutes tending to his horse. First he led the stallion out onto the wide balcony overlooking a spacious courtyard. Alec found a bucket of hot water and set to work getting his horse cleaned up and dried off. As he worked, he realized that he had almost completely forgotten about his twisted ankle. It seemed to hurt hardly at all now. Maybe he hadn't injured it as badly as he thought.

His gaze stretched to the opposite end of the courtyard. Beyond a line of carefully trimmed trees, he could see a much larger building, like a palace, crowned with gables and royal-blue tile. It was rectangular and framed by a long row of columns. In front was a wide patio. Figures dressed in white climbed up and down the stone steps between the palace and a sculpture garden in the courtyard below. Around the courtyard were small buildings and guest wings, like the one where Alec was staying. Everything beyond was bordered by the high stone wall separating this place from the world outside.

Where were they? Alec wondered. It looked like some incredible lost city hidden from the world for centuries. Of course, it couldn't be that; it had to be some theme resort. Whatever it was, this place was unlike anything Alec had ever seen.

He rubbed down his horse with a soft cloth, the warm touch snapping him back to the present. There was a quiet alarm ringing in the back of his mind that told him to be careful and stay alert. Alec spoke to the Black in soothing words as he brushed the stallion's coat, drawing on the touch of his horse to give him strength.

After cleaning the stallion's feet with a hoof pick

that looked like it was gold-plated, Alec brought the Black back inside. The stallion seemed more curious than wary now. He nosed at the grain in his fancy ivory manger. Alec covered him with a stable blanket. It was made of a plush blue cloth, almost like velvet. As he pulled the blanket over the stallion's back, he saw an image woven into the fabric, a rearing white horse with a Greek inscription written beneath. The figure resembled the horse depicted in the statues he had seen earlier. Alec had also seen the image on banners that hung from some of the buildings they had passed.

Alec double-checked everything, then left his horse and crossed through the connecting door into his own room again.

He picked up the clothes that were laid out for him on the bed, a white tunic, a rope belt and a blue cloak, the same sort of getup everyone else seemed to be wearing. Leather sandals were placed neatly on the floor by the door.

Alec took off his wet clothes and stepped into the bath, wondering who had drawn it for him. There was an ornamented faucet plated in gold at one end of the tub. Fine copper piping etched with designs led from the faucet into the wall. Despite the ornamentation, the plumbing seemed primitive and not what a guest would expect in a first-class resort, Alec thought. The toilet was little more than a marble-lined hole in the floor. The room was lit by oil lamps hanging from the ceiling. He wondered if the people here even used electricity, as he hadn't seen anything electrical anywhere.

After a quick bath, Alec dressed and opened the door to the balcony. The terrace spanned the entire upper floor of the building, and Xeena was standing over by the edge. Like Alec, she had washed up and was now wearing the uniform of everyone he had seen so far in this place—a sleeveless white tunic tied at the waist by a blue cord.

She laughed when she saw Alec. "You look good in a dress," she said.

"At least it's dry," Alec said.

"How's your boy?" Xeena asked, and then followed Alec to the stallion's room to see for herself. The Black lifted his head from the ivory feed trough for a moment as they stepped inside. He came to Alec and eyed the girl briefly, then gazed out to the courtyard and the mountains beyond.

Alec glanced at Xeena and smiled. Gradually it seemed that the beginning of a friendship was growing between Xeena and the Black, Alec noticed. He didn't pull away from her anymore when she approached, and he even let her stroke his neck from time to time.

Alec pointed at the Black's gold-plated bucket. "Did you see that? It looks like gold."

"Looks like it."

"Same with the hoof pick."

Xeena shook her head. "Could it be real?"

"To be honest, I have no idea what real gold looks like," Alec said.

The Black snorted and Alec moved to his horse. "And did you see this blanket?" he said. "It feels like velvet. What's that say there? Isn't that in Greek? Or is it Russian?"

"It's Greek," Xeena said. "Old Greek. The classical kind that no one uses anymore." She read the words sewn into the blanket. "I think it says, 'House of the White Horse, particularly beloved of the gods.'"

"The gods?" Alec said. "Like the Greek gods?"

"Who else could it be?" she said. "It looks like whoever runs this place is trying to re-create a classical Greek city."

"They certainly have the money to spend," Alec said, "way beyond anything I've ever seen. I mean, who can afford a golden hoof pick?" He glanced at the Black and the white horse figure sewn into the blanket. "Any idea who this horse is supposed to be?"

"It might be Poseidon. He was the god of horses for the Greeks."

"I thought he was the sea god," Alec said.

"The god of horses too," Xeena said. "But there were other horse gods and demigods, too, like Pegasus.

Zeus supposedly gave Achilles an immortal horse—I forget its name—and there were other horse-type creatures besides immortal horses too. Some of them weren't always so friendly, like the centaurs that would get drunk on wine, crash wedding parties and carry off the brides."

Alec took a deep breath and looked at his horse. They had to get out of this place. The Black needed to get checked out by a vet. He looked at Xeena. "You sure you're okay? We're lucky to be alive after getting dragged into that underground river."

"I don't know if it's shock or what, but I feel pretty good now."

"So do I," Alec said, "but don't ask me why. My leg doesn't even hurt anymore." He shook his head. "But we still need to get word back to the others. And I haven't seen a sign of a telephone or anything electrical since we've been here."

"No mirrors either," Xeena said, "at least not in my room." They both returned to the balcony and gazed over the wide plaza, which was completely empty except for a few distant figures, perhaps gardeners pruning a tree.

What sort of place had they stumbled into? Alec wondered again. For the first time, the thought struck him that perhaps this wasn't a resort at all, that it was something else, someplace that really did belong to another time, a real-life Shangri-la. Who could say where that underground river had swept them to? Maybe, like Dorothy in the *Wizard of Oz*, they really weren't in Kansas anymore.

8

Fire-eyes

There was a soft knock at Alec's door, and he and Xeena stepped inside the room to see who was there. At the door were four attendants, young women in white tunics. They entered the room bearing vases of long-stemmed white flowers. With small steps, they brought the flowers to a table, eyes downcast, silent, with heads bent low deferentially.

Xeena spoke to the girls in Greek, then in what sounded like Italian. They looked at each other, and Alec thought he saw the glint of recognition in one girl's eyes before she averted her gaze and her face became sullen and empty again. Whether she understood and didn't want to answer or really didn't understand what Xeena was asking her, the girl only smiled and shrugged. Then the mute attendants set the vases down and left the room as silently as they had come.

A white envelope accompanied the gift of flowers. Inside was a note written in formal-looking English script. Alec picked up the note and showed it to Xeena. She read it aloud. " 'Medio bids you welcome and requests your presence at a banquet to celebrate the coming of the full moon. Spiro.' "

Alec couldn't believe it. "A banquet? After everything we've been through, we're supposed to get dressed up and go out on the town? This is just too much."

Xeena shrugged stoically, as if nothing could surprise her anymore.

Alec paced the room a minute, trying to collect his senses. What a day it had been, he thought. So much had happened already it made his head spin just to think about it all. He pondered the possibility of slipping out on his own and trying to find a phone somewhere but decided against it. He didn't feel comfortable leaving the Black just then, even with Xeena there. They didn't seem to be in any danger. In fact, they were being treated extremely well here, almost as if they really had been expected guests. Aside from the fact that there did not seem to be any phones, there was nothing to complain about, except . . .

Except there was tension looming in the air, and something told him to be careful, as if he, Xeena and the Black might have walked into an attractive trap. As it was, there wasn't much more he could do about it but sit tight and see what developed. And patience was something Alec was practiced at, a skill required every day at the track, especially at the jumbled start of a horse race. Somehow, at that moment, he could feel the same sense of anticipation, as if everything was about to bust loose. He told himself to be patient, watchful and ready to move when the time came.

A soft breeze blew across Alec's bare calves. He looked down at the sandals on his feet. He wished his jeans were dry so he could get out of this ridiculous outfit. It was like walking around in a knee-length T-shirt. He stepped over to where his pants were hanging on a chair and touched them. Still soaked. He felt the pockets and found a few coins inside one of them that had miraculously remained there through the ordeal in the river. They might be useful if he could find a pay phone somewhere. Meanwhile, he and Xeena passed some time pitching pennies against a wall while recounting to each other the events of this extremely strange day.

About a half hour later, Alec brought the Black out of his room and onto the balcony, letting him take a look around and scent the fresh breeze. The stallion peered out over the courtyard. His ears were pricked, his nostrils flared, his eyes alert. Alec watched his horse, and it gave him some comfort that the Black's light feed seemed to have agreed with him.

In the courtyard below, long shadows fell from the

towering colonnades of the palace and cast themselves in black bars over the steps. Farther back, beyond the environs of the acropolis and the high Acracian walls, the last flashing streams of late-afternoon sunlight purpled the mountain forest. Alec lifted his gaze to the horizon and the mountain peaks that rose up on all sides around them. A few specks of firelight twinkled like stars in the black night of the distant forest.

The breeze wafting in from the courtyard now brought with it the faint sounds of live music, the soft, faraway strains of a harp and flute. The music sounded off-key and ethereal, one more thing that seemed as if it belonged in another time. Alec looked in the direction the music was coming from and noticed the glowing of lights inside the palace. More people were gathering on the patio in front of the central building, on the steps and in the courtyard garden.

"Looks like something is going on over there, all right," Xeena said.

Before long, Alec heard steps coming down the hall, and there was another knock on the door. Xeena went to see who it was while Alec stayed on the balcony with the Black.

It was Darius, the guide who had led them to their quarters. Two attendants followed him into the room and out to the balcony. The Black turned his head and eyed the strangers suspiciously as they came closer.

Alec moved to his horse and put a hand on the stallion's halter. The attendants gazed up at the Black warily as Darius spoke with Xeena in Greek. Darius bowed and then beckoned for Alec and the others to come with him.

Xeena translated for Alec. "He says he will escort us to the megaron," she said. "I think that is what they call that large building. He says to bring the Black with us."

"Did he get in touch with your dad and the crew back at the monastery?"

"He says they sent a message."

"We don't need a go-between in this," Alec said, his frustration boiling over at last. "Where's the darn phone? I'd like to explain what happened in person. I also need to arrange to have the Black checked out by a vet when we get back. What am I supposed to do? Send smoke signals?"

Xeena relayed Alec's request to Darius, who only smiled, lowered his eyes and gestured to the hall door. The two attendants stood to one side, quietly waiting for the strangers and the giant black horse to pass. Alec hesitated.

Darius gestured again. "Come, please," he said.

Xeena looked at Alec. "Shall we?"

"Why not," he said. "Maybe we can find that

Spiro guy. I need to speak with someone in charge around here, someone who understands English."

Alec led the Black from the balcony and out to the hallway. They followed Darius down the hall to a ramp descending to the plaza below. The two silent attendants trailed behind them. Darius led them along a path of flat stone that cut through a lush lawn to the courtyard garden fronting the megaron. Young people were congregated there, including a group of women playing flutes and small, handheld harps. The music stopped and a hushed silence passed over the group as they turned their attention to the strangers and the magnificent black stallion.

The Black seemed to enjoy the notice he was getting, throwing out his forehooves, almost swaggering as he walked beside Alec and Xeena. His ears were pitched forward as he listened to every sound.

They climbed the stone ramp running through the center of the steps and up to the patio. As they reached the top level, the two attendants suddenly rushed up and stopped them before they could go any farther. Their quick movements startled the Black. He tossed his head and jerked on his lead line. Alec held the stallion tight while one of the attendants stepped over to him. The young man said something and touched Alec on the left shoulder.

"Hey," Alec said. "Back off."

The young man pulled back and lowered his head apologetically. Alec turned to Xeena. "What's this guy want?" Alec said.

Darius spoke up and said something that sounded like an apology. Xeena seemed to understand. She smiled and laughed.

"It's your cloak," she said. "It's supposed to hang over your left shoulder. I think it is some kind of protocol here in the megaron."

The attendant held up his hands politely to show he meant no harm. Alec fumbled with the cloak and then acquiesced to let the attendant pull it from his back, where Alec had been wearing it like a sloppy cape, and adjust it so it draped evenly over his left shoulder. The attendant gave Alec a courteous nod and stepped over to Xeena. She gave him her cloak, and he folded it carefully, then slung it over her left shoulder, fussing with it a moment until it hung evenly. When that was done, Darius gestured them ahead toward the torch-lit interior of the megaron.

Alec looked up at the Black and touched the stallion's well-groomed coat. Just pretend you're going to a costume party, Alec told himself. And however silly he might be dressed, at least his horse looked great.

They started down a long hall toward a wooden door. Decorative vases stood on the floor or on

pedestals. Much of the interior walls, cornices, paneling and doors were painted in blue and gold. There
were few people here. The Black's hooves clicked
sharply in the quiet.

The big doors swung open from the inside as if by
magic, and Darius beckoned them ahead to a reception room. Tapestries decorated the wall, covered with
picture writing and strange symbols. There was a bust
of a young man's head on a pedestal, the stone painted
in flesh tones for the skin and red for the lips. From
the next room came the sound of a crowd.

They passed into the main room, where more statuary of ghostly white horses stood like sentries on either side of the door. A golden cage sat on a pedestal
of sculpted stone. Inside the cage, two blue birds trilled
a welcome.

The room was as big as a football field and lit by
thousands of candles burning in stands. At both ends
of the enormous room, logs blazed inside fireplaces the
size of small houses. Guests sat on the floor and at tables and on couches grouped around the three sides of
a long slab of raised marble laden with platters of
food. White-robed musicians strolled about playing
lilting tunes on harps and flutes.

"Look," Xeena said. "There are other horses
here."

It was true, Alec saw. On the other side of the

room, a chestnut Arabian mare stood beside a man re-
clining on a couch. A finely attired attendant carrying
a tray of food offered appetizers to the man and then
to the horse. Both declined.

Among the horses and people were three mares,
all colored a powdery white, all strikingly similar to
the albino mare he had seen at the waterfall that morning. These horses were not albinos, though. They
looked more like a cross between a Lipizzan and something else, maybe Arab, with dark eyes, fine heads and
short backs.

Perhaps he had been mistaken about the mare at
the waterfall being an albino, Alec thought. Maybe
it was one of these mares that had lured the Black
into the cave. Except for those red eyes—he certainly
couldn't have imagined those. And Xeena had seen
them too. No, Alec thought, that mare was not among
these three. Their coats were not the same impossibly
white color as the mare that had taunted the Black,
though they could have all been sisters they appeared
so incredibly alike. Their finely groomed coats shone
like pale sheets of smoked glass in the candlelight.

"People eat together with their horses in this
place?" Xeena said with surprise.

"I guess so," Alec said.

Well, Alec thought, maybe it wasn't all that
strange after all. He knew from firsthand experience

that Bedouins sometimes shared their tents with their horses. So did the Mongols and probably other people too. The big difference here was that this place looked like a king's palace, something far from a tent in the desert.

Darius directed them to one of the tables of honor near the long marble serving board. There were four finely carved wooden chairs with gold trim and gold velvet cushions, and there was plenty of room for the Black.

Alec stood beside his horse. The stallion was always unpredictable, but his years at the racetrack had instilled in him a high tolerance for crowds when necessary, and Alec was thankful for that now. The Black gazed around at the assembly, his eyes sparkling brightly. He was relaxed, Alec thought, and seemed to be enjoying all the attention he was receiving.

The guests' voices were a jarring mix of languages from all over Europe and beyond, from Russian, to German, to Greek, to Italian. Like the people, the dozen or so horses gathered in the hall were a mixed group, from enormous draft horses to elegant Arabs to tiny Shetland ponies. All seemed as at ease as the people in the luxurious surroundings of the banquet hall.

The aroma of spices and fine cooking filled the air. Xeena looked around the great hall, gaping at it all in openmouthed wonder, and Alec understood how she felt. It would have taken hours to ask about everything that caught his eye here. He lifted his gaze to the ceiling and saw murals depicting scenes out of mythology and a diagram of the orbits of the moon and seven planets.

At the sound of a gong, all the guests, horses and humans, took places at the dinner tables. The Black was served a bowl of fine oats that seemed ordinary enough to Alec when he gave them a taste test. Alec couldn't tell what the other horses were eating. The human guests were brought samplings of meat pastries and spiced vegetables. Alec and Xeena were tasting their appetizers when suddenly Spiro and a tall, blond woman arrived to take the empty chairs at their table.

"Mr. Spiro," Alec said casually. "Just the man I was hoping to see—"

Alec's words were cut off by the blare of trumpets, a fanfare to announce the arrival of the governor. Everyone stood up, and a man strode in leading a white horse by a golden rope. Instantly Alec recognized her as the albino mare they had seen at the waterfall. It seemed it had been a week ago but in truth had been only that morning. Behind the governor and the albino, a groom walked a young, gray stallion. He was of the same breed as the mares, seemingly similar in every way except for the color of his coat and his virile, masculine swagger. The gray pranced in proudly, then tossed his head and glared toward the Black's side of the room.

Alec had a hand on the Black's lead and quickly stepped up to his horse's head to keep him steady. But much to Alec's surprise, the stallion remained still, as if he was too mesmerized by the appearance of the ghostly albino mare to even notice the young stallion with her. The mare tossed her head but did not acknowledge the Black or the other guests.

The governor, the mare and the young stallion all took up places beside the three white mares at the center table. A hush fell over the assembly as the governor looked out among them like a king surveying his subjects. He was a big man with a soft, young face, almost like an overgrown baby, dressed in a velvet robe over a white tunic and wearing expensive-looking gold rings and bracelets. He addressed his guests in Greek and raised a goblet in the air. Everyone in the room stood up and raised their glasses as well. Attendants held bowls of water for the horses to share in the toast. The same attendant that had adjusted Alec's cloak approached the Black with a bowl, and Alec intercepted him before he came too close.

"Hold on just a second here, pal," Alec said as he took the bowl from the attendant and tasted the contents, just as he done with the Black's oats. It seemed to be nothing more than water.

A cry went up from the crowd. *"Chalazi to spiti tou Diomidi!"*

Alec glanced at Xeena. "It's a salute to the house of Diomedes," Xeena whispered.

Alec turned to see the governor on his feet and waving his cup. He was a giant of a man, easily six and a half feet tall, much taller than anyone else in the room, and yet his face was that of a child. *"Na Diomidi,"* the man called, gesturing to Alec's table and beckoning from across the room. All eyes moved to the strangers and the big black horse.

"He wants us to drink," Xeena whispered to Alec. "He's making a toast to Diomedes."

Alec raised his own glass and took a swallow. "I did," Alec said, holding up his glass and gesturing to the governor and his guests.

"I think he means the Black too," she said.

A murmur went up from the crowd, and some of the guests used their hands to pantomime lifting up a bowl and drinking. Alec looked out over the smiling, expectant faces at the tables around him. The governor raised his glass again. His gesture was more insistent this time.

The Black's bowl had been refilled. Alec sniffed at the water and tasted it once more. It looked clean and tasted fresh enough. He held the bowl so the Black could drink again. The stallion sniffed the water and took a sip. A roar went up from the crowd. Then the toasters sat down, and more trays were brought in. A moment later, everyone was once again merrily enjoying their food.

Spiro introduced the tall blond woman beside him as his wife. "Are you an American?" she asked in English, all smiles. Like Spiro, her accent sounded German. She had a boyish face with little blue eyes.

Alec nodded, then turned to Spiro and asked about making his phone call. Spiro told him that he had been in touch with the monastery and alerted them of their whereabouts. He promised to get Alec to a phone tomorrow morning, first thing. For now, Spiro said, Alec should relax and enjoy his food and the hospitality of Governor Medio.

Alec spoke, eager to share his thoughts with another English speaker. "What is this place?" he asked. "Where do these people come from?"

"All over the world," Spiro said.

"How do they find out about it? Do you advertise?"

"Acracia does not seek out patrons," Spiro said. "Word of its existence is known to but a few secret societies, the knowledge shared only when an initiate has reached a certain level of awareness."

"Why did those men attack us in the woods?" Alec asked.

"Strangers are not welcome here," Spiro explained.

"It is Medio's law. As his subjects, we are honored to do his bidding and pay him homage."

"Are you kidding me?" Alec said. "I thought this was a resort. And what do you mean 'we'? I am no one's subject. Who is this Medio person anyway? Can I talk with him?"

"You do not talk with that man; you listen to him." Spiro gestured out at the gathering. "He has brought us all this, and the waters of life."

"Waters of life?" Alec said. "What are you talking about? No one makes any sense around here."

"You cannot judge the governor as you would an ordinary man," Spiro continued, oblivious to Alec's comments. "The inexperienced cannot understand him. I am his chamberlain, and even I do not know him. Glory to the gods, we are all his vassals here."

Alec looked at Spiro's face. If the man is acting, he is doing a very good job, Alec thought. Plainly it didn't occur to Spiro that Governor Medio was no idol of Alec's.

"He lives here?"

"This is his home, though he retires to the shrine up on the mountain with his horses most of the year. These days he only returns to the acropolis for special occasions like tonight."

"He lives with his horses?"

Spiro pointed to the white mares at the head table.

"The sacred mares are normally sequestered atop Mt. Atnos," Spiro said, "at the temple of Diomedes. At this time of year, they sometimes come down to the palace for a visit during the full moon. Doubt me not when I say that it is with the mares' wondrous milk that the waters of Acracia are blessed, the reason the water here has such miraculous powers to restore vitality to all who drink it."

Alec started to laugh. "Is that what you people are selling here? The Fountain of Youth? I figured you were selling something."

Spiro lowered his head deferentially and spoke. "I beg your pardon, Herr Alex, but have I not heard that you were injured in some way before you arrived at the acropolis?"

Alec suddenly recalled his sprained ankle. He had forgotten completely about it.

"I grant you that it sounds mad," Spiro said, lifting his head and holding Alec's gaze, his eyes cold and sharp. "I would never have believed it myself before I came here from Berlin." His glare softened. He smiled and glanced at his wife. "I was a doctor there, a modern-minded man of science." Spiro sighed and took his wife's hand in his. "How life can change. This is our home now. Here we are among friends." He waved his hand to the other guests. "Could we ask for better company?"

Alec again looked over the people gathered in the banquet hall. It was true that everyone in the room appeared to be young, healthy and happy. In fact, there wasn't anyone here who was anything but young, healthy and happy. It didn't seem natural.

Spiro nodded across the room to the head table. "The White Ones are stabled in the finest quarters whenever they come to the megaron and are catered to like royalty," Spiro said. "She that stands to the governor's right is named Celera. Some call her Fire-eyes. She is Medio's favorite."

"Fine-looking animals," Alec said, glad to talk about something a little more down-to-earth.

"They are much more than that," Spiro said.

"Are they working horses?" Alec asked.

"Far from it," Spiro said. "The sacred mares live an easy existence in the woods and groves around the temple sanctuary. There they are pampered and live a pure life, free from any taint of earthly labor. Their only job is to be harnessed to a sacred chariot once a year or accompany Medio at court."

Another course was brought in then, skewers of meat, platters of finely chopped vegetables, bowls filled with delicate sauces. As the people ate, the musicians took up their harps, flutes and lyres again and began to play. A masked poet appeared and sang in Greek verse. Xeena leaned over and whispered to Alec that the poet was praising Medio's ancestors and insinuating they were connected to the gods. Xeena said he seemed to be making up the flattering verse as he went along, even suggesting the Black and Alec were connected to the gods as well.

After the poet was through singing, tables were moved and an area was cleared before the governor. Then a red carpet was spread out over the floor. An attendant walked the albino mare called Celera onto the center of the carpet. Alec leaned closer to the Black and put his hand on the stallion's neck.

The assembled guests grew quiet again as a veiled woman entered the room and moved ceremoniously toward Celera. The young woman walked with measured steps, draped in a cloak, treading proudly, deliberately, her head held high. Suddenly she opened her bare arms, threw them above her head and then swayed back and forth as though possessed by some uncontrollable desire to touch the ceiling.

The woman removed her headscarf, but her face remained veiled. Her raven-black hair fell down upon her bare shoulders. A man with red hair at the governor's table called out a question to her, and she laid her hands on Celera's neck. The mare shook her head and twitched an ear. The woman stepped back, staggering a bit, and then began speaking some words in a deep, sleepy-sounding voice.

"What is she saying?" Alec asked.

Spiro leaned forward. "This last part of the evening is for those who seek omens and monitions," he whispered. "The red-haired man asked the priestess, Cyrene, if the coming of the full moon tomorrow and the positions of the planets in the zodiac are an auspicious sign for him. The Oracle said that it was so."

"The Oracle?" Alec asked. "Is she an oracle?"

"The woman is only interpreting," Spiro said. "It is Celera who is speaking. Fire-eyes is the Oracle."

Other guests asked more questions, and the priestess interpreted the mare's murmurings and body language into words for the governor and his guests. For the next few minutes, the bizarre ceremony continued, the oracle Celera divining omens and dispensing advice to a half dozen different questions by way of her human interpreter.

At last the governor stood up and asked one final question.

"What is he saying?" Alec asked.

Xeena translated the Greek for Alec's benefit. "It's something about a messenger."

The priestess's deep voice uttered some more words. "My messenger is the message," Xeena interpreted. "The message my messenger brings is that the gods have sent Acracia a messenger."

Alec glanced at Spiro. The chamberlain said nothing, only watched him and smiled.

Alec looked at Xeena. "What's that mean?"

"I have no idea," she said.

The crowd took their eyes off Celera and once again turned their attention to Alec and the Black. Voices rose, and some guests stood and raised their glasses. The musicians suddenly redoubled their efforts. Drummers joined them and the tune became rhythmic and lively. People began singing. Medio left his place at the head of the table, and he and his entourage of horses joined Celera and the priestess on the floor.

The horses formed a small circle around Medio and pranced to the music, throwing out their hooves in short, mincing steps. They were quickly joined by other horses and guests. Soon the entire hall was filled with moving bodies, horses doing stylized leaps or skipping back and forth while the dinner guests spun and dodged between them like matadors in a bullring.

It was a scene out of a dream, Alec thought. All his senses told him to get out of there, but before he knew what was happening, he and the Black found themselves on the floor with the others, swept up in the carnival atmosphere. Alec didn't have much choice. There was no way out but through the crowd.

"Alec," he heard Xeena cry after him. "Wait."

Xeena caught up to them, and with the girl running interference, Alec did his best to guide the stallion to the exit, pushing his way through the dancing people and horses. The Black bucked around at Alec's side, trying to pull away, more playful than angry, enjoying the chaos and instability in the air. All around them were shouts, laughter, noise and the sounds of scuffling feet as people and horses jostled each other to squeeze into the crowd of dancing bodies.

In the middle of the room, the white mares were performing a finely choreographed dance that was central to the spectacle, occasionally springing into the air and twisting their bodies from side to side. The humans and other horses moved among them casually and with practiced skill. A deafening clamor filled the great hall, and the entire room seemed alive.

Alec looked about him as the horses became an incredible living carousel, a merry-go-round of real-life dancing horses circling faster and faster. Suddenly the music stopped and the carousel came to a screeching halt. Standing before the Black now was the young gray stallion, the one that had followed the governor and Celera into the room. A look of hate burned in his eyes.

The gray shrilled a challenge to the Black and deftly spun around, lashing out a hind hoof that just missed the Black's shoulder. "Whoa," Alec called out angrily as he hauled on the Black's lead. A gasp went up from the crowd. The uncontrolled gray turned again, reared and then brought his hooves crashing to the ground, as if daring the Black to step forward.

The Black strained to free himself and join the battle. Alec grasped the shank in his hand and threw all his weight downward, trying to turn the Black away and keep the stallion's hooves on the ground. Somehow he managed to hold the horse back.

Two men bravely dashed forward and got a grip on either side of the gray's halter, pulling the young stallion away. Then he was gone, lost in the crowd. As quickly as it had stopped, the music started again and once more the floor was a sea of people and horses meshing together.

Alec held tight to his horse's lead, but the Black seemed more shocked than angry now. What had happened to the gray? Alec thought. Then he heard a furious uproar coming from the other side of the crowded room and saw the young stallion, still bucking against his handlers defiantly. The Black saw the gray but did not make a move toward him, nor did he answer the cry of his attacker. Instead he twisted his head, unconcerned about the young stallion's threats, searching for someone else in the crowd, undoubtedly the albino mare Celera.

Alec felt someone tugging at his arm. It was

Xeena. "This way," she cried. Xeena pushed her way through the dancers. Alec pointed the Black in her direction and did his best to get the stallion to follow. A few of the revelers stared at the Black but otherwise went on with their celebrating, as if the confrontation between the two stallions was of no importance and best forgotten.

The crowd swallowed them up again. No one tried to stop them from leaving, but neither did they make much effort to stand clear. Xeena nudged, pushed and shoved people out of their way, and at last they burst through the swarm of revelers and into the reception room.

Alec stumbled ahead, keeping a firm grip on the Black's lead, still dazed by all he'd seen. They approached the exit, and the doors to the banquet hall opened as if by magic. The Black threw his head and cried out wildly as they passed through. Then the doors closed behind them and the clamor of the throng receded.

9

Dust to Dust

"How do we get out of here?" Alec said.

"I think it's this way," Xeena said, pointing down the corridor to the gallery they had passed on the way to the banquet room.

Alec kept a close hold on the Black's lead and spoke to his horse softly, trying to keep him settled. The words came in a steady stream that lasted until they had returned to the Black's room.

"What in the world kind of party was that?" Alec said to Xeena as he took off the Black's halter.

"Wild," Xeena said. "Really spectacular, except for when that crazy gray stallion went after the Black."

"He didn't concern me so much," Alec said. "The Black can handle himself with other stallions, and no one there seemed too surprised about what happened. I suppose that with all those horses and people bumping around together on the dance floor, a confrontation between horses wouldn't be unusual, no matter how well they are trained." Alec shook his head. "It's not the gray," he said. "It's that albino mare I'm thinking about. She's poison and the Black can't see it. If he gets another chance at her, I'm not sure I can keep them apart."

Alec walked through the passageway to his own room. He could see someone had been there while they'd been away. There were fresh blankets on his bed, and a fire had been lit in the corner fireplace. He splashed some water from a wash basin onto his face, then returned to the Black's quarters, picked up a brush and gave his horse a light grooming. The Black didn't need it, but the routine and familiar touch of his horse always made Alec feel better. Xeena stood at the connecting door, her eyes fixed on the stallion watching her.

"Pretty cool when you think about it," Xeena said after a minute.

Alec laughed. "Certainly unusual. That Medio really knows how to have a good time. Want to go back?"

"No thanks. I need to get some sleep now. But that was fun."

Could it all be just that? Alec thought. Just harmless fun? He had to admit that from the safety of his room, things suddenly started to look different. Could any of this be more than some kind of strange role-playing reenactment of ancient times, a place where people could get dressed up in costumes and pretend they were somewhere other than the modern world? He remembered hearing about people who reenacted famous Civil War battles in period uniforms. Maybe it was all just something like that. Some sort of club. Sure, Alec thought. That must be it. The only difference here was that these folks seemed extremely serious about it all, almost too serious, like actors who could not get out of character.

Perhaps he had overreacted, Alec thought. The gray was no threat to the Black. As for the albino, perhaps she was nothing more than a pretty white horse, a genetic oddity of nature on the outside but like any other horse inside. All the same, Alec still felt wary about everyone in this place, people and horses alike. There were no locks on the door, so he propped a chair against it for a barricade in case someone tried to slip into the room when he was asleep.

"If it wasn't night and I wasn't so tired, I'd say we should try to get out of here *now*," he said.

Xeena shivered. "I wouldn't want to go anywhere near that river tonight," she said.

Alec had to agree. He stepped into Xeena's room to help block her door with a chair, and then they said their good-nights. Alec returned to the Black for a minute and then went outside on the balcony. The megaron was aglow with amber light, and he could hear the sounds of the festivities continuing in full force. He sat down in a big, comfortable, wooden chair, leaned back and closed his eyes. Images from the day flashed through his memory: the waterfall, the albino mare, the swirling black water of the river, a sea of people and horses dancing together . . .

The world was certainly a funny place, he thought. And if these folks got their kicks out of dressing up and pretending to be ancient Greeks, who was he to judge them? Anyway, he'd be out of there in the morning. After checking on the Black one more time, he went back to his own room. Crawling into bed, he soon fell into a deep sleep.

The next morning, Alec was glad to see his jeans and shirt had dried by the fire so he could get out of his oversized T-shirt and put them on. Then he fed and tended his horse, just the same as he would have any morning anywhere. The sleep had done them both some good, Alec thought. The stallion leaned into Alec's brushstrokes with pleasure and shuffled his feet in the soft bedding, anxious to get outside.

"Okay, big guy," Alec said to his horse. "Just hang on a minute." He ran his hands over the Black's legs and was grateful to feel no excessive heat or swelling that might indicate an injury of some kind. It was truly amazing considering all they had been through the previous day. Even the scratches that raked his side seemed to be healing, almost as if they'd never been there.

Alec brought the Black out into the corridor and walked him up and down the length of the empty hall for ten minutes so he could stretch his legs. Then they returned to the Black's room.

Last night, Spiro had said he would get Alec to a telephone in the morning, so there was nothing to do but wait. The Black turned his attention to the feed in the ivory trough. Alec rattled around the room. Fifteen minutes passed, then a half hour, then an hour. He gave the Black another grooming and going-over with a rub rag just to pass the time.

The sun climbed higher over the mountain peaks, and there was still no sign of Spiro. Alec stepped out onto the balcony where Xeena was standing by the railing and looking out over the patios and gardens of the acropolis. No one seemed to be up and around anywhere. The place looked like a ghost town.

"I can't believe this," Alec said.

"I guess everyone is sleeping in after the big party last night," Xeena said.

Alec paced around on the balcony, waiting for a knock on the door. He was starting to get frustrated and wanted out of this madhouse. "Where in the heck is that Spiro guy?" Alec said. "It must be midmorning by now. He said he'd be here first thing."

"Maybe they reckon time differently here," Xeena said. "The monasteries do that. Morning to the monks is a completely different time than it is to people in the outside world. They use a different calendar too."

Alec looked out over the balcony railing to the megaron and the gardens and courtyard, the fountains and white statues. His gaze lifted to the ramparts beyond the gardens of the acropolis. High along one section of the fortified walls were figures moving about, perhaps lookouts or sentries of some sort. From the summit, one could probably see all around the acropolis, Alec thought. After a minute, he decided to go up there and take a look around. Even if he couldn't find a telephone, maybe he could get a lead on an exit out of this labyrinth. Alec told Xeena what he was doing and asked her to stay there and keep an eye on the Black while he slipped out to take a look around.

Soon Alec had wound his way through the maze of colonnades, patios and garden hedges to a walkway that led to the walls edging the acropolis. He'd seen no one along the way there, no sign of life at all except the trails of smoke drifting out of a few chimneys.

He followed the base of the wall until he came to a series of steps cut into the side and leading to the summit. He climbed the stairs to a narrow path of flat stones topping the barricade. If there had been anyone there before, they were gone now. All he could see were two small trees overhanging the railing, their white flower blossoms dangling in the branches.

Alec walked over to the trees, stopped and looked out over the mountains. From this vantage point, the walls looked as if they might encircle not just the city but also the entire top of the mountain. He saw a couple places where there were breaks in the wall, but only because cliffs and gorges made access impossible there.

Nothing seemed to be moving anywhere. The whole of nature seemed asleep—the woods silent, the sky empty of birds, no sign of life at all. He searched in vain for signs of commercial air traffic, or even Bateman's helicopter. Nothing. About the only movement he could see was a horse-drawn wagon on a road going up the mountain behind the acropolis. Alec wondered where it was going and if there were settlements closer to the summit.

Dark clouds were gathering around the mountain peaks, and it looked like a storm was approaching. A brisk breeze blew in suddenly, rattling the branches of the two trees beside him. Alec leaned over the edge of the wall as a white flower blossom fell from one of the trees and was swept away in the wind. He let his gaze follow the blossom as it twisted in the breeze and floated off. Then, as the blossom reached the other side of the stream beyond the wall, a peculiar thing happened. The flower seemed to vanish into thin air.

Alec blinked to clear his eyes and looked again. He picked up a fresh blossom from the ground and tossed it into the air. The wind caught the flower and carried it over the moat, and once again the flower disappeared, only this time Alec thought he could see a faint trail of dust falling through the air where the flower had been. He tried one more time and watched again as the soft white petals seem to dry up in midair, then crumble and dissolve to dust.

What could have caused that? he wondered. Was he still dreaming? Again he looked out to the world beyond the acropolis, his eyes searching for some sign of life in the forest. Where were the animals? He could see a few birds in the far distance but none close by. There were no squirrels in the trees, or on the opposite bank of the moat, or in the grass area bordering the woods. All of nature was fast asleep.

Strange, wild thoughts dashed through his mind. It was almost as if some invisible wall of death stood between Acracia and the outside world, a dead zone that drained away the life of whatever passed through it. Hadn't that pamphlet he read at the monastery said something about an enchanted forest that could hide whole cities and a poison river in the woods? And then there were those tall tales about the magical healing waters that Spiro had been going on about at dinner, waters blessed by mare's milk.

Waters of eternal life, winds of sudden death— could any of it be true? Alec knew that the stories were just crazy enough to be real. He had seen enough in his young life by now to know that most anything was possible. Understanding the how and why of it all was a different matter.

Alec retraced his steps to his room, determined now to forget everything else but getting the Black and Xeena and making a run for the main gate as soon as they could. From what he'd seen atop the barricade, that was the only certain way out of this madhouse. But when he reached his room, he found the Black alone. The girl was gone.

10

Forbidden Pastures

Alec checked the rooms, the balcony and out in the hall. "Xeena?" he called. "Where are you?" The Black was safe enough, but Xeena was nowhere to be seen. Surely she wouldn't have left the stallion alone unless it had been an emergency, Alec thought. He stepped out into the hall and looked up and down the corridor. "Xeena," he called again, and again no answer came.

Now what? Alec thought. Maybe she just went outside for a minute. He could wait here and hope she turned up. Or he could take the Black and try to find her. Alec moved to his horse. The Black was starting to get restless and pacing the luxurious confines of his room like a boxer gearing up for a big fight.

Alec looked out over the acropolis and the advancing storm clouds in the sky. After a minute, raindrops began to fall softly on the balcony. It would start raining now, he thought.

"Easy boy," he said as he pulled the halter over

the Black's ears and clipped on the lead line. Thunder rumbled and the pattering of raindrops quickened. He opened the big wooden door and walked the stallion out into the hall. Rain or no rain, there was no use hanging around here anymore. He had to find Xeena and get out of this place.

The Black's hooves clopped down the empty marble halls as they made their way to the entrance and the path to the grounds outside. The rain was falling harder now. Soon Alec saw a figure carrying an umbrella and approaching up the path from the other direction. The stallion tossed his head and gave a shrill warning cry. Alec tightened his grip on the lead and spoke to his horse to keep him calm.

The figure came closer, and Alec saw it was Spiro. "What are you doing out in the rain?" the bald-headed chamberlain asked. "I was just on my way to find you."

"I was waiting," Alec said, "but that doesn't matter now. Something has happened to Xeena. She's not in the room. She probably just went for a short walk and got caught in the rain or something but . . ."

"I just saw her a few minutes ago," Spiro said. "She was running up the road to Tarta."

"You did?" Alec said. "To where?"

"To Tarta. It is the next settlement up the hill."

"Why would she go there?"

"I believe she said something about her father," Spiro said, "seeing him in a wagon heading up the mountain. She wanted to catch up to him and would not stop to say more."

Karst? Alec wondered. What would Xeena's dad be doing here? Then he realized that Karst might have received the message about what had happened at the river and had come to get them. Either that or Karst had come here looking for them after they'd gone missing. Alec didn't trust the chamberlain, and there was no telling if Spiro really had sent the message last night as he said he had.

"Where is this Tarta place?" Alec asked. "Is it far?"

"Not too far," Spiro said. "But the girl will be fine, I am sure. Come. Let us breakfast together and wait for the rain to stop. Summer storms in the mountains aren't unusual. It should blow over momentarily."

Spiro gave Alec a kindly smile, but his animal eyes were cold and dark. The Black tugged on his lead, and Alec held him still. He shook his head. "Thanks, but I'd like to find Xeena. I know her father. Perhaps he came to take us back."

"Perhaps," Spiro said.

Alec again tried to read the man's expression but could see nothing there.

"Maybe that really was Xeena's dad she saw in the wagon," Alec said. "But maybe it wasn't. Either way I better go after her. How do I get to this place you say she was headed?"

"Follow the road up the mountain," Spiro said. "But you shouldn't worry yourself about the girl."

"I'll feel better if I know where she is," Alec said. "We've been through a lot since yesterday, and I feel responsible for getting her home safely."

Spiro bowed his head formally. "As you wish, Herr Alex." He pointed up the road behind him. "The turnoff to Tarta is no more than a couple kilometers. Bear left at the fork. But please remember to stay on the road. You will be passing through the pastures of the sacred mares. They are forbidden to all. You must not enter there."

Alec thanked Spiro for the help. He took hold of a hunk of black mane, stepped back and then vaulted onto the stallion's back. Following the road in the direction Spiro had indicated, they soon found the fork and headed left. Alec kept his horse to a steady walk. The Black seemed to be carrying his weight well. He moved easily beneath Alec, the rhythm of his steps even, his ears forward and alert.

The rain was slowing now, but Alec kept his head down and tucked his face into his horse's mane, letting the Black lead the way. Then, just as quickly as it had started, the rain shower stopped. A moment later the clouds parted and the sun was shining upon them.

Again Alec noticed the woods around him seemed to be completely void of animal life. It was unnatural, he thought. A place like this should be teeming with life, especially after a summer rain. The silence around him was unsettling as he recalled what he'd read about the poison river and remembered what he'd seen happen to the flower blossoms that had fallen from the top of the city wall. Some part of him just wanted to turn his horse around and get out of there right now. If it wasn't for Xeena . . . but he couldn't leave without her. Alec inhaled the smell of his horse. He would be all right, he knew. He was with the Black.

The road switched back and forth but remained fairly easy going for them at this pace. He saw no road signs, and if there had ever been any wagon tracks here, they had been washed away by the rain.

Alec wondered what time it was. Half the day was probably already gone, and the sun seemed to be getting lower in the sky. The Black raised his head and sniffed the wet air, then pawed the ground. "Easy, boy," Alec said, leaning forward and pressing his chest close to his horse's neck. "We'll get ourselves out of this place soon."

Around the next bend, the road ahead dipped and

entered a lush meadow with unfenced fields on either side of the road. These must be the sacred pastures, Alec thought, the place Spiro told him was off-limits. Alec had no intention of trespassing there whatsoever, though the pastures certainly did look inviting, with acres of green grass that ran all the way to the edge of the forest.

On the uphill side of the pasture, about fifty yards off the road to the right, Alec saw a small stream winding down from the mountain peaks. Beneath a towering oak on the other side of the stream were three horses. They looked to be the same mares he had seen the day before. They raised their heads and turned to watch Alec and the Black. One of them half reared and broke away from the others. She splashed through the stream and cantered across the field toward the road.

The Black stamped his forehooves suddenly. Alec pulled him to a stop. "Hold on, now," he spoke softly to his horse.

The mare ran up onto the road and careened to a stop in front of them, then stood there boldly, as if to block their path. Alec did his best to keep the stallion still. He could feel the Black tensing up, but only slightly, almost as if the sudden appearance of the mare was expected.

Alec spoke to the mare so she could hear his voice and know that there was no threat or fear in it. The mare whinnied and pawed the ground. The Black tossed his head in reply.

All at once, the mare began to move, stepping in place, then bobbing and weaving like a boxer, then prancing in a little circle, then backing up to pivot side to side in dressage-like movements. It was a display of true grace and beauty, a version of the same courtship dance Alec had seen at the banquet last night.

The Black seemed curious about the mare but also unmoved, or perhaps he was wary of her. She stopped dancing, then turned away and lowered her head submissively, now playing the shy coquette.

This was a distraction they didn't need right now. "Better get back where you belong, girl," he called to her. "Go on. Get."

The mare swished her high-set tail but otherwise did not move. Alec touched the stallion with his heels and turned him to the edge of road so they could step around her and get on with their business. The stallion resisted a moment but answered Alec's signals, perhaps as suspicious of the mare as Alec was. She waited for them to pass. Pretending to sulk, her head hanging low, she began following a few lengths behind them, almost like a lonely dog. In the field across the stream, the other two mares watched silently.

"Go home," Alec called to the mare on their tail. She raised her head, her soulful eyes fixed on the Black.

Alec kept his horse pointed ahead. "Come on, fella," he said. "We are in enough trouble already. We don't have time for this."

Alec pushed the Black into a trot, but still the mare followed. She began to canter and moved up alongside them, pushing her head close to the Black. "Hey," Alec shouted at her. "Back! Get back!"

The mare pressed closer, almost touching the Black's neck with her soft gray muzzle, then nipping the air next to him playfully. Alec kicked out his right foot to push her away. The mare swung her head and deftly avoided Alec's foot. Then with a flash of teeth, she lunged.

Alec threw out his foot once more, and this time the mare caught hold of it with her mouth. He felt her teeth through the shoe leather and jerked his foot back, losing his shoe. The mare shook her head and dashed up the road ahead, triumphantly gripping Alec's old running shoe in her mouth.

"Hey," Alec cried. "Give me that back!" He couldn't believe the mare's behavior. She was acting more like mischievous dog that had just snatched a bone from the kitchen table than a horse. It was all very peculiar, Alec thought, but more importantly the mare had his shoe, and he needed it. He wasn't about to walk out of this place barefoot. Alec put the Black into a gallop and chased after her.

"Give me that back, you nut," Alec cried.

The mare bounced up the road in front of them. It didn't appear that she was really trying to escape; it was more as if she was simply teasing and wanting them to chase her. The Black carried Alec close enough so he could lean down, reach over and get a hand on a part of the shoe that was sticking out of her mouth. The mare tugged back playfully as he yanked on the shoe, trying to free it from her clenched teeth. Finally she let go.

Alec pulled the stallion to a stop and couldn't help but laugh at the absurdity of it all. The Black snorted and drummed his hooves in the dirt. The mare squealed triumphantly and then dashed away. She veered off the road and across the open field to return to where her sisters were waiting by the side of the stream. A moment later, all three vanished into the trees bordering the far side of the pasture.

Alec jumped off the Black, mashed his shoe back into shape and then put it on again. He gave the horse a pat on the neck. "Shoe-stealing mares," Alec said. "You don't want to get mixed up with them."

He took a step back and remounted. Pointing the Black up the road, he touched the stallion with his heels and they were off. The road twisted around a sharp bend, and a short distance away Alec could see several small cottages among stands of tall trees.

Larger, gable-roofed houses were clustered around a central courtyard farther on. Alec heard a baying sound and saw sheep pastured in a field to one side of the settlement. Animals at last, he thought. What a relief. It was the first time he'd seen any animals, aside from horses, since he'd been here.

They passed through an open, unmanned gate. Outside one of the cottages, a young woman was raking leaves in the yard. As she stared at the passing stranger, Alec noticed something odd about her. Somehow her pale, pinkish skin seemed to be pulled too tight over her face, like a person who'd had bad plastic surgery. She stepped back as Alec passed, retreating all the way to the shadow of her doorway.

Alec looked around for more signs of life. Two ordinary-looking draft horses were yoked to a wooden wagon loaded with straw in a field beside the road. It was odd he hadn't seen any machines, not even a bicycle, since he'd been here, Alec thought. It really did seem as if he'd stepped back in time a couple hundred years.

They came to a village square. At the center was a marble fountain and statuary in a small garden. If this was Tarta, Alec thought, the village didn't look to be nearly as fancy a place as the city of Acracia. This neighborhood appeared a bit run-down; the gardens were smaller and not so carefully tended, and the statuary was less elaborate and buildings less imposing. A flock of geese and a herd of pigs roamed loose around a small amphitheater.

Alec slid off the Black's back, and the stallion immediately turned his attention to munching on the garden grass. A half dozen villagers who had gathered on a nearby porch now cautiously made their way toward Alec, plainly wary of the visitor and his black stallion. As in the city below, the men and women here were all attired in sleeveless gowns with cloaks draped over the shoulder. They appeared to be about the same age, perhaps in their early thirties, and all slightly older than the dwellers in the acropolis. One of them raised his hand in a salute, then stepped forward and bowed almost to the ground. Alec wasn't sure what to do, so he bowed in response.

He was a big guy, with bulked-up muscles and long, flowing blond hair; yet his eyes were old-looking, his face crinkled with age around the edges. "English?" the man said.

"American," Alec said. "Speak English?"

The man smiled but shook his head no. He bowed again, then called out in the direction of the cottages on the other side of the square. After a minute, Alec saw Xeena hurrying his way. Karst was with her.

"Alec," she called, beckoning to him.

"Xeena! Karst!" he answered. "There you are."

Alec shook Karst's hand. Xeena's dad smiled but did not speak. He was looking at the Black as if he'd never seen the stallion before. Xeena took Alec by the arm, then turned and pulled him back in the direction of the cottages. "We need to talk," she said softly.

11

Popi

Xeena cast a look over her shoulder. She smiled and waved to the group who had met Alec and the Black inside the village square. Then she turned to Alec and lowered her voice. "Just keep walking," she said mysteriously. "I'll explain in a minute."

"How did you find us, Karst?" Alec asked. Alec waited for his friend to answer, but Karst only kept marching forward. Xeena's dad still barely seemed to recognize Alec or the Black. He kept his eyes on the stallion, his gaze wide with wonder. Alec asked again, and when Karst finally spoke, the tone of his voice sounded odd, nothing like the man Alec remembered.

"This is my home," Karst said, his English almost without accent and completely unlike Karst's normal voice. Then he bowed his head in that way everyone seemed to do around here and that usually translated into "that's all I have to say."

They came to a white cottage surrounded by big,

old trees and a lawn and garden run to seed. Xeena waved them through the open front door. Karst paused and turned to face Alec and the Black. "My home is humble but clean. Please do me the honor of allowing me to pay my respects." He showed them to a corner bedroom, and Alec held the Black steady as Karst pushed the narrow bed against the wall. Xeena covered the floor with straw. A minute later the bedroom had been transformed into a makeshift stall for the Black.

Inside the cottage, as everywhere in Acracia, the dominating theme was horses. Everything in sight was decorated with them—horse heads, rearing horses, running horses. Renderings of horses were embroidered on the pillows, carved on the posts of the banisters leading to the attic and adorned either end of the mantelpiece.

Xeena brought in a towel for Alec to dry off with and a blanket for the Black. Then she spread out a bucket of oats over a table for the stallion to eat. The Black sniffed the oats a moment and then set upon his feed.

"Welcome to my home," Karst said, his English perfect with barely a trace of accent. "All Acracia has been expecting you." Again the voice sounded unfamiliar to Alec and not at all like Karst. Could this be the same man he'd known on the film set, the one who always seemed jovial and ready for a laugh?

"Expecting me?" Alec said in exasperation. "Karst. Wake up. What's wrong with you? It's me. Alec. Xeena must have told you what happened to us."

"Yes, she told me. You are both lucky to be alive."

Alec glanced around him. "Who lives in this house? What are you doing here?"

"I told you," Karst said. "This is my home."

"Your home?" Alec said. "I don't understand."

Karst smiled again.

"You better sit down," Xeena said, pointing Alec to a chair.

Alec took a seat, and Xeena explained what had happened since he left her in the megaron. Her words came quickly as she told him how she had been on the balcony when she thought she saw her father passing by in a wagon. She'd followed him up here and then—

Alec held up his hand. "Wait a minute, Xeena. What do you mean thought you saw . . . Isn't this your dad?"

Xeena blinked and shook her head. "This is my grandfather, Popi."

Alec gazed at the man sitting in the chair opposite him, someone who could not have been much more than thirty-five years old.

"At first I thought he was my dad too," Xeena said, "just as you did. I don't understand it myself.

Popi has been trying to explain it to me ever since I got here. Popi, you tell him."

"My name is Nicholas Balastritis," the man said. "Karst Balastritis is my son. This is my granddaughter."

Alec glanced at Xeena. "It's true, Alec," she said. "He knows things that only Popi could know."

"It is going to be difficult for you to believe this," the man said, "but you must try."

"You can't be Xeena's grandfather," Alec said. "What are you, thirty-five? Thirty-six?"

"I am seventy-two years old," the man said without blinking an eye.

"I tell you it's true," Xeena said. "This is Popi. I asked him about some things that happened when I was little, and he knew all about them."

Alec held up his hand. "Please, Xeena," he said patiently. "Lots of professional fortune-tellers and phony psychics can do that, and usually it is part of some sort of scam. This place looks like a big-budget health club selling salvation and magic cures to vulnerable people. Someone is making money out of all this, believe me."

"This is no health club," the man who called himself Nicholas Balastritis said. "Acracia is a Garden of Eden. The waters here are truly blessed. Drink deeply."

"Let's talk about the money for a minute," Alec

said. "Are you saying everything is free here? How do you people pay for it all?"

Nicholas smiled, as if amused by Alec's skepticism. "Upon arriving in Acracia," he said, "people deposit their money in the bank and are given credit in the city's shops and eating places. Guests are welcome as long as they obey our laws. Strangers and trespassers are not. Once here, most guests stay for the remainder of their lives."

"Do you mean that no one ever leaves this place?" he said.

"It would be impossible to leave Acracia for most of us. And why would we even want to leave? You can keep your modern civilization, its ravages of time and old age, its wars, famine and disease. Here in the Realm, life is good. We citizens of Acracia accept that this is the best of all possible worlds. You will know this to be true if you stay with us."

"Thanks but no thanks," Alec said.

With a bow, Nicholas spoke again, his voice more humble now. "Of course, you are not an ordinary guest and may do as you wish here, but please do not dishonor my house by leaving before you can truly be made welcome." He gestured to a small empty field outside an open window. "Look, please," he said. "Allow your horse to graze a few minutes before you go. The grass is rich and green here in Tarta."

Alec welcomed the chance to get outside and try to digest all he had just heard. He led the Black to the pasture and realized that it was later than he thought; the sun was already descending behind the mountains. Once again, ominous-looking rain clouds were gathering in the sky to the north and a not-so-distant rumbling filled the sky. A minute later, it started to rain.

Alec brought the Black inside, toweled him off and rubbed him out again. Nicholas watched Alec as he worked. "He is a fantastic animal, your Bucephalus," Nicholas said. "One truly worthy of Alexander and the messenger of the gods of Greece."

"I am from America, not Greece," Alec said.

Nicholas smiled. "No matter. The fact is you are in Acracia now. Your coming was foretold by the Oracle, and you are here."

"We got caught in a river, were swept through the mountain and almost drowned. That is the only reason we are here," Alec said.

"That is also a sign that was foretold."

Alec looked at Xeena. From her mesmerized expression, it appeared that she really did think this man was her grandfather and that the wild things he was saying could be true.

"Okay," Alec said, "believe what you want. You are right. I am a messenger from the gods. My message is that you guys are great. Thanks for everything.

Keep up the good work. Now how the heck do we get out of this place?"

"Please, Alec," Nicholas said. "Do not be so quick to judge us. There is much to learn here." His words were punctuated by another long rumble outside.

More thunder, Alec thought, though he was surprised that it shook the furniture and rattled the dishes.

The Black whinnied. "Easy boy," Alec said. The stallion bobbed his head and leaned into Alec's shoulder. "That's it. Just some thunder. Easy now."

The sounds of wind and rain grew stronger. Not much sense in trying to make a run for it now, Alec thought. He watched the Black nose around in the fresh grain Xeena brought him. The stallion didn't seem anxious to go back outside just yet either.

No, Alec decided. The smart thing to do was to wait. However nutty this place seemed, he couldn't see harm in anything they were doing. Alec trusted the Black's instincts far above his own, and the stallion didn't seem to be too alarmed about being here.

Later that evening at dinner, they ate corn and potato soup, grapes, cheese and yogurt, everything fresh and flavorful. As they ate, Xeena told Nicholas about their jobs on the *Young Alexander* film set and about meeting Alec and the Black. She explained that the

Black was a famous racehorse and that only Alec could ride him.

"Like Bucephalus and Alexander," Nicholas said. "Again I say this is no mere coincidence. It is your destiny to have found your way here."

Alec started to say something and then held back. Better to go along, he thought, at least until he could find a way out of here. It wasn't up to him to prove Nicholas was a fraud, and who knew? Maybe he wasn't.

Alec looked down into his glass and swirled the contents. The water tasted so clean and pure it was almost sweet. Certainly it contained minerals of some kind. Alec figured he'd been drinking it since yesterday with no ill effects, so there didn't seem to be any reason to stop now. Quite the opposite, he thought. In some ways he couldn't remember when he'd felt as strong and clearheaded. There was no disputing that he had almost forgotten about the twisted ankle that had troubled him so much yesterday.

Nicholas raised his glass. "Blessed by the milk of the sacred mares, the waters of Acracia will cure sickness and will restore youth and health. It seems an inexcusable loss that the secret of the water is not shared with mankind. Science could tell us much if studies could be made—if only we could get the message out."

"Why don't you?" Alec said.

"It's not that simple," Nicholas said with a wry smile. Despite his youthful appearance, his face was that of someone who had seen that life is a much greater riddle than most people suspect.

"Perhaps you are the one Fate has chosen to do just that, the courier who will take our message to the outside world," Nicholas said. "Perhaps that is what the Oracle meant about a messenger. Perhaps Acracia is sending the message, and not receiving it."

Night had fallen and the rain continued. Alec cleared the dishes and Nicholas made coffee while Xeena set up a backgammon board. Alec sipped a cup of thick, sweet coffee and went into the Black's room and looked out the window. He could hear water dripping and leaves rattling and could see dark branches swaying in the wind as it rose and fell.

As he gazed at the world outside, his supper settled in his stomach and mellowed his mood. What a fascinating place this is, he thought. The Black seemed to be enjoying it too. Maybe Nicholas wasn't so off base, after all. Maybe he should spend a little more time here and try to find out what this place was all about.

Lightning flashed across the sky and more thunder rumbled. The sounds snapped Alec back to reality. What were these thoughts in his head?

Stay here, in this place? What was he thinking? He didn't belong here. The people in Acracia weren't just guests in a resort. They were part of some bizarre health cult. Even more alarming was the realization that something inside him was on the verge of succumbing to the idea of staying here. It was almost as if some unknown force was trying to rub away all his concerns and responsibilities. His thoughts about the past were jumbled and confused, though he felt incredibly alert in the present. Deep in the back of his mind, a voice told him this wasn't right, that he wasn't thinking correctly, that these weren't his thoughts inside his head but someone else's.

He went to the basin to splash some water on his face, water clear as winter ice in the candlelight. Whatever was happening to his body, it was his imagination that now needed soothing more than anything.

He returned to the living room where Xeena and Nicholas continued their board game on a low table by the fire. It was a lovely domestic scene—a cozy room lit by the soft glow of firelight, everything warm and safe and dry. Even the Black seemed relaxed. Alec fought to keep his mind alert and his guard up.

As the night wore on, Xeena and Nicholas talked together over their game, easily switching back and forth between English and Greek. Soon Alec found he was getting sleepy. Nicholas offered up his bed, but

Alec said he wanted to stick close to the Black. Nicholas said he understood and brought blankets to keep Alec warm. Xeena found a place on the couch in front of the fire.

Alec lay beside the quietly dozing stallion. He resolved to be up before dawn so they could start the journey away from here, rain or no rain. Pulling his covers up to his chin, Alec listened to the raindrops falling outside like plucked violin strings. Soon he was drifting off, again returning in his dreams to the banquet in the megaron. He could see the swirling figures of dancing horses and people, the slender form and veiled face of the priestess Cyrene as she ran her hands over the albino mare. Then they were soaring up over the gardens together, circling higher and higher, past the guard tower, past the acropolis wall. Around them flower blossoms blew through the air like dry leaves caught in an updraft. . . .

Alec was awakened by an explosion of sound, first the fierce cry of the Black and then another sound even more forceful.

At first Alec thought it must be thunder, until he realized he had been thrown out of bed and was now lying on the floor. No mere thunderstorm could do that. There were crashing noises coming from the other side of the house and sounds of breaking glass.

The floor beneath him was rising and falling as if washed by rippling waves. Hunks of plaster were breaking loose from the walls and ceiling. It wasn't the first time Alec had experienced something like this, and instantly he guessed what was happening.

Earthquake!

He looked around the room. The door was off its hinges, and there was no sign of the Black.

Alec screamed for his horse. The ground was so unsteady beneath him that he didn't even try to move. All he could do was hang on to the floor and wait for the tremor to pass. Again Alec heard the wild clarion call of the stallion from out in the night, only this time another horse shrilled a reply.

Finally the floor ceased shaking enough that Alec could move. He leaped to his feet and raced outside over the still-unsteady ground. The rain had ceased, and a bright, full moon illuminated the shapes of two rearing horses. One was the Black. The other was the ghostly albino mare Celera. They seemed to be dancing in the air, several feet above the rolling moonlit earth below. Then they turned and dashed away across the field.

12

Nocturne

The Black tore into the night. He was free again, and the ground had ceased to shake beneath his hooves. His nostrils filled with the unearthly scent of the mare running before him. She sped toward a high wooden fence spanning the far end of the pasture, glimmers of moonlight splashing her pale white coat.

The mare barely slowed as she gathered herself for the jump. Then she sprang into the air and was flying over the top rail to come down lightly on the other side. Instantly she was off again in full stride, galloping along the road out of Tarta. The Black burst into a run and charged the fence behind her. He leaped forward, taking the fence at a gallop. Touching down, he skipped into the air again, stretching out his neck, his great strides swallowing up the dark ground beneath him.

There was a sharp curve in the road ahead, and the mare followed it. The Black rounded the bend less than a dozen lengths behind her. Straightening out again, he extended his stride and continued on at full speed.

The Black threw back his head and gave a piercing cry, calling in vain to the ghostly apparition running before him. As he closed in to overtake the defiant mare, the albino suddenly broke off the road, vanishing where a trail led into the woods. The Black ducked under a branch to follow until his way was slowed and finally blocked by snakelike vines hanging from the branches overhead. All at once, he could barely move. The vines caught his neck and pulled at his legs. Thorns stung his flesh. He fought to break free, finally escaping the tangle of vines and bolting up the trail.

The path led to a moonlit clearing. Breaking into the open, he began sniffing the air, seeking some scent to tell him where to go. Not finding it, he cried out in frustration and burst into a run, dashing off in one direction, then another. He pulled up finally and waited. Soon his ears caught faint, tinkling sounds in the wind. There was an odor there as well, something unknown but somehow familiar and inviting.

Following the strange signs in the breeze, the stallion could soon make out the dark shapes of horses moving in a glade at the far end of the clearing, a pair of mares dancing in the moonlight. They passed each other with even strides. Their tails flicked back and forth, whisking to a soft rhythm pulsing in the air.

loaked figure of a young woman stood on
k near them. She held a horseshoe-shaped
close to her chest. From it emanated the soft
raindrop-like sounds that had led him there. The Black
watched and waited as the mares moved in time and
revolved around each other. Though the albino wasn't
there, he sensed she wasn't far off.

For many moments, all was still but for the
padding of hooves in the grass, the relaxed breathing
of the horses and the soft strains of music floating on
the air. The mares were aware of the stallion, but they
did not stop their dancing or break their formation.
Then one turned to him. She pranced in place and
bobbed her head as if inviting him to join them. The
other mare continued her soft parading and watched
him with sly, secretive glances.

There was a sudden drumming of hooves. The
melodic strains of the strings stopped. A cry cut the air
and standing beside the cloaked woman's perch was
the albino. Her cry and sudden appearance unsettled
the intricate passage of the two mares, and they suddenly collided into each other.

The Black replied and stepped into the center of
the glade as the mares retreated. He sensed more than
saw the albino who stared at him from the far end of
the glade. An aura completely unknown to him surrounded her, and the Black stood spellbound, his gaze

fixed upon her. She switched her tail, but that was the only part of her that seemed to be alive. Her legs and even her mane were as still as lifeless stone. She stood silent, not even seeming to breathe.

The stallion gazed at the vision before him. Her ruby eyes were open, yet they were not focused on anything. It was an unseeing gaze, as if turned inward. The other mares clustered to one side, nickering to each other and content to stand by and watch the confrontation between the two silent, motionless figures locked in their moonlit reveries.

Finally the albino broke from her pose and noticed him. The stallion caught the look and cried out. The mare replied with a fierce neigh of her own, a high, defiant cry let loose upon the night. It was not a call for solace or a cry for understanding, but a claim of dominion.

Rising up on her hind legs, the albino pawed the air, as if trying to claw her way up into the starry sky, into the lonesome depths of night. When at last she came down again, she glared at the stallion. Her eyes seemed to burn like red-hot coals. Then she was off and running over the moon-splashed grass. With a playful whinny, she taunted the stallion to follow.

The Black raced after her, but cautiously. Somehow he felt as if he had been here before, as if he had returned to some long-lost place that now welcomed him home after a long, weary journey. All was quiet in his ears. Even his hoofbeats sounded muffled and distant to him now. Ahead of him, the mare seemed to float over the dark ground as she dashed away.

With blowing breath, the stallion accelerated after her, and the speed broke the spell that had been holding him back. All at once, his nostrils caught new smells in the air, scents that spoke of others, and of danger, but he did not stop or slow his headlong charge. All his senses were focused ahead as he closed to within a length of the mare. Just as he was about to overtake her, the pair of horses reached the end of the field.

The mare swung hard to the right. Suddenly they were sprinting along a line of fence and toward a narrow passageway opening into the adjacent pasture. The mare squeezed through the gap in the high fence. The Black followed a step behind.

The two horses burst into the pasture. Immediately they were running neck and neck toward a cluster of moonlit shadows in the center of the field. It was a herd of grazing horses, mares and their foals. The startled herd burst into motion, sprinting for a dark line of trees looming in the distance. Leading them was the young gray stallion who had challenged the Black the day before. The herd raced ahead in a mad frenzy. The smells from their steaming bodies told the Black they were running out of blind panic.

The Black and the albino rushed ahead to join the others, and in an instant the herd was racing as one. The horses' fear pushed them to frightening speeds. An overpowering instinct drove the stallion's headlong rush to lead them. Heaving bodies rolled beside him, plunging forward, matching him stride for stride.

The pasture narrowed. Suddenly there was a loud clamor, and a new smell fueled the air—fire, the element the two-legged beasts held so sacred. There was a burst of light, and in front of the herd stood a line of men. They were standing shoulder to shoulder, shouting and waving torches and long, pointed sticks. The horses careened to a jumbled stop.

The appearance of the men made the mares scatter. Before the Black could join them in their flight, the young gray stallion wheeled and struck out at him. The Black turned to face his attacker. He rose on his hind legs, and the gray reared to meet him. Their heavy bodies collided with a terrible impact. They hung together in the air a moment and then crashed to the ground.

The Black was moving forward to renew the fight when the pack of men came toward him. Distracted by his arrogant pursuit of the mare and the attack of the gray, the Black was caught by surprise. The stallion reared as the men formed a circle around him. He had known their kind before, two-legged creatures who would rather fight than run. A long, snakelike rope flew through the air suddenly. It opened its mouth and coiled around his neck. Another flying snake hissed overhead and wrapped around him.

Soon the rest of the herd was gone, and the Black was left fighting the snake ropes and the men who held him. The stallion boldly threw off one of the ropes, but another caught his hind leg. More men came to join the others. The Black could see the albino running off behind the men. She paused to look back. Lifting her proud head, she uttered a high-pitched, almost sorrowful neigh, then turned and bolted into the night.

13

Dark Visions

After watching the Black race off with Celera, Alec had run inside the cottage, pulled on his sweater and jumped into his shoes. Nicholas and Xeena followed him as he dashed back outside.

"It's that mare again," Alec said. "She's lured him off, just like she did at the river."

"We'll help you find him," Nicholas said. "Wait a moment for me to get some shoes on and—"

"I can't wait," Alec said. He looked at the broken door and a deep crack that had formed in the wall. "What happened? Was that really an earthquake?"

"I am afraid so," Nicholas said. "We have had tremors before but never anything like this."

Without another word, Alec turned and ran out into the night to search for his horse. A stiff wind was blowing away the last few clouds, and a full moon brightened the landscape. To one side he could see the tower of Tarta was still standing, but he could also hear the distant sounds of voices shouting. Smoke was swirling up into the sky, and there was the glow of light as if a building had caught fire.

Alec turned away from the town and jogged off into the night, quickly picking up the trail of the two horses. He followed the tracks to the road leading down to Acracia.

Everywhere along the road were signs of devastation from the earthquake that had shaken the mountain. Fences were down and stray sheep and goats gathered in the road bleating. A giant cedar tree had been lifted out of the ground and lay toppled on its side. A barrier wall next to the road had collapsed. Alec ran along, trying to stay focused, following the trail the stallion and the mare had left in the wet dirt.

All at once, Alec heard the drumming of hooves behind him. He turned, thinking it was the Black, but it was not the stallion or Celera. Charging down upon him was the shoe-stealing mare he and the Black had met on the road earlier that day.

Alec held up his hands. "Whoa," he called to her. The mare splashed to a stop in a mud puddle only a few feet away. As before, she wore no tack whatsoever, not even a halter. The mare beat her forehooves on the wet ground.

"What are you doing here?" Alec said.

The mare bounced back and forth on her hooves, then side to side.

"Sorry, girl," Alec said. "I don't want to dance right now, and your boyfriend already took off."

The mare lowered her head and came to Alec. She stopped jigging and stood still before him, as if inviting him to mount up and go for a ride. Alec didn't need to think about it long. If he was going to catch up with the Black and Celera, he would do better on horseback than on foot. Alec trusted he could handle this unfamiliar horse as he had so many others, green ones to mean ones, at the farm and on the track.

Alec spoke to the mare, then touched her and leaned his forearms on her warm, wet back. Her coat felt coarse, almost like rough fur. She did not move away from him.

"Okay, Shoe Thief," he said. "You behave now. That's it. You're a good girl." The mare looked over her shoulder at him, listening to his soft words as if she'd heard them a thousand times before. Then she straightened her neck and waited for him to make his move.

In one swift step, Alec pivoted his body and vaulted onto the mare's short back. The instant his legs wrapped around her, she was off and running, not in the direction the Black and Celera's trail was leading but in the opposite direction, back toward Tarta. Using soft pressure from his legs, hands and voice, Alec finally managed to get her slowed down and turned in the right direction.

Soon they were splashing ahead through the puddles and loping along the road back to the citadel. The mare moved willingly, but Alec was not fool enough to believe he had much control over her. Even the best riders could be unseated while riding bareback, even on a horse they knew well. And this horse was unlike any Alec had ever ridden. He gripped the white mane and pressed himself closer to her neck. There was a strange, heavy smell about her, a wet muskiness more akin to some wild forest animal than a horse. He tried to stay in rhythm with her shuffling strides. At least he was covering some ground, he thought. He shifted his weight in response to the mare's action, trying to keep his body centered and his legs ready to answer any sudden change in direction or speed. The wet mane whipped back into his face as the mare broke into a gallop. She was not fighting him, but there was something more than untamed about this petulant mare who had stolen his shoe earlier that day. Had she ever carried a rider before? Alec wondered. Through his legs and seat, he could feel shudders of pleasure running through her like intermittent waves of electricity. To Alec it was almost like a purring sensation, as if he were seated atop a contented mountain lion rather than a mare. The shoe thief glided smoothly along, barely seeming to notice the human clinging to her back like a giant bug.

Alec had no idea where she was taking him but could only hope that her instincts led her to the other horses and that the Black was with them. Her ears were angled back, and she bounded ahead, not like a flight animal but with all the intense focus and grace of a predator on the hunt.

The muddy ground passed beneath him in a blur as the mare carried Alec past the sacred pastures to a place where the road forked, one fork descending to the acropolis, the other leading farther up the mountain. Alec wondered if the Black and Celera had come this way.

The mare barely slowed as she swung her body hard to follow the fork climbing up the mountain. She careened forward along the moonlit road, running fast and close to being out of control.

A cloud covered the moon, and too late Alec saw what looked like a dark wall ahead. It was a fallen tree stretching from one side of the road to the other. Alec could tell the mare wasn't going to stop, and he had no time to prepare for the jump. The mare took off without hesitating, soaring into the air, her legs brushing through the tops of the branches. She staggered only slightly as she touched down, but it was enough to bounce Alec forward and unseat him from her slick back. Jarred loose from his mount, Alec was launched into the air. He just managed to pull his legs up under him before he slammed into the ground, rolled and came to a stop.

Alec lay motionless for a minute, gasping for breath as the mare continued flying up the road. He crawled to his feet and for a moment could not even remember who he was or how he came to be here. Then the buzzing between his ears slowly subsided, and he recalled the wild ride on the mare and his search for the Black. He tried to keep his mind focused, but his thoughts remained as scattered as wind-blown leaves.

Alec stared into the night, trying to get hold of himself. He'd had the wind knocked out of him and was scraped up and covered with mud, but otherwise he was unhurt. He took a cautious step forward, testing each leg before putting weight on it. Satisfied that everything seemed to be in working order, he immediately began searching the road for tracks. After a minute, he found one set of hoofprints, then another, then a third. One set Alec felt fairly certain were those of his horse. In spite of the moonlight painting the muddy road, it was still too dark to be positive.

Alec continued on, not sure of where he was

going. At least there were still tracks on the road, Alec thought. If the trail had broken off into the woods, it would have been almost impossible to follow. He hurried along the route up the mountain, again asking himself how in the world he ever ended up here.

The road wound through the forest, and soon he came to a long row of neat, orderly houses that seemed to be leaning into each other for support. The dwellings were made of white stone and built in low two- and three-story stacks against the base of a cliff wall, like small apartments. The arched shadows of their doorways stood out against the white walls in the pools of bright moonlight. Not a single light shown in any of the windows. There were none of the ornate fountains or plazas here as in the city below, or even the lush but overgrown gardens of Tarta. Here all was simplicity itself, white and clean-looking but humble. Smoke rolled out the chimneys, and there was a smell in the air Alec could not identify. All was still except for the sound of his own footsteps. Just keep moving, he told himself.

The trail of fresh hoofprints led straight down the center of the village. Alec saw no signs of collapsed walls or buildings here, or anything that even looked damaged. Perhaps the earth tremors had not reached this high up.

At the other end of the main street was an old

man shrouded in a blanket and sitting on the ground, his back propped up against a wall. The man looked very skinny, little more than a skeleton in ragged clothes. He was the first person who appeared much over thirty years old that Alec had seen since he came here. Alec spoke to the man, but the old guy seemed to be asleep.

Alec passed the last house on the far side of the strange little town and looked toward the summit of Mt. Atnos, home to the Oracle and the temple of Diomedes. He could see little dots of light moving around the faint outline of the temple. What were they? Alec wondered. People carrying flashlights? Perhaps a rescue party of some sort? Was that too much to hope for?

The street became a wide path that led farther up the mountain. There were more rocks than trees here. In the pale moonlight splashed over the ground, he could see telltale traces of horses—fresh manure and muddy hoofprints along the path.

Alec heard something that made him stop, the distant cry of a horse coming from somewhere among the lofty peaks. Could it have been the Black? He waited in vain for some clue telling him where to go, straining his ears in the dark, his heart pounding in his chest. Gazing up to the temple, again he felt as if he had stepped back in time and was now locked on some

predetermined path, one he had no choice but to follow, one leading unstoppably upward to the summit
of Mt. Atnos and the temple of the ancient horse master Diomedes.

The passage to the top zigzagged higher, and Alec
saw more lights. People were carrying torches, he realized, though it was difficult to make out much more
than that. The lights were clustering around a dark
shape, what Alec at first thought might be a small
windmill built in a cleared area along the slope of the
mountain. Or perhaps it was a very large statue of
some sort. Despite the bright moonlight, it was impossible for Alec to tell exactly what the object could be.

All at once, the torches were tossed onto the structure. Even from a quarter mile away, Alec could hear
a whooshing sound as the windmill burst into flame. A
moment later he smelled burning oil in the wind.

The fire spread rapidly, running along the edges. It
was only after the object was completely consumed by
fire that Alec could finally see what it was—an enormous wooden horse that now burned like a beacon in
the night.

Built into the mountaintop above the flaming
horse figure were columns that rose to a domed roof,
the temple of Diomedes. Alec couldn't see what was
inside, but he could hear a chorus of voices singing
somewhere not far off in the dark.

Alec crept closer. The moon was very bright, and now the burning horse also added light to the nocturnal landscape. He kept to the shadows, unsure of what he should do next. He could see movement on the lawn in front of the temple, people dressed in robes, and there were horses, too, all riderless. It must be some sort of ceremony, he thought. Perhaps the burning of the wooden horse was an offering of some sort, or perhaps it was meant to invoke the legendary Trojan horse.

The droning murmur of chanting drifted in the air and was soon joined by the soft beat of drums. Alec could make out figures circling the towering effigy, swaying and waving their long arms across the glow of the fire.

Then, above the noises of the ritual, Alec heard a sharp, piercing sound ring through the air, the war cry of an enraged stallion. It was the Black—he was sure of that now—and he was close by.

Alec followed the sound. The Black was surrounded by a crowd of Acracian guards bearing spears and torches. The men had managed to get ropes around the Black's neck and one hind leg and were trying to force him into submission. They swarmed around like insects as they tried to overpower the enraged stallion. The Black twisted his body. Rearing up, he fought the ropes that held him and screamed again.

Alec picked up a stick from the ground for a weapon and charged headlong at the men in a desperate attempt to free his horse. He ran into the crowd, swinging the stick like a club and crying out at the top of his lungs.

Alec slammed into one man and clubbed at the hands of another. The Black shook one of the ropes loose and reared again, his coat gleaming like black satin in the firelight. Throwing all his body weight back onto his forelegs, he brought his hooves to the ground with an explosive crash. The men scattered and the stallion broke free. A moment later he was running off into the night. Two of the men chased after the stallion, and the others turned their attention to Alec.

14

The Temple
of Diomedes

Suddenly a voice from beyond the group barked an order and the guards backed off. It was Spiro. He shouted a reprimand at the men and dismissed them with a wave of his hand.

"Dear, dear," the governor's chamberlain said, his voice softening as he addressed Alec. "I am terribly sorry, Herr Alex. Please forgive those overeager fools. They were only acting under orders."

Alec had a hard time keeping his anger in check. "Fools?" he said. "Those men are dangerous. This *place* is dangerous. This is the second time my horse has been attacked."

"Medio is very protective of this area. The temple of Diomedes is the heart of Acracia. None may come here unless they are granted special permission by the governor himself."

"I didn't want to come here in the first place, and neither did my horse," Alec said. "We are just looking for a way out of here. If those security guards of yours hadn't interfered, we'd be long gone already. Now the Black has taken off again and—"

"Yes," Spiro said. "I would imagine that neither the bonds of human love nor Acracian walls could hold the likes of him for long. But Fire-eyes is here. Perhaps your Bucephalus is with her. At any rate, he cannot be far off."

Spiro gestured to the temple and beamed at Alec with polite courtesy. "It is good to see you here, and I am glad you could join us, oh messenger of the gods."

Alec shook his head. Here we go again, he thought. "No, I'd rather not . . ."

Spiro smiled and took Alec by the arm. "Now that you are here at the temple, I really must insist," he said.

Alec shrugged off the man's hand, losing his patience. "No," he said. "Now *I* must insist. Who are you anyway? How do I get out of this place?"

Spiro stepped back and bowed his head apologetically. "You came by way of the white road and must leave by way of the red road, through the gateway at the temple of Mt. Atnos. Thus spoke the Oracle."

"There is a road to the other side of the mountain?" Alec said. "That's terrific. Red road. White road. I don't care if it's the pink road with purple polka dots on it, as long as it gets me out of here."

"That's the way out for you," Spiro said, "the best and only true way. But I was hoping you would change your mind and stay with us a time. If you really must go, be assured we will await your return."

"Fine," Alec said. "We will all get together next year and have a big reunion. Right now I need to get back to work, and I am not leaving without Xeena and my horse."

Spiro nodded. "Of course," he said.

"So where is this road?" Alec said. "How do we reach it? Is it this way?"

"This way," Spiro said, leading Alec onto the temple grounds.

Spiro gestured up to the moonlit temple as they walked along. "I beg you to take stock of this place while you can, messenger," he said. "The ancient world has been reborn here. Not retold as in a play or mocked in a show, or even imitated in some meaningless ceremony, but born again in the flesh, as you will be. Wait and see, young Alexander, your destiny will be fulfilled again."

Alec's frustrations boiled over. "You people are crazy," he said. "Please listen to me, Spiro. One last time, I am not a messenger and my name is not Alex. It is Alec. Alec Ramsay. I am a jockey. I was born in New York. My horse's name is the Black, not Bucephalus."

Spiro looked at Alec. His face hardened, and it

appeared that Alec's words were finally sinking in. He shook his head with disappointment. "Do you mean to say you still believe your coming here was just an accident, that it wasn't preordained somehow?"

"Preordained by whom, the gods? I just can't buy that."

"Then the time has come for you to leave," Spiro said.

"That's fine with me," Alec said. "I appreciate your hospitality but—"

"Of course, Alec," Spiro said, bowing his head, then gesturing to the fire on the mountain summit. "This way, please."

Alec knew he wasn't arguing with a lunatic. The man's intelligence was perfectly clear, and Alec knew he was sincere and believed what he was saying, as mad as it might sound.

Spiro led the way ahead and spoke to Alec as they walked along. "Of course, you may do as you wish here, messenger," he said, his voice becoming more serious. "But it is my duty to warn you. If you fail to pay homage to the gods and ask their blessings, you will never see your land, your friends or your home again. Once you have honored the gods of heaven, then and only then will they grant the passage you desire."

"And how am I supposed to pay homage to something I don't believe in?" Alec asked.

"Once you have seen the truth," Spiro said, "perhaps you will believe."

"The truth?" Alec said. "What is that supposed to mean?"

Spiro did not answer.

The ancient temple was clearly lit by the glow of the burning horse effigy. Vines climbed up the stone columns all the way to the domed roof. Even the steps leading up to the temple were covered with a tangled web of vegetation. Small crowds of Acracians grouped together at the temple base and spread out around the clearing. All wore masks, and some were crowned with goat and deer horns. Others wore simple pasteboard masks cut in the likeness of wolves and mountain lions. Many were in costume.

At the top of the steps was a small pavilion and throne where a figure sat presiding over the spectacle. By the man's size, Alec guessed it was Medio, though it was impossible to tell for certain as the person was wearing a mask, a grotesque thing made of metal with a wide-open mouth. A small, gilded sword hung at his side.

Medio rose from his throne and descended the temple steps. As he reached the bottom step, he was joined on his right by the albino mare Celera, her red eyes gleaming in the firelight. Then a cloaked figure stepped from the crowd gathered around the flaming horse. She alone was unmasked, wearing only a sheer veil over her face. It was Cyrene, the priestess who had interpreted Celera's prophecies during the banquet. She moved with small, even steps to stand at Medio's left.

At a gesture from their leader, the crowd proceeded up the stairs and into the temple. Alec joined them. Once inside, Medio raised his arms and beckoned for Alec and Spiro to approach him. "I believe King Diomedes would like to have a word with you," Spiro said.

"King Diomedes?" Alec said. "Isn't that Medio?"

"Here at the temple mount, the governor is the earthly embodiment of Diomedes," Spiro said.

"Fine," Alec said, trying to sound as brave as he could. "I'd like to speak with him too."

Spiro touched Alec on the back to gently urge him forward.

The masked monarch pronounced a greeting, and Spiro translated the message—that Alec was an honored guest and that his message would be heard.

Alec looked at Spiro. "Tell him thanks," he said. "This is a great place he has here, but I really must be off. Tell him I have business to tend to elsewhere, other messages to deliver, a family back home."

Spiro translated as a chant went up from the crowd, words Alec did not understand. Then the masked monarch spoke again, his tone stern now.

"He says he understands your concerns but that you must ask for guidance from the Oracle before you go," Spiro said. "With your permission, I will ask her if it is an auspicious time for you to travel."

Upon hearing Spiro's question, Cyrene moved closer to Celera. She lowered her eyes and pressed her cheek against the mare's ivory neck. She uttered some words, and Spiro turned to Alec. "The Oracle says the time has not yet come for you to leave us."

Alec took a deep breath, mindful of the power in the ritual that was going on around him. Yes, he believed if there was magic anywhere, it was here, and something inside him ached to go with it, to let go, to join in and be part of it. The sensation thrilled as much as frightened him. Celera held him in her gaze, her head tilted slightly, her ruby eyes glowing orange in the moonlight, a vision of imperious equine beauty. From deep within him, Alec found the courage to speak up.

"What does she want?" Alec asked.

"Do you mean what does she want of you?" Spiro said.

"No," Alec said. "I mean what does *she* want, the Oracle."

Spiro looked at Alec with surprise. "The Oracle? The Oracle does not want. She only sees the future."

"I don't care to know the future," Alec said. "I am only asking what she wants, she herself. Could you ask her that for me, please?"

Spiro reluctantly translated Alec's words, and the priestess read the mare's soft murmurings, the tapping of hooves and flicking of ears. The priestess dropped her head, her voice quavering and soft as she interpreted the Oracle's words. When she stopped speaking, a collective gasp went up from the throng gathered there. Medio raised his arms and gave a command for quiet. Finally Spiro turned to Alec. "The Oracle says she wants to be with you," he said, "to be like you, to be as you are, to live as you live, but most of all to die as you will die."

To die as he would die, Alec thought. What did that mean?

Spiro bowed his head and backed away. The crowd pressed back and turned their masked faces to avert their eyes as the mare looked out upon them. Only Medio and Cyrene dared hold their ground in her presence now. The mare fixed her attention on Alec. Again she locked him in her fiery gaze, and at that moment he knew he was looking at an animal unlike any other. Despite her beauty, there was an aspect of deadly violence about her, a quiet threat that he never sensed in any horse before, even in the most war-like of stallions.

Medio's voice rang out in the silence to break the spell that the Oracle's words had cast over the gathering. Then the governor turned and led the way to the far end of the temple and down the stairs on the other side. Alec and the rest of the crowd followed him.

A natural basin was tucked into the mountain on this side of the temple, a large amphitheater with a hundred-yard-wide, crater-like pit in the center. Some of the masked revelers hurried to take up positions on the slope of the mountain above the steep walls of the pit. Medio, Celera, Cyrene and the rest of the governor's entourage strode ceremoniously through the amphitheater to the rim of the pit, stopping at a stone-pillared gate with a flat roof built at its edge. The gate loomed large in the moonlight, more than twelve feet wide, the carved stone covered with inscriptions and astrological signs.

Alec watched and waited, knowing he must play along and stay ready for the appropriate time to make his move. He was determined to find the Black, get back to Xeena and make their escape. But if there was another way out of this place, a road or some passageway through the mountain, he knew he must find it.

From out of the crowd behind Medio came two

people shrouded in white robes, a skinny, frail-looking old man and woman. They stepped forward and stood before the governor. They were by far the oldest people Alec had seen since he came here. Alec wasn't sure but the man could have been the same one he had seen sleeping in the streets of the village he had passed through earlier.

The couple bowed their heads as Medio spoke. Cyrene moved to stand before the couple and drew back the veil hiding her face. It was the first time Alec had really seen what the priestess looked like, as she had remained veiled throughout the banquet in the megaron. As with the mare, Alec felt almost helpless before her, unable to look away from her. A chill ran down his spine as he realized he was looking at the most beautiful woman he had ever seen, a goddess as impersonal as a force of nature. It was as if Cyrene *were* Nature herself. What was the woman's connection to Celera? he wondered. Master? Servant? Equal? Twin?

In the young woman's hands was a simple wicker basket full of flowers. The blossoms were strung together into necklaces, like Hawaiian leis. Medio reached down into the basket, took out two of the necklaces and draped one each around the necks of the old couple. They bowed again and backed away humbly.

A moment later, the old couple was escorted by a

pair of guards to the gate. The guards stood back as the couple held hands and hobbled silently through the stone pillars like sleepwalkers. Then they disappeared within the dark, yawning shadows falling from the slab of carved stone roofing the gate.

There was a noise Alec couldn't identify that was quickly drowned out by a cheer from the crowd rimming the arena. A chorus of voices broke into song. Drums and pipes sprang to life, stirring the air with frenzied rhythm.

Alec didn't understand. "Where did they go?" he asked Spiro.

"See for yourself," the chamberlain said.

Alec walked to the edge of the pit and looked inside it. The drums hammered louder, joined by more singing. Now he could see inside the gate where a path led out to the precipice and to a steep chute made of weathered stone. The slide ended at the floor of the pit, which was like a bowl-shaped arena about the size of the banquet hall of the megaron.

Something was moving over the floor of the pit. It looked like a small herd of horses, some of the same ones Alec had seen at the banquet in the megaron, including Shoe Thief and her two sisters. The young gray stallion was there as well.

What had happened to the old couple after their big send-off by Medio and Cyrene? Had they fallen down the slide? Where were they now? He finally noticed them in the shadows near the bottom of the slide.

The spectators raised their voices, calling out the horses' names, encouraging them on like racetrack fans at the finish of a big race. A sick feeling rose inside Alec as he suddenly realized the true nature of the drama being played out here before him.

The horses had spotted the man and woman now, and Alec watched in disbelief as they ran down the old couple. In seconds, the horses began tearing into their victims' flesh with their teeth, shaking their prey as a pack of hungry wolves or pride of lions might. It was a scene out of hell. This was the red road that Spiro had been talking about, Alec realized, the road to sacrifice and violent death. The red road was the road of blood.

After a moment, one of the mares looked up from her ghastly meal, her muzzle smeared with gore. Throwing back her head, she screamed wildly in her triumph, her savage cry ringing out into the night.

Alec reeled away from the horrific sight, but he didn't get far. Medio's authoritative voice boomed a command, and Alec was taken in hand by two strong-armed Acracian guards and ushered to where the mad governor was standing at the foot of his throne.

Alec fought against his captors, but the guards held him still and he could not break free. Medio stepped closer, close enough that Alec could smell his foul breath. In his hands was another necklace made of flowers. Medio raised the necklace ceremoniously above him and gestured to the moon. He said a few words to the gathered throng and lowered the ring of flowers over Alec's head, pressing it down onto his shoulders. Then Medio signaled to the guards, who instantly began dragging Alec toward the gate, the sacrificial pit, the road that Alec now understood led to imminent death, a horrific death unlike any he ever could have imagined. To be torn limb from limb and eaten alive . . .

Alec searched for an ally in the crowd of masked faces edging closer to the rim of the arena. The demon revelers stamped their feet. They elbowed each other out of the way, coming as close to the precipice as they dared, swaying to the music and nodding their horned heads. The scent of blood filled the air.

In a desperate effort to survive, Alec cried out and struggled against the arms forcing him forward. Outnumbered and alone, he was lifted off the ground and carried over to the ceremonial stone gate and the top of the slide leading down into the pit.

He jerked his body against the tight grips on his arms and legs, determined to fight until the end. Slipping one leg free, he brought his heel down as hard as he could on one of the men carrying him. It struck something that felt like a man's leg. The man stumbled and lost his hold. The others became unsteady. Alec wrenched an elbow free and kicked his foot again, then brought his elbow down as hard as he could on whatever was in reach. The fury of Alec's resistance startled his bearers, and they collapsed in a pile.

Alec landed on his back, but at least he was on top of the others. He rolled off, crawled back through the gate and looked for a place to run. . . .

15

The Red Road

After his escape from the man-beasts, the Black had resolved to stay hidden. He did not fear the two-legged ones or their rope snakes or pointed sticks, but he had no intention of seeking revenge for his treatment at their hands. He had found his way to this rocky peak where he could see all that passed beneath him. Here he would wait and watch. The pain in his shoulder was minor. The stick had only grazed him, and the bleeding had already ceased to flow from it.

The stallion gazed out into the starry night beyond the mountain peaks and then down at the dark world of rocks and trees below. It seemed the man-beasts had given up the chase. And if they came again, he knew he could evade them. The Black tossed his head and gave a fierce snort. The time had come to move on, even if he remained unsure which way to go. Somehow, he would find his way out of this place.

He started down a path, knowing he could circle

around the herd of man-beasts. As he moved along, a fresh wind brought with it a familiar smell that stopped him in his tracks. It was the boy. There was fear there, he scented, as well as the smell of fresh blood. The stallion turned his head into the wind and let the telltale signs lead him to where his heart told him he must go—to the boy.

Soon the stallion was close enough to see the fires burning and the gathering of horses and men. His flight instinct warned him to avoid these men who were ruled by creatures that looked like horses but acted like hungry wolves. Still the stallion continued along the path, following the scent in the breeze.

The Black moved down the path, unafraid. He was a stallion, desert-born. What he could not outrun he would fight, and he could stand his own with any. If his enemy could stalk him, he could stalk them, these predators who lived for blood. And if he had to, he would match them in their violence. He had killed horses. He had killed men. If necessary, he would kill again. Let *them* fear *him*.

The sounds of the pounding drums filled the air as he descended the trail. The scent of the burning fire became stronger in his nostrils, but so did the scent of his boy.

Preoccupied with each other, those gathered by the pit did not see the stallion as he crept closer, hiding

in the shadows of the trees and rocks. He was a predator now, like his enemy, waiting and watching for the
time to move.

The mare was here, too, the Black knew. He could
smell her close by. He wondered if she could sense him
as well. Then, among the crowd, he could see the boy
struggling with a pack of man-beasts.

The stallion did not hesitate. With two quick
steps, he bounded into a gallop, trampling the ground
and rushing ahead, bearing down on the man-beasts.
A cry went up from those in his way as the stallion
burst in upon the throng. The boy was there on the
ground, alone, just as the stallion had been alone,
cornered as he had been cornered. But now they were
together, and together they would fight. And together
they would win. And together they would escape.

Alec scrambled to his feet among the shouts of men,
cries of anger and pain. Then there was a shrill whistle, a drumming of hooves, and like an avenging angel,
the Black crashed in upon their enemies. The stallion
reared up, higher and higher still, until his raven mane
unfurled like a flag in the moonlight, his hooves beating the air, his eyes like lanterns of hate.

Does he even recognize me? Alec thought.
"Black," he called. "It's me!" If the stallion heard him,
he made no sign of it. Alec was knocked back to the

ground as the Black careened past him and burst upon the others, charging back and forth and flailing his hooves.

To get clear, Alec crawled backward until he felt someone taking his arm and lifting him to his feet. It seemed like a gentle gesture, and for an instant Alec thought perhaps help had arrived at last. He turned his head to look over his shoulder, and his hopes collapsed.

It was Medio behind him. The mask had fallen from the mad governor's face, and his sharp eyes glared at Alec. He tried to pull free, but the baby-faced giant easily managed to keep Alec's arms pinned to his sides. He whispered some words Alec did not understand, his tone soft and menacing, his breath foul on Alec's neck.

Alec threw back his head with a grunt but wasn't close enough to connect. Crushed in the man's embrace, Alec felt his feet lift inches off the ground. As Medio carried him to the gate, Alec threw his weight from side to side and kicked his legs. Nothing seemed to help. He was trapped as surely as a fly in a spiderweb.

Just as they reached the entrance to the gate, there was an explosion of hooves. It was the Black. Behind him, two guards lay unconscious on the ground; the rest had scattered. Medio called to the stallion and pushed Alec forward, holding him as a shield between him and the black demon. Alec looked into the Black's eyes, trying to read what he could but seeing only black rage.

Medio shouted fearlessly as the enraged stallion moved upon them, pushing them both back against a pillar and then through the gate, closer to the precipice.

The Black coiled back on his haunches and charged again. Medio spun around. He raised an arm, trying to avoid the blows from the stallion's hooves, and Alec pulled himself free. Medio snarled as Alec escaped but did not try to pursue him. All the man's attention was focused on the Black.

The stallion struck on one side of his cornered prey and then the other, pushing him closer to the edge of the cliff. Medio moved backward, waving his arms and cowering from the blows. In desperation, he tried to break to the side. Tangling his feet, he lost his balance as he came too close to the edge. He seemed to hang in midair for an instant, a look of surprise on his face. Then, with a cry of disbelief, the Lord of Acracia tumbled over the precipice and down into the pit.

A gasp fell over the party of revelers lining the rim of the crater, followed by a great silence. Alec looked out at the masked faces as they stared into the pit. No one moved or made an effort to help their fallen leader.

At the bottom of the slide, Medio clutched his

thigh. He struggled to his feet and limped toward a doorway in the wall of the arena. Alec watched as one of the white mares approached Medio. The Acracian emperor said something and held up his hand. The mare hesitated a moment, then moved closer.

Medio called out again and reached out to the mare as if to caress her. She brushed past his hand and lowered her head to sniff at the fresh blood staining his bare legs. Then she licked it. Medio suddenly drew back. He tried to push the mare away but she persisted, licking at the blood and quickly taking hold with her teeth. Medio struck at her head as she raked his arm with her teeth. The rest of the herd circled closer and then moved in to join their sister.

Medio staggered backward until the gray stallion lunged at him, knocking him to the ground. The fallen governor stared up in terror as the circle of death tightened in upon him. He cried out and reached for his sword, but it was already too late.

Alec turned from the awful sight and rushed back through the gate. The Black stood alone, waiting for him. The stallion watched Alec approach, then reared and pawed the air.

Alec stopped short and stood still until the stallion's hooves were on the ground again; then he stepped in close. The Black snorted but did not move away as Alec stepped closer and raised his hand to the black mane. He spoke some low words and then, drawing on every ounce of energy he could muster, hurled himself onto the stallion's back. A second later they were off and running. Alec buried his head in his horse's mane, wanting nothing more than to get away, to get anywhere, as long as it was far from here.

16

Escape

The Black carried him at a gallop through the village at the mountaintop, slowing to a trot as they reached the road down the mountain. Again Alec could see the fallen trees, collapsed walls and other signs of the earthquake that had shaken the mountain earlier that evening.

Alec stroked the Black's neck, trying to calm both of their nerves. He could hardly believe what had just happened. Could he have come any nearer to death than he had been only a few minutes ago? If it wasn't for the Black, he would probably be dead right now.

Soon the eastern mountain peaks started to lighten, and Alec realized it must be close to dawn. All his senses told him to escape this place as soon as he could, but he knew they couldn't leave Xeena here, especially after what he'd just seen up at the temple.

Alec took a deep breath and tried to take stock of what he needed to do now. Medio was dead. There was no way to tell whether Spiro and the others would blame the Black for causing his death or spoiling their ceremony. No one had tried to prevent Alec and the Black from escaping the place or made any attempt to pursue them when they left. The entire gathering, even the Acracian guard, had just stood there stunned, as if in a collective trance, while Alec had mounted his horse and ridden off. Surely they'd come out of their stupor before long, and Alec didn't want to be around when they did.

He leaned forward and spoke softly to his horse. They pulled to a stop, and both looked back toward the mountaintop. Alec could see the flaming horse effigy still burning on the distant mountainside. He watched for signs of movement on the road behind him and saw none. Nor could he hear anything but the unnatural silence that always seemed to permeate these woods.

The Black held his head high, his ears pricked. Alec watched the stallion for any signs that the horse sensed something in the wind. After a moment, the stallion dropped his head, seemingly unconcerned. Perhaps Medio's followers weren't as loyal as they were professed to be. Certainly no one seemed to be chasing after him, Alec thought, at least not yet.

Questions raced through his mind, and he forced himself to think ahead. He still had no idea how to get out of this place. Would the guards try to stop them when they passed through the acropolis? Were the citizens of Acracia evacuating the city after the quake, or was the main gate still closed?

They reached the fork in the road, and Alec turned the Black toward Tarta. He could only hope Xeena was still there.

In the distance he could see the tower, and soon they reached the outskirts of the town. Alec found his way to the cottage where Nicholas lived and was relieved to see Xeena in the yard with her grandfather. Nicholas was trying to get the front door back on its hinges. He stopped working when he saw the Black and Alec.

Alec jumped down from his horse's back.

"You found him," Xeena said. "Where was he?"

"Don't ask," he said, "I can't even begin to tell you."

"Come have a glass of water," Nicholas said, leading Alec through the open doorway. "It will clear your thoughts."

Xeena stayed with the Black, who lowered his head and began grazing hungrily on Nicholas's overgrown lawn.

"You were at the temple ceremony?" Nicholas said as they stepped through the open doorway. Alec didn't answer, but the man must have read Alec's expression and guessed the truth. "Then you know," he said.

Inside, the house was in shambles, with piles of broken dishes and glass, collapsed shelves and cracked walls. Alec took a drink of water and felt new strength spiral through his head and body. It made him talkative suddenly, and Nicholas listened as Alec told him what had happened at the temple atop Mt. Atnos.

Nicholas smiled. "So Medio is no more," he said. "The king is dead. Long live the king." He gave Alec a deferential bow of his head. "You will be a wonderful governor, and all Acracia looks forward to your reign."

Alec laughed at the thought.

Nicholas's expression became serious. "That is not a debate, Alec, or a request," he said. "You and the Black were chosen. You cannot insult the gods by refusing to take your place among them now."

"We can't, huh?" Alec said, and laughed again at the absurdity of it all. "Why can't Spiro be chosen? He is the chamberlain."

"True," Nicholas said. "He was the next in line, until your arrival here. But such is Fate. Spiro could never command if you fled the realm. There would be chaos. For Spiro to rule, you would need to meet your fate as Medio did, via the red road—an offering to the sacred mares."

"Chaos?" Alec said. "That would be an improvement from what I've seen around here. This mixed-up paradise of yours could use some chaos."

"Please consider your position," Nicholas said. "You cannot defy the will of the gods."

"Do you seriously think I want to give up my life and stay here, as governor, or king, or guest, or anything else?" Alec said. "And what about Xeena? Do you really believe this is the best place for her?"

Nicholas did not answer, but the mention of Xeena plainly troubled him and he looked vulnerable suddenly. Alec walked back outside and Nicholas followed.

"We have to go," Alec told Xeena. "We have to get out of here."

Xeena looked at him. Her voice was stiff. "We can't leave yet. People could be hurt. They need our help. And what about Popi?"

Alec shook his head. "You don't understand. We have to get out of here. Right now."

Nicholas glanced at Alec, a steely serenity in his expression now, as if he had resolved his inner conflicts and made up his mind. Then he put his hands on Xeena's shoulders and looked her straight in the face. "Alec is right," he said. "You must leave, child."

"I'm no child," Xeena said. "I'm—"

Nicholas gave Xeena a hug. "You are unafraid,

Xeena," he said, "and I respect that. But listen, you must go. It is too late for me. You have drunk only lightly of the water here; perhaps it is not too late for you."

"We have to go now," Alec repeated firmly.

Xeena untangled herself from Nicholas's arms. "I am not going without you," she said stubbornly.

Alec looked at the young man who he now accepted was indeed Xeena's grandfather in the body of a man less than half his age. How that happened, he hadn't a clue, but he had to accept it.

Nicholas shook his head. "I could not join you, even if I wanted to. The effects of Acracian waters come at a price. Without it, not only would the benefits of the blessed nectar be reversed, but also whatever illness, injury or age had been masked by the effects of the water would return, and be compounded." The young-old man sighed wearily. "I suppose no one really knows. No one has ever left Acracia and returned to say otherwise."

"That doesn't matter," Alec said. "We have to try. We are not staying here."

"I don't understand, Popi," Xeena said. "Your family loves you. You have to come with us. You have to try."

"Do not grieve for me, Xeena. I am comfortable here. When my time comes, I will go the way of the others before me."

"But why?" Xeena pleaded.

"I am a citizen of the Acracian realm, loyal in heart, mind, body and soul. Here we do not die from old age or disease, but for loyalty. It is our responsibility to keep in step. If we have violated Nature's law, we must wait for her judgment."

Alec listened to Nicholas. He didn't understand the reasoning, and it didn't matter anyway. There was no more time to waste.

"We have to go, Xeena," he said. "Come on."

The Black suddenly stamped his hooves, lifted his head and shrilled. "Ho," Alec cried.

Approaching the yard was Spiro flanked by the three white mares and the gray stallion from the temple pit. The horses' eyes were alight with hunger, their muzzles smeared with blood.

"Salutations, Governor Alexander," the chamberlain called out. "Your chargers await you."

Nicholas took Xeena by the hand, and they stepped closer to Alec and the Black for protection. Then, at a vocal cue from Spiro, the four horses spread out and took up positions around the black stallion and the three humans huddled in his shadow. The horses moved at a slow, unhurried walk, their noses close to the ground, like slinking wolves, predators zeroing in for the kill.

These were not horses as Alec knew them, and he

couldn't help but be fascinated by the sight. How could he fight creatures he could not understand, horses with human blood on their lips?

The circle tightened. With a savage cry, the Black bolted for Nicholas's cottage, as if trying to draw the flesh-eating horses away from Alec, Xeena and Nicholas. But the mares remained where they were, and only the gray followed. The Black ducked through the open front door of the cottage, and the gray rushed in after him. The sounds of smashing plates and splintering furniture mixed with the screams of the two stallions. A few seconds later, they came bursting outside and the battle spilled into the front yard.

The three mares watched as the Black broke off the fight and circled around one side of the ruined cottage. The gray stallion responded by climbing a ramp made of sections of fallen roof and slinking over to the edge. As the Black came into range beneath him, the gray leaped down upon him like a mountain lion pouncing on its prey. Then both horses were on the ground, rolling and thrashing their hooves as they tried to get up again.

"Popi!" Xeena cried out.

Alec whirled to see Xeena caught between Nicholas and Spiro. Nicholas had her by one arm and Spiro by the other. Both were pulling her in different directions. Alec rushed at Spiro and knocked him to the ground. Nicholas fell upon Spiro and they began to struggle. Instantly the pack of mares returned to claim their captives.

Xeena dashed away as Nicholas and Spiro wrestled each other on the ground. Alec sprang to his feet. There among the horse pack, he saw the shoe-thieving mare from last night. Her attention was focused on Nicholas and Spiro, her lips pulled back in a wolfish snarl. Both Nicholas and Spiro seemed unaware of the mare as she closed on them and moved in for the kill. The two men were fighting on their knees now, each trying to pin the other to the ground.

Without thinking, Alec took a quick step back and leaped astride the mare's back. She immediately reared and Alec leaned forward, his legs wrapped around her neck. He locked his ankles and began squeezing with all his strength.

The mare pounded her forehooves in the dirt and then suddenly stopped her bucking and thrashing. She reeled around, shrilling defiantly. A piercing cry answered her. It was the Black, returning from his combat with the gray, who was now nowhere to be seen.

All three mares turned their attention to the stallion charging into their midst. Spiro and Nicholas continued their fighting, Nicholas pleading desperately for Xeena to stay away. Shoe Thief bucked, then shot into the air.

The Black reared back, plainly startled by seeing Alec astride the mare. Shoe Thief lunged at the Black, and the best Alec could do was swing his free hand at her head to try pushing it away from the Black. She pushed back and fought to take hold of the stallion's neck with her teeth. Alec struck again, and this time the blood-maddened mare turned away from the Black. With one great heaving of her body, she threw herself into the air again. Alec lost his seat and flopped to the ground. In an instant, Xeena was standing over him, giving him a hand and pulling him to his feet.

"Get up," she cried. "It's Popi . . . He pulled me free and then . . ."

Alec looked to where Nicholas and Spiro had been fighting. Both had fallen beneath the mares' hooves. The two mares squealed and sparred with each other as they fought over the broken bodies and bloody, ripped-up clothes.

Alec put his arm around Xeena and turned her away. Only a dozen yards off, the Black was still battling Shoe Thief. She reared up, her lips pulling back to show long, sharp teeth. The Black rose on his hind legs to meet her.

Shoe Thief flicked her head and came at the Black's neck, not trying to take hold this time but nipping almost playfully, letting the stallion feel her teeth, as if it was all just a game. The Black pounded the earth with his hooves. The mare collected herself and stood ready to attack.

There was the sound of onrushing hooves, and Alec spun around to see yet another horse crashing toward them. It was Celera, the albino mare, her head and tail held high. With a defiant war cry, she thundered to a stop, then stepped between the Black and Shoe Thief, her neck arched in disdain. The two other mares trotted over to join their sister and face the albino. Alec took Xeena by the hand and pulled her closer to the Black.

Celera screamed at the mares, and they replied in a chorus of frenzied whinnies and animal snarls as she stood between them and their prey. Celera stood her ground, keeping the other mares back, as if to protect Alec, Xeena and the Black from the flesh-eating white sisters.

The mares hesitated before challenging the ruby-eyed albino. One finally lowered her head and thrust forward. Celera easily sidestepped the charge and let fly with her hind hooves. The white mare crashed to the ground with a squeal of pain. After another moment's hesitation, her sisters tried to move closer. Celera stamped the ground threateningly and then lunged, striking out with the skill of a practiced warrior.

As the mares fought among themselves, Alec pulled the Black away and swung onto his back. He grabbed Xeena by the arm and pulled her up behind him. "Hang on," he cried over his shoulder.

The stallion whirled and took off, racing for the road as fast as a horse carrying two riders could run.

"Go, Black, go!" Alec cried.

They startled a herd of goats as they zoomed past. As they turned down the road to the acropolis, Alec heard something behind him, the defiant call of a horse. He turned to see Celera racing after them. Alec urged the Black faster, hoping beyond hope that Xeena could manage to hang on as the stallion lengthened his stride on the open road. He glanced back over his shoulder again. The albino was still there, chasing after them and getting closer. At least there was no sign of the other mares on the road behind her. That was something to be grateful for.

As they reached the outskirts of the acropolis, Alec could see more signs of destruction from the earth tremor here—broken columns, collapsed pillars and stone debris. The Black had to slow down, but so would Celera. What the Black couldn't get around, he jumped over. Somehow both Alec and Xeena remained on his back.

Celera closed in behind them as they reached an open field that led to the acropolis. Alec spotted a fissure that had been rent in the wall from top to bottom. It was a miracle. The earthquake had opened a passageway to the outside!

This was their only chance, and Alec turned the Black toward it. The stallion saw it, too, and needed no further urging from Alec. He knew where he was going now. The albino kept up her pursuit. Unburdened by one rider, much less two, Celera was soon only a length away and closing.

Celera cried out as she narrowed the gap between them. It was not a war cry this time but a haunting, forlorn, almost pleading sound. Whatever it meant to the Black, he did not stop.

Soon the two horses were running neck and neck toward the jagged opening in the wall. Careening through the passage, they emerged on the stretch of grass lying between the wall and the moatlike canal bordering the city. At last the Acracian walls were behind them, and they were free. What a relief!

The two horses rushed to a place where the canal narrowed to little more than a stream. Reaching the edge at the same instant, the runners leaped into the air, flying across the enchanted waters to the other side.

Out of the corner of his eye, Alec could see something happen to Celera as they touched down on the opposite bank. A whooshing sound filled his ears, like something bursting into flames, much like the sound Alec had heard when the wooden horse caught fire.

The mare didn't fall, but something was clearly wrong with her. She stumbled to a stop. The Black, too, stumbled and slowed to a halt, breathing hard. Alec let go and both he and Xeena tumbled to the ground, rolling through the grass.

All at once, Alec's left ankle throbbed with pain, the one he thought he had twisted days before. As Nicholas had warned, all the pain that Alec hadn't felt for the past few days was returning with a vengeance. His entire body ached as if he had suddenly been struck by an intense case of altitude sickness.

Alec looked up at the Black standing unsteadily beside him, clearly shaken, his body trembling. Xeena lay groaning on the ground. The stallion threw back his head and whinnied to Celera as she tried to come closer.

The mare teetered on her legs and could barely move. She was still standing but was also transforming before Alec's very eyes, aging years in seconds and then even faster. It was as if she were drying up, as if all the moisture was draining from her body. Suddenly her magnificent white coat seemed to turn to paper, wrinkling and cracking and finally dissolving into a heap of dust.

"Alec," Xeena called. "Are you okay?"

Alec heard Xeena but he didn't turn to see the girl. His eyes remained fixed, as the Black's were, on the pile of dust that was all that remained of the albino mare.

"Did you see . . ." Alec started to say. He blinked, still disbelieving his own eyes. It was true, he realized. Celera was gone.

"What happened to the albino?" Xeena said. "Did she fall in the water?"

Alec shook his head. "She just . . . vanished." He pointed to all that was left of the mare, little more than ashes and dust. The Black paced back and forth, waiting and watching, as if trying to reason what was happening. The stallion cautiously approached the ashen remains of Celera, sniffed the ground, then whinnied and pulled back.

A mountain breeze blew up around them suddenly. The breath of wind picked up the pile of dust, and the particles flew into the air, becoming a grayish puff. Alec watched as the dust swirled along like a tiny dust devil, floating back across the stream to the other side. Once there, the swirl turned inside itself, becoming what looked like a cluster of windblown paper, quickly taking on thickness and shape and the form of a white horse. Once returned to the other side of the river, the dust reassembled into Celera, just as quickly as she had dissolved.

The reconstituted albino mare reared up and

shrilled to the Black. The stallion cried an answer and charged to the river's edge but did not jump. He threw back his head and called to the mare again.

Celera stood still, watching him silently. Then, with one last, plaintive cry, she spun around and ran off to vanish beyond the city walls.

The Black watched her go. He cried again, but no answer came. The stallion paced back and forth on the embankment, neighing wildly and pawing the ground as if anxious to jump across the river to the other side.

Alec tried to call out to his horse, but he could barely find the breath to speak. In a minute, the Black stopped his pacing, raised his head and sniffed the wind. Then he turned to where Alec lay sprawled on the ground.

"Black," Alec managed to call, his voice a hoarse croak. He tried to stand up, but his legs felt incredibly weak and collapsed beneath him. Crawling over to an outcropping of rocks, he pulled himself high enough so he could mount the Black again. Once he was on the stallion's back, he gave Xeena a hand and swung her up behind him.

Alec felt weak, spent. His body ached and his sore ankle throbbed. He looked around him, wondering what direction was home, finally letting the Black decide which way they should go.

17

Home

How long they wandered in the woods Alec wasn't sure. He felt dazed, but the pain in his leg kept him awake. He and Xeena barely spoke as they rode along, hunched together over the stallion's back. From time to time, Alec could hear her weeping behind him, and once he heard Xeena calling her grandfather's name softly to herself. Alec didn't know what to say, so he didn't say anything. The Black was strong enough for all of them, carrying his riders up one trail and down another, sometimes stopping in his tracks to retrace his steps and take a different turn.

Finally they emerged from a tree tunnel to a gently sloping field. At the bottom of the field was what looked like a road. Alec lifted his head to the sky, and from the position of the sun, he could see that it was already early afternoon.

"Whoa," he called to the Black as the stallion started to break into a quicker pace in the open field.

"I think it's a road," Xeena said, her voice excited suddenly.

Alec pulled the Black to a stop. Xeena hopped off and Alec slid gently to the ground, his legs still shaky beneath him.

"We didn't pass by this field before," Alec said, "but I bet that road leads somewhere if we just keep following it down the mountain." He took a step and staggered as his injured leg buckled beneath him.

"You better ride," Xeena said. "I'll walk."

Alec got set to remount, but before he did, he glanced over his shoulder to where they'd just been. The mouth of the tree tunnel seemed to have vanished, swallowed up by the forest as if it had never existed.

Alec pulled himself onto the Black's back, and they started down the mountain. He still felt dazed and thankfully was able to keep the stallion to a slow pace. Xeena walked beside them in silence and apparently deep in thought.

It was Cleo that found them, Xeena's sleepy-eyed pony. Amazingly, she was still tacked up in saddle and bridle, exactly as she had been when they left her at the falls three days ago. She was sauntering up the path in the other direction, jogging lightly toward them as if she'd just come outside for an afternoon stroll. The mare whinnied as she saw them. Xeena dashed ahead to greet her horse and threw her arms around the mare's neck.

"I can't believe this," Alec said as he joined her. "What is Cleo doing here? Didn't she go back home after we went into the falls? Has she been out here all the time we were gone?"

"I guess so," Xeena answered, glad to be with her horse again. She leaned her forehead against the mare's neck to breathe in the smell of her. Alec watched her and smiled. At least they were closer to home now than they had been an hour ago.

Xeena swung herself into the saddle, and a minute later they all were making good time down the trail. The path ahead wound past rocks and trees, at one point edging along a steep mountain pass Alec had never seen before. At last the path straightened and widened to a dirt road. Soon Alec could see the monastery walls in the distance and the film crew's trucks parked in a row outside the visitors' compound. There was movement around them, people from the crew.

At last it was over, Alec thought. The long and terrible journey through the lost city had come to an end. He felt exhausted, too tired to think of food or anything else but lying down and going to sleep.

Soon they were passing through the gate to the

compound. No one seemed to pay them much attention. The gaffers and electricians who had been hanging out around their trucks barely gave them any notice at all. It wasn't that Alec cared or expected a big reception, but hadn't the crew been alerted about Xeena and Alec going missing? Hadn't their unexplained absence caused some concern among the crew?

Reaching the Black's tent, Alec carefully dismounted and put the Black in his stall. Then he set to fixing the stallion's feed and water. The Black waited and watched him patiently as Alec hobbled around the tent. There was a look of dark sadness in the stallion's eyes, and Alec spoke to his horse in singsong to brighten their spirits. He gave the Black a few swipes with a soft brush, then stepped out of the stall and sat down on a tack trunk to catch his breath.

Xeena had walked Cleo to her own tent, and a few minutes later she returned. Karst was with her. The sight of Xeena's dad startled Alec. For a moment, Alec thought he was back in Tarta looking at Nicholas. Then Karst put on a playful smile, and when the man spoke, Alec knew that this was the real Karst and no one else.

"How was your walk?" Karst said in his thick Greek accent. "I hear you take a fall."

"How was our walk?" Alec said, hardly believing his ears. Alec glanced at Xeena, but her expression revealed nothing. "Didn't she tell you what happened to us?"

Karst looked at Alec's ankle. "Not broken?"

"I don't think so," Alec said. "Maybe I sprained it."

"We get you fixed up with nurse. Be good as new, no time."

"Yes, but . . . Karst, didn't you get the message about what happened to us? Haven't you been wondering where we've been? Wasn't any sort of search made?"

Karst looked perplexed. "Why search? You not gone so long. Maybe two, three hours. You okay?" Karst said, a hint of concern coming into his voice.

Alec looked at his friend, the shock he was feeling surely visible on his face. "Two or three hours?" Alec said. "Are you saying this is still Tuesday?"

"You okay?" Karst repeated. "You hit your head? Yes, Tuesday. Crew on break; we sit tight, still waiting for director. Chopper broke down. He be here tomorrow." Karst pointed at Alec's swollen ankle. "You take it easy. We get you to nurse's station and then you rest."

Xeena glanced at Alec, and she shook her head slightly, as if signaling him to stop. "Go ahead," she said. "I'll stay with the Black."

Karst unclipped his walkie-talkie from his belt and put in a call to Jeff. The young Australian soon drove up in his golf cart. "Heard you had a little accident," Jeff said. "Hop in and I'll take you to Lana. She can get you fixed up."

Alec climbed into the golf cart beside Jeff, and they drove to the nurse's tent.

The nurse washed and bandaged Alec's ankle, then sent him on his way with a walking cane and a pocket full of extra-strength aspirin. "That'll do until we can get you back down the mountain tomorrow night," she said.

Jeff was waiting outside in his golf cart as Alec left the tent. "Where to now, boss?" Jeff said amiably. "Do you want to go back to your room?"

"Think I better check on my horse," Alec said.

Jeff nodded and eased the golf cart in that direction. "Well, you missed a good card game after lunch," Jeff said as the cart hummed along. "We are having another one tonight, if you're up for it."

Alec glanced at Jeff a moment and then turned away. He still felt dazed by all that had happened, and he knew it probably still showed on his face.

"You feeling all right?" Jeff said. "You look sort of sick."

"I'm okay," Alec said. "It's just . . . this has been the strangest day. I don't think I'll ever be the same again."

Jeff laughed. "Oh, you will be all right," he

said. "I didn't hear how you took your fall. What happened?"

"I'm not sure," Alec said. There was something in him that wanted very much to confide in another person about what he had seen, if only to try to assemble some kind of sense out of it. Besides that, he didn't have the energy to think up an alternative alibi.

Alec started talking and Jeff listened easily. They arrived at the tent. Jeff switched off the motor, a half smile on his face, plainly not sure if he was being kidded or not. Even to Alec's ears, the story he told sounded incredible. Perhaps that was because they were here, safe in the monastery compound surrounded by tents, trucks and their fellow crew, not lost in the wandering woods around Mt. Atnos. Alec recounted what he could, though he intentionally left some parts out, mainly the part about Nicholas's recovered youth and the horror he had seen at the temple of Diomedes.

They sat there in the cart for many moments until Alec finished his story. Then Jeff asked him straight out, "You wouldn't be pulling my leg, would you, Alec? Is this some kind of joke?"

Alec shook his head. "I wish it was. The woods here are . . ."

"What? Magical? Like a magic forest? I don't know, Alec. This sounds like something right out of

Alice in Wonderland. Maybe one of the monks slipped some forest mushroom into your eggs this morning. It is a great yarn, though."

Alec looked at Jeff. What was the use? he thought. Who could believe such a far-fetched tale? And Alec had not one shred of evidence to back up his story. He thanked Jeff for the ride. "No worries, mate," Jeff said lightly as he glided off in his cart.

Alec stepped into the Black's tent. Xeena was idly cleaning some tack that didn't need it, just to keep busy. Alec told her about Jeff's reaction to the story of what happened on their walk that afternoon. "He thought I was making it all up," Alec said. "I don't know what else I expected."

Xeena shook her head. "I know what my dad would say if I told him."

Alec nodded. "Hard to believe we'll both be out of here tomorrow and all this will just be a memory. I just wish I understood. . . ."

Xeena's walkie-talkie crackled to life, and Karst's voice broke in over their conversation. Xeena stood up. "I better go," she said stoically, the serious kid back on the job.

"Take it easy, girl," Alec said.

"You too."

Alec looked in on the Black, then sat on his tack trunk and tried to read a little. He began to feel tired again, so he set up his stable cot to lie down for a minute and take a quick nap. In minutes he was fast asleep, and he stayed that way for the rest of the afternoon, through dinner and long into the night.

Everyone was up extra early the next morning. Bateman had choppered in at first light, and shooting was supposed to be completed by noon, at least according to the schedule Alec had seen. He, the Black and most of the crew would be leaving the monastery shortly thereafter.

Alec's head hurt a little for some reason, but at least his ankle wasn't bothering him too much. He fed and watered the Black, then led him outside so he could stretch his legs.

Jeff caught up to Alec as they circled the animal tents. "Feeling better this morning?" he asked. "How's the head?"

"Yeah, I'm okay. Thanks. But don't we have to rehearse or something for the scene we're supposed to do? I'm still not sure. . . ."

Jeff smiled. "No worries, mate," he said. "Your scene should be a snap. We'll block it out when we get to the location. For now, just go get into costume. We'll be ready for you when you're ready."

An hour later, Alec and the Black were suited up in their Alexander and Bucephalus outfits and waiting with Karst and the rest of the crew on the set. It was the same location they had used before, the place with the spectacular mountain backdrop only a few minutes from the compound.

The place looked like a construction site. Black cables snaked across the ground between humming generators and the sound and lighting equipment. The crew called back and forth, adjusting camera tripods and positioning stands of lights. Two separate camera teams had taken up vantage points along the route. Bateman shuttled back and forth between cameras in his golf cart, crouching down and peering through the lenses, backing up and moving from side to side, checking every possible angle.

Jeff waved to Alec and jogged over. "We are about ready," he said. "This is the layout. Do you see Xeena over there?" He pointed to a spot a couple hundred yards away where Xeena and Cleo were positioned up the hill. "Think of her as a marker. Stiv wants you to lope along straight toward her. The first camera team will track you from the start. When you pass the second team, you should turn to them and point as if you have just noticed some riders in the distance. Got it?"

"Sounds simple enough."

"Places, everyone," called the assistant director over a bullhorn. "Quiet on the set."

Another assistant stepped in front of the camera

holding a black slate clapboard. "*Young Alexander,* scene twenty-one, take one."

"Action!"

Alec urged the Black ahead, and they loped toward Xeena and Cleo, turning and pointing as they passed the second camera team.

"Cut, cut, cut," Bateman called over from a bull-horn behind him. "Back it up. Do it again."

Alec turned the Black around, and they returned to the start marker where Karst was waiting for them.

"Okay," Bateman called out after a moment. "Let's take it from the top. A little faster this time." The assistant with the clapboard stepped in front of the camera again. "*Young Alexander,* scene twenty-one, take two."

"Action!" Alec and the Black took off again, Alec pushing the stallion into a slow gallop. "Cut! Do it again," came the orders over the bullhorn.

Alec thought he and the Black were doing every-thing that was asked of them, but Bateman wanted more footage, so they kept retaking the scene. Every few takes, the camera crews tried a new shooting angle. As much time was spent adjusting cameras and lights between takes as the actual filming. Finally, after fifteen takes, the director seemed satisfied. "That's a keeper, people," Bateman said. "Set up for the next shot."

Alec and the Black started back to the wardrobe tent to get out of their costumes. They were through for the day, and now all they had to do was get packed up and ready for the trip down the mountain. It felt good to be busy and working, Alec thought, good to not think too much about what he had seen, or thought he'd seen, in the Acracian woods yesterday.

All at once, he heard someone calling his name from behind. It was none other than the director, Stiv Bateman. Alec pulled the Black to a stop and swung down from the saddle.

Bateman glanced at the Black and then turned to Alec. "Can I walk with you a minute?"

"Sure," Alec said. "It'd be a pleasure."

"I wanted to thank you for your help on the shoot," Bateman said. "The footage looks great, and I think the Black has a future in pictures if he wants it. But there is something else I'd like to talk to you about. Jeff told me an interesting story this morning, a story he says you told him yesterday, something about a lost city in the forest. Were they ruins?"

Me and my big mouth, Alec thought. But the cat was already out of the bag, and there was no sense in being coy about it now. He spoke up and tried to be as honest as he could. "They weren't ruins," Alec said. "It was a city, like an ancient Greek city, a place unlike anything I've ever seen."

"Tell me about it," Bateman said. His expression was intent, his eyes focused. Alec repeated the version of the story he had told Jeff. Bateman walked beside him and listened quietly all the way back to the Black's tent.

"I don't expect you to believe me," Alec said at last, "but since you asked . . ."

"Believe you? Who says I don't believe you?"

The director's reaction was not at all what Alec had expected. He was actually taking Alec seriously. "I just figured . . ."

Bateman laughed jovially. "Why not? Life is still a mystery to me. And you don't look like the sort of guy who would make up a yarn like that just for fun. I think I'd like to see this lost, time-wandering city of yours for myself."

"Seriously?"

"Sure. It sounds fascinating. Don't know how I'd get in there, though. It was hard enough getting permission to film here at the monastery. I might try it guerilla-style, like we used to do back in film school. Go in light, take some money for bribes. It just might work." Bateman looked at his watch. "Gotta go, kid," he said. "And thanks for sharing. If I go, I'll let you know how it turns out."

Alec led the Black to the tent entrance and then turned and watched the director hustling off back to the set, already barking orders into his walkie-talkie. He wondered if Bateman was really serious about what he had said. Bateman did have a reputation for shooting in the most out-of-the-way places imaginable, in deep jungle and at the bottom of the sea, so it made sense that he might be tempted to do what he said he wanted to do.

For the next hour or two, Alec busied himself packing and getting the Black ready for the van ride down the mountain. Xeena gave him a hand stowing his gear in the van, and he told her about his talk with Bateman.

"I guess some people are like that," she said. "I wouldn't go back into those woods for a million dollars. But to tell you the truth, right now I am starting to think it might have been just some incredible dream after all."

"If it was a dream," Alec said, "we were in it together."

Xeena nodded. "That makes me feel better for some reason. Let's leave it at that."

"Fine with me," he said. Alec stepped over to the tack trunk. "Can you give me a hand with this? My ankle still hurts a little."

Xeena smiled. "Sure," she said, taking up the other end of the trunk.

"Thanks," Alec said. "At least I know I didn't imagine this twisted ankle of mine."

An hour later, the Black was safely loaded up and Alec was sitting in the van's passenger seat as Karst eased the van out the driveway and through the monastery gate. Xeena was riding with Cleo and some of the other horses in Thomas's van, so it was just the two of them. Karst waved to the monks standing watch, but the sullen-eyed men took no notice of him. He shook his head and laughed. "Friendly guys."

Alec leaned forward in his seat and turned to look out his window to the peaks of Mt. Atnos, now shrouded in thick clouds. He wondered again about Celera and the white mares. Were they still there, grazing on the lush grass in their sacred pastures? He thought about Cyrene and the temple of Diomedes and wondered if the citizens of Acracia were rebuilding their city walls. Or had chaos fallen upon the realm, as Nicholas had foretold? A gentle wind drifted through the open window, and Alec heard the sounds of singing birds. For an instant, he thought he could hear the faint, faraway strains of a handheld harp playing a melody from another time. Taking a deep breath, he leaned back in his seat and turned his mind to the road ahead.

◆　◆　◆

One cloudy afternoon, several months later, Alec was sitting at his desk in the office of the stallion barn at Hopeful Farm finishing up paying feed bills. It had been some time since he'd even thought about the *Young Alexander* shoot and all that had happened to him and the Black when they were there. With all of his scenes completed, Alec had ended up spending only a few more days in Thrace. The trip home had been painless, first-class all the way, and Alec had quickly settled back into life at Hopeful Farm.

After filling out the last check and addressing the envelope, he stood up from his desk and walked to the window. Outside he could see a pair of foals playing tag in the late autumn sun. Their dams stood nearby in the shade of an oak. He watched them a moment, then took a seat on the office couch. Picking up a news-paper from the coffee table, he scanned the headlines and then turned to the entertainment section to see if there was an interesting movie playing at the local theater. Before he could turn to the listings page, a headline caught his eye:

STIV BATEMAN MISSING IN BULGARIA
Stiv Bateman, renowned screen director of such epic blockbusters as *Underworlds, Amazon Beaming,* and *Beyond Mars,* has been reported missing while location-scouting in a

little-known area of Thracian Bulgaria. The director had recently returned to Thrace after completing postproduction work in Los Angeles on his latest film, *Young Alexander,* a much anticipated work about the early life of Alexander the Great that is due to open next week. Bateman's last communication with the outside world was more than three days ago, and it is feared he is lost and may not be on hand for the opening of his new film. The region where Bateman was last seen is one of the least explored areas of Europe, unmapped and obscured by clouds most of the year. Local district sources say that the eccentric director was traveling in a restricted, unsafe area without permission.

The newspaper fell from Alec's hands and hit the floor. Without thinking, he stood up and walked over to the stallion barn. He picked up a halter and lead shank, then stepped outside again.

"I'm going to check some fences," Alec called to Deb, the barn manager, as he left the tack room. "I'll be right back."

"Okay, boss," Deb said.

The fences didn't need checking, and both he and Deb knew it, but Alec wanted an excuse to get away from the farm for a few minutes. He figured a ride with the Black to a friendly neighbor's back property might give him some time to reflect.

It had been an effort, but so far he had done a pretty good job of putting behind him what had happened to him in the woods around Mt. Atnos and keeping his mind focused on everything he needed to do here at the farm. He hadn't even tried to tell his parents or anyone else about his adventures in the lost city. Now, with the news about Bateman's disappearance, it all came thundering back.

Alec jogged out to the upper pasture where the Black was spending his afternoons these days. Soon he and the stallion were winding their way along a back trail into the woods. As they rode over the soft grass, Alec remembered what he had read about Diomedes since he'd been home. The local library had had hardly any information on him. The only reference to the demigod Diomedes of Thrace was a short paragraph in a kids' book on Greek mythology. It was all there, though, and the words had chilled Alec's blood as he read them: the flesh-eating horses, Diomedes's tyranny and his ultimate death at the hands of his own mares.

The Black carried Alec all the way to a field beyond the woods and a small pond that was a favorite getaway spot for both of them. Alec dismounted and stood beside his horse. The Black slopped his tongue over the back of Alec's sweaty neck.

"What am I, a salt lick?" Alec said, pushing the stallion's head away. "Or are you just working up to the big bite, like one of your girlfriends? Drink some water from the pond if you want something to drink."

They walked to the water's edge. The stallion bent his head to sip from the shallows, swishing his tail in contentment.

Alec thought about Bateman and wondered if he would ever return. Had Stiv really been swept back in time to the lost city among the wandering trees, as he, Xeena and the Black had been? Was the director being made a guest of the realm at that very moment, wondering at the marvels of the acropolis and the lush gardens of Acracia? What would someone like Stiv make of it all? The thought made Alec smile. Bateman would probably love it. At least for a time.

Afterword

Much of the folklore referenced in this story is based on known history, legends and myths. Alexander's Bucephalus was believed by many to be a direct descendant of Diomedes's sacred mares. There were a Sybaris and a Croton in ancient times. The Sybaris cavalry included dancing horses, and they were defeated in battle when the Croton pipers played the horses' favorite dancing music. In Thrace to this day, folktales exist about forests with wandering trees that can hide anything and anyone, and about poisonous rivers and pools of water that will madden any animal or person who drinks from them. Incitatus, the Roman emperor Caligula's horse, was an elected priest and member of the Council of Rome. He ate from an ivory manger, drank from a golden pail and had eighteen attendants. Celer, owned by the Roman emperor Verus, ate nothing but almonds and raisins and was stabled in a suite of apartments in the emperor's palace.

SF

Steven Farley, the third of Walter and Rosemary Farley's four children, was born in Reading, Pennsylvania. He was brought up near there and in Venice, Florida. In both places, there was always a horse in the backyard. *The Young Black Stallion,* cowritten with his father, was Steven's first novel. He followed it up with several more Black Stallion novels, including *The Black Stallion and the Shape-shifter,* which first explored the author's fascination with the great horses of myth.

Steven studied journalism at New York University and has worked as a writer and editor for magazines and TV. Currently he divides his time between New York, Florida, and Mexico.

IT LOOKS
LIKE US

IT LOOKS LIKE US

LIKE US

alison ames

PAGE STREET
PUBLISHING CO.

PAGE STREET
PUBLISHING CO.

Copyright © 2022 Alison Ames

First published in 2022 by
Page Street Publishing Co.
27 Congress Street, Suite 1511
Salem, MA 01970
www.pagestreetpublishing.com

While certain characters in this book are inspired by real people, the incidents
and events in the book are entirely fictional.

Distributed by Macmillan, sales in Canada by The Canadian Manda Group.

26   25   24   23   22   1   2   3   4   5

ISBN-13: 978-1-64567-618-8
ISBN-10: 1-64567-618-8

Library of Congress Control Number: 2021953067

Cover and book design by Julia Tyler for Page Street Publishing Co.
Cover illustration © Julia Tyler

Printed and bound in the United States

Page Street Publishing protects our planet by donating to nonprofits
like The Trustees, which focuses on local land conservation.

for Emily

You think that thing wanted to be an animal?
. . . No, you don't understand.
That thing wanted to be *us*.
—John Carpenter's *THE THING*

Nobody will ever know
I came here for a reason
Perhaps there is a life here
Of not being afraid of your own heart beating
Do not be afraid of your own heart beating
Look at very small things with your eyes
& stay warm
—"The Way to Keep Going in Antarctica," Bernadette Mayer

THE VICTORIA STATION BURNS SO FEROCIOUSLY
that the man with the binoculars can feel the heat from his perch
in the helicopter.

The pilot's voice crackles into his headset, but he's not
listening. He's sweeping his gaze back and forth across the
Antarctic landscape, blinking away afterimages of flames only
to have the sharp white glare of the sun thrown back into his
eyes by the endless snow beneath them. The fire roars and the
sound is amplified by the cracking of ice, the shriek of metal as it
buckles. Something moves at the corner of his field of vision and
he jerks the binoculars away, then jams them back to his face so
hard he will later find bruises along his orbital bones.

There is something happening at the edge of the facility.

As he watches, a shape separates itself from the bulk of the
domed structure shimmering in the heat below him. He loses
it almost immediately, swallowed up into the goddamn *light*
everywhere, and he wonders for a second if it was even there,
but then he yells into his mic and the pilot swings the chopper
around.

They dip closer to the inferno, the collapsing skeleton of the
building silhouetted against the flames. Orange light glances off
the helicopter blades. He shields his eyes, squinting, trying to see

through the glittering maelstrom of sparks and ice and smoke, and then he sees it. He yells again and the pilot banks lower, and he doesn't lose it this time, he keeps his eyes pinned on that tiny dark slash across the white. They sink like a knife through a plume of smoke and the smudge gets bigger, resolving out of the chaos into a living human being, her face upturned toward them like a flower to the sun.

She can't be much older than his daughter, this girl, as far as he can tell through the blood streaked across her face. Her small frame looks tilted, like all her weight is on one leg, and she's cradling one hand at a strange angle against her body. He knows it's not possible, knows she's not seeing anything but blinding light everywhere she looks, but it feels like she's looking right at him. She stares for the space of a breath, not even long enough for him to blink, and then she turns away and lowers her head and *sprints*, arms pumping, trailing sparks from her hair and coat and everywhere else she's on fire.

"What the fuck?" the pilot yells, slamming the yoke up. They descend, gaining on her easily. She weaves from side to side, glancing over her shoulder as she flees, and as they close in on her he can see the panic on her face. She keeps running even as they pull ahead. She staggers as they bank in front of her, whipping ice and snow off the ground and into her eyes, but she keeps running. She doesn't stop until the chopper touches down less than fifty feet ahead of her, blades icing over before they've even gotten the harnesses unbuckled.

She watches the man with the binoculars step down onto the ice and falls to her knees, her face a mask of frozen tears and blood. She raises her hands above her head.

2

Riley Kowalski sits silently in the makeshift interview room, picking at an empty Styrofoam cup. Her jacket is melted into her flesh in several places. They've left it on her until they can get her to a burn unit on the mainland, but they've pumped her full of morphine, and she floats comfortably atop what she knows is the deep, dark ocean of pain that awaits her. She knows they're going to question her, and she knows she won't be able to lie convincingly with the drugs in her system. She crumbles another piece off the edge of the cup and pinches it between stiff, swollen fingers. The rat squeaks. She puts her hand over the edge of the container and pets its head.

She has almost completely destroyed the cup by the time the cops come in. One of her fingers is turning black at the tip, which she's pretty sure is bad, but she doesn't feel it. She flexes the hand idly as the cops remove their hats, coats, gloves. The tall lady cop has a fresh cup of coffee, which Riley wants, and a cigarette, which makes her nauseous. She makes a big show of lighting it and takes a long drag, staring at Riley as she does. Then she flicks it into the coffee. The smell is almost enough to make Riley retch. The shorter one sits down and leans forward in his chair, and she guesses he's Good Cop. He looks like her sophomore English teacher. She realizes neither of them are wearing uniforms.

"Wait," she says as Good Cop opens his mouth. "Are you real cops?"

He closes it, seemingly unsure how to answer.

"We work for SladeTech," Bad Cop says.

"That doesn't answer the question," Riley says. "Do I get a phone call?"

"We're actually the ones who get to ask questions," Bad Cop snaps. She puts her hands on her hips.

"Does anyone know we're here?" Riley asks. The painkillers are making her fuzzy, vocal, much more up-front than usual. "Anyone that doesn't work for Slade? Any, like, FBI or . . . who owns Antarctica, anyway? Who does security?"

"Riley," Good Cop says, making eye contact with her. "We need you to tell us what happened, okay? Walk us through it."

Riley pulls at the ends of her hair, rubbing her fingers together as they come away black with soot.

"Riley, a—a lot of money went into this expedition," Good Cop says. "The facility is destroyed, and as far as we can tell you're the one who destroyed it, so we need you to explain this in a way we can understand."

"Did you know?" she asks. The rat pokes its head out of the Tupperware again and she strokes it with a fingertip. "Did you know what he was doing?"

Bad Cop makes a huffing sound. "Just answer the question."

"He wanted the monster," Riley says, lifting her eyes to Bad Cop's. Her voice is hoarse from smoke inhalation and screaming. "He didn't—I don't think he knew it was a monster at first, but Asha told him, and he . . . he wanted it anyway. Even if it—if we—"

She falls silent.

"The monster," Good Cop says carefully. "What was—"

"Out on the ice," Riley says. "It watched us for the first two days. Breathing. Waiting. Little clicky-scratchy sounds as it circled us."

Bad Cop is tapping her foot.

"Then it came inside," Riley says.

"Where is everyone else?" Bad Cop slams her hands onto the table. "Slade told us you had five student volunteers, a supervisor, and an expedition leader. There should be six charred corpses in that fucking building and there are *none*. Explain it to me."

Riley licks her blistered lips. "We shouldn't have come here."

Bad Cop looks like she's gearing up for a rampage, but Good Cop holds out a hand.

"Okay, Riley," he says quietly. "Are you hungry?"

She nods once, a quick jerk of the head. Her nails have left little marks in her palm that match the holes in what remains of the cup.

"I'm going to find you something to eat," Good Cop says as he pushes back from the table. He tilts his head at Bad Cop and then at the door. She sighs explosively, mutters something that sounds like *fucking teenagers*, and follows him out. Riley stares at herself in the black mirror of her dead phone. There's a flash of white peeking out of her light-brown hair that she's afraid is bone, but she's too tired to lift her arms to feel it. She settles for picking at the blisters on her hands until both cops come back in. Good Cop puts a container of soup in front of her, tosses a plastic spoon and a packet of oyster crackers across the table. She takes off the lid and drinks half of it, then shakes most of the crackers into what's left and starts stirring them around. They watch her do this in silence for a few minutes. Good Cop waits until she's given the rat a few crackers and then makes his move.

"Riley," he says gently. "I know you can't give us all the answers, but will you talk to us? Will you tell me what you remember? You never know what might come up as you go through it."

She holds his gaze for too long, her widely spaced gray eyes assessing him. She spoons the crackers into her mouth and drinks the rest of her soup. Bad Cop seems to be fighting the urge to scream at her, almost vibrating as she holds herself still in her chair. Riley wipes her mouth on her half-melted sleeve and winces at the smell. She puts her hands on the table in front of her, letting them relax.

"We got here a week ago," she says.

THREE FLIGHTS: PORTLAND TO ATLANTA TO MIAMI
to Punta Arenas. Twenty-five hours dragging herself from plane
to plane. Seven soft pretzels, fifteen refills of her gigantic water
bottle. Ten packs of gum, ten cuticles. By the time she sets foot
in the final airport she's chewed her lips and fingers to shreds,
but she's made it. She follows a series of Slade-branded signs to a
door that leads to a tarmac, on which is parked a very small plane.

She sighs. She's almost made it.

She's still not a hundred percent sure what made her apply for
the trip. It was a sponsored post, a suggestion that came up amid
the Instagram pictures of beaches and dogs and food, people
who don't talk to her anymore. A simple picture: an ice floe in
the foreground, snow and mountains in the background, and
superimposed gently over it all was the stylized *S* that she knew
from hood ornaments. SladeTech, producer of everything from
electric cars to AI companions, the corporate baby of multimil-
lionaire techbro Anton Rusk, was offering a chance to spend two
weeks in Antarctica as part of a data collection expedition.

Are you ready to be part of the climate solution? the caption
asked. *Join SladeTech on a new venture into the heart of the
Earth's remotest continent. This is a special opportunity for high
school students to take part in a research expedition unlike any
before it. Spend your winter break in Antarctica collecting samples*

*of snow and ice; help us determine the extent of plastic pollution in
one of the most isolated places on Earth.*

Riley had clicked on the caption, trying to expand it, and was
taken instead to the application page. She watched as pictures
flicked across the screen, a slideshow of tents and snowshoes and
glaciers. It looked calm, somehow, and quiet, and big enough to
hold her. *Why not?* she thought, and fished out her debit card.
She filled everything out, pausing for a moment on the "Why
do you want to join this expedition" question before settling on
"To change my life." *Was* that what she wanted? Close enough.
It felt too vulnerable to say *To change myself.* She had stared at
the words for a moment before pressing Submit, and then she'd
promptly forgotten about it. Until the acceptance letter was
hand-delivered to her parents' door.

Her parents were surprisingly into it, which said something
Riley didn't particularly like about the way she'd been acting.
She wanted to believe she was holding it together, that they
couldn't see her loneliness, her grief, the way she was mourning
her old self. The new, quiet, constant fear of her own mind and
body. Her mom had said *Oh this looks like so much fun, I've
always loved the idea of Antarctica* and her dad had said *Great,
you can tell that Rusk I'd buy one of his cars if they didn't cost
as much as a midsize house*, and they had signed the permission
forms after less than an hour of private, murmured discussion.
Her mom handed her the sheaf of paper with a smile, the
corners of her eyes touched with worry and nervous, tentative
hope. *It'll be good for you*, she said. *To get away for a little while.*
She didn't say they didn't know what to do with her now that
she was broken. She didn't have to.

Maybe the whole thing should have scared Riley more, the
idea of being alone with strangers so far away from home, but
as she slipped the papers into the prepaid return envelope all
she could think about was the fact that no one on the expedition

would know her. None of them would have watched her fall apart, whispered about her in the cafeteria, shared the video of her gasping on the hallway floor like a hooked fish. She would be a blank slate, *normal*, someone a curious gaze would skate right over. They wouldn't really see her, and maybe inside that smooth, frozen shell she could piece herself back together. Maybe she could find a way back to who she used to be.

She sleeps until the tiny plane touches down on King George Island, then follows everyone out into the glaring sunlight. She looks around, realizing that this must be the group. There's nowhere else they could be going at this point.

"Are you all—are we all here for the Slade thing?" she asks, offering a small smile. The cold slices at her cracked lips and she pulls her scarf up higher.

"Indeed we are." The boy has a strong English accent.

"Let's wait until we're on the boat for introductions," a tall older woman says. She's probably thirty, with a strong red lip and a ponytail that rivals Ariana Grande's. Riley has no idea how her face hasn't frozen all the way off, but maybe the gigantic fluffy earmuffs keep her warm enough. She looks extremely bored and extremely mean.

"She's from Slade," another boy whispers. "Chaperone."

It's hard to tell what anyone looks like, swaddled as they all are, but once they're in the boat's little cabin everyone unbundles and Riley starts trying to memorize names.

"I'm Nelson," the British one says. "I suppose I'm here for adventure."

He tells them his mother hadn't wanted him to come, had actually cut off his access to his trust fund right after the check for the plane tickets had gone through. She said he needed to focus on his studies; he said he was a student of life. She'd mentioned his stint in rehab, he'd mentioned his father, she'd thrown a highball glass at him and missed so nearly that an ice cube hit him in the eye.

"But I'm here," he says with a wry smile, pulling a tiny flask from inside his coat and toasting them. "Mostly unscathed. Ready to find my purpose." He tilts the flask toward the girl next to him. "International waters," he says. "Legal even if you're not from the UK."

The girl shakes her head slightly. "My name is Ilse," she says, unwinding a shockingly long braid from inside her hat. "From Germany, but moved to the US when I was ten. In case you have questions about the accent."

Riley has to admit, she would have wondered.

"I am here because I want to be a part of the climate change solution," Ilse continues. "This experience will be very good for me."

Riley throws herself into the fray. "I'm Riley," she says. "From Oregon. I'm here because . . . I thought the project sounded cool. And I didn't really have anything else to do over break." She winces. Was that really the best she could do? *Oh, well.*

They all turn subtly toward the two remaining guys. One of them is fidgeting with a small notebook; the other is executing what looks like a very complicated drum riff on the bag perched on his knees.

"Luke," says the one with the notebook. He's built like a jock, captain-of-the-football-team prom-king handsome, but he has purple bags under his eyes so deep they're almost bruises. "I lost someone close to me. Thought it might be good to get away from— from where all the memories were." The corner of his mouth twitches like he's trying to smile. "This felt like far enough."

The final guy pulls his earbuds out and says, "Are we doing

intros? I'm Dae-sung, Dae is fine, I'm trying to get a new angle on Slade. I'm applying to journalism schools next year, and all the major outlets are so far up Rusk's ass that you can't get a straight answer as far as where all his money goes, you know, what the company's *actually* doing. If I can get anything like that, I'm golden." He grins. "But on my application I just said 'penguins.'"

"Have any of you met the scientist?" Luke asks. "I saw her up top when we were on our way in here, but we didn't talk."

"Not yet," Riley says, trying unsuccessfully to bring up the welcome email on her phone. "I think her name is Greta, though. What about the chaperone?"

"Asha," Nelson says. "Tall and mean, be still my heart."

"What's her deal? Why is she here?"

Nelson rolls his eyes. "Technically the scientist is an independent contractor, so no one can accuse the study of being biased. But Rusk obviously isn't just going to let us fuck about all over the continent without some kind of, of . . ." He waves a hand.

"Insurance," Ilse says.

He beams at her. "Thank you, love. Insurance. She's here to make sure we don't break all the fancy instruments and kick in the TV and generally go all Sex Pistols on everything."

"You're like a cartoon of a British person," Luke says. "Say something about the Beatles."

"Lick my bollocks, how's that," Nelson bounces back, not looking even faintly upset. "I know the whole handsome-rich-sole-heir-to-a-fortune thing has been done to death, but unfortunately, it is my life. I mean, not unfortunately, it's objectively very good, but, you know."

"Why aren't there more of us?" Riley asks, looking around the little room. "Doesn't it seem like there should be more of us?"

"Only the cream of the crop for this trip." Nelson grins.

"Only the people stupid enough to pay the second-richest man in the world for the opportunity, more like," Luke murmurs. He flicks a glance at Riley. "That was a little weird, right? I mean, I've never been on a research expedition before, but it seems like at the *very* least we should be unpaid interns."

"The application fee wouldn't cover even half a week's supplies for one person." Ilse sounds slightly annoyed, but Riley thinks that might be the way the accent clips her words into unfamiliar shapes. She doesn't *look* annoyed, anyway, and her face is soft as she continues. "I think it was a good-faith thing, you know? Only those who truly wanted to be here would be willing to pay. They want the people who actually care."

"I think—being reasonably cynical, I'd say—that it's cheap labor and it looks great on paper," Dae says with a wry smile. "He's shaping the future scientists of the world or whatever, he probably gets to write it off as some kind of charity, and five teenagers to two adults is probably the safest ratio they could get away with."

"High school classes are like, twenty to one," Riley says.

"Yeah, but out here they can't exactly show us a video if we start getting rowdy. He's gotta keep it manageable. What if we run out of Tang and there's a mutiny?"

"Tang is for astronauts," Luke says, sliding his notebook into his bag.

"Hot cocoa, then. You get what I'm saying."

Riley still feels a bit unsettled, but she guesses it doesn't actually make a lot of sense to bring a full classroom's worth of kids to the literal end of the Earth to do data collection. Two weeks of sampling, even with just the five of them, should give Rusk more than enough information to start doing whatever it is he plans to do.

"Plus," she says as the thought comes to her, "there's probably going to be more expeditions. We're like the preliminary run, to prove there *is* something here, and when he gets what he needs from our trip he'll send a whole, like, squad of scientists."

"Didn't want to spend scientist money before he had to," Dae says, nodding. "That tracks."

They all look up at the sound of shoes on the metal stairs. The chaperone—Asha—ducks into the room.

"We're almost ready to dock," she says. "Start putting your gear back on."

The cold is like a living thing, slapping Riley in the face as she emerges from the hold. She yanks the face guard of her coat up as far as it will go and steps carefully out onto the little bridge connecting the boat with the dock. She shuffles slowly downward, clutching her bag tightly, and after an agonizing minute she's standing on the ground. The *ice*. It stretches in every direction, blinding white and disappearing up into the sky. She understands the need for the heavily tinted goggles now. She walks gingerly toward the sledges loaded with their supplies. A smaller person that Riley guesses must be the scientist—Greta—emerges from behind one of the sledges' towering loads, waving them toward her. As Riley gets closer, she can hear her talking.

"It's about an hour inland," Greta says. "Maybe a little longer depending on how the terrain is today."

Riley shifts her weight nervously. She's not exactly in *good* shape anymore, and she can feel a nosebleed coming on. Hiking for an hour isn't on her to-do list even when she's at home in the temperate Pacific Northwest; her right ankle sprains too easily after years of soccer and her emergency brace is stuffed deep in her bag somewhere. She closes her eyes and hopes she hasn't made a mistake coming here.

Someone prods her gently in the side. Or maybe they prod her aggressively, and the force of it is deadened by the six cubic feet of goose down stuffed inside her coat. Whatever. She turns to see—whichever of the others it is, they're all covered from head to toe.

"Luke," he says, patting himself on the chest. *Blue mask. Luke, blue mask.* "You good?"

She nods. "Riley," she says, assuming he also can't tell who she is.

"Energy gel?" he asks.

She shakes her head in confusion. He holds up a plastic thing the size and shape of a ketchup packet and presses it into her gloved hand.

"Just rip it open with your teeth," he says. "Hurry, before it freezes."

She wrestles her coat away from her face, wincing at the cold air snaking around her neck, and stuffs the end of the packet into her mouth. She gnaws off a corner and the strong flavor of synthetic grape hits her tongue. She does her best with it. As she pulls her coat back up and tucks the scraps into a pocket, Luke pats her on the shoulder.

"You look, uh, wobbly," he says. "Just let me know if you feel like you're gonna pass out."

"Have any of you driven a snowmobile before?" Greta asks. Luke raises his hand. She lobs a set of keys attached to what appears to be a Beanie Baby at him. He snatches them out of the air.

"You take the one with the passenger sledge," Greta says. "I'll take the one with the supplies."

She turns away and starts the process of getting herself onto the snowmobile. Luke turns to the rest of them, and they look at the passenger sledge.

"There are only three seats," Asha says.

"Rochambeau for who has to stand," Nelson says.

"Absolutely not." Asha stamps toward the sledge and flops

into the first seat, holding one of her bags in her lap and tucking the other under her feet. Nelson and Ilse follow her, leaving Riley and Dae to perch on the back of the sledge, arms wrapped around the metal caging that keeps the seats upright.

"We can switch out after a bit," Ilse says, turning her head a bit to see them.

The roar of an engine cuts through the air. "Stay in my tracks!" Greta yells at Luke over the noise. He gives her a clumsy, mittened thumbs-up. Greta motors away from them slowly, the sledge scraping against the ice, and Luke puts the snowmobile in gear and follows.

It's definitely more than an hour, but it feels like no time at all. Riley's never seen anything like this. The wind-blasted expanse of the ice dazzles her; everywhere she looks glows sharp white and blue. The snowmobile jounces as they pass over ridges of ice, the sledge juddering beneath their feet. Riley keeps her arms locked around the metal bar, but she's too distracted to be scared. The ice is frozen into waves like a choppy ocean in certain places; in others it's smooth like glass. They pass a jade-colored rift and Greta stops, turning off the snowmobile so they can hear as she excitedly explains how the ice splits and refreezes to form these frozen rivers. Glaciers rise around them, mountains in the distance, steppes and valleys and gravity-defying spires of ice and snow. Shadows pool pale blue across the emptiness, sometimes the only indication that the ground is not a flat white sheet beneath them. It is so empty, so open. Riley is used to trees and moss and close wet clouds. Her sky is always at least a bit obscured. It feels within reach. This sky is something new and distant, huge and a little terrifying, but exhilarating. She takes a deep breath, scanning the horizon. Then there's a shout from somewhere ahead of her.

"Look over there!" Greta yells, waving wildly as she cuts her engine once more. Luke follows suit. "Everyone! To the west!"

Riley's at the perfect vantage point to see everyone turn in a different direction. She stifles a laugh. Greta points, and all their heads swivel.

"That's the Leviathan Station!" she calls. "Empty right now for the off season! It means we're close!"

The structure is big and boxy, crouched low to the ground with its second story overhanging the first. A line of flags is planted in front of it, spanning the width of the building, and there's a little metal blob that looks like a silo off to one side.

"Weather monitoring!" Greta yells. "No summer crew at this one!"

"Why not?" Riley yells back.

Greta makes a gigantic shrugging motion that looks more like she's trying to fly away than anything else, but it gets the point across. *No idea.* The station passes out of view as they move up a slight incline. They climb for a few more minutes, crest a ridge that ends in a curl like an ocean wave, and there it is.

The building that will be their home for the next two weeks rises from the ground in a bubble, studded all over with strange paneling and protrusions. It almost looks like a planetarium, but its irregularities aren't uniform. Riley's sure they serve a purpose but has no idea what they could be. As they get closer she can see a long, flat building stretching out behind the dome and another, separate building behind that one. It almost looks like her high school campus.

"Where's the bleachers?" Dae asks.

She laughs. "Right?"

"I think the dome part was the original," Dae says as they start down the hill. "Rusk really went hard on the expansion."

"I wonder why."

"Who knows with him? It's not like the five of us need the space. Maybe he's gonna rent it out once we're gone. Airbnb it."

They cruise slowly past a brand-new sign staked into the

ground: WELCOME TO THE SLADETECH ANTARCTIC RESEARCH FACILITY.

"He does love to put his name on stuff," Dae says.

"What was it called before?"

"Victoria Station," Dae says.

The inside of the Victoria Station—Riley wants to call it that; it deserves the dignity of its real name—looks more like a spaceship than anything else. If a spaceship had been furnished almost entirely by Pottery Barn. The dome area is a combination living room, dining area, and kitchen, divided by an angular bar that appears to be topped with real marble. Part of the wall has been replaced with floor-to-ceiling windows, which Riley can only hope are made of something stronger (and warmer) than glass. There's a Slade-brand robot vacuum charging in the corner next to a fireplace so big Riley could easily stand inside it. A gigantic sectional couch is set in the middle of the room, in a sunken area two steps down from the rest of the floor that is carpeted in the thickest plush she's ever seen. The coffee table is shaped like the Slade logo, a stylized curl that reminds her of a scorpion's tail, and atop it is a real live orchid in a porcelain vase.

"Holy fuck," one of the boys says from behind her. She realizes she's been standing in the vestibule—it has a *vestibule*—for almost a full minute. She jerks her bag off the floor and moves farther into the room.

"Sorry," she mutters, sliding around the island. The sink, which is apparently motion-activated, turns on with a pleased little chirp.

"This is insane," Luke says, peeling off his coat. "This is like . . . like a fancy hotel."

"It's important to Anton that we have our creature comforts," Asha says, brushing past them all. "Why should we rough it if we don't have to?"

"God knows I'm not complaining," Nelson says, "but the cost of doing this had to have been . . . astronomical. Staggering."

"Short-term loss for a long-term gain," Asha says. "If you're a researcher and you have your choice of who to work for, you're gonna pick the lab with the single group espresso machine and the fireplace, no?"

"I suppose," Nelson says as Riley tries to process the words *single group espresso.* "I think he spends money even more indiscriminately than I do."

Asha's face takes on a slightly pinched look. "The dorms are down that hallway," she says, looking at her phone and then pointing. "There's bunk beds, but I think there are enough rooms that you don't have to double up. There are only a few bathrooms, though, so those will be shared."

"No sauna?" Luke catches Riley's eye and they both suppress a grin.

Asha doesn't even look at him when she says, "There's a steam room."

"Of course there is."

"I'm gonna put my stuff away," Riley says, ready to be alone for a minute. She starts toward the dorms without waiting for anyone else to say anything. "So if anyone has a room preference, speak now or forever et cetera."

"I want one connected to a bathroom," Ilse says, darting across the room behind her. The rest of them follow suit, Luke and Nelson jogging ahead to scout out the quarters. Dae hangs back near Ilse and Riley as they walk down the hall.

"Looks like you're already finding out where the money goes," Riley says, looking at him.

He snorts. "Yeah, seriously. Can you believe this?" He stops in the doorway of one of the dorms. "It's like being on the Titanic."

Ilse makes a little disapproving *tsk* sound and he looks at her. "I just mean, like . . . this is first-class accommodation, you know? And I think we were all expecting, you know, whatever one Leo was in."

"Still," she says. "Don't invite the comparison."

She stalks down the hall and turns into a bedroom, closing the door behind her. Riley and Dae glance at each other.

"Superstitious?" she asks.

"I guess. Better safe than sorry, though." He reaches out, raps his knuckles on the wooden door. "See you at dinner."

"See you," she says to the closing door. She turns and walks down the hall. She puts her stuff in the first still-open room she finds and flops onto the bottom bunk, wondering if everyone will get friendlier or if she's destined to end this trip with the same amount of friends she had when it started. She pulls her headphones out and clamps them over her ears, squeezing her eyes shut tight. *No tears.*

"You all right?"

She pulls one of the headphones away from her ear and sits up. Luke is leaning against her doorframe, eating a banana.

"I think maybe I shouldn't be here," she says after a moment.

"Why not?"

"I don't know," she says. "I feel . . . unqualified."

"They picked you," he reminds her. "They picked all of us." He does a bad British accent. *"The cream of the crop."*

She smiles. "Maybe *unqualified* isn't the right word. Especially since we've basically decided we're guinea pigs, or worker ants, or whatever. I don't know. I feel like I don't . . . fit, I guess."

"I don't know how any of us fit here, honestly," Luke says. His eyes go distant for a second before he focuses back on her. "Their algorithm might need some work."

She pulls her headphones all the way off and sets them beside her. She tilts her chin at the foot of the bed, hoping he'll get the idea. He sits.

"Look, I'm . . . I do, like, extreme sports," he says. "I was at the X Games this year instead of junior prom. My grades are garbage. I don't have any kind of, I don't know, science-career aspirations. But they decided I should be here, so I gotta assume there's a reason. Even if the reason is that no one else applied, you know? They could have rejected us all, started over. There's something that we have, some kind of *Fifth Element* thing or whatever, that isn't based on what we look like on paper."

"A vibe," she says. "As the young people say."

He huffs a quiet laugh. "Yeah."

They sit there for a moment.

"I felt like I needed to be here," she says. She picks a point on the wall and stares at it, afraid to look at him. "Maybe that's why I'm all nervous. I need—"

She stops herself before she can say *I need this to work*. Blank slate. Smooth. Normal. "I need some sleep," she says. "I'm probably just jet-lagged."

She glances at him. He's staring down at his hands in his lap, rubbing his thumb along a braided bracelet around one wrist.

"No, I . . . I get it," he says, head still lowered. "Needing to be here."

Right. God. She's an asshole. It's been less than six hours since he told them why he's here, and she'd already forgotten. Too inside her own head, worrying about herself. Too busy trying to be normal.

She wonders if she should ask about the person he lost. Ask if he's okay, if he wants to talk about it, if she can do anything for him. But she doesn't know him like that, and he's got no reason to trust her, and he looks so sad. She leans toward him for a second, just long enough for their shoulders to bump together, hoping he understands what she means. She's still staring at her spot on the wall, but she feels him lift his head. He bumps his shoulder into hers.

"Are you hungry?"

Greta coaxes them all into helping her cook, and by the time the food is ready the atmosphere is less awkward. It's still too quiet while they eat, but Riley catches Luke's eye a few times and they smile at each other. She's aware that it's pathetic, how happy this makes her, but it does. *Friends.*

"So how does it work tomorrow?" Dae asks through a mouthful of beef stew. "The hunt for the mysterious miniplastics, or whatever."

"Microplastics," Asha corrects in a bored monotone, not looking up from her tablet. "Microplastics leaching into the ice from the polluted atmosphere and refreezing."

"Right, my bad, the microplastics—"

"It will be very straightforward," Greta says. "You will take at least one hundred samples per day within the quadrant you are assigned. You will tag the specimens each night and store them properly. At the end of your time here we will package everything to be airlifted directly to Slade headquarters and then begin the journey home."

"Yeah, um," Dae says, looking somewhat sheepish. "Sorry, I literally just meant, like, what are the actual things we'll be doing."

Nelson snorts.

"I'll demonstrate the process in the morning," Greta says. "You will each get a drill and a corer, as well as a sampling kit. Then you'll take the snowmobile and passenger sledge out to the day's quadrant, and each of you will have GPS coordinates to hike to within that area."

"And we're just . . . eye-droppering up the snow?"

"More or less," Greta says. "The tool you'll be using is most similar to what I believe they call a post-holer."

"Care to define it for those who don't do a lot of manual labor?" Nelson asks with a grin he's definitely been told is charming.

"You plug it into the ground and it punches a hole," Greta says. "Essentially. But you'll need to drill down a ways first. We need to sample at a variety of levels to determine how long the plastic has been leaching out of the atmosphere."

"And why is Slade interested in this again?" Dae asks, leaning back in his chair. He's trying to sound bored, but there's a keen edge under his words that Riley wonders if Asha can hear.

"Why is Slade interested in the deterioration of the polar ice caps?" Asha asks, narrowing her eyes at him. "Because it's a company that values the planet we live on."

"But if we confirm there's microplastics in the ice, what then?" Riley asks, hoping she doesn't sound stupid. "I mean, we can't, like . . . remove them, right?"

"No, but if we prove plastic pollution is reaching the most isolated place on Earth, we can use that evidence to lobby for climate control legislation," Asha says tartly. "As well as funding for future research here." She pushes back from the table, scooping up her tablet and cradling it close. "And anyway, *we* won't be doing anything with it. *You* are just here to collect samples, and even that's only because Anton thinks youth outreach is important. I'm going to bed."

They watch her stomp away down the hall and there's silence. After a few moments, Nelson sighs dreamily. "I think I'm in love."

THE SUN IS ALREADY SHINING (*ANTARCTIC SUMMER*, she reminds herself as she pulls back her curtains, *it's always shining*) when the smell of coffee lures Riley from bed after a night of fractured sleep. She's still more nervous than she wants to be, and she laid awake most of the night worrying that she would take the samples wrong or label them wrong or drop them down a crevasse or somehow otherwise ruin everything, and then the ice caps would melt and the Earth would be destroyed and it would be her fault.

Thinking this, she takes her meds.

They have breakfast together, all of them in various stages of jet-lag hangover. No one says a word until Asha swans in wearing a floor-length black robe. She rummages in the little fridge, emerges with a bottle of pressed juice, and retreats back to her room.

"Morticia seems a bit on edge this morning," Dae murmurs to his bagel. Ilse chokes on her juice.

Greta clears her throat somewhat disapprovingly and sets down her fork. "If you're all finished," she says, and it's not a question. "Let's get started."

Greta's mood improves as she shows them how to take the samples. "You'll use the drill—see it's marked all the way down? You sample at each mark." She holds up the corer. "Then you use this and bring up a full core, and you seal that entire thing away as well. And you record coordinates and depth for all of this!"

She smiles at them as she hands out their equipment. "I will be going back and forth from the sample site and the station," she says. "If you have any questions, or if you need anything, I will never be too far away. You have flares in your kits if you need them, although I can't for the life of me think why you would. Though, better safe than sorry, no?"

Her enthusiasm is catching, and Riley starts to feel less like she's doomed to tank the entire expedition. As they pile into the passenger sledge, this time with Nelson standing, she lets herself get a little bit excited. She's in the Antarctic, for Christ's sake. She's part of a research team that will make history, probably, and even though she's only collecting samples that a real scientist will use later to make some kind of incredible *actual* discovery, that still counts. There is a reason for her.

She looks out across the ice as they travel, watching the light play across its surface. It refracts almost like a prism, and the shadows bounce and melt as the angle of the light changes when they pass by.

"Sastrugi," Ilse says. Riley turns to her. "It's what it's called when it's in waves like that. The terrain. The wind shapes them."

Riley nods and looks back at the snow, the long harsh grooves carved into it. She hasn't thought about the possibility of a windstorm until now. It's summer, true, but a whiteout can happen almost out of nowhere. She doesn't know how they'll get back to the station if the wind whips up and cages them in. She doesn't know how to stake down a tent in the midst of something like that, or what to do to protect the samples. Will the flares be visible? Will they be able to find their way back? She feels herself starting to spiral, to circle the drain, and she forcibly redirects her thoughts. She digs out her phone and earbuds and puts on an audiobook, turning it up until she can hear it over the snowmobile. She breathes and counts and tries not to worry, and eventually they reach the first sampling site. They break apart into a staggered arc across the area and settle in to work.

The audiobook finally sucks her in, pulls her all the way under, and she can't hear anything above the soothing rasp of the narrator's voice. She falls into a rhythm, her movements smoothing out as she thinks less about them, and her bag fills rapidly with sample tubes. Then a hand comes down on her shoulder and she yelps, toppling sideways and scrambling to her feet in a defensive stance before she registers that it's Luke. She yanks her headphones out.

"What the shit, man?"

He points across the ice to where Nelson is jumping up and down, waving his arms like he's starting a drag race. Riley follows Luke across the snowpack. As they get closer she can hear Nelson yelling.

"I fucking swear, it was like a fucking snake or something, it went *right* there—"

Ilse is crouching next to a divot in the snow. It looks like someone stabbed a trowel into it and then moved it away.

"It couldn't be a snake," Riley says. They all turn to look at her. She pulls her face back, into her coat, and her voice is muffled when she says, "Cold-blooded."

"Well, it was slithering," Nelson says. "And it went down there."

They all look at the little divot.

"It's solid ice down there, Nellie," Dae says. "For miles."

"I saw it," Nelson says stubbornly, glaring at him. "And don't call me Nellie."

"Maybe you need to actually wear your goggles," Ilse says,

gently flicking the lenses perched atop his head. "Maybe you have eye fatigue."

Riley pokes the tip of a gloved finger into the snow. "Did you drill after it?"

"No," Nelson says, eyes lighting up. He crouches next to her and sets the tip of the drill next to her finger. She pulls her hand back and he squeezes the trigger, the high, thin whine of it vibrating through her teeth like it has been all day. He pushes the drill as deep as it will go and then pulls it out. The bit is caked with ice, which he starts sealing into tubes inch by inch, labeling each one as he goes.

"There's gonna be something in here," he says.

"Well, unless it's microplastics, I don't think Slade will care," Ilse says.

He ignores her.

The next day it's Riley who sees something in the corner of her eye, almost like a floater. She turns and there's nothing but the vast expanse of ice, but it feels . . . not empty. The feeling gets stronger throughout the day. She does her best to talk herself out of it. *Anxiety is a liar*, her therapist says in her memory. She concentrates on the world around her. The sound of metal biting into ice, the ache in her back. These things are real; they have weight and texture. She turns her music on loud enough to drown out her thoughts, pulls her next core up, and keeps taking samples. There is nothing behind her, nothing out on the ice watching her.

Nothing.

But all day long there's a small jitter at the edge of her field of vision, almost an eye twitch, but as if the world is contracting rather than her muscles. Every time she turns around it's too still, like something has just stepped out of view. The base of her skull tingles and she has the sense that something, somewhere, is wriggling toward her. Low and flat and writhing, a ribbon of a leech invisible against the snow, *under* it, surfacing with a razor-edged mouth open wide—

When they finally make it back to the station that night, her entire body aches from clenching her muscles all day. She wants nothing more than to shut herself in the steam room until her bones and her heart and her fear dissolve, but Asha has other plans.

"One of you needs to keep your coat on," she says as they crowd into the living room. "Slade is sending one more sledge."

Riley doesn't know what Asha does all day. She hasn't left the station once and all she's done is type on her laptop or stare at her tablet. Probably taking notes for Rusk, sending a daily report, but it seems like a lot of time to spend on something that might as well just say: *Still ice.* Riley wonders how much she gets paid for what amounts to babysitting.

"We have all our supplies," Greta says. "What—"

"I don't know." Asha's eyes are already back on her computer. "Just someone go get it."

"I'll go," Greta says. "I was very specific with the requisition forms, very careful, I don't want—if I get charged for something I didn't order, I'll . . ."

She stomps back out into the snow, still talking to herself.

Riley's heartbeat ratchets up a notch at the thought of Greta going out alone at night. She doesn't know why, but she starts after her, catching the door before it can close. "Do you—do you need help?" she yells. Greta turns back.

"If it's only one sledge it will be fine," she calls. "Just go tag your samples."

Again the coiling sensation in the back of her head; again the feeling that something distant is rushing toward her. She closes her eyes, reasoning with herself. The sun won't set, not really; there will still be light. Greta is perfectly competent with the snowmobile, and the track they made two days ago is still clear. She'll be fine. Riley punches the dread back down into the pit of her stomach. *And stay there.*

"I can do us a curry," Nelson says, finally fully free of his coat. "If that sounds agreeable."

"Yeah," Luke says. "Riley, first shift in the lab?"

They've set up a buddy system, two of them at a time in the lab and then Ilse alone, as she prefers. Riley likes Luke more and more each day; he's big and solid and he moves slowly, and she feels settled around him. They spend an hour in the lab, the rat—Greta brought a rat, somehow, shrugging as she unbundled its cage, *every lab needs a rat*—watching them from the corner of the desk. Then they go their separate ways to clean up before dinner.

Riley presses herself into the corner of the steam room and tips her head back, letting the tension seep out of her. Hopefully she'll get some rest tonight. It's been hard to sleep while the sun is out, even with the little porthole window covered against the lower light of nighttime. The wall timer dings and she stands slowly, trying to preempt a head rush. She ducks in and out of the shower, puts on her pajamas and slipper booties, and walks out toward the main room. She remembers at the very end of the hallway that her hair is still clamped on top of her head in a hot pink claw clip and yanks it loose, darting back to fling it in the general direction of her room.

"Look, Riley!" Nelson says, looking up as she walks in. He's gotten the fireplace lit. "It's like a ski chalet!"

Asha snorts. "I thought you were making curry."

"I was distracted, my dove, by the need to make sure you were cozy," he says, doing a little bow in her direction. She makes a face, still staring at her tablet. Riley moves toward the fire. It's almost funny how big it is. It's covered with an ornate screen, with mesh behind it; sparks snap at her but don't make it through. She wants to flatten herself against the metal. Her heart's still beating fast from the steam room; it's making her nervous, her body leading her brain. She lifts a hand to her mouth, ready to bite at her cuticles, then yanks it away. *No.* She starts to walk the length of the room, making sure her steps are even, and then the lights flicker and go out.

Without even thinking Riley sinks to the floor and pulls her knees tight to her chest, counting her breaths. She's glad she hadn't made it too far from the fire.

"Does one of you know how to do the generator?" Asha asks. She's still so monotone, sounding only faintly annoyed. Riley wonders if she's on tranquilizers or something. She taps her phone screen and something chimes.

"I probably do," Luke says. "My family's big on camping."

"Does anyone think it's weird that Greta's not back?" Riley hears herself ask from a distance. "It's been, like, too long, right?"

"You have to drive slower once it gets toward dusk," Ilse says. "It hasn't been that long."

"Okay," Riley says. "Okay."

"Let's have you come with me to look at the generator, okay?" Riley looks up to see Luke holding a hand out to her. She lets him pull her to her feet. "You gotta get some layers on, though. Go do that and I'll find some flashlights."

She shakes her head, then nods, then walks toward her room with her phone held out in front of her. Once she's in there she stands still for a moment, trying to get a grip on herself. She pulls on the first set of thermals she can find, two pairs of socks, and a hoodie, and when she opens the door Luke is waiting.

"My sister has panic attacks," he says quietly. "You okay?"

Riley nods. "Yeah. Thank you. That was—thank you."

"No prob," he says. They walk down the hall to the back door, which leads to a dug-out path to the outbuilding that houses the snowmobiles and the generators. It's not quite dark enough to need a flashlight, but Riley is nervous enough to turn it on as they enter the space. The building is big enough that the light doesn't reach the ceiling, but the beam throws everything it can reach into sharp relief, shadows wobbling crazily behind the outlines of the stuff strewn across the space. Everything is haphazardly arranged, draped in tarps and shoved against walls; it's like a freestanding junk drawer full of whatever Rusk didn't think was important enough to keep in the actual station. It reminds Riley of a disused barn.

Luke threads his way through the space to the insulated box on the wall and pries it open. "I'm gonna flip all these first, just in case," he says, and starts toggling things.

Riley looks over her shoulder, back out the open door toward the station, and waits for a light to come on. The building stays dark. "Nothing," she says.

"Plan B," he says. "Shine it over this way."

She catches him in the beam and follows him toward the generator. It doesn't seem nearly big enough to power the whole station. He runs his hands over it, searching, and finds the starter pull. He yanks it once, twice, and it roars into life with a shudder she can feel through her boots.

"Ta-da," he says. She grins.

As they walk back along the trodden-down path she feels a tickle between her shoulder blades, rippling up toward her neck. She turns around, sweeping the flashlight out across the snow.

"You good?" Luke stops to watch her as she completes her circle.

"Yeah," she says. "Just thought—yeah. Fine."

"Don't go all Jack Torrance on me yet, Kowalski," he says. "It's only been two days."

She puts the flashlight under her chin and makes a face, and his laugh makes her feel a little warmer. As they clamber down into the little space where the back door has been dug out, she hears a faint scraping sound to her right and snaps her gaze that way. Without the flashlight, everything is the same gloomy color, the ground barely distinct from the sky except where the sun hovers above it. As she stares toward the horizon, she sees a flicker of movement. Two dark dots, low to the ground, almost undulating as they vanish, and as she steps back into the station she has the thought: *Eyes.* She shakes it off immediately, tells herself she's seeing things, but her breath comes quick and shallow as she closes and locks the door behind them.

It's much dimmer inside the station now, and there's a soft throb to the lights that makes Riley start grinding her teeth. Asha's abandoned the tablet and is once again clicking away on the laptop, Nelson's returned to cooking, and Dae is lying on the couch with headphones on, only one of them over his ear.

"The conquering heroes have returned," Luke says. "You're welcome."

Nelson blows them a kiss with the hand not holding a wooden spoon. "Savior to us all."

"Is Greta still not back?" Riley asks. None of them look at her. "Hello?"

"I'm sure she's fine," Asha says in a very beleaguered voice.

"I'm serious," Riley says. "I think we need to go look——"

"What is that?" Ilse is standing at the far end of the room, hands cupped around her eyes, pressed against the window. "There's something out there."

"Very funny." Asha hits a key with particular force.

"No, I mean it. There's an animal."

"Polar bear?" Nelson exclaims, coming around the counter.

"We're Antarctic, not Arctic," Dae reminds him, standing. "It would be a penguin if it's anything."

"Well, it's not a penguin." Ilse's voice is muffled, trapped in the space between her arms.

Riley laces her fingers together, holding her own hand. She walks toward the window slowly, trying to match her breaths to her steps, and looks out.

"Do you see it?"

She leans closer, her breath fogging the Plexiglas. She swipes the condensation aside with her sleeve and squints. There is . . . *something*. Long and sloping and almost the same color as the snow. She keeps losing it as it moves, but it looks almost like it's pacing. It walks—*is it walking? crawling?*—back and forth, back and forth.

She loses her breath in a gasp when those two black dots appear again. "It can see us."

"Yes," Ilse whispers.

"What is it?"

"We're sure there's no bears?" Nelson asks, his voice hushed. "Leopards, maybe? Really big, erm, seals?"

"It's a trick of the light," Dae says. "On the snow."

"It has *eyes*," Riley says, and the end of the sentence is dangerously close to a sob. She's breathing too hard, unsteadily, and her head is spinning. *Anxiety is a liar.* There is not an animal watching them. Her pulse beats hard in her forehead and she presses a hand against it like she can control her one jumpy vein. She wants to scream, and she *knows* that's not the right reaction to this situation but she doesn't know what *is*, and so she just breathes and breathes and breathes.

Asha speaks, and she's so close behind them that Riley actually jumps.

"Show me," she says. Suddenly she's alert, interested, craning to see what they're staring at.

Riley puts a finger to the window where the eyes are. As soon as she does, they vanish. "It must have turned away," she says. "Did you see them?"

Asha makes a disgruntled sound and pushes closer to the glass. "Hey," she says. She knocks.

"Stop it," Ilse hisses. She's got her whole body pressed against the window, taut like a bowstring, nose mashed against the glass. Her hands still frame her face as she stares out into the night.

Asha knocks again, harder. The black dots open up and Riley can feel them on her. Her left hand closes on her right wrist and digs in hard, pressing the tendons until her fingers curl. *Real.*

"I see it," Asha whispers.

Riley is trying to make herself speak, but her throat is too tight. She fights back tears. "We—" she whispers. "Greta."

"It's probably smoke from one of the other stations or something." Dae has returned to the couch. Riley can't read him, can't tell if he saw anything. *Not real.* He picks up his phone and starts typing.

"I wonder what it is," Luke says.

"We have to—" Riley starts, her voice too quiet to hear.

"I want to know what it wants," Ilse says. Her tone is markedly sharper than Luke's.

"Greta is out there," Riley finally manages to say. She's trembling so hard she can't get her arm into her coat the first few times she tries. She would rather die than go outside where those eyes are, but she can't risk another person's life. She slides one foot into a boot, then the other.

The door opens.

The light catches and flares, flashing back at them as if from an animal's eyes in the darkness of the shape in the doorway. For a moment all Riley can think is *what could be that tall, what is it, what* is *it* and a sharp burning smell curls through her nostrils and then Greta steps into the room and it's Greta, only Greta, of course it is.

"Come unload the sledge," she says.

All the air in Riley's lungs rushes out of her as she deflates, and for a moment she worries she's going to simply crumple to the floor like an empty bag. She walks to the door and wills herself to step outside. Greta, bless her, has brought the sledge right up against the building, so they don't have to go far. It's half-full of food, toiletries, and notebooks—supplies they have in excess. The other half bears a large covered box.

"What's that?"

"That's mine," Asha says. "Nelson, drag it around to the door on the west side and I'll get it inside from there."

Nelson leaps to his feet, gets into his coat, and vanishes out the door in a matter of seconds. Asha pulls a key card out of her robe pocket.

"Luke," she says. "Come help."

Riley trails a few feet behind them, unsure why she feels compelled to follow, but unable to stop. Asha winds them through the hallways until they're at a locked door with a flashing red light beside it. She taps the card on the panel and the light flicks to green.

"You don't need to come," she says to Riley, barely turning her head.

"Why is this door locked?" Luke asks, flashing Riley a sympathetic look.

"Rusk divided the station into two halves," Asha says, bored again. "For smaller groups, like this one, who don't need the whole space. It's on a separate power grid, so it's all turned off and locked down. No reason to keep the lights and the temp control up if no one's in there. It's just other labs and dorms and stuff."

"Why is the box going in there, then?"

The look Asha gives her could freeze lava. "It's a delivery for the next expedition," she says. "It's easier to bring it in with other supplies. Is that okay with you?"

"Sorry," Riley murmurs, wondering if she's going to spend the whole trip feeling this stupid. She watches them go through the door, and then she trudges back to the kitchen.

Greta looks tired and a little shaken, and she doesn't say anything as she takes off her gear. She sits at the table and eats three bowls of curry one after another, utensils moving mechanically back and forth between her mouth and the dish until the pot is empty. Riley has to look away after a while because the sight is making her increasingly anxious. Every scrape of metal against teeth zings up her spine. Finally she shoves her chair back and darts down the hall to her room without saying good night. She closes the door behind her, locks it, flattens herself against it. Inhales for four, holds for four, exhales for four. *Mammalian diving reflex, baby,* she thinks with a humorless laugh.

There *is* a normal amount of fear to have. She knows this is true like she knows the sun rises in the east. She doesn't know how to find it, though. For instance: It's her third night in a new place, thousands of miles from her home and her parents. It's normal to be nervous about that. On the other hand: She is on an island in the middle of an ocean of ice. There are no animals for miles, unless they are penguins or the occasional seal, but she saw eyes in the snow, and she wasn't the only one. Surely there is an explanation they haven't yet found, but.

But.

She wakes without knowing why.

The room is dark; her phone says it's approaching 3:00 a.m. She sits up slowly, trying to figure out why her heart is thudding in her chest. She hears a soft thump and a rustling sound from out in the hall.

One of the boys, she thinks. *Up to get a drink or something.*

The explanation isn't enough to still her thoughts.

She swings her legs out of the bed, creeps across the room, and pokes her head into the hallway. She looks down toward the other dorms, then back toward the common area. The safety lights along the floor cast a shadow like a waveform, rippling away in either direction.

She steps out of the room.

It's cold, she realizes. Really cold, outside cold. She hopes the power hasn't gone out again. She doesn't know if she can do the generator on her own. She doesn't know if she can even go into the outbuilding alone, if she's being honest. She walks toward the common room, wishing she had more than one pair of socks on, pulling her fingers into her sleeves and tucking her hands into her armpits.

"Luke?" she whispers into the dimness.

No one answers.

She walks into the kitchen, does a slow circle as she takes in the room, and stops.

The back door is unlocked.

Not open, not ajar, but the deadbolt is pulled all the way back and there's the faint shine of snow through the crack where the seal hasn't met. She moves slowly toward it, puts her fingertips on it and pushes. The tongue clicks as it settles into its groove; the rubberized edging on the door meets the wall. She pulls the deadbolt across into its home. She stands there for a moment, fingers resting on the cold metal. She turns back into the kitchen, thinking maybe about a cup of cocoa, and freezes with one foot in the air when her gaze catches on something through the window.

Greta is standing in the snow in her thermal underwear, breath steaming away from her uncovered face. Riley squints as she walks closer. Greta looks—*wrong* somehow, the bones of her face crowding behind her lips, almost protruding like a muzzle.

She bends her knees slightly, then bends them back the other way and falls onto all fours.

Riley claps her hands over her mouth. She drops to the floor behind the couch and scrambles to look around it, not wanting to take her eyes off Greta. When she pokes her head out she doesn't see her at first. She's still down in that animal crouch; her sleeping clothes are pale blue and she blends into the landscape. She shakes her head vigorously, strands of drool flying from her mouth, and pushes herself back to her feet unsteadily.

She straightens to her full height, clothes sparkling with ice, and looks around. Her head turns just enough that Riley can see that too-long jaw, watch her mouth drop open to reveal too many teeth. She presses her hands to her face and rubs at it like she's cold. Her fingers push and knead, scraping across her skin, and through it all her mouth opens and closes. Her breath clouds away from her in little puffs, and Riley thinks she might be talking.

Greta's hands slip away from her face and drop back to her sides. She bounces on the balls of her feet, turns in a small circle.

"Is she sleepwalking?"

Riley barely manages to stifle a scream. She jerks back behind the couch to see Luke blinking at her sleepily.

"Oh my God," she whisper-yells at him. "You scared me."

He looks out the window. "Should we go get her?"

Riley gets to her feet and finds herself standing close enough to him that their arms touch. She looks at Greta. She's opening her mouth to ask if Luke thinks she looks strange, but she . . . doesn't, anymore. She's standing still, her face in profile, and she looks completely normal.

What the fuck? She jams the heels of her hands into her eye sockets and rubs hard, then stares back at Greta.

Still normal.

"What?" Luke asks, elbowing her gently.

"Sorry," she says, realizing she must have made a sound. "I

thought—I think I scared myself." She laughs a little. "Overactive imagination."

"We gotta go get her," Luke murmurs. "I don't know if we can get her inside without waking her, but she'll freeze if we don't."

Riley nods, reassured by how calm he's being. Surely if Greta's face—her bones, her body—surely if it had been doing something, he would have seen it. This wouldn't be the first time Riley's talked herself into a state of absolute terror based on nothing, even if it has been a while since the last instance. They get their coats on quietly, pull gaiters and hats over their heads, and make their way out the front door. They walk toward Greta slowly.

When they're about ten feet from her, her head turns sharply toward them. Her face doesn't move at all; her body doesn't move at all. Aside from the turn of her neck she could be a statue. Riley has a flash of memory: an art festival in the park, by the river, a woman she thought was a sculpture suddenly moving fluidly into another shape and going still again. Greta's eyes are open.

"Her eyes are open," she whispers.

"That's normal," Luke whispers back. "Just—I'm gonna go behind her, okay?"

Greta's looking toward Riley, but whether she sees her is unclear. Her eyes don't move at all as Luke circles slowly behind her.

"Call her," Luke says. "Not like a dog, but not . . . not like a dog."

"Greta," Riley says. "Greta, come inside. Let's go."

Luke puts his hand between her shoulder blades and pushes just a little, just enough that she leans forward slightly, and Riley has half a second to wonder if she's going to fall and shatter like she's made of glass before she stumbles into motion.

"Good, that's good," Luke says. "We're gonna just go inside, okay?" He keeps talking quietly, soothingly, urging her forward as Riley coaxes her toward the station. "Come on, Greta," she says. "Let's go in. Let's go to bed."

They get her inside, close and lock the door behind them, and shed their gear. Riley has to take a minute to fight with her boot before she can wrench her foot free, and when she turns around Luke is leaning against the wall watching her with a faint smile.

"Did she——?"

"Yeah," he says. "Watch your step. She dripped on the floor."

There's a small puddle where Greta apparently paused before going directly back to her room.

"We did it," Riley says, spreading a towel across the floor. "Scientist rescuers."

"Rusk will have to give us jobs now," he deadpans.

"I think that's only if we rescue Asha," she says. "Greta's, like, a contractor. No benefits."

"Good point."

She looks at him for a moment. His hair is rumpled where he pulled off his hat. He's still half smiling, but he has a faint, hollow look around his eyes that she recognizes.

"You okay?" she asks. "Like . . . in general."

He lets a breath out sharp, fast, almost like a laugh. "Nah."

"Wanna talk about it?"

"Nah," he says again. "But thanks."

"Well, I'm around," she says.

"I'm not trying to be weird," he says. "Can I hug you?"

"Yeah," she says. He puts his arms around her and hugs her tight, a really back-cracking one, and she returns it fiercely. He lets her go and turns to walk back to his room.

"Night, Kowalski," he says.

"Night, Wheeler," she says. "See you in the morning."

She doesn't wake again until her alarm goes off.

"AH, LAKE VOSTOK," NELSON SAYS CHEERILY. "WHAT a beautiful day to sit on top of the last truly undiscovered place on Earth."

Ilse rolls her eyes and steps on the flange of her corer, pushing it deeper into the ice.

"What are you talking about?" Riley asks. She's still got another quarter mile to walk before she's at her coordinates for the day, but she's surprisingly starved for conversation. She leans on the handle of her own corer and waits.

"Lake Vostok," he says again. "Three miles below us, and probably three miles deep after that. An entirely closed ecosystem."

"You mean it's liquid?"

"Yes, yeah, because of the pressure," he says, eyes alight. "And also because it's so close to the, um, the core, you know. The lava."

"Magma," Ilse corrects absently. Nelson flaps a mittened hand at her and continues.

"They're still trying to get down there," he says. "The Russians, especially, but everyone's interested. Could be a bioweapon down there."

"Please," Ilse says.

"Anything that's down there has survived in a completely closed environment since the beginning of time," Nelson says.

"Like those crawlies that live on the bottom of the sea, the ones that . . . eat . . . sulfur, or whatever, just a totally different life-form than anyone could possibly imagine."

"A bacterium, maybe," Ilse says. "Not the fucking megalodon."

"A bacterium, my Type A princess, could wipe out the entire human population."

"Anyway, it's not since the beginning of time," she says, removing the long spike of her drill from the ground. "Just since the Pole froze."

"So it was on the surface once," Riley says.

"Right."

"So it *could* be the megalodon," Nelson says.

He holds up a hand and Riley stares at it for a second. "I don't think I want to high-five the megalodon," she says.

He shrugs and puts it down. "I'm just saying," he continues. "Knowing that we're up here, just little teeny-tiny sitting ducks, on top of this gigantic underground lake, I mean, it's . . ." He spreads his arms. "Eerie."

"Really, though," Riley says. "What do they think they'll find?"

"Really," Nelson says, "bacteria. Amoebas and shit. Something that humans have never been exposed to, and then they're going to take it and make it into fuel or bullets or some horrible combination of the two. They'll come in and put a big fucking drinking straw down through the ice and drain it dry."

"It will be a long time." Ilse punches another hole in the ice. "There is a ban on any more drilling until they can figure out how to keep the holes from freezing around the drill. They contaminate all the samples because they use kerosene to keep it liquid. It flows right down into the lake."

"Christ," Riley says. "So they've actually gotten to it before?"

"Few times," Nelson says. "Never found anything good, though. I keep saying they've got to make a bigger hole, but you know no one listens to me."

"Structurally they can't—"

"I *know*," he says to Ilse. "I was making a joke."

"Why do you know so much about it?" Riley asks. "Did you do research before you came?" The thought makes her feel insecure. She should have done research.

"I have a little bit of a, mm, compulsion problem," Nelson says. "Fixation. I get interested in something and I go all the way down the rabbit hole. The *ice* hole, ha." He elbows Ilse, who makes an annoyed throat-clearing sound. "I just read and read and absorb everything I can and then I get bored, or distracted, or a combination of the two, and that's that. On to the next." He shakes his head. "Can't be helped. It happens, it passes, and then I'm left with an arsenal of useless information about something I no longer really care about. This is . . ." He waves his arm. "Fortuitous coincidence."

"Huh," Riley says. "Well, that makes me feel better about not knowing anything about it."

"I'm on cryptids now, if you're interested," he says. "Everyone always wants to talk about Mothman this, Bigfoot that, but England has cryptids too, you know. Have you ever heard of the Black Shuck?"

Riley just shakes her head.

"Of course not. But you know Mothman." He points at her. "That's all I'm saying."

"Okay," Riley says. "Well. Cool. I'm gonna . . . go, then. Try not to fall into the underground lake. Unless you think we can all go for a swim later."

She laughs, but neither of them do. *Yikes.*

"Well, all right," she says, hoisting the corer back onto her shoulders. "See you in four hours."

Nelson gives her an odd but charming salute. Ilse just keeps tweezing crystals of ice off her drill. Riley resumes her journey across the snow toward her own little patch of science.

They break for lunch in the pop-up tent, which by the end of the half hour is so warm inside it feels like a greenhouse. Riley takes a deep breath as she emerges, the whiplash of the temperature change making her lungs seize in her chest. She feels her nose hairs freeze immediately and pulls her gaiter up over her face.

She looks down at the ice as she makes her way to her next sample site, imagining a subterranean lake. Closed ecosystem. Dark water, like the river near her cousin's house that they'd both come out of covered in leeches. She wonders if there's something down there, something eely and sinuous. Rows and rows of teeth. She shivers.

"Can't be cold yet," Luke says from behind her.

She turns and flips him off. "Can you tell what this is?" she asks, grinning. "I know it's a mitten, but you should be able to feel it."

He snorts. "The classiness is overwhelming."

She does a little curtsy, the best she can manage in three layers of pants. "Anyway, I'm not cold," she says. "Nelson freaked me out, is all."

"What, did he start talking about the Parliamentary houses or something?"

"No, he said, um, he said we're above a lake," she says. "Like, an underground one. Way down there."

"Oh, shit, are we really? Lake Vostok? I didn't realize we were that close to it," he says.

"Does everyone just know everything?" she asks, only half joking. "I feel really painfully un-smart around you all."

"No, there was . . ." He laughs sheepishly. "There was a *Predator* movie set here, and they went down underground, and the lake was . . . mentioned."

"That makes me feel better."

"Very cool, though, that we're nearby," he says. "I wonder if that's why they have us taking samples up here. The ice probably freezes and refreezes pretty often."

"Ilse said they use stuff to keep the holes from freezing when they take samples of the water," she says. "Kerosene and stuff. I wonder if that's going to get into the samples."

"Huh." He stands still for a moment, chewing on the edge of his gaiter. "That is . . . weird, actually, that they would have us take samples here if they knew that. Unless maybe they're doing it on purpose?" He starts walking, circling around her as he does. "What if Rusk is like, trying to figure out how to start drilling again? Trying to figure out how fucked everything is so he can use more chemicals to get down there?"

"I thought you were, like, a Rusk guy," Riley says. "No?"

"I mean," he says. "I like hybrid cars and rockets as much as the next person, but he's not . . . I don't know. He's not a *good* guy. People just think he is because he throws every, like, fourteenth million dollar he makes toward a charity."

"Hmm."

"He shot a boat into space, Riley," he says. "Just because he could. Did you ever read, like, any Spider-Man comics?"

"No," she says.

"There's one where this supervillain is trying to turn people into dinosaurs, right? And Spider-Man is confronting him and he's like, 'You could cure cancer with this technology!' and the guy's like, 'I don't want to cure cancer, I want to turn people into dinosaurs!' That's the vibe I get from Anton Rusk."

"He wants to turn people into dinosaurs?"

"He wants to do whatever *he* wants," Luke says. "Regardless of whether or not it helps or hurts anyone else."

She looks at him for a moment. "Will you tell me what happened to the person you lost?"

He smiles painfully, tucks his chin deeper into his coat.

"Maybe. Not today, though."

She nods and watches him walk away, hunched against the light wind that's kicking up. She returns to her patch of ice and sets up the windbreak to protect the samples. She puts her headphones in, starts her audiobook back up, and loses herself in the slow, mindless rhythm of the work.

"Have any of you seen Greta?"

Asha is waiting for them in the middle of the living room, laptop cradled in one arm, the other hand on her hip.

"We've been outside all day, Asha," Ilse says. "The door has just now closed behind us. You might have noticed."

"Well, she was supposed to give me a report, and I haven't been able to find her."

A thin sliver of fear lodges itself in Riley's chest. She thinks about that feral eyeshine, the sharp sizzle of acid in her throat as Greta's knees bent the wrong way in the moonlight. *Real.*

"Is she in her room?"

"Oh, gee, I didn't think to check her room, maybe I'll just— no, she's not in her room, Nelson, Jesus."

"Okay," he says mildly, eyebrows lifted. "I'll just fuck off to the lab, then, shall I?"

"I wish you would," Asha snaps. "Any of the rest of you have any bright ideas?"

"We're close to the Leviathan, right?" Dae asks. "Maybe she went over there for the day."

"To the empty research station," Asha says flatly.

"Maybe she wanted to be alone," Dae says, tone just neutral enough. "Did you check the outbuilding?"

"No," Asha sighs. "Can one of you go out there? And if she's not there, can you—ugh, you're the little science monkeys, can't you call one of the other stations or something? See if she's there? Surely she wouldn't have just gone totally off the grid, right?"

"We have the number for her SATphone," Riley says, fumbling in her pockets. "Somewhere, anyway. Maybe it's in my room—"

"Her SATphone is on the charger," Asha says.

"Shit."

"I'll check the barn if one of you wants to get started on reaching the other station," Dae says.

"Yeah, I can fuck with the radio," Luke says.

"I'll go look for tracks," Ilse says. They all turn to look at her. "What? She wears a distinctive boot, and if she left the station, her prints will still be there."

"Good point," Asha says reluctantly.

"I'll go with her," Riley says.

"I'll . . . make some hot chocolate," Nelson says. "For when we all reconvene."

They stand in a rough semicircle around the prints.

"It just ends," Ilse says. "It's like she started rolling or something."

Greta's boot prints crisscross the area around the station, looping back on themselves and meandering away in new directions, but Ilse has determined that this trail is the most recent because it ends in the middle of the snow.

The prints get closer and farther apart as Riley looks back across the space, as if Greta had been alternately running and walking. Riley turns her gaze back to the flurry of prints at her feet. Boot prints give way to smooth snowpack, marred every so often by crumpled ridges or little holes.

"This looks like a dog print," Dae says from behind her. She turns to see him a little ways off staring down at something that, yes, does look like a dog print.

"Dogs are banned here," Ilse says.

"Wait, what? Really?" Luke sounds appalled.

"Disease vector," Ilse says. "Focus."

"What should we do?" Riley asks quietly. She looks at the others. "The snowmobiles are all still here, so we know she's walking. She could be—when we saw her outside last night, she wasn't even wearing a *coat*—"

She presses her hand hard into her sternum, breathing against the resistance.

"We have to look for her," she whispers. "Out there."

Out where the eyes are.

"We do," Luke says, putting his hand on her shoulder. "But I think we have to wait for morning. It won't do her any good if we all go out and get lost, right?"

"We have to make a grid," Ilse says. "A search pattern. We can't just drive out into the snow and hope we are lucky enough to find her."

Riley knows they're right. She does. But she can't shake the feeling that something terrible is going to happen if they don't find Greta, and *soon*.

"Can we light a flare?" she asks. "So she can see it, and maybe she'll come back during the night?"

"Couldn't hurt," Nelson says. He jogs back inside and returns with his bag. They spend a tense five minutes bickering over the instructions for loading the flare gun, and finally Riley is pointing it at the sky and pulling the trigger. The flare burns high and bright overhead, its arc slow and graceful as it starts to fall.

Come on, Greta, Riley thinks. *Come back.*

It's 3:00 a.m. again. There is a scratching, clicking sound coming from the hallway outside Riley's door, and it has woken her up, and now she can't go back to sleep.

You're fine, she tells herself. *It's locked, and it's nothing, and if it's not nothing, you know, it's locked.*

This works for all of five minutes, during which time Riley loses a battle with meditation, and the scratchy-clicky, vaguely insectile sound keeps seeping under the door. She scans the room, looking for something she can use as a weapon, and finds nothing. She puts on her shoes, steels herself and flings open her door.

Greta stands in the hallway, looking lost. She turns slightly, one way and then the other, as if she's trying to figure out where to go.

"Greta?" Riley asks. "Are—are you all right?"

Greta's focus shifts slowly to Riley, her face turning toward her, and Riley sucks in a breath. Greta's face is—*hanging* wrong, almost like it's sliding off her skull. Everything droops; crescents of wet red flesh peek out under her eyes where her eyelids sag down.

"What—" *This is not real.*

"Hmmmmm," Greta says.

Riley is sliding her foot backward, trying to find the courage to take a step, hands reaching desperately behind her like she can summon Luke from his room. *You saw her last night and she was sleepwalking. Her face did* not *change. Her bones did not change.*

"*Hmmmmmm,*" Greta says. Her lips open farther. Her tongue flops out of the side of her mouth.

"Luke?" Riley's voice is shrill and high. She reaches back, back, until her knuckles brush the door and she thumps on it hard. *Please don't be wearing headphones.*

"Greta," she says. "I think—I think you're sick."

"Shhhick," Greta says. Her lips won't close all the way. Her hands dangle and Riley has the strange thought that they're too close to her knees, too close to the floor, like her entire body is just losing a fight with gravity—

"'M shick," Greta slurs. "'M—feel—haaanh. Greh."

"Luke!" Riley yells, throwing caution aside. "Luke!"

"Haaah. Gree. Hah."

"Hungry? Greta, are you trying—are you hungry? I can get you—"

She hears the door open behind her.

"Luke, thank God, I think she's having a fucking stroke or something—"

"Whoa, Greta, you look—Jesus, that's—Riley, can you turn on the lights?"

She slaps around on the wall until she finds one of the push buttons for the timed hallway lights and jabs it. The bulbs flicker and then glow, bathing the three of them in soft yellow light, and Riley bites her tongue so hard she feels the flesh part between her teeth.

Greta looks like she's *rotting*, like her skin is separating from the rest of her, sliding down her skeleton like a flesh suit to puddle on the floor. She shudders, and it's probably a trick of the light, but it looks like her bones are shifting under her skin. *Something* is shifting under her skin. Ripples course up and down her arms.

"Luke," she whispers. "What the fuck is happening to her?"

"Hhhungreee," Greta says. Her voice rattles as it comes out of her, like her voice box is collapsing along with the rest of her body.

"Well, let's—Greta, let's walk toward the kitchen, yeah?"

Luke steps past Riley, holding his hand out to Greta. She fights back the urge to grab him and pull him away. This is Greta. She's like fifty, and she's a scientist, and she's probably having some kind of terrible medical issue. She's not *dangerous*.

Luke pauses in front of Greta, hand still extended. Greta looks at him, eyes tracking across his face and down to his fingers. Something pulses in the middle of her forehead and moves down her face, under her eyes, and wriggles down the side of her throat. Her head tips forward like she's fallen asleep, then snaps back upright. Then it starts to tip backward.

"Um, Greta, let's—maybe let's just get you to bed, actually," Luke says nervously, inching toward her. "Do you feel like we can do that? Can we walk down to your room?"

He turns his head slightly to whisper over his shoulder, "Go get Asha. And the radio."

Riley nods and turns away, trying to move quickly without drawing Greta's attention, and she's almost all the way down the hall when she hears a muffled cry. She whips around in time to see Greta's hand snap up from her side and close around—*all the way around*—Luke's neck.

"Greta!" she screams, running toward them. "Greta, stop!"

Luke's feet kick as she lifts him off the ground. He scrabbles at her hand, trying to pry her fingers away, but she's got him so tightly—they're actually overlapping in the back, where they meet at the nape of his neck—and Riley acts purely on instinct.

She lashes out with a closed fist, hoping desperately that this is how to punch, and hits Greta smack in the elbow. She feels a wet, sliding *give* inside the joint and Greta howls, fingers unclasping from Luke's neck. She retracts the limb, holding it to her chest, and Riley feels a wave of nausea as she realizes that Greta's elbow is just below her waist, even as she grips her shoulder with those long fingers.

"Are you okay?" she says, spreading her arms, trying to get between Greta and Luke. She can hear him coughing.

"Fine," he says. "But something is really—*really* wrong with her."

Greta looks at Riley, cradling her wounded arm.

"Hrrrrr," she says. "Hurrr. Hurt."

"I'm sorry, Greta," Riley says. "I'm really sorry. But you're not—you're not thinking straight—"

Greta's head tips back again, too far, *way* too far. Riley watches in horror as the skin on her neck stretches and folds, pulling taut as her head just keeps falling backward. Luke is muttering "Oh my God, oh my God, oh my God" somewhere behind her as Greta turns, shuffling her feet, until her body is facing away from them. Her head hangs down squarely between her shoulder blades, eyes still fixed on Riley.

"Luke," Riley whispers.

Greta's head keeps descending, folding farther down her body, and then her spine starts to follow it, starts to bend backward as she sinks toward the floor until she's basically folded in half. Her hair brushes along the carpet. Her arms unfold with the sound of popping cartilage, hands slapping wetly against the floor. Her mouth is still hanging open; her tongue lolls.

Riley takes a step back, then another.

Greta starts to walk toward her.

"What the *fuck*?"

Nelson's voice is clear and loud as a gunshot. Riley whips around to see him standing at the end of the hallway holding a cup of tea.

"Nelson, get Asha," she yells. "Get the radio!"

He stands there, wide-eyed, and then he drops the mug and bolts away as it shatters. A crunching sound comes from behind her and she turns back to see Greta's throat contracting and expanding like a breathing lung. Luke is gone.

"Luke!" she screams.

Greta takes another lurching step toward her. Her face is sliding again, toward the floor, pulling the flesh up around her forehead. Something is happening to her mouth. Her teeth are pushing forward, her jawbones shuddering as they move, and for a moment it almost looks like she has a snout. Then her hair catches on something, some pull in the carpet, but she keeps moving toward Riley and her head folds all the way underneath her.

"Oh, Jesus Christ in heaven," Riley whispers. "Oh, mother of God, fucking shit, holy fucking shit—"

Greta moans low in her throat, the sound compressed in her folded windpipe.

"Rrrrrr," she says into the floor. "Rrrriii."

If she says my name I will go insane, Riley thinks. *I will go fully, completely, batshit fucking insane.*

The muscles in Greta's arms and legs flex as she moves, and as Riley watches they start to slide toward the floor, shifting around her body. Her joints crack and pop and there's a horrible wet *squishing* sound that seems to be coming from inside her. Her knees buckle and then break, bending underneath her until she's on all fours, and then her elbows do the same. Her head starts to pull, starts to try and lift itself off the floor. Her torso ripples and shudders and then almost collapses, and suddenly Greta looks like an animal, crouched low to the ground. Her eyes lock on Riley, and her body tenses as if she's about to leap—and Riley thinks she *can* leap now, like a fucking predator would—and then something whooshes past her ear and connects with what remains of Greta's chin with a hollow thunk.

The corner of the microscope digs into her under her chin, caving in the bones of her face and tearing a hole in her skin. Riley screams and so does Greta, the sound bubbling out of her on a tide of blood and black liquid.

"Oh my God," Luke says, breathing hard. "Oh my God. Is she—did I—?"

"*Hurt,*" Greta snarls, blood dripping down her face. She lifts one long-fingered hand and puts it over the wound, holding her flesh together, and then scrabbles toward them like a spider.

Luke seizes Riley's hand and yanks and she stumbles into a run behind him and they tear down the hall, through the common room and into the pantry. He slams the door behind them and leans against it.

"What do we do?" Riley pants.

"I have no fucking idea," he says. "Do you think Nelson actually went to get the radio, or do you think he just bailed?"

"Fuck," she says.

Both of them fall silent as Greta moves into the kitchen, limbs thudding and creaking as she searches for them.

"Hurt," she whines. "Hun. Gree."

"What is wrong with her?" Riley whispers.

"I don't know, but it's not . . . she should be fucking dead," Luke whispers back. "The weight of that microscope—I mean, at the very least her neck should have broken—it doesn't make any sense."

"Last night," Riley whispers. "Before you came out. She was different, her face—I thought it was a trick of the light, but she looked . . . her bones, they looked . . . wrong."

Luke puts a finger to his lips as Greta pauses outside the pantry door.

"Haaaaah," she growls. "Grrrrh."

Then she does something that sounds almost exactly like a bark. Riley flinches, her elbow knocking against the light switch. The light flickers and dies as she yanks her arm away. She looks at Luke, eyes wide with horror.

Greta has been standing outside the door so long that her blood is starting to seep under it. The black liquid curls through it, writhing like a leech, and Riley has a thought. She pokes Luke in the arm.

"Sick?" she whispers, barely a breath, as quietly as she knows how. "Infection?"

He nods, looking thoughtful. Greta's hair drags through the blood on the ground as she snuffles along the bottom of the doorframe. Luke and Riley retreat deeper into the pantry as slowly as they can, clutching each other tightly. After another minute she moves away. They wait until they can't hear her anymore and then Luke cracks the door open.

"One of us has to get the radio," he whispers. "I can distract her if you run."

They emerge from the pantry slowly, holding their breath, heads on a swivel. Greta is gone; she's left a trail of blood and ichor.

"We have to get the others first," Riley whispers. "She could be contagious."

Luke nods. They move back toward the sleeping quarters. Riley slips into Ilse's room to see her waiting, back ramrod straight as she sits on the bed.

"What is happening?" she asks.

"Greta's sick," Riley says. "Really bad. And she's dangerous. We had to hurt her, and we don't know where she is now."

Ilse nods, her face eerily blank. She stands up, then runs one hand under her mattress and comes up with a folded knife. She flips it open, flips it closed, and then tucks it into her waistband. "Let's go."

Luke and Dae are waiting in the hallway. The four of them move slowly toward Asha's private suite, which is a spare lab that Rusk outfitted specially for her comfort while she supervised their operation. Riley has time to roll her eyes mentally as Luke pushes the door open. There's a leather couch, a TV, and an aromatherapy diffuser hissing away on a little vanity table with movie-star mirrors. Her laptop is open, email pulled up, perched on the coffee table in front of the couch. The shower is running.

Dae sits down on the couch and pulls the computer into his lap.

"What are you doing?" Riley hisses. Luke walks toward the

bathroom door and knocks gently. "Asha?" he calls. "Asha, sorry, we've got a problem——"

Riley tunes him out and sits next to Dae. He's scrolling through Asha's emails to Rusk; they seem to correspond almost constantly throughout the day.

"I don't trust her," Dae says. "I don't like it that she's here. It feels weird that Rusk would fund this entire thing and then send a chaperone. Like he didn't vet us all to hell and back. I just don't know . . . I don't know."

He keeps scrolling until the shower turns off, then shoves the computer away from himself and stands just in time. Asha slams out of the bathroom, hair in a towel, draped in the Morticia bathrobe.

"What the fuck?" she says by way of greeting, disappearing behind a screen—a screen! A little folding screen, like she's a fucking Regency heroine!—and keeps talking. "This had better be goddamn serious, I already finished the report for the day, and he hates it when I send addendums, okay, so it has to be *extremely*——"

"Addenda," Riley hears Ilse whisper half a second before Luke interrupts Asha.

"Greta tried to strangle me," Luke says. "And her bones are all bending the wrong way."

Asha steps out from behind the screen in sweats, face like a thundercloud. "Are you fucking high?"

"No," Riley says. "I saw it. He hit—she got hit in the head with a microscope, and she's still—she might have left the station——"

"I'm sorry, you *hit her*——"

"She was going for Riley!" Luke says.

"She is a middle-aged woman," Asha mutters, shoving her feet into slippers.

"I don't know if she is anymore," Riley says. "Her blood . . .

it wasn't only blood."

Asha rolls her eyes, pulls her wet hair into a ponytail, and motions for all of them to leave the room. They file down the hall, Asha turning on every light as they pass, and when they get into the kitchen and the light comes on it illuminates the trail Greta left behind and all of them stop moving very abruptly.

"Oh, shit," Asha whispers. "Oh, Anton is going to fucking kill me, what—"

Blood, streaked with the strange black stuff, straggles through the station in a wide, wavering arc, as if its creator was stumbling. Riley wonders if Greta is outside. If she is, she's probably dead. *Would that be so bad?* says a voice in the back of her mind.

They start to move into the common area, following the blood without touching it. Asha has her phone out, recording everything as they go.

"Where could she have gone?" Ilse asks. "The blood goes to both doors, but I don't know if we should follow it out."

"We have to," Luke says. "She's hurt."

"She tried to kill you," Riley says.

"She's not herself."

Ilse shakes her head, folds her arms tighter against her body. "This feels very bad," she says. "This feels very dangerous. I don't think we should—"

The door opens. All of them turn at once.

Nelson stands there, coat unzipped, radio in hand. He's unplugged the entire set from its place in the outbuilding.

"Sorry," he says. "I didn't mean to just run away from you."

"Where is Greta?" Luke asks, crossing the room toward him fast. "Let me have that."

Nelson hands him the radio reluctantly and Luke starts hunting for an outlet.

"Did you find the SATphone?" Dae asks. "Does Greta have it?"

"I don't know where she is," Nelson says. "I heard her in the hall and I ran, and then I got back in here just now."

"Did you see any blood outside?"

"Or anything," Riley adds. "Did you see anything?"

"No," he says, looking faintly puzzled. "Just our tracks from the last few days, you know? Nothing new."

"She's still in the building," Luke murmurs. "We have to find her. Everyone get something you can use as a weapon, and then we have to split up."

"What's the signal if we find her?"

"Scream really fucking loudly," Asha says darkly.

Nelson shrugs his coat off, picks up his flashlight, and starts down the hall toward the lab. Riley gets a kitchen knife; Luke is holding a lamp, and Dae has a textbook thrust in front of him like it's a crucifix. Asha is still just filming, filming, filming.

"What are you doing?" Ilse asks her, delicately flicking her knife out.

"Documenting," Asha says. "For when I have to explain exactly how and when this whole endeavor went fully fucking sideways."

"He's not gonna fire you because Greta got sick," Riley says.

"If she disappears into the fucking Antarctic he will fire me, eat me for dinner, and pick his teeth with my bones."

"Not an 'all press is good press' sort of guy, huh?" Dae grins halfheartedly.

Asha turns in circles, capturing the streaks and splashes of blood. "She's in AA," she says. "I wonder if she fell off the wagon."

Unease flickers in the back of Riley's mind. *How would she know that?*

"Everyone pick a hallway," Luke says. They split up.

Riley steps into her little spoke of the station. The running lights are on; the overhead lights are on. There are virtually no shadows anywhere. It makes the hallway look like it's vibrating slightly, very quickly, and she feels queasy as she moves forward. She thinks about a haunted house she went to once, when she had friends, and they had to walk down a long hallway toward a gigantic jack-in-the-box puppet. As they approached it, a strobe light flashed, and every time it did the clown's leering face seemed to jump closer to them. The light in the hallway is constant right now, but it *feels* the same as that long-ago light did.

She walks down the hall, head turning from left to right and back again, looking for—what, exactly? *Clues?* She has no idea what she's supposed to be doing. She pokes her head into something that turns out to be a utility closet, investigates another door that leads to more labs, and gets her mental footing. She tries to understand where she is, the places near her that she could hide in. Thinking this, she looks over at the air vent set directly into the wall, just above the floor.

She moves toward the vent. There is a thin smear of something next to it, an almost-oval shape of something greasy. It looks like someone leaned on this wall, bracing with the palm of their hand. And they did it recently.

Riley wants to yell for Luke, but she doesn't want to scare Greta. She runs her fingers around the edges of the vent, feeling for a catch, but the whole thing just falls into her hands like it's been waiting for her. Greta probably climbed in and pulled the grate up after herself; no way to lock it from inside. Riley puts the grate aside and leans down to stare into the darkness of the air shaft. Her breathing echoes back to her doubled, tripled, until all she hears is a rush like the ocean and her heartbeat like hummingbird wings.

"Greta?" she calls softly, her voice bouncing around the aluminum panels. "Greta, it's Riley. I'm going to come in and get you, okay?"

She climbs into the vent.

"NOW, HANG ON," GOOD COP SAYS.

Riley looks up from the pile of cracker crumbs she's been mindlessly assembling as she talks. "Hmm?"

"Why would you go after her?" he asks. He seems like he genuinely wants to know.

"What do you mean?"

"He means, if you're telling the truth, that she tried to kill you and the others and then scuttled away into the night like some kind of Cronenberg monster," Bad Cop snaps. "And given your whole, you know—"

"Anxiety," Riley says evenly.

"It seems as unlikely as the rest of what you're saying that you would follow her into a confined space," Bad Cop finishes. Something somewhere on her person beeps. She pulls out a phone and looks at it, then hands it to Good Cop. He nods and gives it back to her, then gets up and leaves.

"I felt bad for her," Riley says. "She was sick. And—I don't know, when Asha said she was in AA—I thought maybe she was having some sort of backslide, and my cousin is in AA, and if she couldn't reach her sponsor—"

"Then it would make her *bones* go the wrong way?"

"I don't know!" Riley snaps. "I just felt like she was probably really scared, and I couldn't leave her, okay? She's just a person.

Just a nice older lady trying to—do you hear that?"

There's a faint humming sound crawling along the edges of the room.

"What? No. Stop stalling."

"What else is in this building?" Riley asks.

"Who knows?" Bad Cop says, glancing at her phone again. "It's just another old station Rusk owns."

Riley shakes her head and the sound retreats. Maybe she has tinnitus. There's certainly been enough loud shit happening to cause it.

Good Cop comes back in with a bottle of water and another packet of crackers, both of which he sets down in front of Riley. "Working on more soup," he says. "This place is a maze."

Bad Cop gives him a look Riley can't read, and he gives her one back that's just as impenetrable. Riley rips open the crackers and drops another one into the Tupperware for the rat. She looks at the cops and raises her eyebrows.

"Go on," Bad Cop says wearily.

IT'S WARM IN THE AIR SHAFT, A SOFT CURRENT moving past Riley's face. She pulls her phone from her pocket and turns on the flashlight. She shines it left, then right, looking for the blood trail. There's another dark smear down to her left, where the shaft seems to drop lower. She pauses for a second, trying to figure out if there's a way she can put her phone in her mouth and still use the light. Finally she just starts crawling one-handed, holding the phone out in front of her. The air shaft slopes down, then levels out, then starts to angle toward the right. She follows the trail until she comes to a vertical section of the shaft. She peers up. There is another glistening handprint six feet above her head, next to an opening she assumes is another horizontal shaft.

"Fuck," she whispers. She tucks the phone into her bra, which isn't a bra as much as it is a compression bandage with soft cups, and moves it around until the light is at least partially shining out of her shirt. She stands up carefully, putting her palms flat against the walls on either side of her in the narrow space. She takes a deep breath, braces herself, and pulls her feet up. She wedges the toe of her sneaker into a corner and pushes until her back is against the opposite wall, hands still braced, and then she starts to shuffle upward.

She's drenched with sweat and panting when she shoves

herself into the next flat section of the air shaft. She lies there on her back for a moment, trying to catch her breath, feeling her overworked muscles tremble.

"I guess I gotta go back to the gym, Greta," she says in a low, soothing voice. Like she's trying to catch a stray dog, almost, trying to coax it into the car with her. "I used to be strong, you know? Not so much anymore."

She rolls over, takes the phone out of her bra, and starts crawling again. She passes a few more dark smears, contorting herself to avoid touching them, listening intently for movement in the vent. She can hear the murmur of voices beneath her and she knows it's the others, doing their own search, and she resists the urge to thump on the floor of the vent and yell *Be* quiet *so I can hear!*

This stretch of the air shaft is long and claustrophobic, and the heat quickly becomes overwhelming. Now that Riley's started sweating she can't stop, and she keeps blotting it off her face before it can roll into her eyes, but every time she does that split second of darkness when her arm passes over her eyes terrifies her. Every time she pulls it away she's more convinced that the Greta-monster is going to be right in front of her, stretched out and grinning like a lizard, waiting for her. She shakes her head and keeps crawling. As she makes her way deeper into the network of vents that run through the station she counts her breaths, thinks about the expanding eight-count polygon, *inhale, hold, exhale, hold.* She is calm. She is calm.

She stops herself half a second before she puts her entire hand into a puddle of ooze. The phone slips from her other hand and clatters loudly to the metal beneath her. Her heart rate spikes. She snatches the phone, flattens herself against the wall of the air shaft, and slithers past the viscous liquid. Distantly she thinks that she felt heat radiating from the stuff in the moment before she yanked her hand away. Was it warm from the vent, or was it fresh? Is Greta even still warm-blooded?

What is happening to her?

She thinks about zombie movies, apocalypse movies, humanity-ending plagues. What could Greta be carrying, and how did she come into contact with it? Is she dying? Is it killing her? Can she be saved? Riley has never liked zombie movies, except for *Shaun of the Dead*. She doesn't like that they essentially reward people for being willing to murder their loved ones at the first sign of infection. What if you killed your mom, or your best friend or something, and then the very next day they announced a cure? They're too shortsighted, and too violent. She didn't mind when Luke hit Greta with the microscope, though, and that probably makes her a hypocrite. She guesses it's different when the danger is standing right in front of you.

She turns another corner and sees a faint square outline ahead of her to the right. She shines the phone at it. The grate is covered in blood.

"Okay," she murmurs. "Okay."

She crawls toward the grate slowly, dread rising bitter and metallic up her throat. Half of her brain is caught up in the idea that Greta has somehow—somehow *melted through it*. Why else would it be coated in blood from top to bottom? Where else could she have gone? It's a dead end otherwise, and this is where the trail goes. It's the only explanation, as insane as it sounds. The back of her mind, though, is blaring sirens, telling her that *however* Greta got out of the vent, she didn't get very far, and she's waiting for Riley on the other side.

Whatever's wrong with her, her mind's not so far gone that she didn't put the grate back after she climbed out.

Unless she went through it.

Unless whatever is coursing through her in that inky, viscous fluid that poured out of her mouth, whatever made her body fold all the way in half and still move, let her go soft and liquid and shove herself through it like a ricer, bones and blood and all.

Fuck.

Riley shifts onto her butt and braces the bottoms of her shoes against the sides of the grate, pressing her back against the other side of the shaft. She pushes, wincing as the metal scrapes in its frame. She closes her eyes and kicks out with all her strength, slamming the back of her head into the metal. She barely feels it, can't even hear the sound of it over the triumphant rush of blood in her ears as the grate shudders out of its housing. She leans forward, wedging her fingers into the spaces she's made, avoiding the still-drying fluid. It's definitely warm; she can feel the heat in the metal. Her hands tingle like the grate is vibrating. She pushes and pulls, tiny motions that shift the grate farther and farther out until she feels the bottom of it slip completely out of the frame. She holds on to the sides as tight as she can with the tips of her fingers, sliding forward as she does, and when she's right up next to the opening of the vent she starts lowering the grate to the ground.

She realizes she has a problem as soon as she pokes her head out of the shaft. This vent isn't right above the floor, like the one she crawled into. This one is up by the ceiling, and when she lets go of the grate it's going to drop ten feet to the floor and make a horrible sound. She debates pulling it back in, trying to find another exit, but this is the one Greta took, and she doesn't want to lose the trail. She can see faint traces of offal moving away from the vent down the hall, and she needs to follow it.

She looks down the hall, back in the other direction, and back again. No Greta. She listens, breathing slowly and evenly, not holding her breath even though she wants to because she knows then she'll just hear her heartbeat in her ears and that won't help anything. She doesn't hear anything moving, or breathing, or doing anything else. She's also not sure exactly what part of the station she's in.

She has to risk it.

She leans as far out of the vent as she can, pressing her ribs against the edge of the vent and stretching her arm down the wall. She lets go of the grate one finger at a time, winces as it clatters to the floor, and then turns and shoves herself feetfirst out after it, rolling over as she kicks her legs out so her front is pressed into the wall. She slides until her fingers catch the edge of the vent and then lets go, dropping the last few feet. She almost lands it, but something in her ankle rolls as she comes down on the edge of the grate and she crumples, pressing her hands over her mouth so she doesn't scream. It's been over a year since the last time she rolled it, but oh God the pain is bright and familiar and immense. She clasps her hands over it. *Please don't be that bad. Please don't be that bad.*

She stands up, bracing herself against the wall, waiting to see if the throbbing will subside. She takes the phone out of her bra and sweeps it back and forth, taking in her surroundings. From the total darkness, she assumes she's in the unused half of the station. Hopefully there's a breaker box somewhere she can use to turn on the lights, unless Rusk somehow does that from the control room he no doubt has.

She smirks. Luke is rubbing off on her.

A new and more pressing concern surfaces as she follows that line of thought. *What if the key-card door is locked on both sides?*

She'll cross that bridge when she gets to it.

She takes a tentative step. Not horrible. Not good, not by any stretch of the imagination, but she can move. She can get back to her room, get her emergency brace, get her stiff new boots and lace them all the way up. She moves slowly, carefully down the hall, following Greta's trail, which is growing fainter by the moment. The bloodstains get smaller and lighter, as if she's healing (*or running out of blood*, her brain supplies hopefully, *and dying before she kills one of us*). There is a larger puddle in front of one of the closed doors, as if Greta paused here for a moment.

Riley doesn't touch the doorknob—it's slicked with goo—but she leans toward the little window in the door and peers through.

The first thing she notices is that this room has power. There's a soft blue glow, kind of like the one that comes from a sleep screen on a game console, and for a moment she can't tell where it's coming from. Then her gaze focuses on the thing in the center of the room, which appears to be a gigantic glass box.

"What the hell?" she whispers, leaning closer.

The box has lights set into it, illuminating the empty space inside, and they're what's giving off the weird glow in the room. They almost look like black lights, or UV lights, and she's reminded of her friend Shane's older brother, who had a weed plant growing in his closet until his parents cut the lock off and found it. The light he kept it under had the same glow.

Riley shakes her head, trying to understand. *Is this the thing that was on the sledge last night, the mystery box for the next expedition?* It has to be. Why else would there be a glowing box—easily big enough to fit several people inside it—in the back half of the station? But if it's for the next group, why does it have power *now*, and where is it getting that power from if the rest of this half of the station is still dark? She stares at it. The soft blue light looks like it's pulsing, a slow cycle from bright to brighter, almost hypnotic. She turns away. It makes her deeply uneasy to look at, and she doesn't know why. Something about it feels malignant. Whatever its purpose, it's not a good one.

She hobbles down the hall, following the spatters on the floor, shining her phone around every so often to make sure she's still alone. Keeping her weight mostly off her injured ankle is draining, and she's already so tired from the surges of adrenaline ebbing and flowing through her over the past few hours. She desperately wants to lie down.

"Keep it moving, Kowalski," she mutters.

After what feels like an eternity of following her increasingly shaky cell phone light she arrives at a door. There's a slick of blood underneath it. Riley takes off her hoodie, puts her hand in the hood, then grabs the doorknob with it and turns.

Locked.

She clamps down on the swell of panic before it can get ahold of her, wrestles it back under her ribs where it belongs. She hammers on the door.

"Luke!" she yells. "Nelson! Dae! Ilse!"

She waits, listening for footsteps, pointedly not thinking about how if Greta is still in this half of the station somewhere she can definitely hear her. After another minute she bangs on the door again, harder, putting all her weight into it. The dull clanging echoes around her.

"Hey!" she yells. "Someone!"

Before the sound of her voice fades completely, the door swings open and light spills over her.

"Thank God," she says, shoving her phone into her pocket. She leaves the hoodie on the floor and darts through. She wants to leave her sneakers, too, knowing they're caked with whatever Greta is shedding, but she's not about to risk having to run out into the snow in her socks.

Luke is standing in the hallway, looking so solid and normal it almost brings tears to her eyes. He blinks at her, bemused, and then pulls her into a hug. Then he holds her out at arm's length and looks at her.

"How did you get in there?" he asks. "You're lucky I hung on to that key card."

"I was in the vents," she says.

"Jesus fuck," he says. "She went in the vents?"

"She came back out, though," Riley says. "I followed the blood trail. She came back into this half of the station. Can I— can I lean on you?"

She braces herself against him as they walk back to the others gathered in the common room, and then she tells all of them about the glowing box. Ilse looks extremely troubled, like she's on the verge of remembering something she can't quite reach, but she doesn't say anything. Luke sits down next to her and scrubs his hands over his face with a sigh. Nelson looks nauseous, and Dae is typing something into his phone.

"What are you doing?" Ilse snaps, looking at him. "Do you have texts to send right now?"

Dae *tsk*s, keeping his eyes on the screen as he flicks through pictures. "You know we're locked down on that NDA. I saved a bunch of stuff to my phone before I left. I'm trying to see if I have a map of the whole station. With the vents." He grimaces. "We might need it."

Ilse nods, her lips thinning as she takes in what that means.

"So none of you saw her?" Riley asks, looking at each of them. "Anywhere?"

"No," Nelson says. "No joy."

"So where is she?" Her voice is shriller than she wants it to be.

"We don't know," Ilse says. "But she is not in the station."

"She has to be," Luke says. "She's hiding. She can't have gone outside. She'll freeze."

"We don't know that anymore," Ilse says.

"You think whatever's wrong with her is gonna make her, what, ice-resistant?"

"We don't know *what* is wrong with her," Ilse says, glaring at him. "Why would we assume anything that makes us feel more comfortable? Why not assume she is ice-resistant and flame-resistant and bulletproof? Better to be too prepared, I think."

"Did anyone check the barn?" Riley asks. "The outbuilding, I mean?"

"She wasn't there when I got the radio," Nelson says. "And there's still no blood trail out there, so she can't have slipped out after that."

"Would she have covered the trail?" Riley asks. "Or—when I was following it, it was getting lighter. Maybe she's stopped bleeding?"

"Then she's dead," Luke says shortly. He catches Ilse's glance. "Or not. Sorry."

"I think we should check outside," Ilse says. "Two of us to go around the station, check for prints and traces of blood, and the others to wait at the doors in case she tries to come inside."

"Or leave," Dae says.

"Yes."

"I have to get my boots," Riley says. "And my brace. I rolled my ankle."

"I'll bring them to you," Luke says, and jogs away down the hall.

"We should stay together!" she yells after him, but it's too late. She sighs. "The brace is in the bottom of my bag," she calls halfheartedly, in case he's not out of earshot.

"Macho man," Ilse sneers. "He will get us all killed."

"Okay, look, you don't have to be a ray of sunshine tonight, but at the very least you need to not be the one-woman doubt parade, all right?" Dae snaps at her. "There's being cautious, and then there's being so depressing that we all just lie down and wait for her to come eat us, or whatever."

They all stare at him. This is the most he's ever said at once, and certainly the most emotion he's shown.

"We're all scared," he says. "But fighting with each other isn't going to do anything."

Ilse folds her arms and looks away, but she doesn't say anything else. Luke reappears with Riley's boots and she slides from the couch to the floor to put them on. She runs her fingers over her ankle as she takes her sneakers off, checking for swelling. It's warm, but it's still normal-sized. A good sign.

"I couldn't find the brace," Luke says apologetically.

"It's fine," she says, unlacing the right boot. She redoes the top few eyelets in a lock-lace pattern, then slides her foot into it gingerly and yanks the laces as tight as they'll go.

"Who's going outside?" Nelson asks. "Shall we draw straws?"

"I'll go," Luke says.

"Obviously," Ilse mutters. Dae makes an aggravated sound.

"Straws for the rest of us?"

"It was *my* idea," Ilse says. "I'll go."

"You sure?" Nelson asks, looking at her intently. "I'll do it, I really don't mind."

She clicks her tongue. "Fine. I don't care. Just be thorough."

"Oh, always," he says, winking at her. She rolls her eyes. Riley wonders briefly how much of his saucy-flirty-carefree-devil persona is real and how much is him putting on a brave face.

They walk through the common room in a circle, backs together, everyone facing outward. It feels painfully silly, but it also makes Riley feel much safer. Luke and Nelson bundle themselves up, then Luke grabs two knives from the butcher block and hands one to Nelson.

"Just in case," he says. What little Riley can see of Nelson's face drains of color, but he takes the knife nonetheless. He pulls down his gaiter and flashes them all a cocky grin.

"Off to slay the dragon," he says. His goggles are mirrored, so Riley can't see his eyes, but there's the faintest shake in his voice. She feels a rush of fondness for him, for his goofy bravado. "Back in a tick."

Luke knocks him gently on the shoulder. "Come on, James Bond," he says. "Let's get this over with."

Riley watches nervously as the boys step outside. She takes her spot by the door behind them and locks it from top to bottom, bolt by bolt. She looks around for a weapon.

"Use this," Ilse says. She's taken the lampshade and the bulb off one of the table lamps, and she hands the heavy metal base to Riley. Then she takes the knife out of her boot, opens it, and moves across the kitchen to the back door.

"I'll just go back and forth between you, I guess?" Dae asks. "Stay by the windows, maybe, in case they try to—"

"Those windows are reinforced against Antarctic windstorms," Ilse says. "They can't come in through there."

"Well, fine, I just—"

"Just stand with Riley," Ilse says. "That door's a bigger target."

Dae takes his place silently, almost sulking, muscles flexing as he clutches the other lamp, swinging it as if to test its weight.

"Can you see them?" Riley calls across the room. "Through the window?"

"Not yet," Ilse says. "They must have gone around to the right."

"You don't think they split up, do you?"

"I hope not," Dae says. "I don't think they're that stupid."

Riley doesn't say anything. She also hopes that, but Luke has a reckless streak, and his eyes go bleak and vacant when he thinks no one's looking at him. Whoever it was, his friend that was killed—that's broken him more than he's willing to admit. She's not so sure he's got his own best interest in mind. She turns her head toward the windows, waiting for them to come around the building.

"What do you think is wrong with Greta?" Dae asks.

"I don't know," she says quietly. "Some kind of infection, right? A virus? Something that's . . . eating her flesh, or something. Breaking it down. Her bones, they weren't—they were going in all the wrong directions."

"A flesh-eating bacterium," Ilse says. "It's not impossible, but where would she have picked it up out here? Nothing could survive."

"The lake," Riley says. "Down beneath the testing site. Like Nelson said."

"There hasn't been any drilling done in years," Ilse reminds her.

"But what if they brought it up when they *were* drilling? It could have frozen on the surface and then one of us picked it up in a sample."

"The samples stay frozen." Ilse's lack of inflection grates on her.

"Well, on our clothes, then," Riley snaps. "Our boots. The drills. Maybe one of us scooped it up in the pot to boil water for lunch. I'm just saying, if we're looking for explanations, we could do a lot worse than bacteria."

Ilse doesn't have anything to say to that.

"So it could have been any of us," Dae says quietly.

"That brought it back?"

"That caught it," he says. "It just happened to be Greta. I mean, fuck, the rest of us could probably still catch it. We should—we should probably tell someone, I—they're gonna have to shut all this down." He pulls out his phone and starts typing.

"What, are you taking notes?" Ilse's voice is derisive. "Got to make sure you get the story? Your big break—"

"What do you think it's doing to her brain?" Riley interrupts, trying to defuse the tension. Dae's face is tense and cloudy in the glow of his screen. "Why does she want to hurt us?"

"If it is literally flesh-eating, and it's in her brain, then it's eating her brain," Ilse says flatly, turning her gaze to Riley. "Severing neural connections as it goes. Synapses are firing wildly, no longer connected to the proper reactions. She may not have any idea what she's doing."

"She can't be saved, can she?" Riley's voice trembles. "I mean, we can't—there's no way we can fix her."

"Not without immediate medical intervention," Ilse says. "Is the radio working yet?"

Riley turns to look at the box in the corner of the room. Nelson plugged it in at some point, but the lights are still flashing randomly, unable to settle into the calm, steady pattern that means the receiver has found a signal. She shakes her head. "Not as far as I can tell."

Ilse mutters something to herself in German. "Could we get anything on the SATphone?"

"We could, if it works, but we don't—there's no numbers saved," Dae says. "We wouldn't know who to call. Greta and Asha have—"

Riley gasps. "Asha. Where the fuck is Asha?"

"She had to have heard us yelling," Ilse says. "She's probably hiding. Writing an email to Rusk." Her voice is cold. "Maybe her little suite has a panic room."

"But you don't think—what if Greta found her?" Dae spins away from them, pacing back into the center of the room. "What if she's been infected?"

"You're welcome to go check," Ilse says acidly.

"Ilse," Riley snaps. She's surprised at herself, but she's had enough. "Stop being such a brat."

Ilse's eyes widen slightly. She turns away from them, looking out the window of the back door again.

"They're coming around," she says. "I can see the flashlight beams."

"When they're back inside we'll find Asha," Riley says to Dae. He comes back to her side and she puts a hand on his shoulder. It feels weird to be the one providing comfort, but she kind of likes it. She feels strong, somehow. Less like her usual self.

They watch through the big windows as the boys make their

way around the final side of the building. They're moving almost in unison, flashlights sweeping back and forth in smooth arcs across the snow. Their heads turn one way and then the other, breath pluming into the air above them. She's fiercely glad they stayed together. They disappear from view and a few minutes later there's a knock on the door. Riley starts unlocking the bolts.

"Anything?" Dae asks when the door opens.

Luke shakes his head, stomping snow off his boots onto the floor. Cold radiates off him. Nelson's right behind him, a crust of frost on his gaiter where his breath condensed.

"It's clean out there," Nelson says. "All the way around. Just our boot prints and the sledge tracks. Nothing that looks like it was made by someone without gear."

"Did you go in the barn?"

"No," Luke says. "But we went right up to the door, and there's no trail."

He's very careful to keep the *I told you so* out of his voice, but Riley imagines Ilse can hear it anyway.

"So she's inside," Nelson says. "Has to be."

"I think she's with Asha," Riley says. "We—we forgot about her." Shame floods through her. Asha can be a pain in the ass, but she's still a person, and the five of them hadn't given her a single thought.

"Oh, shit, Asha," Luke says. "Jesus. Yeah. We have to find her."

"Then let's go," Ilse says. "Bring the weapons."

They move down the hall toward Asha's quarters.

"She was recording," Riley remembers. "Maybe after we split up she went back to her room to get in touch with Rusk? Maybe she's getting him to send help."

"I don't know about you, but I sort of feel like we might not be high on his list of priorities," Luke says darkly. "I don't think he's gonna be sending a jet, or whatever."

"The research is important to him," Ilse says. Dae holds his phone out in front of them, filming.

"The research, yeah," Luke says. "Not the nobodies collecting it."

Ilse makes an aggravated sound and motions them forward. Asha's door is closed.

"Should we knock?" Riley asks. Ilse looks at her with disdain and then puts her hand on the knob. She turns it slowly, silently, and eases the door open. They file into the room behind her. It looks the same as before; no obvious signs of a fight, no blood. No weird, prickly black stuff. The laptop is open, but the screen is dark. Dae immediately sits down in front of it and tries to wake it, propping his phone in his lap.

"Does anyone know her password?"

"Try '*I love Rusk 99*,'" Luke murmurs.

"You really don't like him," Dae remarks, clicking around. "Maybe I can—huh. There we go."

The screen blinks to life.

"Weird," he says. "The password screen just went away."

"Gift horse," Luke says. "What's she up to?"

"Still just email," Dae says. "It looks like she was actually in the middle of writing one."

He frowns at the screen, leans a little closer.

"She says the specimen may have been contaminated."

"Like Greta got into the lab?" Ilse asks. "Or does she mean that only the samples Greta collected are compromised?"

"I don't know," Dae says. "But it seems like . . . she's not talking about the ice samples. She keeps talking about *the specimen*, singular, and she says—she says right here that it's not yet been *contained*."

"Is it possible that she's talking about the virus?" Riley asks. "Bacteria, or whatever? Maybe she told him what was happening to Greta and he wants to study it."

"Maybe," Ilse says. Her face is troubled.

"Asha?" Luke yells. "Are you in here?"

There is only silence from the room.

"Should we check for a panic room?" Riley asks, only half joking. Ilse starts running her hands over the walls, pressing and feeling for some kind of secret door.

"Wait," Dae says. "She just got an email." He stares at the screen. "Holy shit."

Riley stoops down to read what he's looking at. The email is from Rusk, and it's only two lines long.

CONTAIN SPECIMEN **ALIVE** AT ALL COSTS. ALL PARTICIPANTS EXPENDABLE.

"What the fuck," she whispers. "What the fuck? How would he—how would he even *explain* this? If all of us fucking *died* on his little—his little research trip? What the fuck?"

She jerks upright and starts pacing, pressing her hands against her sternum like she can calm her racing heart from outside her body. Luke watches her with concern in his eyes.

"So where is she?" Ilse demands. "She's hiding from us? Or maybe preparing to kill us? What the fuck is going on?"

"I have no idea," Dae says. "But I think we need to investigate. Are we alone in here?"

Luke does a quick circuit of the room, ducking into the bathroom and closet. "Yes."

"Lock the door, then," Dae says. "We can hide out in here while we figure out what's happening."

He starts opening files. Riley watches the others while he clicks around. Ilse sits perfectly still, an economy of movement that suggests something tightly wound and ready to snap. Nelson is drifting around the room peering into corners and feeling along the edges of things. Luke catches her eye and winks, somehow managing to still look worried, but it's comforting all the same.

"Oh, come on," Dae mutters. They all turn back to him. Riley's breath catches in her throat as she sees what's on the screen.

"Cameras," Ilse whispers. "Cameras everywhere."

Three rows of three boxes each, cycling every few seconds to a new picture. Riley watches her empty room flick by, the kitchen, hallway after hallway.

"What the *fuck*," Luke says.

"This doesn't have to be creepy," Riley says quickly, needing it to be true. "This could just be security. Or, um, documentation. For the, the report. The scientific—"

"In our *rooms*?"

"Is there sound?" Ilse asks. Her posture is somehow even stiffer now. "Can she hear us?"

"I don't know," Dae says. He hits a few keys and a picture of the five of them crowded around the laptop expands. Riley looks at the angle and turns, searching, until she sees the small round black eye watching them from a high corner.

"That's good, right?" she asks. "If there's one in here too, it's probably not . . ." She doesn't know how to finish the sentence. Her skin crawls, prickles across her body like something just under the surface is trying to get out. Her mouth fills with gluey saliva. Asha has been watching them. *Why has Asha been watching*—

"They're not for her," Luke says tightly. "They're for him."

"Rusk," Dae says, minimizing the window. He starts typing again, the low clicking skittering across the back of Riley's neck.

"Why would he need to watch us?" Ilse stands, arms folded. "What could we do? Tamper with the samples? How would we even do such a thing?"

"Maybe he just—maybe it's just one of those things," Nelson says. "Rich tech guy builds something, there's bound to be cameras in it. Especially if he's the one who makes money off the camera sales. He's not, like, sitting at home staring at us labeling slides. It's just, you know, standard."

"Then why is it on Asha's computer?" Ilse demands.

"The program wasn't open," Dae says somewhat reluctantly. "I opened it. So, I mean, Nelson could be right. She wasn't sitting here watching it."

"Not right *now*," Ilse says. "But I'll bet she has been."

"Can she hear us?" Riley whispers. "Is—I mean—is there sound?"

Dae clicks a few times, presses a series of buttons along the top of the keyboard. "I don't think so," he says. "None of the stuff here has any. I think it's just video."

"Fuck that," Luke says. "No more." He swivels around, searching, and snaps his fingers at a discarded shirt hanging over Asha's little folding screen. "Throw me that."

Nelson hooks a finger into it and lobs it overhand. Luke catches it one-handed while dragging Asha's vanity stool into the corner. He climbs up and inspects the camera.

"Shit," he mutters, running his hand along the wall. "It's like, flat."

"What do you mean?" Nelson steps toward him.

"I need, like, tape or something," Luke says. "There's nothing to hang it on. It's set into the wall."

The sound in the room is going funny somehow, getting muffled as if Riley's put earplugs in. The boys' voices fade into a flat soft hum that presses against her eardrums, lays like wet cloth across her face. She's trying desperately to swallow, her throat sticking and scraping like her windpipe is made of sandpaper. She takes a tiny breath through her nose, forces it out through her mouth. Her tongue is a dead, heavy weight in her skull, dragging her head down. She closes her eyes and imagines plunging her face into cold water, drawing it past her gummed-together lips into her dry mouth, feeling the chill of it make its way down into her stomach. The pressure in her head starts to recede. She works her jaw back and forth, puts a hand on her neck and rubs gently. *You're okay. It's okay. It's going to be—*

Her ears pop so suddenly it's painful.

"—doesn't really matter at this point," Luke is saying, frustration sharpening each word. He gets down off the stool and kicks it back toward the center of the room. "They've been watching us for three days already. What else are they gonna see?" He balls up the shirt and throws it halfheartedly at the screen, then sinks onto the arm of the couch and rakes his hands through his hair. "This is so *fucked*. I mean, why would—what?"

Dae is holding his hand up, index finger slightly raised, like he wants to ask a question he might already know the answer to. His voice is hushed when he says, "Asha said Greta was in AA, right?"

"Yeah." Luke shifts down from the arm of the couch to sit next to him. "Why?"

Dae bites his lip, fingers returning to the keyboard. Documents open in a cascade, text flashing onto the screen and off so fast Riley can't imagine how Dae is managing to read it. He leans closer. "I think . . ."

He looks up at Ilse, who is now perched on the edge of Asha's vanity stool with her arms wrapped tightly around herself. "You've been arrested?"

Ilse's face pulls tight and then smooths out immediately, the whole reaction less than half a second long. "What?"

"You . . . you *stabbed*—"

"That is a sealed record," she hisses, standing. "How did you—"

"It's in here," Dae says, not taking his eyes off Ilse. "We're all in here."

Luke stands, intercepting her as she lunges for the laptop. She yowls like a cat as he wraps his arms around her, pinning her against him.

"*Let me see that file,*" she growls, kicking her legs. "How *dare*—"

Her hand scrabbles for the edge of her boot, for the knife, and Riley's voice forces its way out of her in a croak.

"Ilse!"

She's been quiet for so long that it surprises all of them, and Ilse's struggling falters for a moment.

"Ilse," Riley says again. "Stop." Her heart feels like it's beating too slow and too fast at the same time. "Look at me. Look at me, okay? He said we're all in there. All of us. Dae, tell—tell her what mine says."

He looks at her with a question in his eyes. She wants to slam the laptop shut, run away from all of them, lock herself in her room and pretend she isn't who she is, she's not the *way* she is, but she can't. She has to make Ilse see her, make her understand she's not alone with the demons she brought here. She dips her chin slightly. "It's okay," she whispers.

Dae turns back to the screen. "'Debilitating panic attacks,'" he reads. "'Severe, physically symptomatic, barely controlled anxiety. High risk.'"

He doesn't sound disgusted, and when he glances up at her again she doesn't see anything new in his eyes. She doesn't see fear. She can still feel the heat rising in her cheeks, but she stands firm and looks at Ilse. "See?"

"I bet all my drug shit's in there," Nelson offers quietly. He's playing with a tassel on one of the lampshades, trying to sound casual, but he doesn't look at any of them. "I know I put it on the table pretty early, but it's not actually something I'm proud of."

"Suicidal ideation," Luke murmurs, relaxing his grip on Ilse. "For me. Is it safe to fully let you go, or—"

"Yes," Ilse snaps. Luke releases her and she stalks away a few paces, straightening her shirt, then spins around and jabs her forefinger at Dae. "What about—"

"Also arrested," he says shortly. "Doing some questionable stuff to get a story. I'm not talking about it."

"So, what, we're all . . ." Nelson finally lifts his head. "Delinquents? Kind of?"

"Dangerous," Ilse says.

"Unstable," Riley says. "Unpredictable."

"Expendable." Luke's voice is soft and full of hate.

"People would still miss us," Dae counters. "They can't just *disappear* us—"

"They don't have to," Ilse says. "All they have to do is say one of us lost control and did something bad. *That's* why he chose us. If we don't make it back . . ." She ducks her head, wiping a hand over her mouth.

"The cameras," Nelson says, sinking slowly onto the chair Ilse's left empty. "He has footage of all of us. He could use it to—" He looks from Luke to Ilse. "All he would need is two seconds of you squaring up to Dae. He can edit it however he wants, present it however he wants." He gestures at the corner, at the discarded T-shirt, and his face twists with disgust. "Even if we did cover all of them, he's got more than he needs already."

"It was Instagram," Luke says slowly. They all turn to stare at him. He holds up his phone. "That's how he got us. Right? That's where I saw the ad."

"I can't really remember," Nelson says. "Sounds right, though. Why—"

"I saw it there, too." Dae frowns as he turns this over. "You think we were targeted?"

"It makes sense, doesn't it?" Luke stands up fast, like he can't be still for another moment. Tension crackles off of him. "He chose us even before we asked him to. He *made* us ask him. He— you *know* Slade has access to everything. Social media, mailing lists, shopping history, school records. He knew exactly what kind of fucked-up kids he wanted, and he got us." He lifts his hand, curls it into a fist like he's going to slam it into the wall, then lets it drop to his side. "Fuck."

"But *why*?" Riley's question is almost a wail. She feels like they're all on the edge of some great revelation and she's flailing in the dark, trying to grab the end of a power line snapping across the ground, whipping around just out of reach. She takes a breath, trying to ground herself, controlling her tone as she continues. "Why would he *plan* for something like that, for all of us to die? What does he think is going to happen?"

"Not fucking sample collecting, that's for sure," Nelson says darkly.

"It's whatever this . . . *specimen* is," Dae says, returning to the computer and pulling up the email. For a moment, they stare at the words **ALL PARTICIPANTS EXPENDABLE.** "Maybe he does want the samples, maybe he's eventually gonna do something environmental, but this is what he's really after. Whatever it is."

Something starts bouncing at the bottom of the screen and he clicks on it, still talking. "If he thinks people could die trying to get it, no matter how unlikely that is, he wants to make sure it's people he can . . . justify . . . losing . . ."

He trails off, making a small intrigued *hmm* sound as a new box pops open. The screen goes blue, then black. A green command box pops up and Dae looks at it for a moment, then hesitantly presses the Enter key. The entire computer goes dark, even the keyboard, and then it flickers back to its normal appearance. Dae opens the whole directory, the laptop's innards unspooling in a list. He scrolls past PDFs, spreadsheets, a thousand vacation photos, everyone craning over his shoulders, and then there, nestled at the bottom, tucked inside a folder of scanned receipts, is a video file labeled simply "Sequence1."

THE FOOTAGE IS GRAINY, SHOT AT A DISTANCE AND zoomed in. It's gloomy, but not full night; summer of some year. The picture wavers as the camera tracks the object of its focus.

"What is it?" Nelson asks, leaning forward. Ilse wedges herself onto the couch behind him, looking over his shoulder. "It's the specimen, isn't it?"

"It's a monster," Ilse says simply.

There's really no other word for it. It's almost impossible to see against the snow in the low light, but it's there. Riley keeps losing it and then finding it again. It's white, mostly, except for streaks and splashes of blood around its . . . mouth? Face? Teeth? It turns its head as it moves, and it almost looks like a bear, but it's too thin, too long, its snout squared and shortened and almost human looking. Recognition shivers up her spine.

"It's the Terror," Riley says softly. They all turn to look at her. "Something I read in a book. A horror novel. It's like, a bear with a snake neck, I don't know, it does this thing where it—it puts its jaws all the way around your head—"

"Stories," Ilse says. "This is real."

"I know that, Ilse," Riley snaps. "You're the one who said the word *monster*. It just reminded me—"

"Shhh," Dae says tersely, looking at the screen. The camera has zoomed in even further. The monster opens its mouth, saliva and blood dripping from jagged teeth. Its eye sockets are sunk deep into its head, shadowing its eyes and making the skull beneath the skin too visible. It hitches along, its gait uneven and broken, and then lifts itself onto two legs. It keeps walking forward, looking almost like a crouching man, crabbing along with its knees brushing against its distended stomach. A low croaking wail starts to emanate from it as it moves, picking up speed, every so often dropping back to all fours.

"It's like someone took a polar bear and a human and broke all their bones and then smashed them together," Nelson says. "Did Rusk film this?"

"I don't think so," Dae says. "The metadata is all in Russian. *Shhh.* Watch it."

"I'm watching it."

"It's *changing.*"

"What do you mean?"

Dae pulls the cursor back to the beginning of the video. "Look at its back legs," he says. "Haunches, tarsal joint up high. Like a dog, or a horse."

"Okay," Luke says.

"When it starts trying to get on two legs," Dae says. "And it stumbles. Its bones are moving. The legs are longer, the knees lower—"

"Like a human," Ilse says.

"So, what, it's changing its shape?" Luke's voice is quiet, scared.

"Could be a deep fake," Nelson says. "You know. Like that video where Bill Hader turns into Tom Cruise and then back."

"Why would Asha have a deep fake saved in a secret folder?" Ilse asks.

"Well, maybe Rusk thinks it's real," Nelson says. "And he wants to find out for sure."

"You don't think he has the technology to analyze something like that?"

He sighs. "No, I'm sure he does, I'm just . . . trying to be the voice of less panic, I suppose."

"So it's probably real," Riley says hesitantly. Something is scratching at the back door of her mind, waiting to be let in. She's thinking about Greta in the snow, her knees bending the wrong way, her face swelling into a snout. She's still trying to put it together when Dae speaks.

"I think it's real," he says, fingers drumming on the laptop next to the trackpad. "And if it is, I think . . . I think we're in very serious trouble."

"You're thinking about the Vostok probe," Luke says, looking from Dae's face to the creature frozen on the computer. "Right?"

"Yes," Dae says. "Bioweapons."

"Oh, fuck," Nelson says.

"I thought you said it was bacteria or something." Riley looks at him.

"I said it *might* be," Nelson says. "I also said it might be the megalodon."

"It could still be bacteria," Luke says. "Right? I mean, maybe something got . . . infected? And turned into this?"

"I'm not sure it matters at this point," Dae says. "However it's doing this . . . this has to be what Rusk wants. This thing."

"Just because it can change its shape?" Ilse asks, folding her arms.

"It's not about *it can change its shape*. It's about what it can change *into*," Nelson says. He looks almost excited, but in a way that suggests he might also be about five seconds from throwing up.

"Hang on," Luke says.

Ilse scoffs. "Even if that was weaponizable, an octopus can change its shape *and* its color and no one's done anything—"

"Hang on," Luke says again.

"An octopus doesn't have *bones*—"

"Both of you shut up," Riley snaps, watching Luke. His face is so pale it's almost gray. "Luke, what is it?"

He runs a hand through his hair. "That's Greta."

"This video is from——" Dae checks the metadata. "Last year."

"It's the thing that . . . Greta is now," Luke says. "Or, I guess, the thing that is Greta now, I don't know which way——"

"What are you saying?" Nelson stares at him.

Luke reaches out, looking to Dae for approval. Dae shifts out of the way and lets Luke pull the cursor along the bottom of the video, all of them silent as the creature's bones shift again. Luke turns his head. "Ilse. When did they stop allowing dogs here?"

"Nineteen ninety-two," she says promptly.

"And we all agree that's . . . dog-shaped, right?"

Riley nods, watching the others do the same.

"So this thing, whatever it is, has encountered a dog before. Which means it's been walking around the Antarctic for *decades*, and it has some kind of . . . some kind of *memory* of a dog."

Ilse frowns. "But why do you think this is the same——"

"Greta had a snout," Riley blurts. "The first night after she got back. Just for a second, when she was outside, but I saw it. And her knees went the wrong way at the same time."

"So this . . . this creature." Ilse's talking slowly, trying to put it together as she goes. "If it *is* the same creature. You're saying it used to look like a dog, but it doesn't anymore. Now it looks like Greta. But it still has the *ability* to look like a dog if it wants to? Because it"——she throws a glance at Luke——"remembers it?"

Recognition kicks in Riley's chest, drums up her spine to her head. "It's like the Animorphs," she says. "Did you—any of you—"

They all just stare at her.

She sighs. "They're books about these kids who can turn into animals. But the way they do it—they call it *acquiring*—is they basically just touch the animal and absorb its DNA into themselves. So they can turn into it any time they want, for like, the rest of their lives. They always have it."

"But what happens to the animal?" Luke asks. "The one they . . . acquire?"

"They just get kind of sleepy," she says. "And then they usually just wander away."

"Well, we know there's not another Greta running around," Dae says. "We looked all over the station. So what happened to her?"

"I don't know," Riley admits.

"Okay. It was a separate entity from Greta at some point," Luke says. "This video is proof."

Ilse picks up his thread. "But now Greta's gone, and that thing is here, which implies that it . . . what, replaced her somehow? Then where is her body?"

"What if it didn't replace her?" Nelson's face has lost the tinge of excitement; he's now fully in nausea mode.

"How else would—"

"What if it *ate* her?"

Riley's stomach rolls and for a moment she thinks *she's* going to vomit. "Ate her?" Her voice is barely a whisper.

"She kept saying she was hungry," Luke mumbles, putting a hand over his mouth. "And she kept, you know, changing. Falling apart. Maybe it has to eat to keep its shape."

"Christ," Nelson murmurs. "I wonder what it looks like when it's at home with its shoes off."

"But why would it do this?" Ilse asks.

"Why does anything mimic?" Dae asks. "Either it's prey or it's a predator."

"I think we can rule out prey," Luke mutters.

"Wait," Riley says. "So are we saying Greta's—gone? I mean, like . . . you don't think we can get her back? Fix her?"

"I think we need to assume the worst," Ilse says flatly. "Even if it didn't eat her in the sense Nelson means, the monster . . ." She takes a deep breath, straightens her spine. "All we know is there were two separate living things, and now there's only one. So either Greta is inside of it, somehow, I guess, or it put her somewhere we can't find her."

The doorknob rattles. All of them whip around except Dae, who sucks in his breath and starts pressing keys frantically. There's a thud and then a muffled "Ow," and then silence. The doorknob rattles again.

"Are you in my room?" Asha asks, her voice quiet and even. Another rattle. "Let me rephrase: *Why* are you in my room?"

Dae slams the laptop and motions for Nelson to open the door.

"What if she's—you know—" Nelson rolls one eye to the side and lets his mouth sag open.

"She sounds normal," Riley whispers.

"Are you going through my things? One of you answer me," Asha calls. Riley can hear her foot tapping. "Nelson? Are you in there?"

"Coming, my dove," he says loudly, widening his eyes at the rest of them. He lifts his hands, silently asking: *What do we do?*

"Asha," Dae says, raising his voice slightly. "What's your laptop password?"

There's a beat of silence before she tries the knob again. "Why would I tell you that? What are you *doing*?"

"Just tell me," he says. "If you can."

She sighs and kicks the door. "It's 'dangerous woman.' With zeros instead of o's. Now will you let me in?"

Dae looks at Nelson and shrugs. "I don't really have any other ideas."

Nelson opens the door, revealing a glowering, sweaty Asha.

"Where have you been?" he asks.

She shoulders past him into the room. "Leviathan Station," she says, picking up a towel and blotting her face.

"Why would you go all the way there?" Nelson asks.

"How did you know it was safe to come back?" Ilse asks, eyes raking over her from top to bottom.

"I didn't," Asha snaps. "Where's my bathrobe?"

"We might have to run," Riley says quietly. Asha gives her a disgusted look, sighs, and pulls on a sweater.

"I was freezing," Asha continues. "And I hadn't heard anything for hours, and the radio there doesn't work either, so I figured I would come back here and try to get ahold of Anton."

"So you believe us," Dae says. "That something's wrong."

"I believe that you believe it," she answers evenly.

"Right," Dae murmurs. "Of course. And the footage on your computer, the video of the monster, do you believe that?"

The blood drains from her face as she turns toward them. "You—how—"

"You don't get to ask questions," Luke says, voice low and furious.

"You don't understand," she says desperately, hands fluttering in front of her. "Anton—"

"You have files on all of us," he snaps. "How long has he been planning this? How long has he been looking for *expendable candidates*?"

"Why did you even *bother* with us?" Riley blurts. "Why not just—he's got a *jet*, he could just . . ."

She falls silent as Asha's face changes, loses its panicked flush and settles into a smirk. Her voice is calm and cruel.

"You know why you never see a Marlboro truck anymore?" she asks, looking from Riley to Luke and back. "On the highway?"

Riley shakes her head minutely.

"How much do you think an entire semi full of cigarettes is worth?"

"Oh," Nelson murmurs. "Hijacking."

Asha turns to him, face lit with triumph. "Exactly."

"I don't understand," Riley whispers, hating how stupid she feels in this moment. "How are they——"

"They still transport them by truck," Asha says, not looking at her. "They just don't label it."

"You wouldn't risk hijacking a truck if it could be full of cotton swabs, or something," Nelson says. "Right?"

"Right. So if Anton drops everything and gets a special convoy over here, brings the jet and the containment vessel and everything else . . ." Asha raises her eyebrows at them.

"Then everyone knows something's up," Dae finishes.

"But if he sets up a research trip with a bunch of little Outward Bound–type hood rats," Asha says, "then no one looks twice. We're bringing back giant boxes filled with *ice samples*, the most boring, non-valuable thing you could even take out of the Antarctic."

"And he has a built-in explanation in case we die." Ilse's voice cracks.

Asha shrugs, lips twisting back into a smirk. "Did you think he picked you because you were smart?"

Ilse's hands snap into fists.

"Okay, ignoring the absolute——the just *unbelievable* fucking assholery of that," Luke snaps, "let me skip right to the next question, which is *now what, genius?*"

He sweeps a hand out, encompassing the room. "That thing killed Greta. It wants to kill the rest of us. Even if we *were* somehow capable of containing it, which it doesn't seem like we are, why would we help you do that? Knowing you don't care if we live or die?"

"Do you think he cares if *you* live, Asha?" Ilse spits the words with venom. "Why, out of all the people he sent here, do you think *you're* the only one he's not willing to lose?"

Asha's composure seems to falter for a moment, her mouth opening and closing as she tries to think. Her carotid pulses visibly in the side of her neck.

"He—he wouldn't," she whispers. "Anton—"

"He's *playing* you, love," Nelson says, carefully drawing closer to her. "We saw that email. *All* participants expendable. He's counting on the fact that you won't think that includes you, but as soon as that thing's inside a box, I'm guessing all bets are off."

"You're a liability," Ilse says. "He can't risk you coming back, knowing what you know. Even if he didn't plan on letting you die, now that the situation has escalated, he'll probably feel he has no choice."

"But I wouldn't—I'd never—" Asha wipes a bead of sweat from her temple. "I'd never betray him."

She sinks down onto the couch, pulls the laptop toward her. Almost in a daze, she starts typing. They hear the *whoosh* of a sent email and then, almost immediately, the small chime of an incoming one.

"Anton," Asha breathes gratefully, leaning toward the screen. Her eyes dart back and forth as she reads, lips moving slightly. A crease appears between her eyebrows.

"He . . ."

She swallows hard, throat bobbing. Riley watches the blood rise to her face and then drain away, leaving behind a sickly pallor. She's still sweating, the fabric of her shirt darkening with it by the second.

"He says if we don't get it contained I might as well stay here and freeze," she says, her voice hollow. The skin on her neck glistens as her pulse jumps beneath it. "Now that he knows it's alive, that it's nearby . . ."

Nelson makes a *tsch* sound in the back of his throat. "Ouch."

Ilse glares at him. "Don't gloat."

He shrugs. "She chose her man."

Asha buries her face in her hands and moans, low and miserable. Nelson looks at her for a moment, then sits down on the couch next to her and puts a hand tentatively on her back.

"Sorry, love. But now at least you know—ooh." He lifts his hand away. "You're a bit damp there, no shame in that, it's certainly a bit warm—"

"No," Riley gasps. A thin, mucousy strand of something stretches between Asha's wet shirt and his palm. "Nelson, get away from her, *move*—"

Asha's head whips all the way around, mouth opening in a spray of gray-tinged saliva. Nelson screams and leaps off the couch a split second before her teeth snap shut on the space where his hand was. She growls and pushes herself to her feet.

"Asha," Riley says, thinking about how Luke had coaxed Greta inside. "Asha, it's okay, everything's okay, just—"

Asha roars, the sound like a bear and a baby and a cat in heat all thrown into a blender, and slams her fist into the wall.

The wall that's easily five feet away from her.

"Oh, for Christ's *sake*," Nelson wails.

"I," Asha says, breathing heavily. "I, I. Didn't. I didn't know."

"When did you see Greta, Asha?" Dae asks, standing. He's slid the laptop off the table, and now he nudges it under the couch with one foot. Riley can see his phone camera peeking out of his front pocket, and she wonders if he's filming. "When did she—when did it—"

"Don't . . . know." Asha pants. "Radio . . . the radio had . . . blood on it. I didn't know . . . "

Her breathing becomes a high, ragged whistle.

"The Leviathan Station," Ilse murmurs. "Greta must have tried to call for help at some point, and she left—whatever it is that it's made of—on the handset."

"So even its *blood* can infect—?"

"It seems that way," Ilse says. "Asha. Did you ever see Greta, or just her blood?"

Asha's head droops, her chin almost touching her chest. Her hands hang at her sides.

"Greta," she whispers. She reaches up, fingers trailing across her cheeks, pushing and kneading. "Greta."

She lifts her head and Riley almost screams.

Asha's face is gone, warped and mangled into what looks like melting wax. Something about it is familiar, though, as she watches the creature pull at its skin. One eye goes blue, then brown, then blue again, and the cheekbone beneath it flattens, and for a moment Greta's face peers out of the mass.

"Greta," it says again.

"That's . . . that's right," Riley says, voice trembling as she stands up slowly. "That's Greta." She casts a panicked glance at Luke. "Good job."

He nods at her, keeps it going. "It's okay," he says quietly, soothingly. They're all backing away from her in the smallest movements they can muster. "Asha, you're doing great. You're okay. We can figure this out, we just have to stay calm, okay? It's okay. It's all okay. It's going to be—"

The creature's mouth drops open and a tide of black-threaded drool washes out, cascading down its chin and onto the floor. Nelson yelps with disgust and its head swings toward him.

"Nelson," Riley whispers, "don't make her upset."

"Look." Ilse's voice cuts between them before he can answer. "Watch."

They stare at the pool of saliva on the floor. Its surface hasn't settled, most likely because liquid is still dripping from the creature's mouth, but as they watch, something different starts to happen. A tendril curls out, almost lazily, from the larger pool. It reaches toward Nelson, whose booted feet are only a small distance away.

"What do I do?" he whispers, panicked.

"Slide your feet backward," Riley whispers back. "Slow."

He slides one foot back, then the other, keeping his eyes on the floor. The tendril stretches, matching his movements, pacing him. In the corner of her eye Riley sees Ilse's arm creeping down toward her boot.

Then Asha's arm smashes into the center of Nelson's chest.

He screams, the sound bouncing off the walls, crowding against Riley's eardrums. She wants to cover her ears.

"HELP!"

Asha pins him up against the ceiling, shoving until he's wedged into the corner of the room next to the air duct. He scrabbles at her hand, trying to stop her fingers from—it looks like they're *puncturing* him—

"Please," he wails. "One of you, please, *help me*—oh, Christ, it *hurts*—"

His words dissolve into sobbing as Asha's other arm comes up and starts yanking at the cover of the vent. Luke takes a step toward them, but Ilse grabs the back of his sweater before he can move farther.

"We can't touch it," she says. "We can't touch any part of it."

"I have gloves—"

"We don't know if fabric prevents transmission," she says.

"What are we supposed to *do*?" His voice breaks.

A lamp shatters against the wall next to Nelson's head. He shrieks and covers his face. Blood is leaking from beneath Asha's hand where it's sunk into his chest. "Do it again!" he screams. "Kill this fucking thing!"

Riley turns to see Dae lifting a bottle of perfume. He throws it at the creature, hitting it in the side of the head, and it loosens its grip on the grate. Riley scoops up a jar of moisturizer and flings it, hitting the monster in the back. It shudders with annoyance, like a horse flicking away a fly, and slams Nelson against the ceiling. There's a muffled *crack*. Nelson screams again and goes limp, legs dangling. His eyelids flutter.

Ilse looses a bloodcurdling scream, hurling a can of hairspray. It bounces off the wall and into the creature's face, knocking it briefly to one side. It refocuses on Nelson and starts trying to open the vent again.

"Get the other lamp!" Dae yells at Luke. "I'm going to try and get the shower bar——"

He darts past Asha into the bathroom and slams the door. The monster barely glances up as it works on the vent, muscles rippling up and down Asha's frame as it pulls on the metal. Luke rolls across the bed and seizes the lamp.

"Wait," Riley says. "What if you leave it plugged in?"

Understanding dawns on his face and he rips the lampshade off, then smacks the bulb on the table until it shatters. He clicks the button on the lamp's base and electricity arcs between the exposed wires. He shuffles closer to the monster, keeping his eyes on it, and when he's right next to it Riley swings the vanity stool up and throws it. It hits the bathroom door, one leg splintering, and falls to the ground. The monster turns its head to look down at it and Luke jabs the lamp up into its side. There's a hiss and a pop and the monster squeals and then all the lights go out.

"Oh *fuck* me," Luke says in the darkness.

Riley hears the bathroom door open, hears Dae start to say something, and then there's a metallic groan and scrape and she knows Asha has the air duct open, and she knows they have lost.

"The generator should kick on," Luke says. "It's still primed, it should be any second——"

There's a small crunch, and then a wet sliding sound, and all Riley can think is that the monster has shoved Nelson into the too-small opening of the ventilation system. Tears spring into her eyes. The lights flicker, and in the strobing illumination Riley watches the Asha-monster step itself up off the floor, up to the nine-foot-high grate, pull its long limbs into the hole behind it, and vanish into the wall.

There's one last stretch of darkness, and then the lights come back up. The four of them that remain—Luke, Riley, Dae, and Ilse—stare at each other.

"Jesus Christ," Luke says shakily. Riley keeps her mouth shut, afraid if she opens it she'll start screaming and never stop.

"We have to get somewhere safer," Dae says. "The barn, the radio room, maybe."

"The radio is in the main room now," Luke says. "Nelson put it—"

"I don't give a shit about the radio," Dae says, pulling the laptop out from under the couch. "I just want something that locks."

Riley unsticks her tongue from the roof of her mouth. She still half expects a scream, but her voice is surprisingly even. "Wait." They look at her. "What about the other half of the station? Where the box is?"

"The box is for that *thing*," Ilse says.

"So we know it's . . . thing-proof," Riley says. "Right? Or at least they think it is."

"So we get in a box and wait for it to eat us?"

"Do you have a better idea?" Riley snaps, exasperated.

"Not yet," Ilse mutters. "Fine. Lead the way."

THE ROOM WHERE THE BOX IS KEPT IS STILL unlocked, bathed in calm blue light. Riley holds the door for the others and then slips inside, pulling it tightly closed.

"Does anyone have an extra sweater? Something we can jam under it to block it?"

Ilse wordlessly unzips her hoodie, peels it off, and hands it to her. Riley shoves it under the door, wadding it until she can tell herself it's an effective doorstop. Luke walks around the box, running his hands over the sides.

"It's like, bulletproof," he says. "It's like the popemobile."

"He doesn't like it to be called that," Ilse says, somewhat distantly. "It's not dignified."

Riley wonders if she's going into shock or just thinking. Knowing Ilse, it's probably not shock. Dae sits on the floor and opens the laptop.

"I'm going to tell Rusk we have it," he says. "And he needs to come get it right away." He looks at Luke. "Figure out how to get that thing open. We're getting inside it, he's coming to pick it up, and we're all going the fuck home."

"He'll see us," Riley says.

"Not if we soap the inside of the glass or something," Dae says. "He doesn't know what kind of defense mechanisms this thing has. Maybe it's got soap."

"Okay," Riley says. "But——"

"Kowalski, come help me," Luke says, now feeling up the box in earnest. "There's gotta be a way to get inside."

She joins him, pressing her palms flat against the box. The glass—she thinks it's glass, or something like it—is cold and faintly greasy, and it feels like it's humming against her skin. She slides her fingers along the edges of the panels, searching for any irregularity that could be a hidden switch.

"Is there a vent in this room?" Ilse asks, still sounding not quite right. She's turning in slow circles, trying to take in the whole area.

"No," Dae says, fingers flying over the keyboard. "Or at least not one you can get into. I think it's on its own circuit from the rest of the building, even from the back half. I'd bet this room has its own generator and stuff too. Once they get this thing they're *not* letting it go."

"Jesus." Luke makes a disgusted sound. "How long has he been planning this?"

"Since he saw that footage," Ilse says.

There is a distant thump above their heads, followed by a faint scrape. Riley thinks about fingernails scrabbling for purchase on metal.

"Shit," Dae says, typing faster. "Shit, shit, shit, shit."

"What?"

"He saw the video feed," Dae says. "He knows Asha's gone. He's *pissed*."

"Jesus Christ," Luke mutters. "What do we do?"

"We wait for his answer," Dae says. "I just asked him how we can get out of this in one piece."

The computer chimes.

"What does it say?" Riley asks.

"It says . . . it says 'you can't.'"

"We have to get out of this room," Ilse says desperately.

"No!" Dae snaps. "We don't know what's out there. And we don't know that we're *not* safe in here."

"We have to get inside this fucking box," Luke says.

"He can *open the box*," Ilse shrills. "We can't just wait for something to happen. We have to threaten his precious creature. It's our only chance."

"So you want *us* to put *it* in the fucking box," Luke says, staring at her.

"If we show him we can destroy it, he will not hurt us," Ilse says.

"Or he kills us with a heat-seeking drone from his living room," Dae says.

"Okay," Ilse says. "Okay. What if we bargain?"

"What do we *have?*"

"If we can kill it . . . if we can get a piece of it and kill the rest . . ."

"He'll kill us and take the piece."

"Not if it's *in* one of us," Ilse says. "If we tell him we allowed it to infect us—"

"What?!"

"He will have no choice but to take us back to the mainland," Ilse continues. "We become his weapon."

"It would kill us," Riley whispers.

"We will be lying," Ilse says. "Because we will kill it first."

"What if we call someone else?" Riley asks, her mind whirring. "Like . . . like . . . the Coast Guard. Or whoever they have in Argentina. They're the closest, right? We could call that—that little airport—"

She can feel her lungs tightening, feel her throat locking up. *No.* She cannot have a panic attack now. She *cannot.* She closes her eyes and sinks to the floor, covering her face, gasping for air.

"What the fuck—"

"Just leave her alone," Luke says quietly. "Come over here."

Riley listens as the three of them retreat to the other side of the room. She wraps her arms around her knees and presses her face into the corner of one elbow and thinks about the Oregon coast. Cold salt spray on her lips. Breathe in, out, in, out like the tide, pulling back out into the sea and leaving starfish and seaweed in little pockets for her to find. Her mom's yellow hat, her dad's glasses all fogged up.

She lifts her head to see them all watching her warily.

"It's okay," she says. "It's under control."

Ilse presses her lips together but doesn't say anything shitty, and Riley feels a strong surge of gratefulness for Luke.

"We do have to get out of this room," Dae says. "This box won't open."

"There must be a key," Riley says, standing up. "Maybe back in Asha's room. Maybe there's another key card."

"We have to eat something," Ilse says. "It's been almost twenty-four hours."

"But the vents," Dae says.

"We don't know how long it takes for it to, um, change," Riley says. "Right? Greta was normal the first night. Like, she was shaped like herself. Maybe after it becomes something new it can't do anything else right away. Like it needs to rest."

"So since it just got Nelson . . ." Luke grimaces.

"We might have some time," Dae says. "Maybe."

"I'm willing to take that chance," Ilse says. "I need to get out of here. This fucking blue light."

They file out of the box-room clutching each other's hands. Ilse leads, knife out, and they make their way back to the front half of the station.

The kitchen throws them all for a loop.

"Why is it clean?" Riley asks, letting go of Luke. She walks over to the pantry she'd been cowering inside of just hours ago. "I *remember* her blood coming in under the door."

She crouches, looking at the floor. She reaches one fingertip out slowly, carefully.

"Don't," Luke cautions.

She looks at him. "Luke, it's clean," she says. She puts her hand down. "There's not even, like, a residue. How—did Asha *mop* before it got her—?"

"The parts of itself that it sheds must die faster," Dae says, making his own circuit around the main room. "Like, if it doesn't come into contact with something else it can get into, it just . . . evaporates."

"The vent," Riley says. "I can check the vent."

She darts out of the kitchen before anyone can stop her, ducking back into the hallway where she'd emerged from the ventilation system. The grate she kicked out of the wall lies discarded on the floor. She picks it up.

"It's clean," she announces, walking back into the kitchen. "It was *covered* in . . . slime. Blood. Whatever. Top to bottom. It was like she pushed herself through it like a meat grinder."

"Jesus," Dae mutters, nose wrinkling.

"Sorry. I'm just saying I think you're right. It's all . . . infectious, or whatever, but the fringe parts of it can't last."

"But, okay," Luke says, raising a hand like they're in class. "What does that mean as far as, like, vectors? Like, if Nelson had—if her drool had gotten on him, but the rest of her hadn't, would it have been able to, you know, get him?"

"Can the smaller parts colonize a new host, you mean," Ilse says. "Maybe. Or maybe they're in communication with the main body, and they would call it to them. Maybe it hears the parts of itself that are dying and can't go back to pick them up."

"But if they find something it can eat . . ."

"Then it goes to them," Ilse says. "Yes."

"So is it one thing?" Riley asks. "Or a million tiny things?"

"Both, I think," Dae says. "I don't know how that's possible, but . . . that's how it feels."

"How do you kill something like that?"

"Look, let's just . . ." Luke turns in another circle. "I think we all need a minute, okay? Let me just—"

He starts moving around the kitchen more purposefully, gathering pots and pans and cups and silverware, everything he can carry, and then he starts arranging little walls of dishware where the hallways meet the main room.

"I know it won't do much," he says. "I'm pretty sure it's capable of sneaking. But we need to at least try and eat something, and get some sleep, or we're not going to last much longer. If we do this, and then sleep in shifts, maybe we'll feel safe enough to actually rest."

"We should turn off the lights," Ilse says. "Most of them. In case it goes outside. That way it won't be able to see us through the windows as well."

Luke nods and starts flipping switches. Dae goes to the wall where the fireplace is and turns the flame up to a low glow, barely enough to outline the room. Riley starts dragging pillows and cushions and blankets over toward the fireplace, as many as she can find in their immediate vicinity. Then she starts opening cans.

By the time she's warmed up a variety of food, the rest of them have created a little fortress of furniture in a semicircle around the fireplace, like Roman soldiers facing outward with their shields. She hands the bowls over, then clambers over the back of a couch and sits down on the floor with them.

"SpaghettiOs," Luke says. "We cannot die if our last meal is SpaghettiOs."

"Ta-da," Riley says. "A reason to live."

He snorts. They eat in silence for a few minutes before Dae puts his bowl down and says, "Ilse."

She turns her head toward him, chewing, but doesn't say anything.

"The file . . . your file . . . it said you stabbed your dad."

"Dude," Luke murmurs.

"It's all right," Ilse says. "I did."

Riley stares into her bowl.

"He burned my mother," Ilse says. She takes a meatball off her fork with her teeth, delicately, like an animal. "Scalded her. Two gallons of boiling water."

"Jesus," Dae says. "What—"

"It was an accident," Ilse says. "But he wouldn't help her. I went with her to the hospital, to her therapy appointments . . . she needed surgery to sever the scar tissue, so she could move her arm again, but we couldn't afford it . . ." She shrugs. "His life insurance policy was very good."

"How—"

"I made it look like he was trying to kill her," Ilse says. "After the scalding it was easy to believe. Then we took his money and came to America."

"Hang on, didn't you say you came here when you were ten?" Luke asks.

She looks at him levelly, takes another bite of food.

"Holy shit," he mutters.

"Didn't you—don't you feel bad?" Riley blurts. She's trying to imagine stabbing anyone, let alone her sweet, goofy dad. "If he didn't mean to hurt her . . ."

"But he did hurt her," Ilse says. "And then he did nothing to ease her pain."

Riley puts a ravioli in her mouth.

"He refused to help her while he was alive." Ilse shrugs, the motion strangely childish. "So I had to do it, and that was the best way."

"Was she in on it?" Luke asks. "Your mom. Did she—I mean—she didn't help a ten-year-old plan a *murder*—"

"She was in the garden," Ilse says. "She didn't know until she came back inside. But she helped me with the police."

"Was she upset?" Riley can't stop thinking about her own parents. "I mean, she still loved him, right?"

"I loved him too," Ilse says quietly. She eats another meatball and follows it with a sip of water. "I still do. But I had to take care of my mother."

She stares into the fire, eyes unfocused. "I don't think I've ever told that story out loud," she murmurs. "Not the true version, anyway."

The corner of her mouth quirks. "I used to think I got away with it because God knew I did it for a good reason, but now . . ." She lifts her empty bowl toward them like they're going to toast. "Maybe this is a long-delayed punishment."

None of them really know what to say to that. Dae's gaze drops to the floor and Riley feels a shock run through him. He points with his fork.

"So that—in your boot—is that the same knife?"

"Yes," Ilse says, pulling her foot in. She rests one hand on her ankle possessively. "It took months to get it back. I should have just gotten a new one but I felt like, I don't know, *I'm supposed to carry this*. You know?"

Dae nods, and silence falls over them once more. Riley concentrates on threading as many little pasta circles as she can onto one tine of her fork.

"I'm not going to ask," Ilse says after a while. "So if any of you want to talk about what Rusk has on you, this is the moment."

"I don't think any of us can follow that," Luke says.

"What are we going to do?" Riley asks abruptly, setting her

bowl down. "Tomorrow. And the next day. Until we get out of here. What are we going to *do*?"

"We have to get a message out." Dae looks at her. "By radio or SATphone or fucking smoke signal, we have to let someone else on this continent know we're in trouble."

"Aren't there cruises that come through here?" Riley asks. "Could we . . . I don't know, could we hike to a higher point? And see if we can pick up their radio frequency?"

"It's worth a shot," Luke says. She gives him a grateful look.

Ilse is shaking her head, and Riley feels an unreasonably strong pang of annoyance. "What?" she snaps.

"We need to go farther into the interior," Ilse says. She pulls a small folded piece of paper from one of her shirt pockets and sets it on the floor in front of them. She opens it as she talks. "We need to get to one of the manned stations. No matter which one, no matter which country."

Dae slides the paper toward himself, takes a picture with his phone. "Yeah. Rusk can't kill us in front of a full crew of Australian nationals, or whatever."

"Unless he kills them, too," Luke says.

Riley looks at him sharply. "Do you think—"

"It's a chance we have to take." Ilse doesn't look at her as she cuts her off. "There's strength in numbers, especially if we can get to them before Rusk figures out where we are."

"What if he's listening?" Dae whispers, pointing at the ceiling.

"We won't decide until tomorrow," Ilse whispers back. "Outside, away from the station. Even if this place is wired he won't be able to hear us over the wind."

Riley's caught off guard by a yawn that cracks her face open. Luke gives her a small smile.

"I'll take first watch," he says. "Everyone hand me your dishes."

By the time he's done cleaning, the three of them are bundled down into the nest of cushions and blankets. Riley is very glad for the screen in front of the fire; her back is almost pressed flush against the metal, but at least she knows she won't catch fire. *Might be preferable*, she thinks, and then shuts that down. She watches Luke climb back over the couch into their little enclosure.

"I'll wake you up in——" He looks at his watch. "Ninety minutes, okay?"

She nods, then closes her eyes.

"AND THEN THERE WERE FOUR," BAD COP SAYS DRYLY. She looks at her watch. "Any chance we can hurry this along?"

Riley just looks at her. The pain meds are starting to wear off, and there's an unpleasant tingling in her fingers that feels like it's going to be much more than unpleasant fairly soon. She flexes her hand, rests it on the table. The cool metal feels nice against her fingertips.

"Riley," Bad Cop snaps. "Hello?"

"Can I have some more water?" Riley asks, looking at Good Cop.

"Of course," he says, and pushes himself up from the table. When he's gone, she swivels her head and pins her gaze on Bad Cop.

"How much is he paying you?"

Bad Cop's lip curls into a sneer. "Enough."

"What happens after this? Once I tell you the story?"

"I guess that depends on you." Bad Cop leans back in her chair. "And whether or not you decide to stop fucking around and tell the truth."

The humming is back, the distant high-pitched whir almost like a trapped insect. Riley tilts her head, trying to figure out where it's coming from. It doesn't bother her as much as it did the first time she heard it. It's friendlier now, somehow. She wants to know where it's coming from. Maybe the cops are doing some sort of interrogation technique, piping it into the room with a speaker. Maybe there's just a bug trapped somewhere in the hall.

She laughs.

"What possibly," Bad Cop says, "is that about."

Good Cop comes back in with the water. Bad Cop raises her eyebrows as he hands her a bottle, too, and opens one for himself. "It's fine," he says shortly. "Everything's in order."

"What's going on?" Riley asks, interested despite herself.

"Just working on getting you out of here," Good Cop says with a smile.

She doesn't believe him.

IT FEELS LIKE SHE'S BEEN ASLEEP FOR TEN SECONDS
when Luke shakes her awake. She bats his hand away from her
shoulder, then remembers where she is and bolts upright.

"Shit," she whispers, rubbing her eyes. "Sorry."

"It's okay," he whispers back. "Nothing happened. All quiet
on the Antarctic front."

She shuffles around and lets him take her spot on the floor,
watches him pull the blanket all the way over his head. His arm
snakes out from under the covers for a moment and deposits his
watch in her hand.

"Ninety minutes, then get Ilse."

"Gotcha," she says.

She stands up slowly, carefully, and climbs over the couch.

The fire is so low it's basically hidden by the furniture wall,
and the main room is dim and cold. Even with her boots on, Riley
imagines she can feel the cold seeping through her soles. Her
ankle doesn't hurt anymore; adrenaline and terror seem to have
replaced any physical feeling she might conceivably have with a
sort of low static, which is a blessing. She taps her fingers as she
walks around the room, index to thumb, middle to thumb, ring
to thumb, pinky to thumb, and back. Sa, ta, na, ma. Dr. Temple
pats herself on the back somewhere in the distance.

She keeps her gaze moving back and forth as she walks the

room. One of the others is snoring softly, a high thin sound that scrapes at her already precarious composure. She looks outside. The dim gray light makes everything blend together. *That should make it easier to see it*, she thinks. She wonders what it will look like the next time it appears. Like Nelson? Like all three of them? The dog again?

What does it want, anyway? Riley chews this over as she paces. It tricked them. It pretended, it hid. When it was Asha, they didn't realize until it started to change. Is it getting stronger? How did it know how to behave? She thinks about the Animorphs books again. Slug-like aliens spreading their boneless bodies out over a person's brain, sinking into every fold and crevice, *learning* them from the inside out. Impersonating them so perfectly that even their parents couldn't tell. This thing isn't that good, but . . . it seems like it's getting better.

Riley hasn't decided yet if it's malicious. It could be fully amoral, just an organism surviving. A wolf will eat a lamb even though it's defenseless; it doesn't need to justify itself. What if this creature is the same way? It imitates them in order to preserve access to its food source. It hides in plain sight; it doesn't *want* to lose its shape. It doesn't want to reveal itself. So then why does it keep happening? Is it the stress of maintaining a human form? Is that why the dog keeps resurfacing? Maybe the mental strain is too great. Maybe the creature doesn't have a mind the way that humans do, and in human form it's forced to think like them. Maybe the constant barrage of thought weakens it, makes it angry, makes it *hungry*.

Or.

Or it's got more of a mind than they can even imagine, a fully formed consciousness that's actively trying to scare them by letting its mask slip. Wearing faces they know, pretending to be human only to make it that much more awful when it reveals itself. Twisting into horrifying shapes to make sure they're terrified when it consumes them. Hunting for sustenance, yes, but doing it in a way that purposely inflicts pain for . . . fun? She can't think of any animal that does that. She knows orcas fling seals into the air and it *looks* like they're just doing that to torture them, but it's actually supposed to break their necks when they hit the water. Almost humane, compared to getting eaten alive.

A small noise, like a footstep. Riley's head jerks up and she scans the room, nostrils flaring with panic. She sticks to her path, but as she passes the countertop her fingers drift across the marble until they find the knife block and draw one out. She holds the knife tightly, blade up, the way they do in the movies. She always thought it looked stupid—if you were going to stab someone, you'd want the blade pointing down, *Psycho*-style, right?—but she read somewhere that if you're using it for self-defense it's actually much more useful to have the blade up and out, so you can slash with it. She takes a few practice swipes at the air, hoping Ilse isn't secretly awake and watching her.

The sound comes again, a small, metallic tap. Riley moves toward the hallway she thinks it's coming from, stepping carefully over Luke's makeshift alarms. She pulls her phone out of her hoodie pocket, thumbs the flashlight on, and holds it out in front of her.

Another tap. She has a bizarre and almost uncontrollable urge to say *Marco*, see if anything says *Polo* back. The absurdity of it forces a tiny giggle from her lips, and then she freezes.

Two taps. It can hear her. It *must* be able to. She tilts her head, looks up and down the hallway. The emergency lights along the floor have been glowing ever since the power went out for the second time. They throw her shadow up while the overheads throw it down, and the result is a warped, spidery figure that capers alongside her as she moves toward the sound.

Tap.

She stops. She moves toward the wall. She leans in close, presses her ear against it.

TAP.

She shoves a hand over her mouth, bites down on her palm until she draws blood, does not scream. Breathes, chest hitching. *It's in the wall. It's in the vent.*

Why is it playing with her?

"Who's there?"

Nelson's voice floats down the hall toward her, small and hollow, like a recording made on a child's toy.

"It's me," he says. "It's Nelson."

She moves toward the sound. Her hand is shaking so badly that she turns the flashlight off; the flickering, frenzied motion of it is making her queasy.

"Nelson?" she whispers. There's a tap and a rustle, a faint metallic *ping*.

"Here," he whispers back. "In here."

She turns a corner and there is an air duct. This one is close to the ground, not a grate like the others but just a small vent, and she guesses it probably can't be opened. An exhaust port, or something. That's probably a thing. She kneels next to the little slots in the wall, keeping her distance.

"Nelson," she whispers again. "Is that you?"

"More or less," he says.

Riley shakes her head. "It can't be," she says. "I heard—your *bones*—she pushed you into—"

"I know," he says. "And yet."

She shouldn't believe this, *doesn't* believe this, but she so badly wants him to be okay. She so badly wants this whole thing to be some kind of fucked-up shared nightmare, a fever dream, something they'll all emerge from intact.

"Where are you?" she asks, the question coming straight from her heart, fully bypassing her brain.

"I know it sounds mad, but I think I'm underground," he says. His voice is tinny, like it's traveling toward her on a string.

"Is—are you—is she with you?" Riley doesn't know how to ask the only question she needs to ask. She *knows* the monster has him, *knows* he's gone, but she needs him to say it. Admit it. The words *Is it in you?* flicker across her mind in the Gatorade font she's always seen them in and she can't hold back a high, slightly manic laugh.

"She's in here," Nelson says.

"*Here* like, in the vents, or . . ." Riley grimaces. She can't do it. She can't bear to hear him say it. "Nelson, are you—I mean, you know—should we try to find you? Are you safe?"

"I don't think so, love." The words are soft, filled with such despair. "I feel—I feel myself, mostly, but there's . . . it's like there's something else in here with me. I can feel it—not thinking, exactly, but it's like it's *aware*. And I'm so *hungry*." His voice breaks. "I don't know how long it will take."

"Can you—I don't know, can you get into *its* head?" she asks, pressing closer to the vent, forgetting her earlier fear. "See how to get rid of it or something?"

"I'm afraid if I open that door . . ." Nelson sighs. "It'll come through, all the way, and I won't be able to close it back up."

Riley nods. She's chewing on her lip, and she knows it's bleeding, but she can't stop. She needs the clarity that comes with the pain.

"Tell me where you are," she says. "Maybe we can—we can figure something out, maybe if we keep you fed—"

The sigh is longer this time, more like humming, with the faintest tinge of amusement. Riley feels embarrassed and outsmarted, like her mom's caught her in a lie but hasn't told her yet.

"Why is it letting you talk to me?" she demands.

"Because it knows there's nothing you can possibly do to stop it," Nelson says. The metallic, childlike way he says the words reminds her: It has him, no matter how much like himself he sounds. He isn't safe. He might not even be *human* anymore. She thinks about the black tendrils curling through Greta's blood, imagines them spearing from one of Nelson's cells to the next. His outside might still look like him—might walk like him, talk like him, even think like him—but the thing spreading inside him wants to eat her.

"I have to go, Nelson," she whispers, closing her eyes against a fresh surge of tears. "I'm so sorry."

"Where are you going?"

"Back to the others," she says. "We're keeping—keeping watch—"

Terror twists the pit of her stomach.

"Oh no," she whispers, rising to her feet. "Oh, God, I left them—"

Nelson says something else, but she's already started sprinting down the hall, and she can't hear him over the thunder of her own frantic heart.

"Luke!" she yells, skidding into the common room, tripping on every single dish he's set up. She tumbles to a stop in a heap of cutlery and pulls herself up, clambering over the back of the couch, whimpering and reaching out like a newborn kitten. She's greeted, as she slides face-first onto the cushions, by a very aggravated Ilse.

"Are you okay?" Riley gasps, righting herself. She looks at Ilse closely, scrambles over toward the boys, who are somehow still asleep after her tumultuous return. "Are they?"

"Everyone is fine," Ilse says, eyebrows lifting. "Were you not keeping the watch?"

"No, I—"

Riley feels a blush rise to her cheeks.

"I was keeping watch," she says. "But I heard something, and I went to check it out, and I—it was Nelson. I talked to Nelson."

Ilse just stares at her.

"But then I realized that if it could, like, separate itself from him somehow, maybe *he* was talking to me while *it* was going to get you all, and so then I panicked and ran back."

"We haven't seen any evidence that it can split itself," Ilse reminds her.

"Aren't you the one who said we should assume it's bulletproof?" Riley shoots back. "Just because we haven't seen it doesn't mean—"

"I take your point," Ilse says, holding up a hand.

"He sounded so normal," Riley says. "I mean, not normal, he sounded like he was doing one of those tin-can-with-a-string things—"

She pauses at Ilse's expression. "Oh. Sorry. It's like, Americana from the fifties, people used to thread a string between tin cans and then they could talk to each other on them? I don't know. It's in the same area as, like, using a water glass to hear what your neighbors are saying inside their apartment."

Ilse looks like she's trying not to roll her eyes. "Go on."

"He sounded . . . tinny," Riley says. "Like a recording from the twenties, like, the earliest possible version of a recording. Like it was coming from a million miles away. And he said he was underground."

"Underground?" Ilse's voice is sharp and concerned. "How would he be underground? Are there parts of this facility we don't know about? I thought Dae found the blueprints, I thought we knew—"

"I think it's maybe just the ventilation system." Riley tries to placate her. "Like, maybe some of the vents go underground?

For . . . to save space? In the walls?""

"Or there's a subterranean floor of this facility that we don't know about," Ilse snaps, "which puts us at a disadvantage."

"We can't really get more disadvantaged, Ills," Dae says with a yawn as he rolls toward them. "Also, I'm awake now, because you're talking at literally full volume."

"Me too," mumbles Luke, still facedown in a cushion. He props himself up slightly. "Is it even possible for them to build stuff underground here? Isn't the ground, like, too frozen?"

"If they can drill down three miles to get to the lake, they can excavate a subfloor," Dae says. "I'm guessing."

"What if it's, like . . . a tunnel?" Riley asks. "I don't know why it would be, but what if—"

"To one of the other stations." Dae points at her. "Not a bad idea."

"But why?" Ilse asks.

"Inclement weather," Dae says. "If you have to get somewhere else and you'd get blown off your feet trying to get there aboveground, maybe there's, you know, contingency tunnels."

"We should look," Ilse says.

"But what do we do if we find it?" Riley looks at her. "If he really is down there, and it's with him—or in him, or whatever—then we're underground with it."

Ilse makes a face like she wants to argue about this but concedes with a small nod.

"What if we barricade it?" Luke sits up, hair disheveled. "What if we find the door and block it so it can't come back into the station?"

"*That* plan I like." Dae gets to his feet. "That feels like something achievable."

"Then we'll know it has to come back from outside," Luke continues. "We don't have to worry about the rest of the station or the vents or anything, just the outside doors."

"There are three doors," Ilse reminds him. "And the windows. That spreads us pretty thin."

"You said the windows were impossible to break," Riley says. Ilse glares at her and Riley guesses they're back to the *assume it's bulletproof* argument.

"Well, the three of us in here can all see each other," Luke says. "The back door is tricky, but I can—I'll take that one."

Riley feels a wave of anxiety buffet her at those words, but she tamps it down. *Later.* Right now they have a door to find. Unless—

"What if he was lying?"

The others turn to her.

"What if he just said he was underground because he knew that would trick us and while we're all fucking around looking for secret doors he's just—just climbing through the vents, waiting for us to walk underneath him?"

"He's not a Xenomorph, Riley," Luke says gently.

She glares at him. "Don't make fun of me."

His face twists. He looks for a moment like he might cry, and she thinks he's on the verge of apologizing, but then Dae interrupts.

"We won't know unless we look," he says. "There aren't enough dishes in this whole station for us to put booby traps at every potential place he could pop up, so we'll just have to walk back to back like we did outside. It's not impossible that he could still take us by surprise, but it'll be a lot harder for him."

They assemble themselves in a ragged circle. Riley still has her paring knife; Luke and Dae have a knife and a lamp each; Ilse has her switchblade. They start moving down the hall as one.

"What about the flare gun?" Riley murmurs, trying not to move her mouth. "I know it's not a real gun, but—it could hurt it, couldn't it?"

"I don't know where we left it," Dae whispers back. "The last time I remember us having it was outside, and I think Nelson might have put it back in his coat."

"Shit," she whispers. "Okay."

"Don't you feel like Rusk would have given Asha a weapon?" Ilse asks. Riley can see her head turning smoothly back and forth in her peripheral vision. "I know he doesn't care if she lives, but surely he'd want to at least make her *feel* safe, no?"

"We can check her room," Luke says. "On our way through the station. Just in case."

They move down the hall slowly, Dae at the head of the group leading the way, the girls and Luke staring out in the cardinal directions. Riley thinks briefly that it's amazing her phone battery hasn't died, then shoos the thought away as quickly as she can, afraid she's jinxed it.

They reach the vent where Nelson's voice spoke to Riley. Dae turns his head slightly, keeping his eyes on the wall, and asks, "This is it?"

"Yes," Riley whispers. "But he sounded like he was far away. Not right next to the wall."

Dae reaches out, fits his fingers into the little space. He pulls experimentally, watching as the plasticized wall bows out slightly. He steps back, then forward, then hefts the lamp over his shoulder and swings it like a baseball bat.

The lamp smacks into the wall with a dull, bouncy *thud*; matching cracks appear in the wall and the ceramic.

"If you break it, we have fewer weapons," Ilse hisses. "Stop that."

"What's the quickest way for us to figure out where he was?" Dae shoots back. He hits the wall again, deepening the crack, then rears back and kicks at it. The wall flexes against the impact. He puts the lamp down on the floor and starts hitting the wall with his shoulder, driving into it.

"Luke," he pants. "Aren't you a football guy—"

Luke puts his own weapons down and steps up beside him, and the two of them slam their bodies into the wall. Panic bubbles in Riley's throat, and she scans the hallway behind them, slashing the light back and forth too quickly. Ilse's hand settles on her shoulder and squeezes.

"Calm down," she says quietly. Riley is about to snap at her, but as she looks at her she realizes Ilse's terrified. Her face has the pinched, hunted look of someone on their way to a horrible punishment, but she's maintaining her composure. Riley knows it's not a competition, knows mental illness doesn't abide by any kind of rules, but she still feels a pang of guilt mixed with envy. Guilt that she's been assuming Ilse feels nothing, basically, and envy that she's able to function so well when she clearly feels so much.

"Thanks," Riley says after a moment. In her brief, intense consideration of Ilse the panic has ebbed away. She moves the phone in a smooth arc, lighting the hallway evenly, and Ilse nods.

There's a splintering sound and a yelp behind them and they turn to see Dae lodged halfway into the wall. The plastic has finally caved, but not enough; its edges are jagged and sharp and they have his shoulder in a pincer hold. He scrabbles at the wall, trying to find traction to pull himself out. Luke is pulling at his free shoulder, trying to wedge his arm into the wall behind him, but blood is already seeping through the back of Dae's sweater.

"There's"—Dae stifles a sob—"there's nothing back here. I can feel it, it's just insulation and wiring. Unless there's some kind of tiny crawlspace, this won't take us to wherever it's hiding."

Luke cries out as the broken wall snags his shirt and then his skin, pulling back and clamping his other hand over the scrape. "Shit," he whispers, staring at Dae.

Riley moves forward, tucking her phone into her pocket. She puts both hands on Dae's chest. "Hey," she whispers. "Look at me."

Dae's brown eyes are panicked and wild, rolling in his skull, but gradually he focuses on her. She keeps one hand on his chest, sends the other roaming up to where he's tweezed in between the pieces of the broken wall.

"You can't go sideways," she says. "You have to go down. It's got you wedged—you're like, pinched, do you see what I'm saying? If you try to go straight out you're just going into the other side of the pincer. You have to go down, where the tips of the pincer meet."

His breathing quickens and she presses her palm harder into his sternum. "Count with me," she says. Behind him, she can see Luke readying himself. He stands with his hands raised, fists open like a boxer, waiting for her signal.

"Inhale," she says. "Two, three, four. Good. Hold, two, three, four. Exhale, two, three, four. Good. Again."

She meets Luke's eyes over Dae's shoulder. *On the exhale*, she mouths. He nods. She fits her fingers over Dae's shoulder, at the base of his neck, and stares into his eyes. "Inhale," she says quietly. "Good. Two. Three. Good. Hold."

She shifts her weight onto her left foot, stabilizing the base of her left arm, tightening her muscles. She flicks a glance at Luke.

"Exhale," she says, and shoves down with all her strength. Luke's hands descend on Dae's shoulders and he pushes him down so hard that his own feet leave the ground, Dae acting almost as a fulcrum, and there's a horrible tearing sound and Dae screams and then the three of them crash down onto the ground.

"Oh fuck, oh God," Dae is babbling. "How bad is it, how bad is it—I can't feel my arm anymore, I can't—oh my God—"

"Keep breathing," Riley snaps, maybe a little harshly. She's not great with the sight of blood, despite all the horror movies she watches, and the amount of blood here seems to be multiplying exponentially.

"We have to stop the bleeding," Ilse says, jostling her as she kneels next to them. She pulls her sweater over her head and presses it into Dae's wound. "Put something underneath him, on the other side."

Riley is running out of layers, but she peels off her last long-sleeved shirt and hands it to Luke, who shoves it under Dae's shoulder. His skin is rapidly taking on an alarming gray tinge, and she's worried his breathing has slowed not because he's calmer but because he's going into shock.

Luke looks up at her. "Go get some water," he says. "And an actual bandage, or like, a rope or something—get, um, get the tie from Asha's bathrobe, if you can find it—we just have to have a way to keep this on him."

She bolts, noting with chagrin that they barely made it thirty yards from the common room before disaster struck. She runs into the pantry, the motion-activated light flickering too slowly into life as she rummages along the shelves. She remembers Greta telling them about a first-aid kit, somewhere during the tour, and she thinks it was—*there*! She snatches the beige metal box and flips it open.

A box of Band-Aids, a squeezed-out tube of Neosporin, and a stack of cotton gauze pads stare up at her.

"That's *it*?" she asks, the words shrill as they squeak out of her. "He gave us that fucking coffeemaker and *this*—"

She slams the box shut, throws it onto the floor, and kicks it into the corner. Then she changes her mind and picks it up. She runs back to the others, drops the box next to Luke, and starts down the hall in the other direction, toward Asha's room.

"There's basically nothing in there," she calls over her shoulder. "But there's gauze!"

She ducks into Asha's room and stays low, fumbling her phone out of her pocket to use as a flashlight again. She knows they could probably just turn on the overheads at this point, but if the noise she's making hasn't already drawn the monster's attention, she doesn't want to risk making herself more visible to it.

She finds Asha's bathrobe hanging on the edge of the folding screen and yanks the tie out of it. Something clunks as the robe falls back against the metal and she pauses, frowning. She puts her hand into one pocket, then the other, and finds nothing. She takes the robe off the screen and spreads it open on the floor of the bedroom. She can feel something heavy dragging at it as she lays it out, and she runs her hands over the weight, trying to find an opening in the plush fabric. Her fingers graze smooth metal and she forces them deeper into a seam, closes her hand around something and pulls it out. She stares down at it.

A gun.

"So she didn't trust Rusk as much as he thought," she murmurs. She inspects the little gun, as if she has any idea what it's supposed to look like, and then puts it very carefully in her back pocket. She stands up slowly. Her gaze falls on the mini-fridge in the corner.

10

"OKAY," SHE SAYS AS SHE ROUNDS THE CORNER. "I have—"

"What took you so long?" Ilse snaps.

Riley levels a glare at her that actually manages to silence her. She bends down carefully, setting down her armful of glass bottles. There's Coke, Sprite, some kind of gin-and-tonic combination, and water. Then she straightens up and pulls the gun out of her pocket.

"What the fuck?" Dae gasps from the floor. They've moved him so he's propped against the wall. "Where did—"

Luke shushes him and opens a bottle of water, presses it into his hand.

"It was, like, sewn into Asha's robe," Riley says. "Hidden. I don't know if it's loaded or anything."

Ilse takes the gun from her hand and inspects it, flipping various pieces of it back and forth, then finally tilts it above her hand and watches as bullets rain down onto her palm.

"Loaded," she says. "No safety."

"Jesus," Luke says. "No wonder she wanted to put that bathrobe on so bad."

Riley kneels next to Dae. They've taken his sweater off to get to the wound, and her shirt is tied around his shoulder like a weird backward cape. She eases it off, averting her eyes from the fresh ooze of blood, and starts placing cotton pads against his skin. It looks like he's been chewed, almost; the skin is broken and mangled but it's all still *there*. Like something closed its jaws on him slowly and then just sort of ground its teeth together. She swallows a wave of nausea and keeps going until all the gauze pads are gone and the wound is completely covered. She folds up her shirt, presses it against the meat of Dae's chest, where the wound is deepest.

"Hold this," she says. She folds Luke's shirt and presses it against Dae's back, mirroring the other one, and then she takes Asha's bathrobe tie and loops it under his arm and over his shoulder. She wraps it around until she can't anymore, until the dressings are pressed against him as firmly as possible, and then she ties a knot. She picks up his bloody, tattered thermal shirt and hands it to him.

"Put that on," she says. "You have to stay warm."

Luke is already taking another of his off, leaving himself in just a T-shirt. He hands Riley the still-warm henley. She helps Dae put it on, trying to move his arm as little as possible, stretching the fabric over his head. "Did you bring, like, a cardigan?" she asks hopefully. "Something that buttons, or zips, or whatever?"

"Yeah," he says. "In my room."

"I'll go," Luke says. He darts away.

"How do you feel?" Riley asks Dae, watching him nervously. She tells herself his color is better, but he still has deep shadows under his eyes that weren't there before.

"Tired," he says.

Ilse opens one of the bottles of Coke and slides it toward him. He takes it and drains half, then burps.

"Sorry," he says, wiping his mouth.

Luke reappears with a bundle of clothes, which he starts dropping at their feet. He gives Ilse and Riley a few new layers;

he has one of Dae's hoodies and one of his own, both of which get carefully zipped onto Dae. Then he shakes out a faded old sweatshirt and puts it on.

"Oh," he says, digging in his back pocket. "One more thing."

He tosses a bottle of pills into Dae's lap. "Painkillers."

Dae scoops it up and pries it open, shakes three of them into his palm and slaps them into his mouth. He drinks the rest of the Coke, then looks up at Luke.

"You meant, like, ibuprofen, right? Or did I just take . . . three Percocets?"

"I think it's aspirin," Luke answers. "It's definitely not anything that's going to do more than take the edge off."

"Great," Dae says. "Thanks."

They all stare at each other for a moment. Ilse opens the gin and tonic and takes a long drink, then sets it down and reaches for the Sprite.

"Tastes like a Christmas tree," she murmurs. "Piney."

Riley reaches for the bottle. The liquid burns her tongue and her throat, and it does taste like a Christmas tree, but when the heat hits her stomach it ricochets back up to her head and makes everything slower, calmer, softer. She takes another drink, then puts it on the floor. Luke picks it up and finishes it off. He makes a face.

"Of all the gin joints in the world," he starts, waving a hand. "They had to . . . make this one . . . gin."

Ilse hands him the Sprite wordlessly.

"Dae, how are you feeling?" Riley asks, scooting toward him. "Have some more water."

He takes the bottle and cradles it against him but doesn't drink. "What do we do now?" he asks, his eyes holding steady on hers.

"I don't know," she says. She puts her hand under the bottom of the bottle and pushes it gently upward. He relents and takes a sip.

"We should keep looking for a door," he says. "I got too excited about the vent-air-shaft-tunnel situation. But if there was a basement, it would have to be accessible without bashing the wall apart."

"Good point," Riley says. "Do you feel like you're up for that?"

"Probably." He looks at Luke. "Help me up."

Luke pulls him off the floor by his good arm, then inspects him. "We should have made a sling," he says, sounding almost disappointed in himself. "Hang on a sec."

He grabs Dae's discarded, bloody sweater and rips it in half where it's already torn, then ties the halves together. He loops the resulting mess around Dae's neck and tucks his arm gently into it.

"Ta-da," he says. "Now you won't move it accidentally."

Dae looks faintly skeptical, but all he says is, "Thanks, man."

"Let's keep moving, I guess," Luke says. He looks at Ilse. "Do you—this is probably a stupid question, but you know how to use that thing, right?"

She's still holding the gun. She nods.

"Okay, so you . . . be in charge of that, then. Riley, you keep an eye on Dae, and I'll be front guy, and we'll . . . just go, I guess. Yeah."

He schools his expression into something that doesn't look like fear, picks up the undamaged lamp, and walks into the dark.

Ninety minutes later, they've completed a search of the entire facility, including the closed-off half, and found nothing that could lead to a tunnel.

"Should we—"

Riley pauses as she contemplates what she's about to say.

"I've already been in the vents once," she finally continues. "Should I go back in and see if they go underground?"

Luke chews on the inside of his cheek as he thinks. "I don't know," he says. "I think at this point . . . I think at this point we have to start thinking about getting out. Going somewhere else."

"Right," Ilse says. "Even if the air vents do go underground, they won't connect to the other stations, which was sort of the hope, no?"

"Yeah," Riley says. "Yeah, you're right. So we have to—we've gotta figure out what the closest occupied station is. We have to find a radio signal."

They're back in the common room. Dae is stretched on the couch with his eyes closed, a faint sheen of sweat veiling his face. His breathing is even, but too shallow. He speaks without opening his eyes. "The relay in here doesn't work anymore."

"What?"

"I don't think the radio will work," Dae says. "I don't know if it's something Rusk did or it's just . . . actually broken, but we can't—it won't pick anything up."

"So we have to just . . . what, just walk to another station? And hope that there are people there?" Riley's voice goes thin.

"Look." Ilse has Asha's laptop open on the counter. "A map of the continent, including the other stations."

"But it doesn't say which ones are manned right now," Luke says, peering over her shoulder.

"So we go to all of them," Ilse says. "Until we find people, or a radio we can use to find people. We start with the closest and work outward."

"What about Dae?" Riley asks. "He can't—in this condition—"

"We can't split up," Luke says, his voice apologetic. "If we do, then we won't know—you know, whether or not—"

"If it gets me," Dae says with a sad half smile. "Yeah."

"We'll bundle you up really warm," Luke tells him. "We'll take the passenger snowmobile, and you can just sit on the seat and look pretty, okay? No problem. Easy peasy."

"Wait," Riley says. "Wait a second. Asha said the radio at the Leviathan Station wasn't working."

"Right," Ilse says, a slight tinge of *duh* coming through.

"But she was infected!" Riley says. "So maybe she was lying! Maybe it works after all, and we can go right there and be back super quick—"

"Or she damaged it," Ilse says. "To prevent us from using it."

"But if she was lying, would she have bothered?" Luke asks. "Maybe she thought it would be enough to keep us away, so she didn't waste her time disabling it."

"It's worth a shot, right?" Riley asks. "It's the closest station by like . . . miles."

"But there are no other stations in that direction," Ilse says. "So if we go there and the radio *doesn't* work, then we have to backtrack and go a completely different way." She turns the computer around so the rest of them can see the screen, zoomed in on a red dot labeled *Arcturus*.

"We have to go to the Arcturus Station," she says. "It's the closest one to the north, and there are more beyond it. The odds are best if we go in that direction."

"We can still go there," Riley says. "I'm just saying we should check at Leviathan first, it's so close, probably one of us could go alone—"

"No one goes anywhere alone," Ilse growls. "That is how it gets us. If you go to Leviathan Station alone, you come back, you say, 'Oh, the radio is broken after all,' how do we trust you any more than we trusted Asha? How can we be sure you are still *you?*"

"Should we vote?" Luke looks back and forth between them. "I think Ilse's right, I think we need to stay together, so that means the group has to decide where to go first."

Ilse's mouth flattens into a thin, angry line. "We don't know how much fuel we have," she says. "If we go to the Leviathan and the radio doesn't work, we're wasting time *and* gasoline, and—"

"All those for Leviathan?" Luke asks. Riley raises her hand. Dae raises his uninjured hand. Luke swallows and lifts his hand off the counter, leaving it hovering at about shoulder height. A yes, but a tentative one.

"And all those opposed?" Luke asks, his voice quieter. Ilse snaps her hand into the air, mouth twisting as she fights back a torrent of angry words. She blinks fast, shakes her head, and then folds her arms.

"Fine," she says. "Then let's go."

The sun throws rainbows through the ice in the air as they step outside. It's colder today than it has been since they arrived, and Riley feels like that means some kind of weather is coming, but she's probably being paranoid.

Ilse throws the barn door open with a grunt and makes a beeline for the fuel cans, lifting each one carefully, tilting them to see how much is left inside. She opens one and hands it to Luke. He jogs over to the passenger snowmobile, opens the gas cap, and pours carefully until a bubble of liquid pops back at him. Then he hands the container back to Ilse and swings himself into the driver's seat. The little Beanie Baby dangles from the ignition, and he twists it forward hard. The engine coughs and sputters and roars to life and he wrangles the snowmobile backward and forward again until it's pointing out of the barn. He pulls out slowly, carefully, until he's right alongside them.

"Dae," he calls over the rumbling. "Get on."

Dae slides into the front seat of the passenger sledge, holding his wounded arm against himself, curving the rest of his body around it. Riley sits next to him, careful to leave enough space between them that she doesn't jostle his arm. Ilse steps onto the runners behind them and loops one arm around the support posts.

"Ready?" Luke yells.

"Ready," Riley yells back, after a quick confirming glance at Dae.

Luke ducks his head to look at the compass mounted on the handlebars of the snowmobile, turns the wheels, and they're off.

The sense of déjà vu is overwhelming. The landscape slides past them, blue and brilliant and beautiful, and Riley almost can't believe she made this exact journey in reverse less than a week ago. Everything should be different; the things they've endured should be reflected by the wild. The ice should be pitted and gouged, yawning with crevasses to swallow them whole, cracking open to allow monsters to ascend from the depths. But the Antarctic keeps its secrets, its lovely face smooth and blank and close-lipped, and its perfection breaks Riley's heart.

The Leviathan Station looks like she remembers, squat and huddled behind a row of flags. Compared to the Victoria Station you could call it shabby, but to Riley it feels friendly. It feels safe.

"How are we getting in?" Luke asks, his voice too loud in the sudden silence after the noise of the engine.

"Asha had a key code," Ilse says, dismounting the sledge. "In case of emergency."

"How foreshadowy," Luke says wryly. "Lead the way."

Ilse crunches through the snow up to the door, pulls out Asha's phone—*when did she take Asha's phone?*—and taps at the screen. She moves the cover off the keypad and punches in the code. There's a whirring sound and a green light and then the submarine-style door next to her makes a sound like air being let out of a balloon. Ilse spins the wheel and pulls, and it swings open.

"UM," LUKE SAYS AS THEY STEP INSIDE. "DIDN'T Greta say this one was shut down for the season?"

"She definitely did." Riley moves farther into the room. The Leviathan Station is warm; the lights are on and the temperature control system is humming gently. "Maybe Asha turned everything on when she came to check the radio?"

"Do we still think she actually did that?" Dae asks. "Or did she just say she did?"

"She said Greta's blood was on the radio," Riley says.

Ilse pulls off her hat, forefinger tapping against her chin as she looks around. "But in the kitchen in the Victoria Station, when we came through, there was no blood anymore. Because it dissolves or decays or whatever. So she couldn't have left blood on the radio."

"Or maybe she was here, like, five minutes before Asha was." Riley looks at Luke. He's frowning, turning in circles, taking in the space. "What are you thinking?"

"If Asha came here, and Greta was here, she could have just . . . done it here," he says distantly. He's opening cabinets, looking in drawers. He pauses in front of the sink. "Eaten her, or whatever. Absorbed her. Then came back to Victoria."

He leans down, stares at the faucet. "What does that look like to you?"

Riley moves to stand next to him, peers down at the shiny metal. "A Slade logo."

"Why is there a Slade faucet in this station?"

"Because he owns it," Dae says. He's standing in front of the door they just came in. He lifts a hand, taps the plastic box mounted on the wall. A blue light blinks evenly from its top corner. "This is a Slade security system."

"Why would he buy more than one?" Riley asks.

"Maybe he wanted this one originally," Dae says. Riley can't be sure, but she thinks he's starting to sound weaker than he did earlier. "Maybe it was a tougher remodel than the Victoria."

"Maybe it's a backup station," Ilse says. "For when the larger expeditions come." Her lip curls. "Assuming he keeps his little charity act going."

"I still don't understand why Asha would have come here," Riley says. Something plucks at the back of her mind, a high thin sound like a string, and she can't figure out why. She starts walking around the edge of the room. "We're out of the station every day. It's not like she needs to hide from us. Or like, sneak around, or whatever."

"There's not enough gas in the barn for her to be going back and forth like that," Luke agrees. "The snowmobiles would be way closer to empty by now."

"I mean, are there supplies? Is there something here we don't have at Victoria?" She stops pacing. "Wait. What if there *are* supplies? What if there's medical stuff? We can—we can find stuff for Dae—"

She grabs Luke's hand and yanks him with her toward what she assumes is the bathroom. *Two and two, no one's alone*, she thinks. She slams the doors open on a dorm room, some kind of weather monitoring lab, and then—finally—a bathroom. She drops Luke's hand and starts rummaging through drawers.

"More gauze," she says, piling things on the floor that they might need. "More tape, more painkillers . . . yes!"

She holds up a small box. "Stitch kit."

Luke pales. "I don't think I can put a needle through someone's skin."

"Yeah, but I'll bet you Ilse can," she says. He smiles weakly. "Look, there's so much stuff in here. Disinfectant, butterfly bandages—oh, shit, Luke, there's antibiotics!" She snatches up the bottle. "Right? I've taken this." She thrusts it toward his face.

"Yeah," he says, squinting at the label. "Yeah, it's like, for strep."

"Well, it can't hurt," she says. She crams everything into her hoodie pocket and slams the medicine cabinet. "Let's go."

Ilse and Dae are talking quietly, heads together, and Ilse looks up as they come around the corner.

"We found a bunch of supplies," Riley says. "We can disinfect Dae's shoulder, stitch it up. And you should take, like, at least a few of these right now." She sets the bottle of antibiotics on the table in front of him.

"I don't think we should stay here," Ilse says, eyes flicking around the room. "I think we need to find the radio and get back to the Victoria Station. There's a storm coming."

"How do you know?"

Ilse tilts her head at the glass tube on the counter. "The barometer is dropping," she says. "Fast."

"So why don't we stay here?" Luke asks. "Wait for it to pass?"

"I can't explain it," Ilse says. Her shoulders hunch slightly, curving forward like she's trying to protect herself. "I don't feel safe."

"Is this because you wanted to go to Arcturus?" Riley demands. "Just because you were outvoted—"

"We never found the door," Dae says. His breathing is definitely more labored. Riley squints at him. *Isn't it?*

"What door?" Ilse snaps.

"Tunnel door," Dae says. "We never found one. But if there's a tunnel—"

"We can get back even in the storm!" Riley stands, elated, then falters as Dae shakes his head.

"No, you're right," he says, reading her face. "But that wasn't what I was thinking. I was thinking—if there *is* a tunnel—Asha wouldn't have had to take a snowmobile. She could have walked back and forth."

"Which would explain why we never even realized she was gone," Luke says. "And why there weren't any prints outside the station."

"If we can find an entrance on this side we can follow it back," Riley says.

"What if it's a dead end?" Ilse asks, pinning her gaze on Riley. "What if Nelson *wasn't* lying to you and he *is* down there somewhere? Then what?"

"If it's a dead end then he wouldn't *be* down there," Luke says. "It wouldn't connect to the Victoria Station."

"Then we wouldn't be able to get *back*," Ilse says.

"Okay, but if it *does* connect—"

"Then he could be down there!"

"Stop it," Riley says. Whispers, really. Her heartbeat in her ears is louder than her voice, and it's making her head feel hot and swollen. They don't hear her. She makes eye contact with Dae.

"We should at least *look* for it before—"

"There's no time for that, I'm telling you, there's a storm—"

"All the more reason to—"

"If we spend an hour looking for it and *then* spend an hour walking it and *then* find out it goes to some fucking abandoned—"

"But you also don't want to stay here, right? So what's the alternative? Pile onto the snowmobile and hope we beat the weather?"

"It's *not safe here*," Ilse growls, turning to face him.

"But the Victoria Station is? Full of fucking, you know, an entire monster?" Luke throws his hands in the air. "What are we supposed to—"

He cuts himself off with a disgusted shake of his head, and there's about half a second of silence into which Riley, who has been working herself up to interrupt them, literally *shouts*.

"The radio!"

It bounces around the room once and dies away. She flinches. "Sorry," she says, quieter. "I didn't realize you were, um, wrapping up. But we need to find the radio before we do anything else. Or argue about doing anything else."

The two of them look slightly chastened.

"Let's go," Riley says, unsure how she became the one in charge here. "Come on."

They spread out just enough to be able to search separately while still keeping each other in view. Riley circles through the kitchen, looking for anything that looks remotely radio-esque. Her thoughts keep returning to the tunnel, to the idea of the monster scuttling toward them under the ice. She has a flash of Nelson jabbing his drill into the ground, exclaiming *It went right down there!* The end of the video, when the creature had speared its arms down into the ice, pulling itself underground like some kind of pale, burrowing insect.

It wouldn't need a tunnel.

She stops walking and closes her eyes, trying desperately to connect the thought, to make the pieces click. Why does it matter whether the monster travels by tunnel? *Because it wasn't built for the monster. It was built for—*

The cuticle she hasn't realized she's been chewing on rips free, pulling a stripe of skin with it up to her first knuckle. The blood comes before the pain, and it keeps coming, and the pain never does, because there is no room for anything else in Riley's brain except for the thought she's just had.

"Luke," she whispers. "Luke!"

He emerges from the closet he's been searching and crosses the room to her. He pulls her hand away from her mouth—she's been sucking the blood off her finger, she sees—and tilts his head to see her eyes. "Are you okay?"

"What if there's a person in here?" she whispers. "In the Leviathan."

The Leviathan. The perfect name: something dark and hungry rising toward them undetected, jaws opening wide to swallow them. She shudders hard, wrenching her hand out of Luke's grasp, spattering blood onto the floor.

He looks at her, and for the first time since she's known him, she sees a flicker behind his eyes that she recognizes immediately.

"Don't," she says, hating the edge of bitter desperation in her voice. "Don't. I'm not fucking crazy."

"Riley," he says, putting his hands on her shoulders.

"The tunnel is for people!" Her voice spirals higher. "It's not for the monster. It's for people. He could have someone in here *watching* us, going into Victoria while we were *asleep*—"

"He had Asha watching us," Luke says softly. "He didn't need anyone over here. It's okay."

"I—he could still—there could . . ." Riley falters. The panic is ebbing away, and she realizes he's got his thumbs gently dug into the pressure points above her collarbones. She closes her eyes. "Are you fucking acupressuring me right now?"

"Is it working?"

She sighs. "Yes."

"I don't think you're crazy," he says. "I know you're not. But I can tell when someone's spinning themselves out."

"Your sister must hate you," she says. "Can't ever have a good panic attack without big brother interfering."

He smiles. "Yeah, she's mentioned that." He squeezes her

shoulders, then lets her go and steps back.

She wipes her eyes and takes a breath.

"Don't apologize," he says before she can speak. "It's a survival mechanism. Your brain is supposed to see danger. Yours just sees more than most."

A watery laugh escapes her lips. "Way more."

"You're protecting yourself, and you're protecting us, okay? Just try not to let it take over, and if you feel like it's going to, I'm right here."

Ilse clears her throat, and Riley realizes she and Dae have been standing awkwardly in the corner for some time now. *Great.* Now they'll have something to say, and—

"I think we found something." Ilse's voice is slightly softer than usual, like she's trying not to spook Riley, and normally she would take that personally, but for some reason it feels like she might genuinely be trying to help. Riley walks toward her, Luke following close behind. Ilse waits until they reach her, and then she turns and steps through a doorway.

"There's a second bedroom," Dae says, ducking under Ilse's arm as she holds the door for him. "And there's a teeny door in the corner of that bedroom. We didn't go all the way in—we didn't want to get separated—but it seems promising."

As he speaks they move through the dorm, through the connecting hallway into the smaller bedroom, and stop behind Ilse. She stares at the door for a moment, then grabs the handle and turns, pulling it open with a flourish.

"*Yes,*" she whispers, closing her hand into a fist. "Thank God."

The closet is full of blinking lights, and Riley doesn't know what any of them do, but she recognizes the little briefcase sitting on a table in the corner. Ilse opens it and flips a toggle switch. More lights come on, flashing sporadically before settling into a bright green pulse that Riley feels in her own veins. Ilse uncoils the cord, lifts the handset, and presses it to her ear.

"The line is open," she whispers, eyes filling with grateful tears. "I can hear it hissing."

"Now what?"

"Now we find a signal," Ilse says. "Just start turning that." She points at a knob in the corner of the briefcase. It looks like a radio tuner, which, Riley guesses, is basically what it is. She spins it slowly, carefully, watching Ilse's face to see if anything changes. Every few minutes Ilse says, "Hello? Is anyone there?" Sometimes her face seems to sharpen, to come into focus, but then it slackens and goes blank again and Riley knows she hasn't found it yet.

"It's not possible that there's, like, *no* signal, right?" she whispers in Luke's direction. "Like, there has to be *something* it can pick up."

"There should be," he whispers back. "I mean, at the very least—"

"Wait," Dae says. All of them jump and turn to where he's crouched in the corner. He holds up a small laminated card. "This is from, like, the early nineties," he says, "but it might work. It's a list of hailing frequencies for each station."

Ilse takes it from him and stares at it, then hands the receiver to Riley and starts fiddling with the tuner. Riley presses the handset to her ear.

"It's like *The Shining* in here," Luke mutters. "Is there a switchboard we can plug something into? Jesus."

Ilse holds up a hand and, at the same time, something clicks in Riley's ear.

"Hello?" she says, hand tightening on the plastic. "Hello, is anyone there? This is—we're at the Leviathan Station, hello—"

"Well, hi there, Riley," says a smooth, unfamiliar voice. "This is Anton Rusk."

Riley screams and drops the phone. The others look at her with alarm.

"It's Rusk," she whispers.

"*Rusk* Rusk? Anton Rusk?" Dae hisses. "What the fuck?"

She reaches for the dangling receiver, puts it back to her ear. Not all the way, not touching her, like something is going to crawl into her fucking ear, why is she always thinking about the goddamn Animorphs—

"—so I think we can come to a solution that's mutually beneficial," she hears.

"I dropped the phone," she says dully. "Start over."

He does something that sounds like a laugh, but there's no humor in it. His tone is carefully modulated, but she can feel rage simmering underneath every sound he makes, every slow inhale and exhale.

"Are you scared?" he asks.

"Fuck yes, I'm scared," she snaps. "You sent us here to die."

"That's where you're wrong, Riley."

"Stop saying my name."

"I sent you there to do something for me, and I want you to succeed," he says mildly. "It's better for all of us if you succeed."

"And what happens then?" Her hand tightens on the receiver. "We just come home and go back to our lives? Knowing that you have some sort of—of—shape-shifting monster locked in a box? Knowing that *you* know that we know that?"

"Who would believe you?"

She pauses.

"Look, yes, I admit it was a . . ." He clears his throat. "A dick move, if you will. To select you all specifically, for your . . . idiosyncrasies. But I never intended for you to die. It's just a little insurance. If you did decide to start talking . . . I needed people that wouldn't be taken seriously."

"Kids," Riley says viciously. "Fucked-up kids."

"If you insist, but I wouldn't call you that."

"You told Asha we were *expendable*!" she snaps.

He huffs. "Well, technically you are, and I'm *sorry* about that, I *am*, but just because I said that doesn't mean I don't *want* you to survive."

She looks at Ilse, whose ear is almost touching Riley's knuckles as she strains to listen. She mouths *lying*.

"You're lying," Riley says.

"Look, there's no reason you would know this, but—" He sighs. "There's a lot of paperwork involved if you die, and it's really much easier for me and for Slade overall if you just—"

"You motherfucker," Ilse snarls, grabbing the phone from Riley's hand. "You sick, evil—"

She pauses, listening. "Yes."

Rusk's voice is too quiet for Riley to hear without the receiver; all she's getting from here is a spidery crackle as the words slither into Ilse's ear.

"We have the radio," she says. "We'll call another station. We'll call every station on this continent. Someone will come for us."

Riley glances at Luke. He's watching Ilse, eyes shadowed with fear and anger.

"Bullshit," Ilse spits. "There's no way you could afford—"

She falls silent. She closes her eyes, defeat etched across her face. She puts the receiver to her chest, muffling the mouthpiece. "This isn't the only other station he bought," she whispers.

A hot stone drops from Riley's throat into her stomach, curdling everything inside her. She holds out her hand and Ilse puts the phone into it. She lifts it back to her ear.

"Your friend's not doing too hot, is he?"

"You know his name," she says.

"Oh, Riley, hi again. Ilse's a little combative for my taste, but I feel like you and I can talk."

"Fuck you." Her voice is weak and thready, her throat clogged with tears.

"Listen," he says. "I'm not in the habit of negotiating with children, but I have a meeting that I need to get to—"

"Fuck you," she says again. Slightly louder. Still too wobbly.

"Don't fucking interrupt me," he snaps. The fake friendliness in his voice is gone immediately, like it was never there. She feels like she's floating, tethered to the world by this phone and the voice coming through it, the voice of something that looks and sounds like a man but has no idea how to be a human being.

"You belong together," she whispers. Maybe she only thinks it. "You and that thing."

"Asha, unfortunately, is gone. Right? That's what it looks like, as far as the cameras go."

"Yes."

"So it's up to the four of you to get my creature into that box."

"We can't do that." *Don't cry, don't cry, don't cry. Do not cry where this man—this* thing—*can hear you.*

"You have to," he says simply. "Because if you don't, Dae-sung is going to die."

"What? No, he's—what? How—"

"This one is wired, too." Rusk sounds distracted, like he's checking email or something. Riley wants to reach through the phone and claw his eyes out. "They all are. I can see him. He's going into shock as we speak."

She risks a look at Dae. He's still in the corner; he's sunk down from his crouch into a loose puddle, leaning against the wall. He's breathing, but his eyes are half-closed, and his lips are pale.

"What do you want?"

"Go back to the Slade Station," he says. She fights the urge to say *Her name is Victoria.* "Get my specimen into the box. I'll know when it's done. I'll contact one of the other stations and have them send someone with medical supplies, and then I'll get you all out of there."

"I don't believe you," she whispers miserably.

"You don't have a choice, Riley. What are your other options?"

"We can—we can call—"

"Ilse tried that already, dummy. The only call anyone's going to answer on that bastard piece of ice is from me."

"We could go back to the boat—"

"And be picked up by whom, exactly?" Now there's humor in his voice, a sly cruelty curling around the edges of his words. He's enjoying this. "The crew that I sent to take you there in the first place? A different crew that also works for me? Tell me. *Tell* me. I'm dying to know."

"There's a storm coming in," she says. "Is there a tunnel?"

He laughs. "You better move quick."

"Is there a tunnel?"

"Quick, quick, like a bunny."

"*Rusk!*" she yells. "Is there a tunnel?!"

"*Run*, bunnies!" he says. The line goes dead in the middle of a laugh.

She lowers the receiver, lets it slip from her numb fingers.

"We have to go back," she says.

"Is this the wrong time . . ." Dae takes a wheezy breath. "Is this the wrong time to make a *Lost* joke?"

THE WIND WHIPS ACROSS THEM AS THEY EMERGE from the station, everyone wrapped head to toe in protective gear. The sun is still shining, but the air is hazy with ice and snow and it feels like it's getting cloudier by the moment.

"Wait." Luke pauses, one foot already on the snowmobile. "We need a flag line."

"A what?"

"A flag line," he repeats. "We have to put something up between the stations, so we can get back here if we need to. If the storm keeps up. There should be a cable spool somewhere."

"Where would they keep something like that?" Riley asks, turning in a circle. "They don't seem to have an outbuilding like we do."

Ilse steps into her snowshoes and starts carving an arc around the station to the south, where there are a few shipping containers tucked against the side of the building. She disappears into a cloud of swirling ice as Riley watches.

"What if it's not long enough?" she asks, trailing behind Luke as he searches the storage compartments of the snowmobile.

"There should be guide poles on the snowmobiles," he says. "If we run out of cable, we switch to those."

Ilse emerges, dragging something behind her. Luke jogs

toward her as best as he can in snowshoes, takes the other side of the handle, and the two of them hoist the spindle toward the group.

"It says six hundred yards," Ilse says. "I don't know if that's enough."

"We'll find out," Luke says grimly. He tucks the spool onto the sledge, under the seats, and pulls the end of the cable free. He walks it toward the station, making sure the spool spins freely, and weaves it through the door wheel. He yanks on it hard, testing the give, and nods with satisfaction. He comes back to the group and they all load themselves back into the sledge. Riley and Dae squeeze Ilse into the seat with them, and the three of them huddle together for warmth as Luke pulls away from the station. The radio is tucked under Ilse's feet, and the gun is clutched tightly in her mittened hand.

The sky is close and sullen, darker than it's been the entire time they've been here. It looks disappointed and angry, about to mete out punishment. Riley watches the cable spool out behind them and disappear into the white fog, wondering how they'll know when it's about to run out.

She leans toward Ilse. "What is a summer storm usually like here?" she yells over the wind and the motor.

Ilse turns her head and yells through her gaiter. "Katabatic winds!" she says, gesturing with her non-gun hand, swooping it down like an owl onto prey. "From high, to low. Up to a hundred kilometers an hour!"

"How much snow?"

"No!" Ilse says, shaking her head.

Riley stares at her. "What do you mean, *no*?"

"There's not usually new snow," Ilse says. "The wind blows it into the air, but it's not fresh."

Riley closes her eyes, hoping Ilse can't see them through the mirrored lens. She's so tired, and she wants to cry.

"Sometimes they can last for days," Ilse says. "Sometimes just a few hours."

"Great," Riley mutters.

"What?"

"Nothing," Riley says loudly. She huddles into her coat.

The sunlight breaks through the clouds every so often as they travel, and the wind pushes shadows across the ground faster than the snowmobile can move, and the whole thing has a very disorienting effect. Riley feels nauseous, but she can't keep her eyes shut for longer than a few minutes because she's craning her neck, staring into the void trying to find Nelson. Every time her eyes move in a new direction she's convinced he's about to emerge, loping toward them on all fours, tongue lolling out of a distended, snout-like mouth.

She shivers. Dae looks at her.

"You good?" he yells, giving her a thumbs-up. She gives him one back, feeling bad for worrying him. *Get it together, Kowalski.* She returns her gaze to the horizon. A small pink stripe separates itself from the spool and goes rocketing out of sight with the rest of the cable. Riley taps Ilse on the shoulder and points.

"Was that a warning?" she yells. "Pink tape on the cable."

Ilse lurches to her feet, lunges forward over the front of the passenger sledge, and thumps Luke on the back. He jerks upright, hand slipping from the throttle, and pulls the snowmobile to a clumsy stop.

"Jesus, what the hell!" he cries as he turns around in the driver's seat. "What—"

"Pink stripe on the cable," Ilse says. "What is that, fifty yards left?"

He sighs. "I think so. That's what it said on the spool, but who knows if that's even—"

"How close are we to the station?" Riley interrupts.

"I don't know," Luke says.

"Keep going," Ilse says. "Slower. When it runs out we'll leave the sledge and start with the guide poles."

Luke nods and turns back around. He starts the snowmobile and inches forward, barely faster than a brisk walk. Riley digs her nails into her palms inside her mittens and watches the snow fill the air.

The cable runs out fifty yards later, if the pink stripe is to be believed. They're still not back to the Victoria Station. Luke drives the anchor spikes down through the sledge runners and loops the cable around the back posts, then detaches the snowmobile. They help Dae get on first, Ilse and Riley on either side of him, and then Luke climbs up front. Ilse tucks the radio between them and Dae hooks his good arm around Luke, holding onto the zipper pull of his jacket. They start moving at a glacial pace. Ilse and Riley snowshoe alongside the snowmobile, doing their best to keep pace. Ilse plants the guide posts in the ground according to some internal measuring stick, steady like a metronome.

The first time the wind knocks Riley off her feet is about ten minutes later, and she lands so hard it knocks the air from her lungs. It pushes her, the smooth fabric of her coat sliding along the ice, and she rolls and grabs for something to hold on to. Something hits her in the back, then the head, then the ribs as she tumbles. Her mittens snag on tiny points of ice, but they're not big enough to hold her. She's trying to get her foot under her, get the points of her snowshoe into the ground somehow, but again she gets knocked backward, head thudding hard into the ice. She rolls once, twice, the sky and the ground smashing into her goggles, and then she slams into the runners of the snowmobile.

"Riley!" Luke is kneeling over her. When did Luke get here?

"When did you get here?" she asks him. He doesn't say anything, and she wonders if maybe she was only talking inside her head. That happens sometimes.

"Did she hit her head?" he asks. *Who is he talking to?* Ilse crouches down next to him.

"She rolled," she says. "A lot."

"Her lips are blue," he says. "How long has her mask been off?"

"Just since she fell," Ilse says. *Who are they talking about?*

"Come on, Kowalski," Luke says, and he holds out his hand. She figures she's supposed to grab it. She reaches for him and he pulls her to her feet, steadies her against the snowmobile.

"We're almost there," he says, staring at her. His goggles aren't mirrored, and she can see the concern in his eyes even through the blue-tinted lens. "Can you make it? Can you walk?"

"Yep," she says. She gives him a thumbs-up. His eyebrows draw together in the middle but he lets her go, gets back on the snowmobile and starts it up again. Ilse stands in front of her, pulling her gaiter up over her nose, resituating her goggles on her head. She holds up what looks like a pair of tights and hands one end to Riley. She folds both of Riley's hands around it and squeezes. Riley closes her hands on the fabric and holds tight. Ilse takes the other foot and starts walking, stabbing another pole into the ground as she does.

Movement warms her up, and her brain starts to thaw. She keeps getting distracted from her own footsteps by the fear that the snowmobile will tip over, pinning Luke and Dae. Ilse trudges forward, hunched against the wind, and Riley follows behind her, clutching her little leash. She suspects she'll feel embarrassed when they get inside, but she can't really remember why just yet. The wind shoves at her, bullies its way inside her coat, howls around her ears. She thinks about the noise the creature made in the video, that low croaking wail, and she wonders if they'll even hear it over the shrieking of the wind. She looks around, gripped suddenly with fear. *Where is he?* He has to be close. If he was going to the Leviathan Station to find them, they would have crossed paths by now. There's no other way he can get there, unless he took a longer route, and why would he have done that?

She tugs on the leash. "Ilse."

Ilse turns her head just slightly enough that Riley knows she hears her.

"Would he take the long way? To Leviathan? Is that why we haven't seen him?"

"The cold doesn't seem to bother him," Ilse says over her shoulder. "It's possible."

"Why would he do that, though? If he wants to get us?"

"I don't know."

"Do you—"

Ilse stops walking and Riley smacks into her back. They both sway for a moment, but neither of them fall. The snowmobile is parked in front of them, and beyond it—so faintly visible in the blowing snow that neither of them had noticed—is the Victoria Station.

Riley lets out a little involuntary cry of joy and grabs at Ilse, trying to hug her. Ilse takes her gently by the arm and pulls her forward, and they follow Luke and Dae into the warmth of the station.

"Home sweet home," Luke says with a sigh, peeling off his jacket. "We are so fucked."

"I'm going to try to get someone else on the radio," Ilse says. "He could be lying about the other stations."

She picks up the briefcase and climbs into their little nest in front of the fire. *It's still there*, Riley thinks, and then realizes they left it less than a few hours ago. She laughs to herself. Of course it's still there.

Luke turns to her and gently lifts her goggles off her face. "Hey, buddy," he says quietly. "You okay?"

He unzips her coat, lets her pull her arms free while he unwinds her scarf and gaiter, takes off her hat. He rubs her hands between his as he stares at her eyes. Ilse says something in German in the distance.

"Just making sure you aren't concussed," he murmurs, taking her chin and turning her face back and forth. "Eyes on me . . . good. You whanged yourself pretty hard in the face, there." He thumbs at her cheekbone. "Gonna have a pretty serious goggle bruise, I think."

"It's coming back to me," she says, somewhat sheepishly. "Definitely bounced my brain a little bit. That and the cold, I just . . . kind of went away."

"Well, we made it back technically unscathed," Luke says. "Maybe we can all rest for a minute now."

"Guys?"

They look up to see Dae, who's significantly grayer than he has been thus far, swaying slightly on his feet. Riley stifles a gasp and rushes to his side, helping him toward the fire. "Sit down," she says. She tucks blankets around him, touches his cheek. He's cold, but somehow clammy, and the combination sends a little warning chime through her.

"Let me get you some water," she says. "And, um, something warm. I think we still have that soup mix."

She climbs over the couch, feeling strangely rejuvenated, and starts looking for powdered soup. She wonders if it's just being warm again, or if she somehow has sunk so far into fear and exhaustion that she's circled back into adrenaline. Either way, she's going to take advantage of it. She finds the soup and puts the kettle on to boil.

"Luke, give him some more pills," she says as she runs water into a cup. "And this." She hands it to him over the counter. He leans over the couch and bumps it gently into Dae's shoulder.

"Hey, buddy," he says. "Stay awake, okay? You gotta drink some of this."

Dae nods slowly, closing his hand around the glass. He stares into it, eyes unfocused. Riley's warning bell gets louder.

"Dae—"

"*Shit,*" Ilse snarls. She grips the radio handset like she's about to throw it, then takes a deep breath and sets it on the floor in front of her. Then she buries her face in her hands. Riley can see her back rising and falling as she cries, trying to get herself under control, and after a minute of awkward silence as they all watch her, she sweeps her hands back over her hair and lifts her head to look at them.

"I got through to Arcturus," she says. "But Rusk got to them first."

"Shit," Luke murmurs. "What did they say?"

"He told them there was a biological outbreak," she says. "That we've contained the issue, but that the station is under lockdown. No one in or out."

"But—"

"They did say . . ." She wipes her eyes. "They did say he asked them to send an unmanned drone to do a supply drop, so he wasn't lying about that. But it can't fly until the storm breaks and . . . according to their instruments, that's not going to happen for almost forty-eight hours."

It hits Riley like a gut punch; she reels, putting a hand on the counter as if that will stop her from fainting. Her vision constricts, narrowing to a pinpoint. She crouches, bracing herself against a cabinet, willing the blood back into her brain. She listens as they talk.

"He doesn't have that long," Luke says quietly. "None of us do, with that thing roaming around. But he *really* doesn't."

"I know." Ilse's whisper is more of a hiss. "What are we

supposed to do?"

We have to put it in the box.

"What if we go to Arcturus? In person, on the snowmobile?"

"We can't make it in the storm," she says. "Besides, if they think we're carrying something—"

We have to put it in the box.

"—who's to say they won't shoot us on sight? To protect their crew, their station?"

"We have to put it in the box," Riley says to her knees.

"But maybe we could convince them," Luke says. "Bring a big white flag or something, a banner, something they could see from a distance."

Riley wraps her hands around the back of her neck, lacing her fingers together. She slides them up to the crown of her head and squeezes.

"They can't see at a distance because of the *storm*," Ilse snaps. "If any part of the plan involves going outside, it's not reasonable right now. Not now and not for the next two days. We have to wait. We have to take care of him here."

"We have to put it in the box." Riley lifts her head, reaches up for the counter, and pulls herself to her feet. She looks from Ilse to Luke. "We can't survive in here for two more days, not if the monster is just . . ."

"At large," Luke supplies.

"Yeah. We can't take care of Dae if we're constantly on alert for it. We have to get it contained."

"But then we're giving Rusk what he wants."

"Right now we don't have much of a choice," Riley says. The kettle does its breathy pre-whistle noise and she takes it off the burner, fills two mugs. She mixes broth powder into both of them, then takes a big gulp from one. It burns, but it helps. She carries them both over to the nest, hands one to Dae and then climbs down next to him.

He takes a sip. "How do we do this?"

Luke clicks the button on the wall that makes the fire bigger and sits down with them. "I don't know. But I feel like we have to talk about the fact that if we trap this thing, if Rusk gets his hands on it, then we're potentially unleashing whatever it is on the world."

"That's why we need to kill it." Ilse climbs over the back of the couch toward them, leaving the radio case open on the floor. Her nose and eyes are red. "That's the only way we can keep ourselves and everyone else safe."

"Safe from *it*," Dae says. "But then we'll still be stranded in the Antarctic at the mercy of a rich toddler whose toy we just took away. Not to mention, you know." He glances down at his sling. The water has helped a little, but his face still has a tinge of gray, like spoiling meat. "Pretty sure I'm going to become, uh, exponentially less helpful as time passes."

Ilse makes a quiet *shhh* sound, but her mind is clearly elsewhere. After a moment she lifts her head, steepling her fingers in front of her mouth. She taps her index fingers against her lips once, twice, three times. "What if we do both?"

"What do you mean?" Luke asks.

"Trap it," Dae says. "Then kill it. Right?"

Riley nods, turning it over in her mind. "We get it in the box, we tell him it's in the box, he sends help, we kill it at the last possible second."

"We get out of here," Luke says.

"Yes," Ilse says. "I am fairly certain the station is not wired for sound surveillance, only video. We let him see the creature in the box—*look, we did what you want*—and then we knock out the cameras or something."

"The supply drone comes, we get Dae fixed up," Luke says. "Even if he figures it out, if we get you past whatever infection is trying to take hold, we can make it a few more days. We can take the snowmobiles, go back to the dock. Shoot flares at the sky until someone picks us up."

"Get nuked from orbit," Dae says. "When he finds out the monster is dead."

"Okay, wait," Riley says. "Hang on. Hang on."

She shuts her eyes tightly, waiting for the thought to coalesce. "Okay," she says again. "We kill it."

"Yes."

"What do we think happens when we kill it?"

Luke sounds confused when he says, "It dies?"

"To its body," Riley says, eyes still closed. "What happens to its body?"

"If it's like the cast-off parts, it will disintegrate," Ilse says, excitement sparking across the words.

"And he doesn't know that," Riley says. "Even if those cameras are super high-definition, the floor in the kitchen is too dark for him to be able to see blood evaporating off of it."

"Too dark and too shiny," Luke agrees. "So we kill it, and it dissolves or whatever, and . . ." He looks at her expectantly.

"What's the next best thing to having a live monster to do tests on?" Riley asks.

Luke's mouth twitches as it clicks in his head. "Having a dead monster to do tests on."

"So we tell him we killed it," Riley says. "And *then* we tell him that we hid it."

Ilse's face splits in a truly unsettling smile. "*Yes.* We can tell him we'll give him the coordinates of the burial location only when we're safely home."

"That's not bad," Dae says thoughtfully. "He wants it alive, but he might settle for it dead if that's his only chance at it."

Luke's face clouds. "What if it doesn't dissolve, though?"

Riley looks at him questioningly.

"If there *is* a body," he says, "then he has the body. And it might not be as useful as a live monster, but still, who knows what he'll be able to do with it?"

Riley turns this over in her mind while she tries to find the least selfish way to phrase her answer. She doesn't want Rusk to have the creature either, but . . . she wants to live. She wants all of them to live.

"First things first," Ilse says. "We can make a decision once we trap it, but first we have to trap it." She rubs her hands over her face, claps them against her cheeks. Her gaze is hard and direct, and there's a bleak depth in her eyes that makes her look so, so old. "And if we're going to set a trap, we need bait."

13

"THIS FEELS . . . LIKE IT'S NOT GOING TO WORK," Riley says as she puts another slice of ham on the floor of the hall.

"What has it said more than anything else?" Ilse asks around a mouthful of her own deli meat. "Hungry."

"Fair enough," Riley concedes. "It just seems . . . very cartoonish."

"It's a monster that can change its shape," Ilse says. "Cartoons will probably help us more than anything else right now."

"*That's* what it is," Luke says. "Oh my God. Clayface."

"Clayface?"

"I remember that one," Dae chimes in from the room beyond them. He's standing, slightly hunched, in front of the glowing keypad etched in the glass of the box, phone tucked into his sling so the camera points forward. "God, when Asha's arm shot out across the room—"

"Exactly," Luke says.

"Explain for the people who were a different brand of nerd, please," Riley says as she flattens another piece of ham to the floor. She's hoping that if they're difficult to pick up it will buy them more time.

"He's a Batman villain," Luke says.

"I should have known."

"He's like, an actor, right?" Dae pokes at another few buttons,

155

leaning in a bit to create enough pressure that they register his touch. "He has this weird face lotion because his face got, uh, burned up? I think? And so he puts his face on every day with this weird lotion, but then he uses too much—"

"No, no, the bad guy makes him drink it—"

"Right, right, but then his whole body just sort of becomes this squishy—"

"Like a big huge mud-man," Luke finishes. "And he can turn into anything, and impersonate people, and at one point I feel like he has just, like, lobster claws? Am I remembering that right?"

"It rings a bell," Dae says. He wipes his forehead with the back of his good arm.

"But his base form is always the weird clay stuff," Luke says. "So like, when Greta kept trying to be a dog again, that's how he was, but with the clay."

"Right," Riley says. "I'm out of ham."

"Me too," Ilse says.

"Well, that's great," Dae says, "but I still can't get this box open."

"Did you try the key code for the station?"

There's a long silence during which Riley regrets asking, calling attention to what she's worried is Dae's continuing deterioration. He stares at her for another moment, then turns slowly back to the panel on the box. She watches him press the keys laboriously, wanting to do it for him, knowing he wouldn't let her. There's a click and a *whoosh* and then Dae says, "Son of a *bitch*."

"Sorry," Riley says.

"No, I mean, it's—good, objectively, I'm just—I don't know, my head's foggy, you know?"

"You're tired," Luke says. "We all are. Don't sweat it."

He meets Riley's eyes, and the two of them silently acknowledge: It's probably more than that.

"Yeah, well. Okay. The box is open." Dae adjusts his phone and walks toward them, looking slightly embarrassed. "Sling another container of ham over here."

Riley walks toward him, prying open their last pack of cold cuts. She hands him half the stack and they distribute them across the floor in a wide arc, overlapping the edges, leading directly into the box. Riley goes inside it, sticks a few pieces to the rear wall. The blue light unnerves her, as does the quiet, staticky hum. The hair on the back of her neck stands up, and she hurries to rejoin the others.

"How do we close it?" she asks. "Does it swing shut or do you have to enter the code again?"

"We just slam it, I think," Dae says. "But we have to figure out where to hide so it doesn't see us until it's too late. The ham will distract it, and I think probably it'll concentrate on that smell more than ours, but still, if it sees us it might guess something's wrong."

"Or kill us," Riley says.

"Or both," Ilse says.

"On that note," Luke says. "Let's find some blankets. I might have an idea."

"*This* feels extremely cartoonish," Ilse grumbles as they survey their handiwork. The box is now opaque, draped in the giant beach towels that live in the closet outside the steam room. The plan, as far as Riley can tell, is for them to just . . . stand behind the box until the monster goes inside it, then leap out and slam the door. Like a very, very badly planned surprise party.

"There's nowhere else in the room to hide," Luke reminds them, throwing another towel over the top of the crate. "If it can't see through the box, it can't see us."

"We should just put the towels over ourselves," Ilse says peevishly. "Stand in the corners and pretend to be ghosts. We can scare it into the box."

"I know you're being shitty, but honestly, that's plan B," Luke says. "Come on, get back here."

She sighs heavily and joins the rest of them in the small space between the back side of the box and the rear wall of the room. The blue light doesn't shine through the towels, which Riley is grateful for. She doesn't want that weird humming on her skin again, even for a moment. Even through glass.

"Dae, can you get back into Asha's email?" Luke asks. Dae is sitting on the floor, back against the wall, feet braced against the box, propping his phone up to record himself. Asha's laptop sits next to him.

"Probably," Dae says. He slides the computer into his lap slowly, and Riley is struck again by how clumsy and deliberate his movements have become. *He needs to rest,* she thinks. *We all do.* "What am I doing with it?"

"Tell Rusk to tell Arcturus to send the drone," Luke says. "We want it ready to take off the second the storm stops. Tell him this thing is gonna be contained any minute now, and we're not gonna let him see it until we have some real fuckin' drugs for you."

Dae nods and starts typing. The computer chimes once, then again in quick succession. Then a bell starts ringing.

"Shit!" Dae whispers, clicking frantically. "He's trying to video chat."

"Close the window," Luke says. "Close it, close it—"

"It's not letting me!" Dae hisses. "Shit shit *shit*—"

"Just close it," Ilse snaps. "Close the laptop." She reaches for the computer, but then that silky, faintly Scottish-accented voice curls into the air.

"Hello again," Anton Rusk says. "Nice to actually see you. Looking a little worse for the wear, certainly, but the fire in those eyes is still bright. Scrappy little underdogs, the lot of you. Easy to root for."

Dae stares at the screen, unable to move. Riley sits down next to him, leaning into view so Rusk can see her.

"We're doing what you want," she spits. "We set a trap for it."

He makes a noncommittal sound. "Yes, the ham trap, I saw. Not perhaps what I would have expected, but you are children, after all. I'll be very interested to see how it goes."

"Is it in the station?" Riley demands. "You can see everything, right? Tell us where it is."

He chuckles. "I'll do you one better," he says. There's a sliding metallic sound somewhere in the distance. "One of the upgrades I made to this station was blast doors. Only able to be deployed remotely."

Riley glances at the ceiling. There's a thin seam running along the side of the room where the door is.

"What are you doing?" Dae asks.

"Oh, you know," Rusk says, eyes focused somewhere behind the camera. "Closing it in, forcing it toward you."

Sssshhhlunk. Louder now, closer, making Riley think about afternoons at the mall that bled time away until the stores were closing in the slanted sunset light, girls in ripped jeans and halter tops sliding down those metal doors.

"If you could trap it the whole time, why didn't you just *do* that?" Luke snaps, still watching the door.

Rusk arches an eyebrow. "Is that Wheeler?"

"Yeah, it's me, asshole," Luke says, crouching next to Riley. "God, I hate your hair. Ilse, you wanna come say hi? Maybe 'fuck you'?"

Ilse flaps a hand at him and stays where she is, peering around the edge of the box, waiting for the monster.

Rusk just smiles. There's another metallic slam, even closer now, and Riley clamps her hand around Luke's wrist. He leans closer.

"So?"

Rusk inclines his head slightly. "So?"

"The doors," Luke says, and a sliding screech punctuates his words. "Why didn't you just do that in the first place?"

"I can't airlift the entire station out of there," Rusk says. He crosses one leg over the other, folds his hands on his knee, leans back. "I need it fully contained."

"In something you can disguise," Dae says. "Asha told us."

"The box is roughly the same size as the sample containers, true." Rusk nods, like he's proud of Dae for making this observation. Riley wants to scratch him.

"Seems like you could have built some kind of little monster-wrangling robot," Luke says. "I mean, you have the one that can almost do a cartwheel now, right? Surely this is within your reach."

"Try to remember you're talking to an adult," Rusk says acidly. "An adult who, at this point, is your only chance of survival."

"Fuck you," Luke says languidly. "We've got a better chance trying to talk that monster into changing its mind about eating us than we do of convincing you to get us out of here."

"Perhaps if you start making yourselves useful—"

"I mean, you had so many options," Luke continues, as if he hasn't even heard Rusk. "You could have advertised for like, a teen bounty hunter squad." Rusk's fingers tighten on his knee. He's not used to being interrupted. "I'm sure they're out there. Then if they got killed you could just be like, 'Well, it's part of the job.'"

"And then everyone in the free world knows I'm looking for something dangerous," Rusk snaps. "Think. You think Richie Bannon of Bannon Robotics is going to just watch me sending recovery teams to the Antarctic and not come after me? He's been trying to get a military contract for *years*."

Wait.

"You still don't even know if you can use this thing as a weapon!" Luke protests. "You've only seen one video!"

He can't risk drawing attention to this.

Rusk's voice goes low and cruel, almost taunting. "You've seen it up close," he says. "What do you think?"

"Look, you asshole—"

He can't do anything to us until he's got the monster.

Riley pokes her head farther into the frame. "Hey," she says. "I'm having a bit of a thought."

Rusk snorts. "I'll alert the media."

Riley digs deep, finds a smirk, plasters it on her face. "How weird, that's actually . . . that's actually what my thought is about. Because you won't, will you, Anton? You can't." She turns the computer fully toward herself. "We're here, with your monster, and you're not. So we're the only ones who can put this thing in your stupid little box. You with me?"

His eye twitches. God, this camera is good. *Freaking SladeTech.*

"So if we *don't* put it in your box," she continues, "if we let it go, or it kills us, or *you* kill us, then what? Then you have to tell the media how one of us went rogue and killed everyone, and *then* you have to either wait until no one's paying attention to you anymore—which could take years, you know, and in the meantime Richie Bannon is out here under the radar, poking around, scooping up everything you left behind—*or* you say fuck it, you come right back, and *then* you have to explain why you're immediately trying to send *more* unstable teenagers *back* to Antarctica on a clearly dangerous research expedition. At which point Richie says to himself, 'Hey, it seems like Anton is really interested in that whole Antarctica thing, maybe I should check that out.'"

She pauses, trying not to pant. Her heart is beating so fast it must be audible, and she's a tiny bit worried she's about to black out, but when she glances at herself in the little video chat window she looks surprisingly calm. A little prickle of something like pride spreads across her chest. She takes a deep, full breath and the dizziness recedes.

"Or," she says, as if it's just occurred to her, "I guess you could just send a recovery team. You know, like you were trying to avoid in the first place. I'm sure it'll be way less conspicuous, especially when it comes with a side of mysteriously dead or missing teenagers, right? Richie Bannon will be all like, 'Welp, nothing to see there! Back to my robot dog!'"

Next to her Luke makes a muffled choking sound that might be a laugh. She ignores him and barrels on.

"So here's the way I see it, Anton." She clamps her hands onto her thighs, trying to stop their trembling from traveling up her arms and into her brain. "You can ask us nicely to try and get your monster into the box, and then you can tell Arcturus to send us those fucking medical supplies *now*, and then *you* can send the boat back for us and get us the fuck home. Or you can start planning for a new expedition once everyone forgets about this one in, oh, five years or so. I'm sure your monster will still be around. It just might not be yours anymore by then."

She feels like she's just run a marathon. She ducks her head and gasps for air, hoping her hair is shielding her face from Rusk. When she's reasonably sure her nostrils won't flare as she tries to control her breathing she looks back at the screen.

Rusk is definitely pissed, even though he's hiding it pretty well. He's breathing faster than she is. His cheeks are very slightly pink. His pulse is visibly jumping. And his eye is still twitching.

"Your eye is twitching," she says.

"You little cunt," he hisses, slamming himself upright in his chair. "Do you really think I don't have a backup plan? And a backup plan for that backup plan? You stupid, pathetic—"

There's a noise from the hallway. Riley looks up, then back to the computer just in time to see Rusk's eyes flick sideways. His face twists into a smile.

"Here's Johnny," he singsongs, and severs the connection. Riley slams the computer and jumps to her feet.

"And now he's ruined *The Shining*," Luke says, right behind her. "I *cannot* wait to tank this guy's career."

Dae grabs at the back of Riley's leg. She looks down at him. "Stay there," she says. "It's okay, we're hidden."

"That was awesome." His eyes keep falling shut. "You're a badass."

She takes his hand and squeezes it. "Stay with me, okay? It's almost over."

"It's coming!" Ilse stage-whispers, waving the rest of them back behind the box. They crowd into the little space and watch her as she peers out the door, down the hallway. She darts back to them and squeezes in beside them. Luke pulls the extra towel over them and they wait, breathing as quietly as possible, for the monster.

It doesn't sound right as it walks toward the door. It doesn't sound like a person on two feet. Riley thinks about a video she saw once of a vampire bat on a treadmill—which sounds like something she invented in a fever dream, now that she's reminded of it—but the bat could run on all fours, almost the same motion it used to fly, front limbs reaching and scooping forward, pulling back, the back legs jumping up to meet them.

As it walks down the hall, the monster almost sounds like it's doing that.

It's staying remarkably quiet. Maybe it only talks when it's around humans. *Greta did bark at one point, didn't she?* It has to learn how to communicate with what it's pretending to be, after all. A wet, snuffling sound reaches them every minute or so as the creature scrapes the meat up off the floor piece by piece. When it finally rounds the corner into the room it's still audibly chewing. They listen, staring at each other in the faint light that filters through the towels, wide-eyed and silent. The creature moves toward the box and then steps inside. One limb, another, then another. The sounds of its passage are muffled now, but they can feel its footsteps vibrating in the glass of the box. Riley presses one hand against the towel-covered glass and flinches when something scrapes gently against the surface. The monster has found the last few pieces of ham, it seems, and that means that now is their chance.

"Luke," she whispers, barely more than a breath. "Go."

Luke darts out from under the towel and slams his body into the door of the box. The creature makes a startled, almost birdlike noise as Riley rips a towel off the crate, hoping to distract it while Luke shuts the door. Her eyes fall on it for the first time since it was Asha, and she presses both hands over her mouth to stifle a scream.

The monster stands on two legs, mostly, but its left arm is so long that its hand brushes the ground, almost like a walking stick. The other arm is almost comically normal, human-sized and -shaped. It looks like it's still wearing Nelson's watch.

"Riley?" Its voice is muffled as it presses its face against the glass. Literally, flat against the glass. "Is that you?"

She stares at it, still fighting the urge to scream. She takes a step back, then another, until her back is against the wall.

"Is that—"

Luke drives his shoulder into the glass door again and it's almost closed, but at the same time a siren starts blaring, and all hell breaks loose.

A strobe light flashes from somewhere above them.

"We're doing what you wanted!" Riley screams at the ceiling. She knows Ilse said the cameras don't have sound, but the alarm is shredding her brain and she doesn't know what else to do. "We're *fucking getting it, you absolute*—"

The alarm stops wailing for approximately two seconds, and then is replaced entirely by Anton Rusk's voice.

"Did you really think I wouldn't have this room wired?" he says, loud as God. "This room, of all rooms?"

Luke makes a strangled noise and stumbles back, away from the box.

"I want it to know my voice," Rusk says. "I want it to get used to its new master."

Riley spits a laugh. "You—"

"You were right about everything you said, you know," he says, the words shaking the air around her. "That's why I've changed my plan."

"A . . . Anton?"

It's almost, almost, *almost* Asha's voice. Riley looks at the creature, still standing inside the box in the awful blue light. Its skull ripples, the bones shifting and bending under the skin, and for a moment it's almost Asha's face.

"*That's* interesting," Rusk says. "That's *very* interesting."

"Anton," it says again. Asha's face starts to droop, sagging down off the bone as Nelson's face fights to reassert itself. The voice wavers. "What did you do?"

"Asha, sweetheart, is that you?"

The creature takes deep, rasping breaths. It puts a hand on the glass, right in front of Riley's face, and she's transfixed by it. There's something . . . something *wriggling* under the skin of its palm, like it's got a handful of maggots, and the bones of its fingers don't seem fully solid. The whole thing is too big, and slightly translucent, and the veins are too dark. One finger lifts to tap, tap, tap against the glass, and even as she watches, it starts to lengthen and taper until it's a pale, greasy-looking claw.

"Is . . . this . . ." The monster stares at its own fingers, hypnotized by their motion. "What . . . you . . . wanted?"

"Do you want me to tell you my new plan?"

Rusk's voice startles Riley from her own hypnosis. She looks around for Luke and finds him standing pressed against the wall, facing the still-open box. His eyes are closed, lashes flickering. Riley walks toward him.

"I think you'll like it, actually. It's not very elegant, but it's simple, and that seems to work for you."

Riley says Luke's name softly before she puts a hand on his shoulder so she doesn't scare him.

"Luke," she murmurs. "Luke."

He opens his eyes for half a second and closes them again. For a moment she thinks he doesn't recognize her. "Strobe," he says through gritted teeth.

Rusk chuckles. "I actually forgot about that. That's a fun coincidence. Focal seizures, right? Sorry, Wheeler, that one's on me."

There's a slick, lumpy sound behind them, and she turns away from Luke to see the monster emerging from the box. It has one hand over its face, and the other splays flat on the floor as it propels itself. Its knees haven't decided which way they want to bend, bowing in all directions as it propels its weight forward. It's shedding again, skin slipping off of it in long wallpapery strips as it slides along the floor, even though it's just eaten something like three pounds of sliced ham. Riley almost feels bad for it.

It swings its head to one side and sees Luke, and its face cracks open into a horrifying smile. Its *gums* seem to be melting. They have the same insubstantiality as its fingers, the translucence; the teeth look like they're drifting away from each other. Some of them are small and blunt, and she almost recognizes Nelson's chipped front tooth, but the others are all jagged. Some are pointy like wolf teeth, but some just look *broken*. It grins at Luke, and then it licks its lips, and all of Riley's sympathy flees.

"Hey," she says. "No, hey, look at me."

It ignores her and takes a step toward Luke. The strobes are still flashing.

"So my plan," Rusk says. "Are you ready?"

She reaches out to one side, snags the edge of one of the towels. She can see Ilse in the doorway bending sideways, slowly, reaching one hand into her boot. They lock eyes.

"My *plan* . . ." he says, voice filling the room, demanding their attention. He might as well be stomping his foot. "Is . . ."

The strobe stops flashing.

"To let it kill you."

Riley screams and throws herself at the monster.

The towel catches over its head and she yanks down hard, hoping to knock it off balance. She's trying to keep her body away from it, not letting it touch her, but its arm is so fucking *long*—

"Nooo," it howls, clawing at the towel over its face. The sound is filled with such distress. Riley steels herself and pulls harder, trying to pull it down to its knees, and then it makes a sound like knives on metal and pitches forward in front of her.

Ilse stands behind it, and her blade is buried in its back.

"Thank you," Riley gasps, trying to catch her breath. "No, don't—"

Ilse is bending to retrieve the knife.

"You can't touch it," Riley says. "I'm sorry."

Ilse pulls her hand back, a dazed expression on her face. "Right."

"*It's going to kill you,*" Rusk hisses. "It's going to kill you and eat you and then I'm going to come there *myself* and get it the way I should have in the first place."

Riley ignores him as best she can, touches Luke lightly on the chest. "It's okay," she says. "They're off."

He doesn't seem quite in control of his body yet, and his eyes are dazed when they open, but he recognizes her, she can tell. She lets out a tiny sigh of relief.

Then there's a clang and a whir and the blast door starts to slide out of the ceiling.

"Fuck!" Riley yells. "Come on, come on—"

"You psychotic little hood rats are ruining everything," Rusk growls. "I won't allow it."

She yanks at Luke with one hand, grabs at Ilse with the other, wondering how *she* became the functional one in this bunch, wondering even more where the *hell* Dae is because now she's looking toward the back of the room where he was and he's not *there*—

"I'm so glad it's going to kill you in here." The words drip with vicious glee. "I get to see it *and* hear it."

Riley lets go of Luke, shoves Ilse with both hands, and her confusion seems to lift; she throws herself forward through the rapidly diminishing opening into the hallway. Then Riley seizes Luke by the shoulders and pushes with all her strength, sending him stumbling into motion, and he trips and sprawls through the door but he's out, he's on the other side. She takes one last frantic look at the room before she flings herself onto the floor and wriggles through the opening and then she's through, the door thudding down behind her, lungs whistling as she gasps for air. She lies there for a moment staring at the ceiling, the steady weatherproof plastic-domed light. The door whirs, locking itself to the floor somehow. Something about the room tugs at the back of Riley's mind, something important. She tries to review her mental snapshot of the space—

"Hey," Luke says softly, his voice filled with concern. "Are you okay?"

Riley rolls over and looks at him, follows his gaze to see Dae slumped in the far corner of the hallway. There's enough blood on the floor for her to guess that his wound has reopened, and that he's been crawling. He tries to smile, but it's more of a twitch in the corner of his mouth.

"I ran," Dae says. He stares into his lap, shame wreathing his features. "I'm sorry. I was—I got scared."

"That's okay, Dae," Riley says, kneeling in front of him. "You're hurt, and you've been going nonstop for days, and—"

"Take this," he says, gaze lifting to meet hers. He presses a small, square tile into her hand. It's tacky with blood. She swallows hard and tucks it into her bra, the only place she can think of where she won't possibly lose it.

"It's everything. Everything that's happened so far. The story. Video."

"Dae . . ."

"It syncs automatically," he says after a labored breath. "You just click the thing and wait for the light, and the phone will . . . the phone will tell you it's . . ." He exhales, and something inside him rattles.

"You should keep it," she says, knowing what he's doing. Trying to stop him anyway. "For when we get home."

He manages a smirk this time. "When we get home you can . . . give it back to me."

"Okay," she whispers, touching his cheek.

He grabs her hand and pulls her closer, until his lips are almost touching her ear. "In my room," he whispers. "My notebook. My . . . brother. Email him . . . everything."

"We need to get somewhere safer," Luke says, getting slowly to his feet. He keeps looking back and forth, up and down the hallway.

"It's locked in there," Ilse says, gesturing vaguely at the metal door.

"It's not locked anywhere until it's inside that box," Luke says.

"It could be dead," Riley says hopefully. "Ilse got it pretty good."

"I don't think it's dead," Luke says. "Can we just—can we please just go? Somewhere?"

Riley turns back to Dae and asks him wordlessly if he can get up. He holds his uninjured arm out to her and she stands, then lifts him to his feet and braces him with her body. She tucks herself under the crook of his good arm and lets him use her as a crutch, and the four of them start making their way down the hall. As they move she looks up at the ceiling again, thinking about the cameras, and then she reaches out, slaps the button on the wall, and plunges them into darkness. The emergency lights stay on, barely illuminating their feet. She looks at the others. "I don't know if he's got night vision up there, but maybe now he can't see us. Either way, we need to get to the dorms. We can push the beds in front of the door."

"We should have the radio," Ilse says. "Just in case."

"Shit, okay. First to the radio, then to the dorms."

"I know we're not supposed to split up," Dae says. "But I don't think I can make it all the way to the kitchen and back."

"We know the monster is locked up right now," Riley says. "Maybe we can risk it, if you go quick, Ilse—"

Ilse nods slowly, looking in the direction of the kitchen. "He can't watch us all," she murmurs.

"We don't know that," Luke says. "We don't know how many cameras he has in here, or where. We don't know anything except that that *thing* could be waking up any minute now—"

His volume rises enough by the end of the sentence that Riley winces. She puts her hand on Luke's arm.

"You go with Ilse," she says. "Then come back to Dae's room."

He nods, grabs Ilse's hand, and they shuffle away into the darkness. Riley and Dae turn, staggering slightly, and start the laborious journey back to the dorm. He's warm, clammy, and his color is just *off* somehow. In the dark it's better, but as soon as they get into the dorm and the fluorescent overhead comes on she flinches. He's got almost a greenish undertone.

"You don't look great," she says quietly, holding down the light switch to disable the motion sensor. "Come here and lie down."

He shuffles with her to the bed and collapses with a sigh, not even bothering to lift his wounded arm when he bounces down onto the mattress. Riley shoves the balled-up blanket at its foot to the floor, trying to give him more space.

"Does it hurt?" she asks.

"Not really," he says. "Not . . . anymore. I'm just kinda sleepy now. Warm and sleepy."

"Can I look at it?"

He does a wriggle that she guesses is a lying-down shrug and turns away from her on the bed, so his mangled shoulder points at the ceiling.

"Unzip the hoodie," she says, and pulls the sleeve down carefully after he does. She undoes the bathrobe tie and pulls back the gauze. She sucks in a sharp breath and the smell of rot hits her in the back of the throat. She gags and puts a hand over her mouth, turning away.

"What's wrong?" Dae asks, voice worried.

"Nothing," she manages. "Sorry, I'm just—I'm not great with blood, you know—"

She straightens up, still not looking at him. "Hang on for a second," she says.

She ducks into the bathroom and grips the counter, willing herself not to vomit. After a full ten seconds of deep breathing, she takes the stitch kit from her pocket, grabs a bottle of rubbing alcohol from the shelf, puts both on top of the cleanest towel she can find and bundles it all back into the bedroom.

The smell is stronger now, the reek of decaying meat thick in the air. Riley doesn't understand how this has happened, but she knows the creature has to be responsible somehow. Dae doesn't seem infected, but this type of rot—it looks almost like gangrene—can't have happened this quickly without some kind of outside influence.

"Hey," she says, trying not to breathe. "I'm back. Are you still awake?"

His breathing doesn't change, and he doesn't answer.

"That'll make this easier," she murmurs to herself. She almost wants to wake him up, make him take some painkillers and more of the antibiotics they found, but there's a fairly loud voice in the back of her head that says it's not going to make a difference. She saturates the towel with alcohol and presses it against his wound, wiping as gently as she can. He makes an agonized sound deep in his chest, but he doesn't wake up. She pulls the towel away and looks at the wound. She fights back another wave of nausea. The flesh of his back is mottled gray, dark blue veins striating away from the wound and sinking below the surface. The wound itself has stopped bleeding, but the bruising has turned almost completely black, and the edges where the skin has broken are blossoming into curling fronds of some kind of growth that smells almost like mildew. Riley's afraid to look closer, afraid she'll see movement under the skin. She wonders if there was some kind of chemical on the wall, some weird coating, that's causing this reaction. Maybe there's lead in the paint, or asbestos or something. It doesn't have to be related to the creature.

She soaks a new corner of the towel and washes the wound again. It's actually a little worrying to her that Dae isn't waking up; he has to be hurting bad, but the most he does is curl away. She presses down slightly, thinking to purge whatever poison is in him, and blood starts bubbling up out of the holes in his skin. It doesn't smell right; it doesn't look right. It's almost gelatinous, and it smells like seaweed that's been washed up on the beach for days. She keeps wiping at it, pushing it out, trying to get to what she assumes is clean blood somewhere deeper down. It can't *all* be like this.

"Holy fuck," Luke says from the door. Riley straightens up

and turns around, blood-soaked towel clutched tightly in her right hand.

"I know," she says. "I don't know what else to do."

Ilse follows Luke into the room and moves toward Dae, bending down to inspect the wound more closely. She wrinkles her nose slightly, but that's the only indication she can smell anything unusual.

"I think we just have to stitch it and wrap it back up," Ilse says. "You've cleaned it as much as is possible under the circumstances. Ideally, I think, we would leave it exposed to the air and see if that helps, but we may have to run at any moment, so he cannot be unprotected."

"I hate to say this, but I don't know if he's gonna be in any condition to run, wrapped up or not," Luke says, staring at Dae's shoulder. "He didn't wake up while you were doing that?"

"No," Riley says, twisting the towel between her hands. "He made some noise, but that was all."

Luke probes around the edge of the wound, wincing as more beads of jelly-blood come welling up. "His skin feels like it's on fire."

"Well, and you see the blood," Riley says. "It's like . . . like those huge fish eggs you get on top of sushi sometimes."

Her heart drops all the way into her stomach. "Wait. Oh my God, what if—do you think—what if it *is* eggs, oh my God, what if that thing somehow—"

She retches, doubling over. Luke puts his hand on her back.

"I don't think it's eggs," Ilse says. "It looks more like when they lance a cyst on an animal. Sometimes the blood almost curdles, kind of, and it comes out in these chunks."

"Okay, but he doesn't have a cyst," Riley says. "So why would it look like that?"

"I don't know!" Ilse snaps. "I'm not a doctor. I'm just telling you I don't think that creature laid *eggs* in him."

Riley sets the towel aside and brushes her hair out of her face with her shoulder. "You're right," she says. "That was . . . a little too extreme. I just had such a fucking jolt of terror. I mean, imagine."

"I don't like this," Luke murmurs, rolling Dae onto his back. He thumbs up one of his eyelids, lets it flutter shut. He puts his fingers on his neck and looks at his watch, lips moving slightly. After a moment he looks up. "His pulse is slow," he says. "I feel like it's been too long for him to be in shock, but it seems like he's in shock."

"It looks like it's rotting, right?" Riley asks. "Like, the way it looks, like the way it smells . . ."

"It does," Luke admits. "Like frostbite, almost, but it's not on an extremity. It shouldn't be doing this."

Ilse sits down next to him, holds out her hand for the stitch kit. Riley hands it to her and then sets her phone on the side table, angling it so the flashlight shines on Dae. Ilse snaps the kit open, pries out a needle and a length of catgut, and laces them together. She leans over Dae's shoulder and then pauses. After a few tentative touches around the wound she seems to pick a spot. She nods to herself once and then sinks the needle gently into his skin.

Dae keens, the sound escaping out of him like air from a balloon. Ilse freezes, waiting to see if he'll wake or move or both, but the noise just tapers off into a gurgle. He's still unconscious, somewhere far below the surface. Ilse makes her first stitch, then another. The line between her eyebrows deepens as she goes, and by the time she's gotten through about two inches of the wound she's actively grimacing, teeth bared.

"What?" Luke asks, voice low.

"It's not working," Ilse mutters. "It's—the flesh is—look." She leans back so they can see, then pulls at the end of the thread she's holding. The edges of the wound draw together for a moment, but then Dae's skin just *gives*, the holes where the sutures are stretching like taffy. Riley gags.

"It's like it's not even skin," Ilse says. "It's not—the texture is all wrong, it doesn't—it won't hold."

"Can we tape it?" Luke asks.

"We can try," Ilse says.

Riley keeps her eyes averted as she hands the box of butterfly bandages to Ilse, who rips it open and starts peeling wrappers apart. She makes a line of bandages on the side table, then looks at Luke and Riley. "You do this."

She gets to her feet, picks up the radio case, and retreats to the back corner of the room. She plugs it in and picks up the handset. They watch her spin the dial for a second, then turn back to Dae.

"If I sort of—hold it closed," Riley says, trying to keep her voice level, "can you stick them on?"

Luke looks ill, but he swallows hard and nods. "I can do that."

Riley puts her fingers tentatively on the edges of Dae's wound. The spongy texture is familiar, and her stomach rolls as she realizes it's because it reminds her of foraging for wild mushrooms. Sometimes they're warm from the sun, always faintly damp, the meat of them somehow solid and hollow-feeling at the same time. She shakes her head as her salivary glands spark and spit floods her mouth, fighting back the urge to vomit. She pinches the skin together, holding her breath, and she and Luke work their way up and over Dae's shoulder. Pinch, peel off the plastic backing, stick. Pinch, peel, stick. There's one bandage left in the box by the time they're finished.

Ilse sits up straight, drawing their attention. She's staring at the far wall as she twists the dial minutely, trying to sharpen whatever she's found, and then she says something in German. A pause, during which she looks at both of them and widens her eyes, and then her focus snaps back to the phone and she's off, German spilling rapid-fire from her lips. They watch her talk for a few minutes, nodding as she does. She seems . . . resigned, Riley thinks; it's not going badly, but it's not going well, either. Finally she puts the phone down and looks at them.

"He didn't buy all the stations on the continent," she says quietly.

"I knew it," Luke mutters.

"But he did promise most of them funding," she continues. "So they're in his pocket as well."

"Who were you talking to?" Riley asks.

"Arcturus," Ilse says. "I got smart. I just kept speaking German until they put someone on that understood me. And then I lied."

"Lied?"

"I didn't mention Rusk at all," Ilse says. "I didn't tell them what station we're at. I told them we have a very badly injured person with us that needs immediate medical care, and they said we can bring him to them." She reaches up to hook a stray piece of hair off her face, tucks it back into her braid. "They also said that radar has the storm passing in a little less than thirty-six hours."

"Thirty-six," Luke says. His eyes are bleak. "Can Dae make it that long?"

"I don't know," Ilse says.

"Even if we jam him full of antibiotics and he sleeps the whole time, can *we* make it that long?" Luke glances in the direction of the hallway. "We have to assume it's going to get out of the box room, right? So we have to survive two days in here with it?"

"Yes," Ilse says.

"Fuck." He drops his face into his hands.

"No, don't—it's okay," Riley says. "Think about it like camping, like really . . . like really shitty camping." She motions to the now-closed bedroom door. "We can barricade that with the desk and the chair, and the bathroom locks too, so that could be, like, a secondary hiding location. We can sleep on the floor under the bed in shifts. I know we don't have any food or anything, but there's water, and two days isn't that long, right?"

Ilse looks skeptical, tilting her head so her braid swings out from behind her, but she doesn't argue. Luke gets up and starts shoving the desk across the room, pushing until it's wedged against the door. He puts the chair underneath it at an angle, digging the legs into the carpet, and then jams a suitcase behind that. The suitcase is just big enough to fill the space between the chair and the bed, which is braced against the wall.

Riley eyes the barricade approvingly. "Perfect. There's no way it's getting in here."

"Is there a vent in here?" Ilse asks, looking around. "Other than the floor vents?"

The dorms all have tiny openings in the walls above the floors, where the heat blows in. They're long, thin slits, barely half an inch high, and there's one behind the bed. Ilse slides underneath and jams her sweater into it just to be safe, and then they use the blanket to shroud the window. The room is instantly womblike, dark and close and humid with the smell of blood.

"So now we just . . . wait," Ilse says, sitting down on the floor and putting her back against the bed. "For two days."

"We survive," Luke says, joining her on the floor. "And then we get out of here."

Riley steps carefully over the suitcase into the bathroom, fills three of the empty glass bottles, and brings them back out cradled against her. She hands one to Ilse and one to Luke, then raises hers.

"To getting out of here," she says.

14

THEY WAKE UP TO THE THUDDING OF THE BEDFRAME on the floor as Dae has a seizure.

"What do we do?" Riley yells at Luke. "Does someone need to hold him?"

"Leave him alone," Luke yells back. "Just give him space."

Dae's eyes are closed, his lips peeled back from his teeth, heels digging little trenches into the bed. He makes an eerie sound as air is forced past his vocal cords. They watch him spasm and then fall back, completely still. Riley rushes to his side.

"He's not breathing," she says. "He's not——"

Dae takes a huge, gasping breath.

"Oh, thank God——"

"What—where——" He tries to sit up, pushing weakly at Riley's hands, eyes darting around the room as he tries to control his breathing. "What . . . happened? Where am I?"

"Dae," Luke says, moving toward them. "You're in the Victoria Station. In Antarctica. You had a seizure. Don't get up, okay? Just—just stay put; I'll get you some water."

He turns to find Ilse already holding out a bottle. "Thanks," he says, and hands it to Dae.

"I've never had a seizure," Dae says shakily after taking a drink. He's still not breathing well. "What's happening to me?"

"I don't know," Riley says, but she's afraid she has an idea. "I think you have a fever."

"He needs real antibiotics, strong ones," Ilse says. "He needs a fucking fully equipped surgical suite. He's going septic."

"What do you want us to do?" Luke snaps. "You just told us it'll be two days."

"I know that!" she yells. "I know that. But he won't make it."

"I'm right here," Dae says.

"You're dying," she says flatly, turning her gaze on him. "Surely you can feel that."

"I—"

"We have to go to Arcturus now," Ilse says.

Luke sputters. "We can't—the storm—"

"Again, I fucking know that," she snaps. "What do you suggest? Do you want to watch him die?"

Luke's face goes gray and still, and whatever he was about to say gets swallowed up in the weird half-sob, half-choking sound he makes. He turns away from them. Ilse looks at Riley.

"I—I don't know," Riley says, pulling at the strings of her hoodie. "I mean—we can't just let him die. But if we go out there in this storm, I feel like we might *all* die."

"Then we have to decide how badly we want to live," Ilse says.

Luke makes another strangled noise. Riley glances over her shoulder at him. He's got his hands over his face.

"Luke," she says quietly. "Are you—"

"I can't have him on my conscience," he says, the words muffled. "I'd rather die trying to save him than live with that."

"That's a yes," Ilse says, folding her arms. "Majority wins."

"Do I not . . . get a vote?"

Dae's face is even paler than before, and his forehead is beaded with sweat. The rotting-meat smell seems stronger somehow, even though she should be used to it by now.

He looks at them pleadingly. "I don't . . . want to die," he says. He has to take more than one breath in the middle of the sentence. "But I don't want you to . . . die for me."

Riley's chest tightens. She reminds herself to breathe, trying not to focus on the way Dae's struggling to do the same.

"We still don't know how this thing works," Luke says. He's facing them again, his face a little blotchy, but he's gotten himself under control. "We don't *know* it can't get in here."

"Right," Ilse says. "If it is some kind of—some kind of collective creature, a spore or a hive mind or something, it could get in here through a space smaller than we could even see."

"Why hasn't it done that, then?" Riley asks.

"Maybe it hasn't decided to yet," Ilse says. "Does it matter? There is more in favor of us leaving the station than there is for staying."

"The passenger sledge is still out in—"

"We can't take the sledge," Ilse says. "Too slow. Just the snowmobiles. Two and two. We'll tie Dae onto Luke's back."

"How long a ride is it?"

"Three hours in good weather," Ilse replies. "But the pop-up tent is at the sample site, and it's on the way, so we can shelter there if we need to. It's staked down, so it should still be there. We can bring another one just in case."

"How do we keep it from following us?"

"The storm will cover our tracks. And the wind will be too loud for it to hear the snowmobiles for very long. If we can distract it long enough to get a head start, it won't know where we're going. Even with Asha in there. I don't think she has any reason to know about the other stations in the area."

"What if Rusk sees us leave?" Dae's eyes are barely open, but he's fighting to stay awake. "He has satellites . . . everywhere. He can take us out."

"I think . . ." Luke swallows hard and looks at them. "I think we need to start resigning ourselves to the idea that most of these paths are not going to end well for us. Even if that thing doesn't get us, we could still freeze on the way to Arcturus, and if that doesn't happen and we make it there, Rusk will probably incinerate the whole building from orbit."

"But," Riley prompts, sensing it coming.

"But," he says. "If we stay here, then Dae dies, and the rest of us still might, too. If we leave the station, at least we're . . . I don't know, kind of choosing our own terms."

Riley nods, taking this into herself, turning it over. She can't disagree with any of it. For once she wishes she could blame her fear on the chemical imbalance in her brain. She wishes she was just being paranoid, that her racing heart and rapid, shallow breathing were being caused by something in her mind and not something in the world. It's horrible to be scared for no reason, she reflects, but now that she *has* a reason . . . it's infinitely worse.

"You're right," she says. *I wish you weren't,* she thinks. "We have to try." *We're going to die.*

They move out into the hallway slowly, single file. Ilse goes first, then Riley with her phone flashlight, then Luke and Dae. Luke is half carrying Dae, tucked as he is under his good arm, his own arm wrapped around Dae's waist as he supports him. The fastest they can move is a slow shuffle, and every step Dae takes seems to hurt, if the expression on his face is anything to go by. Riley looks back at them every few feet, making sure they're all right, but every time she turns away she expects the monster to be standing in front of her when she turns back. Her heartbeat quickens.

Ilse throws up a hand, fingers spread wide, and her meaning is clear: *Stop.* Riley freezes, reaching backward until her hand hits Luke's chest and she flattens her palm against it. *Stop.* The four of them stand there, the only sound from Dae's labored breathing. Riley shines the light over Ilse's shoulder, trying to see what it is that made her stop, but the hallway is empty. The floor lights stretch away from them in a long, unbroken line. Ilse turns her head so, so slowly, looks over her shoulder until her eyes meet Riley's. Still moving as little as possible, she tilts her head. Her eyes dart sideways, then back. Riley swallows hard and turns the phone. The beam of light catches Ilse's shadow and throws it down the hallway, stretching it into something unrecognizable in the moment it passes over her. Riley holds her breath, still moving the light, and—there.

On the floor, just a few feet ahead of them, where the corridor splits. So small they could have missed it, *should* have missed it, how the *fuck* did Ilse even see it—a drop of blood.

Bile churns up the back of Riley's throat.

Ilse lifts her knife, presses the blunt side of the blade against her lips. *Quiet.* She rolls her eyes toward the bloodstain. Riley strains, listening, and her blood seems to harden in her veins as the sound resolves out of the roaring silence around them. So faint it could be the air-conditioning, barely audible over the rasp of Dae's too-far-apart breaths.

Slithering.

That's the only way she can describe it, the only word that even comes close to what it is. It's a *wet* sound, somehow, but also dusty, like a thousand spiders emerging from a drainpipe, shaking the water from their bodies, hairy legs brushing together as they skitter around and over each other. It feels like it's crawling into her skull, that sound, and as she stares at Ilse in horror she realizes it's getting louder.

"*Run,*" Ilse whispers.

Riley turns to Luke and he's already lifting Dae off his feet, slinging him over his shoulders, bundling him into some kind of army-guy fireman-carry position, and the shriek that Dae lets out as his wounded shoulder takes his weight is the loudest, most awful sound that has ever happened in the history of the world.

"GO!" Luke bellows at her, charging forward. Her terror surges and crests and for a moment she's sure she can't move, will never move again, will stand here frozen and motionless until the creature bursts out of the hallway and swallows her whole, and then one foot lifts and then the other and she takes a breath that feels like drowning and she runs.

15

"ILSE'S FAST," SHE SAYS. "LIKE, SURPRISINGLY FAST. She got to the main room, got all the bolts unlocked, got everyone's coat—"

Good Cop's phone rings. He looks at it in surprise, then puts it to his ear. "Yeah?"

Riley sighs. She's getting tired. She was already tired. She's been tired for a week. But now she can feel herself fading. *Bye-bye, adrenaline.* There's no more fear, no reason to run or fight or do anything, and she just wants to sleep.

"That's, uh, not ideal. Can you—well, I don't know, does it seem—calm down, I'm sure—Goddamn it—" Good Cop thrusts the phone at Bad Cop. "I can't with that fucking—can you deal with him, please?"

Bad Cop takes the phone and sweeps out of the room, slamming the door behind her. Good Cop wipes a hand down his face, then pushes his hair back and smiles at Riley. "Sorry about that," he says. "One of the other guys here, he just . . . he needs a lot of hand-holding, you know?"

Riley nods, then leans forward and puts her head on the table.

"Tired, huh?"

"Are you making that sound?" she asks.

"What sound?"

"The humming," she says to the table. "Nothing. Never mind.

I think I have tinnitus."

His chair scrapes on the floor as he pulls it closer to the table. To her. She can feel his eyes on her.

"Maybe I can get you another pill or two," he says. "In a little bit. If she's not too—" He makes a *grrr* sound. "You know."

The door opens and Riley lifts her head wearily. Bad Cop looks pissed, which isn't new, and she's carrying a tablet, which is. She tilts the screen so Good Cop can see it. He clicks his tongue disapprovingly. She puts it on the table facedown and leans forward, planting both hands flat on the metal.

"I am losing what little remains of my patience," she says tightly.

She reaches into her pocket, takes out a single white pill, and puts it on the table. Riley reaches for it, folds it into her palm carefully.

"What is it?"

"Whatever they gave you before." Her tone is dismissive. "You didn't have a reaction."

Riley shrugs and puts the pill on her tongue, takes a sip of water.

"She's already tired," Good Cop murmurs. "Maybe we should have waited—"

Bad Cop thumps her butt down into her chair and glares at both of them.

"I have a Taser," she says. "Don't fall asleep."

16

IT'S NOT AS LOUD NOW AS IT WAS WHEN THEY LEFT the station an hour ago; the wind is still blowing fiercely but the ringing in her ears has almost gone entirely. She's not too cold anymore, either. *Maybe it wouldn't be so bad to die,* she thinks. Not here, anyway. It's pretty, even with the storm. The snow swirls around them and the sky is darker than she's ever seen it; she doesn't know how Luke is managing to drive the snowmobile. The headlights barely penetrate the wall of ice in the air. There's not really anything for him to hit out here, though, so maybe it doesn't matter. Maybe they'll just drive and drive and eventually bonk right into the station. She laughs. She can't remember why she was so worried. This is nice, the four of them taking a little trip. She feels like they're missing a few people, but they're probably back at the station. Nelson might be making them dinner for when they get back from—wherever they're going. To the sample site? It seems late in the day for them to start working, but maybe it just feels that way because the sky is so dark. Her sense of time is definitely getting a little wonky the longer they're here. She tightens her arms around Ilse's waist, laying her head on her back, and stares out into the snow. Usually this type of thing would make her claustrophobic, the way the dense white fog seems to press right up against them in an endless wall, but right now it feels kind of nice. Like being in a cloud, maybe, or a cotton ball. Her friend Sarah, back when she had friends, had this big, fluffy white duvet that Riley always envied. She loved spending the night at Sarah's because she'd get to curl up under that soft expanse of white. She had asked her mom if she could get one, but her mom had told her *Not if you're going to keep drinking cranberry juice in bed*, so that was the end of that. She giggles again, remembering. Why hasn't she seen Sarah in such a long time? Why did they stop hanging out? Maybe when she gets home she'll call her, ask if she wants to go to the movies. That could be nice.

She jerks upright, a shudder running through her so violently it makes Ilse shove her elbow back into her side. She relaxes her grip and sits up straight, looking from side to side. *What just happened?* Her body is reacting to something, muscles tightening, blood pumping. Her fingers tingle as adrenaline pushes through her, waking her up. What has she been doing? Has she been sleeping? Why is she so—

It happens again, and this time, with her brain fizzing and panicky and *aware*, she sees it.

There is movement out in the snow.

She jabs Ilse in the back so hard she hears her cry out, her body twisting, and the snowmobile handles twist with her. She wrestles the vehicle to a stop, narrowly avoiding tipping them off, and turns as far as she can to look at Riley.

"What the fuck?" she spits. "Are you trying to kill us?"

Riley shakes her head, still staring in the direction where she last saw the movement.

"There's something out there," she says. "Something moving."

Ilse's face is covered, so she can't read her expression, but she nods tersely and turns back, putting her hand on the throttle.

"Wait!" Riley says. "We should—I don't know, shouldn't we—"

Ilse points ahead of them, where the silhouette of Luke and Dae's snowmobile is rapidly vanishing. She guns the engine and they surge forward.

"Just keep watch!" she yells over her shoulder. "Tell me if it gets closer!"

Riley blinks tears out of her eyes and stares out into the snow. The movement could have been anything—a flag, a marker, a coat someone lost—but it wasn't. She *knows* it wasn't. That thing is out there, claw-tipped fingers ticking across the ice, stalking them. She holds on to Ilse with all her strength, sweeping her gaze back and forth as best as she can, trying not to cry. If they can make it to Arcturus—if they can just get Dae some medicine— they can last two days.

She doesn't know how long they've been driving when they come to a skidding halt just inches from the back end of Luke's snowmobile. Luke is standing next to the machine, and Dae is slumped over the throttle.

"Sorry," Luke yells over the wind. "I had to move him. He keeps—he's not staying conscious much anymore, and he keeps slipping—I figure if I keep him in front of me I at least know he's still on the bike—" He shakes his head. "We should be getting close, right?"

"I think so," Ilse yells back. Luke nods and gets onto the snowmobile behind Dae, arranging him so his head is tipped back onto Luke's shoulder. He gives them a thumbs-up and starts the engine, accelerating away quickly. Ilse starts theirs and follows.

Riley sees the monster at least twice more, or thinks she does. Her vision is blurry with cold and fatigue, and the snow whipping past her eyes makes everything look like it's vibrating slightly, but. The first time it's a leg—a *limb*, more accurately, who knows which of its appendages it's using to propel itself through the snow—arcing through the air, a dark blur moving against the wind high in the air. It seems too tall, too pointed, and it reminds her of nothing so much as a scorpion's tail poised above them, but it disappears back into the storm before she can even tighten her grip on Ilse, so she doesn't say anything.

The second time it's a face.

Riley's staring into the white void, eyes darting back and forth as she strains to see any movement beyond the swirling, patternless dance the snow is doing, and all of a sudden, like a fucking Magic Eye painting, it's there. It resolves out of the dizzy blur like ice, almost invisible, but she can see its edges. Again it's too tall, almost ten feet up in the air, and it doesn't look like any human she's ever seen, but she knows. Its mouth hangs open, its insides a dark smear behind the snow, and its cheeks gape and sag emptily. The snow whips against it, for one moment delineating it so perfectly she can see the bones of it pushing at its skin, and it looks at her and she *knows* even with the mirrored lens of her goggles it can see her, is meeting her gaze, is staring directly into her soul. Those twin black dots, the ones that found her the first night, telescoping toward her like empty straws, and she screams and the sound is lost in the wind and she pulls on Ilse's coat and Ilse doesn't even turn around, just guns the engine, and the snowmobile surges forward and the snow kaleidoscopes around them and it's gone.

The tent emerges from the white fog without warning. The snowmobile slows, then stops, and Ilse's hands drop from the handlebars as she stares at it.

"That's our tent," she says. She slides off, sinking immediately up to her knees in the drifting, swirling snow. She wades forward, shaking her head in disbelief. Riley climbs off the snowmobile, throws her snowshoes down and steps into them. She starts after Ilse, carrying her snowshoes.

"Ilse—"

"It's *our tent*," Ilse spits, whirling on her. "Don't you get it?"

"No," Riley says, shame at her confusion spiking her blood pressure. "I'm sorry, I—"

"We've been driving for three hours," Ilse says. "We've been on the same compass heading for three hours."

"You said it was on the way," Riley says uncertainly.

"It is." Ilse's voice is barely audible. The wind whips her braid out of her coat and it lashes across her face hard. She doesn't even move. "You know how long it takes to get to the sample site?"

"Like forty minutes."

"So . . ." Ilse gestures toward the tent.

"We went in a circle?"

Ilse drops to her knees, presses both hands to her face, and curls in on herself. A thin moaning sound reaches Riley's ears and she realizes Ilse is muffling a scream.

"I'm sorry," she says desperately, crouching next to her, clumsy in the snowshoes. "I'm sorry, I don't—"

"He did this," Ilse says, raising her head. Her goggles only show Riley her own reflection, the two of them echoed back and forth in pink and yellow mirrors into infinity. "Rusk. He did something to the snowmobiles, to the compasses, he has to have done something—"

"But where are Luke and Dae?" Riley asks.

"If they didn't see the tent," Ilse says, "they're probably almost back to the Victoria Station."

"You don't think maybe they made it—"

"I've been following their tracks," Ilse says. "Or at least I thought I was, but maybe—maybe the patterns in the ice—"

She hiccups and Riley realizes she's crying.

"Here," she says, and drops the snowshoes next to Ilse. "Come on. Let's get back before we freeze."

Ilse nods but doesn't move to stand, and Riley finally grabs her under the arms and hoists her up out of the snow. The end of her braid is frozen onto her coat. Riley pushes her, trying not to remember Luke herding Greta like a dog into the station, coaxing her into the snowshoes and back to the snowmobile. She gets on and wraps her arms around her. She's shaking, strong convulsive heaves that feel more like sobbing than cold, and all Riley can do is lay her head on her back and wait. After a few minutes Ilse starts the snowmobile and they pull forward, past the tent, back into the gray-white blindness of the storm.

Ilse pulls the snowmobile all the way up to the door, and Riley feels a brief surge of relief that it's shut. Surely the monster would have left it open; surely this means Luke and Dae are safely inside. They hurry inside.

"Luke?" Riley yells, ripping her goggles off. "It's us."

Ilse hisses a *shh* at her so viciously that it stuns her into silence. They shed their gear quietly, Ilse's head turning back and forth like a cat hunting prey the entire time. When they're free of everything she motions for Riley to get behind her, and they walk into the main part of the station.

"There's more blood," she whispers. "On the floor. Don't step in it."

"Is it—human?" Riley whispers back.

"It's still here, isn't it?"

"I don't know how old it is," Riley snaps. "Does it have any weird shit in it?"

Ilse crouches, shines her light around. "I don't think so."

"Dae," Riley whispers. "Oh God."

The blood trail weaves across the kitchen into the hallway, and they follow it. It splits where they should turn to head for the dorms, and Riley feels the dull ache of terror like a fist behind her sternum.

"They went to see if it's still here," Ilse murmurs. "Then they came back and went to the dorms."

"Or they went to the dorms and it fucking came after them and dragged them through the station," Riley whispers. Ilse looks at her, starts to say something, then apparently changes her mind and starts moving cautiously toward the dorms.

The rotting-meat smell hits Riley about twenty feet away from the door to the first bedroom, which is closed. They approach slowly, Riley putting a hand over the pocket where she's tucked the paring knife. Ilse puts her hand on the doorknob. She turns it.

The door clicks open. Ilse puts her fingertips on it and pushes. One inch, two inches, the smell even stronger now, and then the door swings away from her and Luke is standing there covered in blood.

"Oh, thank God," he whispers. "I was so afraid—I thought you were both—"

Riley's gaze lands on Dae and she makes a sound she's never made before, something that catches in her chest and hurts and sends nausea swooping through her. She staggers and puts a hand on the door frame, then pushes past Luke and gets down on the floor beside Dae.

He's panting, slicked with sweat and blood and something gelatinous, and the dark spiderweb of rot has climbed from his shoulder into his face. He looks like he's already dead.

"What the fuck happened?" she whispers. She almost touches his face but folds her fingers back into her palm at the last second.

"It found us," Luke says. His voice is hoarse.

"It—*it?* Found *you?*" Riley looks up at him. "But it was behind us."

Was it? Yes. She had *seen* it. She *had*. She closes her eyes tightly, curling in on herself. *Real.* She knows she saw it.

She thinks she saw it.

Not real.

She whimpers, digging her fingers into her hair. She breathes.

"It might have been, at one point," Luke says. She has enough spare sanity left to appreciate his gentleness. "But then it wasn't."

"Explain," Ilse says tersely.

"I kept—I kept seeing something in the corner of my eye," Luke says. "Every time I looked directly at it, though, it was gone. But I think—I must have turned the handlebars a little bit each time—"

His face darkens with shame and defeat as Riley looks up at him. "It was herding us," he says. "And it worked."

"What about the compass?" Ilse asks. "Didn't you look—"

"It iced over," he snaps, not looking at her. "And then after I switched Dae around I couldn't see it anymore because he was in the way."

"So it caught up to us, passed us, and then started forcing us back here," Riley says. "So it's thinking."

"We know it thinks," Ilse says. "It has at least three different human brains rattling around inside it."

"Right, but . . ." Riley tries to gather her thoughts, follow the slim thread of the idea. "Doesn't that mean it's not getting weaker? When it was in the room before—when Rusk was trying to lock us in—it seemed confused, kind of. It wouldn't have been able to track us and hunt us like that."

Ilse dips her chin in a nod and Riley feels a little twinge of pride.

"So it's gaining control of itself," Luke says. "Of its . . . its form, or whatever. So maybe it doesn't need us anymore?"

"Hey." Dae's voice is small and hollow, barely more than a whisper. "Ow."

Riley scrambles closer to him, leans over his face to hear him better.

"Hey," she whispers, trying not to breathe. "How are you feeling?"

"Bad."

"We're gonna get you out of here, okay?"

"No," he whispers. "Listen."

"I'm listening," she says, blinking back tears.

"My file . . ."

"Yeah," Riley says. Her urge to touch him, to comfort him somehow, is almost as strong as the need she feels to get as far away from him as possible. "You said you got arrested, right?"

"I . . . hurt someone," Dae says. "He was in . . . NA . . . I lied . . ."

"You pretended you were an addict." She's finishing the sentences for him, trying to keep him from straining himself. She knows he needs to tell them, to purge the mental poison before the physical one kills him, but watching him struggle like this hurts more than she could have imagined.

"I told . . ." Something crackles deep in Dae's chest. He clears his throat with an agonizing squelching sound. "Secrets. Used . . . his name."

"You got information for a story from an NA meeting and published it," Riley says.

"He found . . . me." The sound comes again, closer this time, like something is climbing up his spine. "We . . . fought."

"And then you got arrested."

He's managed to lift his head about an inch off the floor, and it thumps down now as the tension in his body releases. "Yes."

"It's okay, Dae," Riley whispers.

"No." He breathes raggedly, the crackling sound becoming a gurgle, and Riley turns her head and flinches back just in time to avoid an explosive spray of frothing, clotted blood. Dae coughs and coughs, his body drawing painfully in on itself. They watch, frozen, unable to help or look away, and finally he slumps flat onto his back.

His next word emerges in a bubble of blood. "Sorry."

"Dae," Luke says.

"Everything." The blood-bubble bursts, painting his chin with black-veined red. "Sorry."

"You're a good person, Dae." Tears slip down Riley's face. "It's okay."

The corner of his mouth lifts, just barely, just enough for her to notice. A single sob escapes her and she presses the back of her hand to her mouth.

"My . . . it . . ." Dae tries to raise his arm. He tries to touch his temple, but his fingertips don't get within six inches of his face. His arm drops back to the floor with an unnervingly squishy sound.

"In here," he says, panting. Fresh sweat has broken out across his forehead, and it trails down his temples into his hair. "It. It's here."

"Dae," Luke says, moving closer. "You're okay. It never touched you, it didn't—"

"I know." His eyelids flutter up for a moment, a brief surge of strength, and Riley bites back a scream. His eyes are *deflated*, like they've been leaking whatever's inside them back into his skull, and his irises . . . they're splitting somehow, dividing and doubling like cells in mitosis. She has a brief flash of a horror movie she watched years ago, a goat walking on its hind legs, sideways pupils flicking back and forth as it stalked its prey. She flattens her hands on her thighs, fighting the urge to run as far away from Dae as she possibly can, looking at Luke instead. His face is frozen, chin trembling, and she knows he saw it too.

"It's just a regular infection, Dae," he mutters. "I swear. It's a bad one, but it's not—you're okay, I promise—"

Dae sucks in a painful-sounding breath. "The . . . mattress. Under."

Luke reaches out and flips the little twin mattress up. Ilse lunges forward, but she's too late.

Her knife is sitting in the center of the unfinished wooden plank that serves as a bed support.

"What the fuck?" Luke looks from the knife to Ilse, back and forth. "What . . . what the fuck?"

It hits Riley in a wave, then, the nagging nervous feeling she's had since they left the creature in the room with the box. As she rolled under the closing door, as her eyes had raked one last time over its form, something had caught in her mind like a fishhook, and now it finally rips free. There had been no knife handle jutting from its back.

"You took it," she whispers, staring at Ilse. "You took it after I told you not to."

"I couldn't leave it," Ilse says. "We needed it."

"We have other knives!" Riley says, aghast. "*You* were the one who was talking about spores, and contamination, and—and—"

"What the *fuck*," Luke says again.

Riley moves closer to the knife, peering over the edge of the bedframe at it. It's still open, and it looks clean.

"Did you clean it, or . . ."

"The blood evaporated," Ilse says. "Or whatever it does."

"So you brought a fucking . . . a fucking monster-blood-covered knife into a tiny room with someone with an open wound," Luke says. His eyes are so cold. "Are you out of your mind? What were you *thinking*—"

"It protected me!" Ilse's voice is thick with tears. "It saved me! I couldn't—I need—"

She drops her face into her hands. "I'm sorry," she cries. "I'm so sorry. I—I can't be brave without it."

Riley almost wants to hug her, and then her gaze falls on Dae again. The cords in his neck stand out as he tries to breathe deeper.

"Have you had it with you this whole time?" Luke demands. "You're probably infected now, too."

"Don't do that," Riley murmurs. "We don't know that."

"I feel fine," Ilse says, wiping her eyes.

"Well, that's great for you, isn't it? I'm so glad you feel fine, because he's fucking *dying*," Luke snarls.

"I *said I'm sorry!*"

Her voice rises almost to a scream at the end. A fresh tear slips down her cheek. "I'm sorry," she repeats, softer. "I really am. I was—that was—selfish."

All of them look at Dae. Riley hates that they can't touch him, can't comfort him. She wonders if they should do something for him, give him whatever painkillers they can find and hope he drifts off—

She shakes her head, appalled at herself. Then she gets to her feet.

"We have to go back out," she says. "We have to get to Arcturus for real this time."

"Dae can't—"

"No, he can't." She glares at Ilse. "So you stay with him."

Ilse presses her lips together and looks at the floor. She folds her arms and tucks her chin into her chest. "Fine."

"Luke, when—when you got back, did you see—"

"It's not in here as far as I know," he says.

"Okay," Riley says. She looks at Ilse. "Block the door again once we leave, and we'll lock everything up tight."

They close the door behind them and stand there for a moment, listening to the sounds of Ilse dragging the furniture around. Then they head back to the main room to put their coats on again.

THE SUN IS CLOSER TO THE HORIZON NOW, STILL
shrouded in clouds and fog, and the wind howls even louder than
before. Luke scrapes the face of the compass, breathes against it
with his hands cupped around it and rubs at it with his sleeve.

"I don't know if it works anymore," he says doubtfully. "But
at least I can see it."

He climbs onto the snowmobile and beckons her to do the
same. She slings her leg over, puts her arms around him. He starts
the engine. She feels him sigh heavily, and then the snowmobile
leaps forward across the snow. She tucks her cheek against his
back and watches over her shoulder as the Victoria Station
disappears into the snow.

She hasn't fully warmed up from the last time they tried this
trip, and her gear is wet with sweat and melted ice. She starts
shivering almost immediately. Luke takes one hand off the
throttle to pat her mittened hand where it's locked onto her other
one across his chest, then guns the engine. She closes her eyes and
tries not to think about the monster.

They've only been driving for an hour when the wind picks
up, shoving at them like a living creature. She can feel the
snowmobile skidding sideways, hear the sound of it scraping
across the ice. Luke starts leaning to his right, trying to counter
the force of it, and Riley copies him. They lean into the wind,

trying to keep themselves upright, and they make it another few feet before the snowmobile lurches up off the ground, slewing wildly, slamming back down onto its runners facing the wrong direction. Luke cuts the engine and slides off fast, pulling Riley along with him, and he's barely yanked her clear when the machine starts rolling.

"Shit, shit, shit, *shit*!" he yells, slogging after it. He stops after a few painful, lurching steps. "Fuck."

"What do we do?" Riley yells at his back.

He turns to face her. "We have to try and get back to the sample station."

"The tent," she says, nodding.

"At least until the wind dies down and we can find the snowmobile," he says, making his way back to her laboriously. "Hopefully it'll get hung up on a big . . . crag, or something."

"We don't have snowshoes," she says, looking down at their buried feet.

"If we were on top of the snow we'd get thrown around worse than the snowmobile," he says. "We have to stay low. It's not that far. It's gotta be just . . . just a mile or so back."

Riley closes her eyes, realizing for the first time how fucking *tired* she is. When was the last time they slept? *Real* sleep, not snatched moments of unconsciousness between bouts of terror? She can't remember. She offers Luke a tiny smile before remembering he can't see her face behind her mask.

"You don't have any more of that weird gel, do you?" she asks.

She lifts her foot, pulling it free of the drifting snow. She keeps her balance, using her arms, extends it forward as far as she can in the confines of her snowsuit. She plunges her foot into the snow. She shifts her weight forward, still balancing, until her back foot can be extracted. She repeats this and repeats this and repeats this, and the world around her is a howling white void, and Luke's coat in front of her is a blue flicker like a mirage. She is pouring sweat and freezing cold; her lungs feel shriveled in her chest and every part of her hurts. There's not enough air inside the frozen fleece of her gaiter; her goggles are icing over as her breath does its best to fog them. She couldn't see anything even if they were clear, but it certainly adds to her feeling of defeat. She tries to keep a rhythm in her head, some kind of beat that will keep her moving forward, and the only thing that will come to her is the fucking *Let's all go to the lobby* song from the movie theater. Left foot, right foot, if she ever makes it home she's going to fight that little dancing bucket of popcorn. *Let's all go to the lobby and get ourselves a treat.* Treat? Snack? Is it *get ourselves a snack? Let's all go to the lobby and get ourselves a—* Why, at the end of the world, are the only things left in her head commercials?

Her foot catches on her other pant leg and she falls forward. It knocks the wind out of her and she lies there for a second, stunned, and then rolls over. She stares up into the whited-out sky. In the back of her head an alarm bell is ringing, but it's so quiet, and it gets fainter and fainter as she lies there. She's so tired, and it's not as cold anymore, and she's never felt further from a panic attack. She's . . . calm. She's at peace. *See, this is what I needed all along. I knew this trip would fix me. Look at me now, everyone.*

She laughs and throws her arms out. "Snow angel," she whispers into her frozen gaiter. The wind pulls at her as she sinks deeper into the snow. It's still blowing hard, but little clumps of flakes are starting to collect on her goggles. She wonders if she'll look nice when she's frozen, or if it'll be like Jack Nicholson at the end of *The Shining.* Icicles on her—

Wait.

The Shining.

Luke!

She sits up.

"Luke," she yells. Her voice is sucked away into the storm. She tries again, paddling her arms, trying to stand. "Luke!"

She squints, trying to find the blue flash of his coat. The whole world is snow, whipping past her at dizzying speeds; she can barely tell where the ground ends and the sky begins.

"LUKE!"

She struggles to her feet. Movement brings some warmth; her blood starts moving, her thoughts sharpen a tiny bit. *I'm dying,* she thinks. *Move. Move, Riley.*

Left foot.

Right foot.

Yell for Luke.

Again.

Again.

Left foot. Right foot. Yell for Luke.

Luke.

She's on the ground again. She doesn't remember falling. It didn't hurt this time. She reaches into her pocket, misses, misses again, realizes it's zipped shut. She unzips it clumsily. She pulls out the flare gun. She aims it at the sky.

"Riley!"

She opens her eyes. She's in the pop-up tent. The tiny stove in the corner is boiling water ferociously, kerosene fumes venting out into the snow. Their coats are spread across the drying rack next to it. Her phone is on the floor facedown with the flashlight glowing. Luke is crouched next to her, eyes worried.

"Hey," she says. It hurts to talk. "Water?"

He hands her a packet of gel as she sits up. Her head feels like it's about to split in half.

"Great," she says, and starts gnawing on a corner.

"Are you anemic?" he asks. "Like, clinically? Do you know?"

"I don't . . . think so," she says around the packet. "Why?"

"You're like, crazy susceptible to cold," he says. "Like, your blood doesn't move nearly fast enough. I mean, I'm not a doctor, but—"

"Did you see the flare?" she asks as the memory surfaces.

"Flare?" He looks puzzled. "The flare gun's back in—in the station, in Nelson's coat, I think, what—"

"I thought I shot a flare," she says.

"No," he says gently. "I heard you yelling and it took me a few minutes to find you. You had one hand in your pocket, but you were out cold."

"Shit." She frowns.

"It's okay," he says. "I found you."

"I really thought I'd be a better apocalypse partner than this," she mutters. "Like, I thought I'd at least have *ideas*, or something. Even if I didn't have skills. So far I've gotten a maybe-concussion and mild hypothermia."

"It's not the apocalypse," Luke says. "You also climbed into an air duct looking for a monster and got us all out of the room when Rusk was trying to trap us, and you wrapped up Dae's shoulder."

"And I made SpaghettiOs." Her eyelids droop.

"And you made SpaghettiOs. See?"

She nods. He takes the empty gel packet from the corner of her mouth and puts it on the floor next to the stove.

"I didn't want you to wake up and be freaked out," he says, "but we need to, um, get warm."

He unrolls the emergency sleeping bag, unzips it, and folds it open. Then he pulls his sweater over his head. His T-shirt catches on it, pulls up to reveal a slice of taut brown skin. Riley flicks her eyes toward the ceiling.

"I'm, um, I don't," she starts, wishing her brain wasn't half-frozen. "I'm asexual, I'm sorry—"

He stops with his shirt halfway off, one arm still pinned by a sleeve. He laughs and she flinches, dropping her gaze to the ground.

"No, Riley, don't—I didn't mean—I'm gay," he says, scooting toward her as he extricates himself from the shirt. "I literally just mean to stay warm. I'm not gonna jump you."

"You're *gay*?" She stares at him.

"Is it that hard to believe?"

"You just look like such a . . . CW star," she says. "Golden boy jock. I just assumed you had a cheerleader girlfriend."

"Look, get in the bag," he says, shimmying out of his snow pants. She pulls off her own sweater hesitantly, then her thermal. She leaves her bra on. She climbs into the sleeping bag next to him and he pulls her up tight against him, bare skin to skin. He reaches around her and zips the bag. She has to admit she's already warmer, although how much of that is searing embarrassment, she doesn't know.

"My friend who died," Luke says quietly. He puts his chin on her shoulder; his breath is warm on her ear.

"Yeah," she says.

"I was—I mean, I don't know for sure, we never—" He sighs. "I loved him."

"Did he know?"

"I was going to tell him," Luke says. "I think he knew, but . . ."

"What was his name?"

"Charlie."

"Charlie," she says. She's so sleepy. "What was he like?"

He huffs a little laugh. "Exasperating. Amazing. He was

incredible on a bike, it was like . . . it was like watching poetry, or something. He was always trying to go bigger, get higher, do *more*. He pushed me, you know? I wanted to be better because he was so good. It was competitive at first, I guess, but . . . I don't know. The more I saw him, the more I thought about him, I realized I wanted to be as good as he was so I'd be good enough *for* him."

"What happened to him?"

He pulls away from her a little, and she thinks he's not going to answer. He tucks his face against her back.

"We were in Utah," he says. "We were racing, up in the mountains, and he just . . . the curve, or something, I don't know . . ."

His breath hitches and she feels wet eyelashes brush across her skin.

"He fell," he whispers. "His bike, he got caught in it somehow, and it pulled . . . it pulled him over."

She puts her hand over his, squeezes.

"He screamed. As he was falling, as he went over the side, he yelled for me, and I didn't—I couldn't—"

"It's not your fault," she whispers.

"I heard—"

She hears him swallow hard and sniff back more tears.

"I heard the sound, when he hit—the bones—when I hit Greta . . ."

She remembers it all too well, the wet pulpy *smack* of it. She thinks about sharp rocks under desert sun. She breathes deep and slow, hoping he'll feel it and follow.

"I wrote him a letter," he says. His voice blurs a little. "I was going to put it on his coffin, I guess? At the funeral? I don't know." He makes a small derisive sound in his throat. "I didn't really have a plan. But I saw his mom look at me, and she was crying, and I just knew she blamed me, and I . . . I couldn't."

"Do you think"—Riley yawns, pulling one hand away to cover her mouth before setting it back over Luke's hand—"do you think he loved you?"

"I want to."

"I bet he did," she says.

A small, stifled sob shakes his body. "Yeah?"

"Yeah." She rubs his arm, hoping it's soothing.

"Sorry," he says after a minute. She can practically feel the walls going back up.

"It's okay, Wheeler," she says, digging an elbow back into his side. "Don't do that."

He sniffs again.

"I freaked out at school," she says. "Like, full-on, hyperventilating, had to be removed from the classroom freaked out."

"Like, you had a panic attack?"

"First one," she says. "I always knew I was anxious, but it was . . . a whole different beast."

"Shit."

"Everyone stopped talking to me," she continues, still rubbing his arm. It's making her feel better, so she hopes it's working on him, too. "I mean, I'm sure it was scary, it was fucking scary for *me*, I thought I was goddamn *dying*, but—my friends, everyone . . ."

She blinks back tears. "I was out of school for two days, I had to quit the soccer team, and no one ever even called. It was like I just disappeared, and no one could see me anymore."

He tightens his arm around her. "People are afraid of what they don't understand."

She nods.

"And they're assholes."

She laughs. "And they're assholes."

"Is it . . . have you had one since?"

"No," she says. "Not a full-blown one. My therapist gives me homework on like, ways to talk yourself out of it. And obviously

I'm medicated now, so . . . it's better. But still."

"The first time my sister had one she fell down the stairs," Luke says. "She thought she was having a heart attack."

That swooping, breathless sensation, the feeling that her body isn't under her control—she remembers. "That's awful."

"It's not your fault either, you know," he says. She doesn't know how to respond to that.

"Well," she says after a few moments. "I know that's like, small potatoes. Compared to, you know."

"It's not—"

"I just wanted to, you know, throw my hat in the ring."

"The sadness ring."

"I didn't want you to feel alone in there."

"Well, it worked," he says.

Darkness snips through the space between them as Riley's phone finally dies. She feels the same nervousness she always does when her phone dies, and the same aggravated amusement at herself—back at home it was always *What, do you think someone's trying to get ahold of you?* Now it's *What, do you think you'd be able to call for help?*

"I think this trip would have been really good for us," she says. A shiver runs through her and she pulls the bag tighter, tucks more of it under her for good measure. "I think it would have made me braver. And it would have given you something else to focus on."

"For what it's worth, I have been pretty distracted the last few days," Luke says dryly. "Thanks, monster."

"I just mean . . ." She considers her next words. "I think we would have found what we were looking for out here. If we'd been able to."

He nods, nose cold on the back of her neck. "I think so too. I mean, after Charlie, I felt like . . . I don't know, I felt—not *exactly* like I wanted to kill myself, but kind of like . . . if I died it would be okay, you know? I kept looking for a bigger risk. Go faster, go higher, let the chips fall, maybe you don't wake up, so what. But now I know I really want to live."

He huffs a laugh. "And that's only after three days. Imagine me after a full two weeks."

"It only takes two weeks if you get the non-monster package," she says. "We went deluxe."

He's silent for so long she thinks he's fallen asleep, and then he says, "Hey."

"Yeah."

"After this, when we're back home, will you call me? Like, can we be real friends?"

She wants to say *There is no "after this."* She wants to say *We're going to die here.* But she wants to be a person who doesn't believe that, and so she squeezes Luke's hand again and closes her eyes and says, "Absolutely," and then she sleeps.

SHE WAKES UP ALONE.

"Luke?" she calls out, sitting up. "Luke?"

She fumbles her clothes on. The stove is still on, water long since boiled out of the little pot. The tent isn't freezing, but she can see her breath. She jams her goggles onto her head, pulls up her gaiter around her face, and unfastens the tent flap.

"Luke?"

The wind slaps her in the face so hard it knocks the breath out of her lungs. She cries out in shock and pain, yanks her head back inside. She blinks hard a few times. The kaleidoscope of wind and ice and sun has immediately made her dizzy. She takes a deep breath, then another, makes sure her boots are laced up tight, and throws herself forward out of the tent.

The wind roars around her, digging cold fingers into every gap in her clothing, curling under her and lifting her away from the ground. She can feel it pulling, sucking her upward. She drops to her knees, and then to all fours.

She lifts her head and sees a flash of orange. A marker pole, the ones they keep tied to the snowmobile. *Luke must have found it.* But why wouldn't he have come back to the tent? Why would he have just *left* her? She crawls forward slowly, keeping her belly hugging the ground, shivering as she goes. She wraps one gloved hand around the pole. She looks right, then left, then back again, craning her neck, trying to find—*there*. Another stripe of orange in the rushing sky.

She starts crawling again.

By the time she reaches the tenth pole she's drenched with sweat, muscles cramping and twitching at the effort it takes to keep herself flat against the ice. She's breathing hard, the inside of her gaiter soaked and frozen, and the skin of her face is definitely stuck to the fleece. She notices distantly she's lost a glove.

What if it's a trap?

The thought surfaces gently, bobbing to the forefront of her mind like driftwood on a wave.

How could it be?

She thinks about her therapist. *For every bad thing you think, Riley*, she says calmly in her memory, *think of five more that are good.*

Luke is my friend.

One.

The monster isn't smart enough to set a trap.

Two. Maybe.

I'm probably getting close to the end of the trail.

Three.

Ilse and Dae are waiting for me.

Four.

Luke is probably coming back for me.

Five.

She pushes herself along, gasping. Her goggles are cracked, she thinks; the right half of the wide mirrored lens is completely iced over. It's skewing her perception, clouding her vision, and every time there's movement on her right side she jerks her head, trembling, to stare into the snow.

She starts crying in earnest when she sees the dim shape of the station. She crawls until she can't bear it anymore and then shoves herself to her feet, sobbing at the strain on her abused muscles. She starts running when she hits the hardpack, slipping and sliding as the wind yanks at her. She falls, falls again, and by the time she reaches the door of the station she knows she can't keep going like this.

She can't leave again. Her mind won't let her, her body won't let her. Whatever waits for her inside, she has to face it.

She steps into the Victoria Station for the last time.

IMMEDIATELY SHE REALIZES LUKE HASN'T MADE IT back. Or—he made it back and then left again, or something else horrible happened, because his gear isn't here. No melting ice puddled around discarded boots, a shed coat. The station looks exactly like it did when they left.

She takes off her coat quietly, staring around while she unlaces her boots. She peels the frozen gaiter away from her face with a wince and a muffled cry. When she looks at it, a patch of bloody skin clings to the fabric. She touches her cheek and her fingers come away wet. She wipes the blood on her pants and stands up, letting her gloves fall to the floor. Then she kneels once more and pulls the knife out of her coat.

She walks into the hallway.

The rotting-meat smell is still there, but it's fainter, and she dares to hope that's a good thing. Maybe Dae is improving. She moves slowly toward the dorms, the floor lights glowing around her. Something ticks in the vents above her head.

The door to the dorm is open.

She pushes it open, knife raised.

There's a soft metallic sound as the blade hits the floor; she barely hears it over the rush of blood in her ears. Her fingers have gone numb.

Dae is lying on the floor of the dorm, arms flung out like he's making a snow angel, and he's dead. He is absolutely, without a doubt, visibly and obviously dead.

But he's breathing.

Riley watches as his chest rises and falls, rises and falls, rises . . . too high. Rises and rises and then contracts with a hard jerking shudder. Rises again and keeps rising, still spasming, clenching like a fist, and then his skin and his shirt rip open at the same time and a fine red mist cracks into the air.

Something is trying to climb out of him.

Something touches the back of Riley's hand.

She screams and jerks sideways, slamming her head into the doorframe. Ilse is crouched on the floor, staring up at her. Her face is drawn so tight that Riley can see her skull. Her eyes are bulging, rolling with terror. She's trying to hold Riley's hand.

Riley grabs her wrist and pulls her to her feet and Ilse burrows into her wordlessly, wrapping her arms around her as tightly as she can.

The thing inside Dae moves again. They both turn to watch, pressing back against the wall. Ilse is whispering something in German and Riley doesn't catch any of it except for something that sounds like "demon."

A limb—an arm, a leg, who fucking knows—lifts itself free of Dae, dripping blood and ichor. It twists upward, and something about it seems . . . questioning. Like a wolf scenting the air. Riley feels like it can see them.

The limb rises and rises, tapering into a long thin point that seems to sharpen as it's exposed to the air outside Dae's body. It reaches almost to the ceiling before it hooks down, bending sharply in three different places, and the point of it digs into the floor. Riley can feel something vibrating in her chest and realizes she's humming, making a desperate low sound that would absolutely be a scream if she let it out. It looks like a spider leg covered in skin, segmented and insectile but horribly, awfully human. Another leg starts to emerge, the first one bracing against the floor as it pulls itself free, repeating the same journey toward the ceiling and back down. The tips of the legs flex and scrape across the carpet as they search for purchase, and then without warning they *lift*.

Dae's body is pulled up off of the floor, head lolling back, hands dangling limply as his back bows into a too-sharp curve, held aloft by the thing in his chest.

"I think . . ." Ilse is breathing shallowly, almost gasping, her voice faint with terror. "Those are—those are his ribs," she whispers.

"How?" Riley whispers back, but as the creature staggers upright she can almost see it. The churned mass of Dae's torn flesh—thankfully mostly hidden by his shirt—is still moving, and she can see more spindly legs starting to lift themselves out of him. His hands twitch and flutter and blur and then his arms are sucked into his body with a wet crackling sound that Riley, if she survives this, will hear for the rest of her life. Ilse gags and vomits on the floor, choking and spitting. The rotting-meat smell is gone now but in its place is something so much worse, something that Riley can only think of as *evil*, like the blood-black ooze of the creature's essence has atomized and is crawling into her nose, her mouth—the open wound on her face—

She grabs Ilse by the shoulders. "We have to move," she snaps. "Come on."

Ilse is rooted to the floor, staring at Dae. There's vomit splashed on her sock. Riley pulls at her hand, trying to get her through the doorway, but Ilse grabs onto the frame with her other hand.

The thing inside Dae—the thing rapidly becoming the thing *outside* Dae, *around* Dae, *subsuming* Dae—stretches a few more dripping legs out. His own legs, his human legs, are curling into him like a dying spider's. His head is mercifully hidden behind the bulk of his own torso but Riley remembers the way his eyeballs sloshed inside his skull and she knows if he were to turn his face toward them now they would be empty, oozing hollows, the soft membranes slipping out and down his face like egg whites. Her stomach rolls and she fights the urge to gag.

"Ilse," she says, her voice low and calm as she can make it. "We have to go. We have to move before it moves."

She pulls again and Ilse lets go of the doorframe. Her eyes focus, tracking across Riley's face.

"Where?" she whispers.

"The box," Riley whispers back.

Ilse grabs her hand and they run.

"THIS IS FUN," BAD COP SAYS. "I'M HAVING FUN NOW. I decided I'm having fun."

Riley looks up, startled out of the memory. She must have been talking for a while now; her throat screams for water. She reaches for the bottle on the table and Bad Cop slides it out of reach.

"It's a fun story, you know? So full of adventure. Danger. Spunky teens!"

She does tiny jazz hands. Riley hates her so much.

"Just a really nice piece of fiction, I have to say. And you're doing it all on no sleep. It's impressive."

"Please," Riley says. Her lips have cracked open again at some point; now that she's back in the room, back in her body, she can feel the sting of them. She can feel a drop of blood making its way slowly down her chin. She wipes it with the back of her hand, wincing at the smell of frostbite slowly claiming her fingertips.

"Meg," Good Cop says disapprovingly. He slides the bottle back toward Riley. She takes it, twists the cap off, wincing as the skin on her fingers catches and sloughs away. She drinks the entire bottle.

"Thank you," she says. Her throat still hurts.

"So after the spider monster climbed out of your friend—"

"It didn't climb out," Riley says. "It . . . it *was* him. Turned inside out."

Bad Cop nods. "Right, sorry, my bad. After the spider monster turned your friend inside out," she says, bright and bubbly and terrifying. "What then?"

21

"WAIT," ILSE SAYS, SKIDDING TO A STOP. "WAIT. WAIT."

She pulls Riley back around the corner. "The lab."

"Why—"

"I have an idea," Ilse says.

"Thank fuck for that—" Riley says, her words getting cut off as Ilse drags her sideways through the door.

The lab looks shockingly normal after everything that's happened, and its tame familiarity makes Riley want to cry. Luke's notebook is still on the counter, his chewed-up pen tucked neatly into the spiral.

"Did you see Luke before I got back?" she asks. Ilse is shoving at one of the sample fridges with her shoulder, trying to get it moving so she can slide it across the floor. Riley leans on it with her and it lurches into motion. They push it against the door and then sink, almost in unison, to the floor with their backs against it.

"I didn't see him," Ilse says quietly. "I thought I heard the snowmobile once—right before Dae stopped breathing—but he never came in."

"He left me a flag line," Riley says. "From the sample tent. We lost the snowmobile and I thought—I thought maybe he found it and came back—"

She presses her lips together as tears close her throat.

"Maybe he did," Ilse says. "Maybe he's in the barn with the generator."

"Maybe," Riley murmurs. She lets her head fall back against the fridge, feeling it throb where she knocked it into the doorframe.

"Do you know what the only constant in nature is?" Ilse asks. Riley rolls her head slightly, just enough to be able to see her. Her eyes are closed.

"What?" Riley asks.

"Fire," Ilse says. "Nothing living likes fire, and nothing living is fireproof."

"Okay," Riley says. "So we light it on fire?"

"We try," Ilse says. "The preserving fluid in here is flammable, and there should be pressurized containers in the barn. I can make a flamethrower, but . . ."

She turns her head toward Riley, opens her eyes. "There's something I have to do first."

Riley has the bizarre thought that Ilse is going to kiss her or something, and in the back of her mind she's faintly surprised to feel that that might not be a totally unwelcome prospect under normal circumstances, but she's just vomited and they're probably about to die, so—

Ilse stands up, walks over to the counter, and starts fiddling with one of the processing machines, breaking off little pieces until she's exposed the interior. Riley watches as best as she can from the floor as Ilse plugs in a heating coil, finds some slides, and crouches in front of her.

"Watch," she says. She holds out her hands and then, lightning fast, she uses her right hand to jab a pin into her left. A bead of blood wells up. She holds the hand steady, using her teeth and her other hand to rip open one of the slide packets, and scoops the blood onto the little glass plate. She sets this on the floor in front of Riley and stands up again. She picks up whatever she's been screwing with from the counter and brings it over. It's a length of wire, wrapped around a rubber mitt and held steady by a microscope clamp. Its tip glows white-hot.

"Ilse—"

"Shhh." Ilse lowers the wire toward the slide, toward the perfect drop of blood on its surface. The blood *shivers*, the bead separating into two even halves. The tip of the wire touches the slide and Riley senses, at the very edge of her hearing, a high whining sound. The blood rolls off the slide, untouched by the wire, and the glass splits in half with a sharp crack.

Ilse lets out a long, wavery breath and sits back on her heels. "I thought so."

Riley looks at the blood soaking into the floor and then at Ilse. "You're infected."

Ilse nods. "I don't know how long I have, but I feel . . . I felt something change." She holds out her hand, motions for Riley to put hers out. "Now we have to check you."

Riley snatches her hand back. "What?"

"We have to," Ilse says. "We can't let it leave."

"What are you saying?"

"When we kill it, I'm . . . I'm hoping that you're right, and all of it will die," Ilse says. "Even the parts that aren't attached to it anymore."

"Okay."

"But if that doesn't happen, we can't let Rusk get his hands on it."

"No," Riley whispers. "Ilse, we can figure it out, we can—"

"If that doesn't happen," Ilse repeats, louder, "we *can't let Rusk get his hands on it*. You have to promise me. You have to promise me you'll kill me, and you have to promise—"

She lunges for Riley's hand, grabs her by the wrist, and yanks her forward. The pin hits the heel of her hand hard.

"Ow, fuck!" she yelps. "Ilse! This is ridiculous, there has to be something else we can do . . ."

She trails off as Ilse rips open another slide and smears her blood onto it. She gets up, still clutching the slide, and goes to the counter to reheat the wire thing. She puts the slide down and lifts the wire, watching a wisp of smoke curl from its tip.

"Ilse, wait," Riley begs. "Please. Please. I can't—if I'm—"

She gasps, her lungs stuttering in her chest. *No. No. Not now.* "I'm too—I'm—" Her heart is leaping, doing roller coaster swoops into her stomach, and she feels like she's drowning. Her vision starts to narrow and sparkle around the edges as she sucks desperately at the air, trying to take a full breath. "Don't—please—I'm scared," she whimpers. "I can't breathe—"

She slumps sideways, pressing her hands to her chest. *Recovery position, recovery position.* She tries to get into a kneeling position so she can put her head down, but the room is wobbling around her. Suddenly Ilse is next to her, helping her up, rubbing her back and making soft soothing sounds. "It's okay," she says. "Breathe. It's okay."

Riley lets her head drop, feels the blood settle inside her skull, pressing against the backs of her eyes. "I'm sorry," she whispers. Her chest aches with constriction. She tries to count, tries to breathe slow, but she just keeps taking those short gaspy breaths and it's making her dizzier. *Fuck.* She puts her hands on her head, curls into a tighter ball.

"I have an inhaler," Ilse says. "I know it's not the same, but—it might help." She feels around in one of her pockets and presses the little plastic device into Riley's hand. "It's a new one. For the trip. I haven't used it."

Riley takes the cap off, puts it to her lips and triggers it, but it's not all the way in her mouth and she sprays a bunch of chemical-scented vapor onto the corner of her lips. She coughs and spits, the taste making her eyes water, and tries again. The second time goes better and she can actually feel her throat opening again, can feel the air as it rushes into her. She triggers it a third time and inhales hard, pulling the mist to the bottom of her lungs, holding it there until she starts to cough again. She puts her head on her knees and lets the inhaler drop to the floor.

"Thank you," she says into her pants.

She looks up to see Ilse's already back at the counter, the glowing wire poised above the slide with her blood on it. Ilse glances at her, concern warring with determination on her face.

"It's okay," Riley whispers. She closes her eyes, squeezes them shut as tight as she can. She wants to put her hands over her ears but she knows Ilse's right, she knows they have to know, but she can't bear it. She doesn't feel different. She doesn't feel like anything is . . . changing inside her, growing or mutating or whatever. Ilse said she felt different, and Riley doesn't feel different, so she's not infected. *So why am I so fucking scared?*

Because what if she *is* infected?

What if she doesn't realize it? What if she's not—not in *tune* with her body enough, too concerned with her brain to notice that something is creeping up the inside of her spine like mold? What if she's been infected the whole time, and she gave it to Luke, and she gave it to *all* of them? She'd followed Greta into the vent, followed her—her *spoor*, her horrible cast-off trail, and what if that whole time she'd just been breathing it in? Letting it coat the inside of her nose, her mouth, her throat, her lungs, sinking in and spreading roots, climbing and twining around her insides like vines. She moans, putting her hands over her face. "Just tell me," she whimpers. "Just say it."

"I—"

The fridge slams Riley forward as something bashes into the door, forcing it open almost a foot. The fridge rocks back, closing the gap, and Ilse screams and drops the wire. Riley lunges for the door, slamming herself against the fridge, shoving it back toward the wall. "Help me!" she yells, trying to brace her feet. Her socks slide against the floor as the door shudders with another impact.

"Let me in," the monster says. "Let me in right now."

It has to be the monster, because there's no one left to say anything except the two of them in that lab, but its voice is all wrong. It's like the creature took everyone it had already consumed and tried to flatten their voices into one sound. It's human, but only barely, and it has . . . layers. It's like listening to two recordings of the same thing, only one is being played at, like, three-quarter speed, like it can't quite catch up to itself. One summer when Riley still had friends, they'd gone down into the caves that only opened up at low tide. Every time one of them talked the sound bounced back into itself until the whole space was almost vibrating with it. Riley had managed to get out and back to the beach before a stress headache set in, but only just. This feels like that, only so much worse.

"Let me *in*," it snarls, slamming some part of itself into the door. Riley wonders what it looks like now. Whose face it has.

"Come on," Ilse says, shoving one of the storage racks against the fridge. "Get into the electrical panel."

She spins away from the door and pulls the cabinet away from the wall, letting it crash to the floor. The noise of it startles an answering shriek from the monster. Ilse pries open the electrical panel and ducks inside, turning to pull Riley in after her. She pulls the panel shut behind them and yanks at it, trying to warp the metal so it's wedged into place.

"Start pulling on things," she snaps, following her own orders. She starts ripping wires out of the wall, yanking at the paneling. "There has to be a way into the vents from here."

The lights flash white and then red, then back to a much dimmer white. Riley starts running her hands over the walls, feeling for some kind of opening. Her fingertips catch on something small and metal, something that feels like it's set into the wall in a depression. She worries at it, digging her nails under it, waiting for some kind of give. Her pinky slips under it and it pinches, breaking the skin immediately.

"Ah, *shit*," she hisses, trying to get another finger underneath. The metal shifts and scrapes against the wall and she jams her hand into the space, lifting and pulling. She bites her lip against the pain, the strained ache in her tendons. The little handle pops free, a small rectangular handhold now standing out from the wall like a drawer pull. Riley shakes out her hand, flexes her fingers, and curls them around the handle. She pulls.

A section of the wall shudders out of true and a breath of cold air puffs over her face.

"Ilse," she says. "Come here."

Ilse steps up next to her, shoulder to shoulder, and slides her hands into the tiny opening Riley's made. The two of them pull hard, and the panel scrapes and shudders and then jerks free, sending them both sprawling backward.

They look up from the floor at the hole in the wall.

"I think it's the vents," Riley says.

"I think you're right," Ilse says. "We have to get to the barn."

"If we go in there, we should be able to get back into the main part of the station," Riley says. "If it connects."

"I have to get the stuff for the flamethrower." Ilse ducks out of the electrical closet. The monster senses her closeness, or her movement, and starts banging on the door again. Riley holds her breath, listening to the clink of bottles and the growling, and Ilse rounds the corner with a plastic gallon jug. Her knuckles are white on the handle.

"Let's go," she says.

ILSE SETS THE JUG ON THE FLOOR AND BRACES herself on the edges of the hole in the wall, then jumps up and tries to get her knee onto the ledge. She slips and swears. Riley steps up behind her and kneels.

"Use my shoulder," she says. Ilse nods, face grim with determination, and puts her hands on the wall once more. She steps onto Riley's shoulder, the bones of her feet flexing as she tries to steady herself, and lunges toward the vent again. This time she makes it in. There's a shriek and a thud and Riley leaps to her feet.

"Ilse?"

She leans into the hole, looking down to see Ilse at the bottom of a five- or six-foot drop.

"Shit. Are you okay?"

"Yes," Ilse says, voice strangled. "I landed on my back."

"Is there a, um, a path? Like a tunnel? Or is it above us?"

Ilse rolls over, wincing, and gets to her feet. Her head is almost level with the bottom of the hole in the wall. She turns in a circle, then crouches. "Here," she says. "It's so small, though."

"Can we get through?"

"I think so," Ilse says. "Hand me the jug."

Riley hoists it over the edge of the hole and Ilse reaches up for it. She puts it on the floor and shoves it forward with her foot. It disappears under the lip of the crawl space.

"Can you get in on your own?"

"I think so," Riley says. Her muscles are overworked, simultaneously feeling too loose and too tight, spasming every time she moves, and her ankle is throbbing, but she has no choice. She takes a deep breath, curls her fingers over the lip of the wall, and launches herself up.

She tumbles over the edge of the hole and, remembering what Ilse said, curls into a ball. She hits the ground with a dull thud shoulder-first, crying out as the bone slams deeper into the socket, and rolls onto her back. She sits up slowly, teeth digging into her lip. Ilse stands watching her.

"Okay?" she asks.

Riley nods, wincing as the movement sends pain shooting up her neck. "Probably."

Ilse lowers herself to the floor, lies down on her back with her head facing the little tunnel. It's *so* small. Riley doesn't know how they're going to fit through it.

"I'm going to go arms first," Ilse says. "So I can push the jug. If I use my feet"—she kicks against the floor, pushing with the soles—"and my hands against the sides, I should be able to sort of wriggle myself along."

"Okay," Riley says. "Just yell when you're far enough in that I can go."

Ilse stretches her arms out over her head and flattens her feet onto the floor, knees bent. She pushes slowly, straightening her legs, and as Riley watches she slides into the vent. Her body is swallowed into the darkness inch by inch and then she's gone.

"It's tight," her disembodied voice says. "I think it will be okay, though."

There's a soft scraping sound. Riley gets herself turned around, lying flat on her back the way Ilse had. She puts her arms up, finding the edges of the vent. She presses her hands flat against the metal, flexing her fingers. Then she changes her mind, pulls one arm back down by her side. If she can push *and* pull, she reasons, she'll have an easier time.

"You okay?" she calls. Distantly she hears the thud of the monster still trying to work its way into the closet.

"Yes," Ilse calls back. Riley waits for something else, something . . . encouraging, maybe, but all she gets is the muffled noises of Ilse moving.

"I'm coming in," she says.

No answer.

She braces her feet on the floor and pushes, keeping her left arm above her head. Her fingers press into the wall of the vent, trying to grip, while her right hand shoves against the floor under her butt. She makes her way forward in slow, hitching movements, watching the dim light disappear beyond her feet.

The vent isn't big enough for her to move her arms now that she's fully inside; she's committed to this one-arm-up-one-arm-down bit. She walks her fingers down the wall, presses her palm into the metal, grateful for once for her clammy skin. She kicks her feet as much as she can, knees brushing the top of the vent every time she does. She wonders how long the shaft is, and whether the monster will be waiting at the end of it. She can hear Ilse shuffling along ahead of her, small scuffly sounds punctuated by the longer slide of the jug across the floor.

"You okay?" she calls. Ilse gives a strained grunt that Riley thinks might be *mm-hmm*. "It's not getting smaller, is it?"

"No," Ilse grits out. "Tired."

Riley falls silent, focuses on her own movement. After a few more minutes she understands why Ilse stopped talking. The motions, small as they are, are quickly becoming agonizing. Every tiny flex of muscles sets off a shivery, crampy ache in the limb she's using. Her breath comes quick and shallow as she inches along, the pain mounting. She stretches and contracts, thinking of caterpillars, wishing dizzily for one moment that someone would scoop her up on a leaf and move her safely to the grass.

They scooch along in the darkness. Sweat starts to trickle from Riley's hairline down into her ears, and she can't do anything about it. She hears the weird ocean-sound of the liquid settling against her eardrums and turns her head, trying to tip it out. The air in the vent is so much warmer than the air in the station; she's sure their combined body heat isn't helping. Every time she stretches her hand out she wonders if she's going to collide with Ilse's foot, but every time she's met with empty space. She doesn't know how Ilse's managed to get so far ahead of her.

"You . . . good?" she asks, forced to stop for breath between the words. There's a knocking sound from ahead, which she guesses is Ilse completely refusing to even try to talk anymore, but at least she's alive. She knocks too, letting her know she gets the message.

Then there's another knock.

This one is right above her face.

"Ilse," she whispers. "Was . . . that you?"

"No," comes the breathless reply.

Adrenaline spikes through Riley's body, sending a fresh wave of shuddering pain along each of her limbs. She squeezes her eyes shut, feeling tears roll down her temples.

Knock. Knock. Knock.

"Go," she whispers. "Go, go, go—"

A choked whimper is the only thing she gets from Ilse, but the sounds of her passage get louder and more frantic. Riley pushes and pulls and shoves herself down the tunnel as fast as she can, breathing so hard and loud she has no way of knowing if the knocking is following them. She keeps her eyes closed, reaching into the darkness again and again, and then she hears a strangled, wordless cry from in front of her.

"Ilse!" she screams.

A hand seizes hers.

Riley screams and opens her eyes and there's light, there's a faint red light and Ilse is kneeling in front of her, pulling her, and then she's birthed into a small round space that feels almost cavernous after the vent.

"Holy fuck," she gasps, staring up at Ilse's red, sweaty face. "Oh my God."

"I know," Ilse says. "I know."

Riley struggles to sit up, her body fighting her every step of the way, and pulls Ilse into a fierce hug.

"Don't," Ilse says, pushing her back. "If you're not infected—"

"Wait, what?" Riley stares at her. The dim red safety light seems to pulse. "Didn't you . . . wasn't my . . ."

"There wasn't time," Ilse says shortly. "I don't know. I didn't see."

"Oh," is all Riley can say. She doesn't feel relieved. She feels . . . maybe not *more* scared, but scared in a new way. She tries to send her consciousness out into her body, poke and prod at everything and see if anything feels strange, but her brain just keeps spiraling back in on itself. *My kingdom for a Xanax*, she thinks, and laughs. Ilse raises an eyebrow.

"Don't gloat," she says.

"No, I'm—sorry," Riley says. "I was just thinking how bad I want a Xanax, and it was, like . . . absurd. Sorry."

Ilse just looks at her.

"Where do we go now?" Riley asks, turning her gaze to the space around them. She's not capable of panicking yet, she thinks, not now that she's free of the tunnel. It will take at least a few minutes before terror and claustrophobia reassert themselves.

"Up," Ilse says. She points. Riley cranes her neck to see what she's looking at. There's a safety light above them, a red bulb in a metal cage, and next to it is what looks like a very old, very rusted metal bar. Riley follows her gaze up, up, up to the shadow of another rung.

A ladder.

"We have to jump again," Ilse says. "I can boost you this time, if you can take the jug."

"Oh, Christ," Riley says wearily.

"I know."

"Why don't the steps go all the way down?"

"I think they used to," Ilse says. "I think this is a much older part of the station. Some kind of access shaft."

"Do you think Nelson was right about the underground system?" Riley turns to her. "Maybe we can get to another station?"

"I don't know," Ilse says. "I don't know how far below the station we are right now, or if we're below it at all. It felt like the tunnel was tilted, a little, but that could have just been dizziness."

"But there's nowhere else." Riley turns in a circle, scrutinizing the walls. The red light is making her eyes itch.

"I don't think so," Ilse says. "And we have to move."

"You heard it, right?" Riley asks. "The knocking."

"Yes."

"Do you think . . ."

"I don't know what else it could have been," Ilse says.

"Pipes? Or something?" Riley knows as she says it she's grasping at straws. "I just . . . we know it could get through the wall if it wanted to, so why . . ."

"It's hunting us," Ilse says simply.

"Herding us," Riley says, thinking about what Luke had said during the storm. "What if we're just going where it wants us to go?"

"We might be."

"But there's nowhere else," Riley says again. "Fuck."

"Fuck," Ilse agrees. "Now let's go."

23

ILSE CROUCHES AT THE BASE OF THE WALL, BELOW
the last usable rung of the ladder. It's maybe seven feet above
their heads; doable, maybe, for a pair of teenagers that haven't
just been run through a wringer. Riley shakes out her arms and
legs, does a few deep squats. She doesn't know what she's doing;
stalling, most likely, but it makes her feel more prepared. She
looks at Ilse.

"I'm gonna run up on it," she says. "It's probably gonna hurt."

"Probably," Ilse says.

"Okay."

She bounces on the balls of her feet, ignoring the twinge of
her ankle. She backs up as far as she can across the little chamber
and charges toward Ilse. Her left foot hits square in the middle of
her back and she pushes up, faintly hearing Ilse's grunt of effort
as she tries to lift her, and then her arm slams up under the bar
and she hooks her forearm back, feeling the rusted metal bite
into her sleeve, and her body hits the wall of the shaft hard. Her
cheekbone smashes into the rung and she bites her tongue but
she holds on, legs pedaling against the wall as she drags her other
arm up and grabs the rung. She wrestles herself closer, jamming
her arm up higher until both elbows are snug around the bar.
Her joints scream with the strain of supporting her weight. She's
panting. She unhooks her right arm, squeezing the other tight

around the rung, and reaches up, stretching and grasping until her fingers graze the next bar. She slides her knees against the wall, hitches her body into a tight curve like the back of a beetle and then *shoves* with her shins, sending her upward just enough to let her fingers wrap around the rung. Her other arm comes up without her even thinking about it, hand slapping onto the bar and snapping shut like a vise. She pulls herself up, a scream escaping through her gritted teeth as her feet search desperately for a hold. When her foot hits the rung she lets out a sob of triumph, letting her weight sag onto it for a moment before bringing the other one up next to it. She's in a crouching position, both hands on one rung and both feet scant inches below, but she's on the wall. She's on the ladder.

"Thank you," she whispers, not sure who she's talking to. She straightens her legs slowly, carefully, pressing her upper body tight against the wall as she reaches for the next rung. After a few agonizing minutes she's fully upright.

"Now what?" she pants, pressing her forehead against the rung and immediately regretting it as the rust pricks into her skin. She looks down, trying to see behind her. "Ilse?"

There's no answer. She grabs the rung tighter and turns around as far as she can, then does the same thing in the opposite direction.

Ilse is gone.

"Ilse!" Riley yells. "Are you fucking *kidding* me!"

She wants to cry.

Not yet. Not now. Get it together, Riley.

She opens her eyes.

"Ilse," she calls. "If you went back—if you're back in the tunnel, can you—will you at least knock? Just knock. Just let me know . . ."

A sob lodges itself in her throat. She waits, holding her breath.

A faint, hollow knock floats up toward her. The sob bursts free and she gasps and hiccups and says, "Thank you."

She doesn't let herself think about the possibility that it wasn't Ilse.

She starts climbing.

She climbs, one hand over the other, legs shaking with effort. Her foot slips and she falls, catches herself with one hand, her body swinging away from the wall. She feels something in her wrist click as she kicks her feet, wrenching herself back toward the ladder. She gets her feet under her, loops her arms under the bar she's holding, and cries. She *wails*. She sobs like a baby whose mother is never, never coming back to it, until she has no tears left to cry.

She reaches up.

She climbs.

One hand over the other.

The red light pulses around her, growing fainter and brighter every time she passes another caged safety bulb. She stops counting after the fourth one, but she wonders in the back of her mind if every bulb is supposed to indicate a floor, and if that's so, why there are no entrances near any of them.

After a lifetime of climbing her hand finds something that feels like another rung, only—only this one is a lip, a round metal bar at the edge of something, the edge of something *flat* and *solid* and she lets out a yell and surges upward, fingers scrabbling across the smooth metal, feet kicking and flailing into open space as she wrestles her body up and over the ledge.

She lies there panting, gasping for breath, and after a minute she rolls over onto her back. She's in a tunnel of some kind, long and flat, safety lights stretching away into the distance. It's cold, but not unbearably. The walls are concrete, not metal, so it's not part of the ventilation system, she thinks. She doesn't know where she is in relation to the Victoria Station; she assumes she's still underneath it, or next to it, or hopefully at least *connected* to it somehow. Wouldn't it be just her luck to have somehow climbed into some kind of, like, abandoned service tunnel that leads to an abandoned station, with no radio, and no snowmobiles, and also the door is locked from the outside, and then she can just starve and/or freeze to death before the monster ever even finds her.

Tunnel pings somewhere inside her, and she plucks the actual thought out of the stream of anxiety. *Service tunnel.*

She rolls over and gets to her feet, then peers back over the edge of the shaft she just climbed out of. She racks her exhausted brain, trying to remember what Luke and Nelson had told her about Lake Vostok. She knows they're not above it, not all the way out at the station, but maybe it goes farther than they thought. Maybe the edge of it is right here.

Would they have tried to drill this far out?

Why not?

She thinks about a murder mystery she read once, something about a woman who was killed in a cave because she discovered the illegal oil drilling that was going on down there. The pipe had gone in at an angle, to avoid detection, but it had smashed through ancient rock formations and destroyed parts of the cave altogether. Riley doesn't know if that's standard, or if something like that would happen in real life, but is it possible that someone has been drilling underneath the Victoria Station?

The answer hits her like a sledgehammer, and she slumps against the wall, still staring down into the pit.

Rusk.

He could have been drilling here for ages, trying to break sideways into the space above Lake Vostok. They had put a ban on it, sure, but he's rich and cocky enough to ignore the rules, and he

usually does. *Bioweapons*, Nelson had said. She had forgotten all
about it when the creature showed up—and clearly that's Rusk's
endgame now, securing the monster—but why did he have
Russians doing surveillance in the Antarctic in the first place?
What had he been spying on when the monster unexpectedly
lurched into view?

"That's why he bought the station," she whispers, turning
back toward the tunnel. She starts walking, wondering if the pipe
ran through here or if—she shivers—she's actually *in* the pipe.
Would they have some kind of . . . service entrance? She visualizes
a big pipe running alongside the drill, little doors perched every
few feet for someone to pop their head through and make sure
everything is working. She has a strong, fierce yearning for Luke,
and grief breaks over her like a wave as she realizes he's gone.
They're all gone, and only she is left, and she's *useless*.

She wipes her nose on her sleeve. The tunnel is so cold. Her
brain feels like it's marinating, pickling in the red light of the
safety bulbs. She wonders if she can break them or if the metal
cages would make it impossible. But no, she can't do that, her
phone is dead. She'd have no light at all. She squints, trying
to keep as much of the light out of her eyes as possible. She
imagines it shining through her pupils, burning her brain like
an ant under a magnifying glass, and settles for keeping her eyes
closed. She opens them for a second every few steps, checks all
around her for a way to escape, and then closes them again and
keeps moving. Her hand trails along the wall, the cold leaching
into her skin. She walks in silence, her steps echoing softly around
her. She tries to think of a plan.

The next time she opens her eyes she can see there's an
incline in the tunnel a few hundred feet in the distance. Another
wave of tiredness crashes over her and she pushes herself back
into motion, keeping her eyes half-open as she goes. The incline
is actually stairs, their outlines becoming clear as she gets closer.

They're concrete like the floor, and there's a rail bolted to the wall at an angle along them. She climbs them slowly, every muscle begging for her to stop, pulling herself up with the rail. The metal is almost too cold to touch, but she ignores the ache it sets off in her fingers. She counts stairs until she gets to thirty and then she stops and slides to the ground. She looks up, trying to find an endpoint. Surely there can't be that many left. Surely she can't be that far underground. She takes a deep breath, then another, inventorying herself for signs of panic. She's surprised to find none, and realizes that she might actually be too tired to have a panic attack. *Gotta tell Dr. Temple about that one*, she thinks as she hauls herself back to her feet. *Miracle cure.*

The air gets warmer as she climbs—still not warm, not by any stretch of the imagination, but warmer. She wonders briefly if she's hypothermic. She's so fucking tired. When was the last time she slept? Or ate? In the sample tent, with Luke. That stupid fucking grape-flavored sports gel. Her stomach actually growls as she thinks of it.

"The first thing," she mutters, "the first thing I'm doing when I get back into the station, I'm finding something to eat. If it kills me in the kitchen, it kills me in the kitchen. I'll die with a fucking . . . a fucking Pop-Tart in my hand. I don't care . . ."

She keeps mumbling to herself as she climbs, no longer really aware she's doing it, the words bubbling from her lips in a slurred stream. She feels distantly like she's losing her mind, like some key part of her is detaching, somewhere inside, from where it should be. Is this what Ilse felt? Is this the monster, taking root inside her? Or is this just her own broken brain, pushed to its limit?

Not broken. Different.

She snorts.

Sure fucking feels broken right now, Doc.

Her feet catch on the steps more and more often, and more

than once she falls all the way down, cracking her knees on the concrete. She gets up again and again. Maybe she's dead; maybe she died in the snow and this is hell. Just climbing these stairs, alone, after everyone else is gone. Maybe she'll never—

She stumbles as her foot, reaching for another step, meets no resistance. She tips forward, slamming the heels of her hands into the ground. The flat, stairless ground. She looks up in disbelief. Another tunnel stretches out before her, another string of safety lights, but—but! There is a small black shape in the distance, and it could be a door, and she pushes herself up off the ground and she runs. She runs, arms pumping, heart pounding against her ribs, and the door comes up so suddenly that she almost runs straight into it.

She puts her hands on it, barely daring to believe. It's cold, and it has a wheel like the door at the Leviathan Station. Does it go outside? If it goes outside . . . she's got no coat, no nothing. She'll freeze in a few minutes.

Does it matter?

She closes her eyes, presses her forehead against the door. She doesn't know why, or what for, but she wants to live. She wants to try. If the door goes outside she'll just stay here in the tunnel until the storm passes. She'll wait and hope that the monster doesn't know about the tunnels, that it doesn't track her into wherever the hell she's gotten herself, climbing—

Ilse.

"Fuck," she whispers, picking her head up just enough to bang it gently on the door. "Fuck, fuck, fuck, fuck."

Ilse knows about the tunnels.

The monster knows about the tunnels.

She can't stay here.

She puts both hands on the wheel and pulls, putting her entire body into it. She lets her knees buckle, lets the wheel take her weight, and slowly, so slowly, it starts to turn. She straightens up, tucking her raw, freezing palms under her armpits for a moment. Then she opens the door.

There's no light coming through it, which is a twofold relief. One: not outside. Two: she can finally get away from that awful red glow. She steps through the door cautiously, holding one hand in front of her, half expecting to feel something slimy and breathing and alive. Gradually her eyes adjust to the slight ambient light.

It's a closet.

SHE STANDS THERE MOTIONLESS, MOUTH HANGING open like she's been slapped. It's a closet. It's a *closet*. There's a fucking pull-string lightbulb above her head, and she yanks on it so hard it snaps off, but the light comes on. Soft, yellow, normal light. She could just cry.

It's a supply closet, she sees as she moves slowly across the little room. Pallets of boxes, cans of fuel, cans of—

"Oh my God," she murmurs, lunging forward. "Please be a pull tab, please be a pull tab—"

It's a pull tab, a pull-tab top on a tin of Spam, and she's never seen anything so beautiful in her entire life. She rips it open and starts shoving chunks into her mouth with her fingers, and she doesn't stop until the container is empty. She opens another and eats all of it, and half of a third, before she finally takes a real breath. Her mouth tastes like salt and meat and she's desperate for water, but for the first time since—*since the SpaghettiOs*, she thinks with a wry smile—she's full. She shoves the empty tins into the corner, knowing what she's about to do and knowing she shouldn't, and knowing she absolutely can't do anything else. She stretches out on the floor, pressing her body against the wall, and then curls into a fetal position. She needs to get out of this closet and figure out where she is. She needs to keep moving, stay ahead of the monster. She needs to, at the very least, open the door and make sure she's not inside a fucking *lair* or something, but she doesn't. She puts her head down on her clasped hands and she falls asleep.

Her first thought when she regains consciousness is *That was a mistake.* Her body has stiffened and cramped; her arms are asleep and yet somehow still ache. She stretches one leg out, then the other, wincing at the way they crack. Every one of her muscles shrieks as she unfolds herself. Her *ribs* hurt. Her *armpits* hurt. Parts of her she didn't even know existed hurt. She moans, low and miserable, and sits up. She rubs her arms, shaking the feeling back into them, the prickle of pins and needles giving way to a low burn that doesn't subside as she moves. She crawls over to the half-empty tin of Spam and eats the rest of it slowly, sucking the salt from her fingers, wishing for water.

It's time, she thinks. *You know it is.*

She stands, bones clicking and protesting, and turns to face the door. The one she came in through, the metal one, is behind her. The one in front of her doesn't have a submarine wheel, or a lock, or even a real knob. It has a push bar, like a diner. She half expects a bell to ring when she opens it.

She pushes the door open and steps through in one quick motion, fists raised in front of her like a boxer. They unclench and fall to her sides almost immediately as she looks around.

"You've gotta be kidding me," she says under her breath.

It looks for all the world like she's in the barn.

She's in the back, behind the gigantic draped silhouette of some kind of machine, but she's fairly certain. There's an electric lantern perched in the far corner that looks exactly like the one Nelson had taken with him to find the radio a thousand years ago, and in the circle of light it casts she can see the tangle of cords where he'd freed it from the wall. It's their barn, all right, and the hulking thing beside her is probably Rusk's fucking drill. She would spit on it if she weren't so dehydrated.

She makes her way through the space. There's one more snowmobile, tucked back against a wall, and she runs her hands over it like it's made of gold. It's definitely older than the others, but if it runs—if it has gas—she can use it. Not yet, not until the end, but she can use it.

What had Ilse said about the flamethrower? What would be in here that she could use?

Riley picks up the lantern and starts pacing around. It would have to be pressurized, whatever it is, some kind of hose with a trigger mechanism, and something that could make a spark. She wonders if the monster destroyed Ilse's little wire heating-coil contraption; that could probably ignite something. She finds a padlocked storage bin, a bunch of empty gas cans, and a discarded coat that she immediately puts on, but nothing that could serve as a weapon. She looks thoughtfully at the shrouded machine.

She has to pull with both hands to get the tarp to move, yanking and hauling as it pools onto the floor around her. The machine doesn't look anything like a drill, but she guesses it wouldn't. The things they used to take the sample cores didn't either, not really. They were designed for *non-scientists*, as Greta had kindly termed it, so they had a recognizable point-and-shoot shape, but even then they didn't look like something you'd use to build a house. This thing is clearly not for non-scientists, and Riley supposes it could do any number of horrifying things, but for now she's going to assume she's right and it's a drill because her entire plan, flimsy as it is, hinges on it being a drill. She's thinking about Nelson again, about what Ilse had said about the kerosene. They had to spray something into that hole to keep the drill moving, and they had to use a . . . a *sprayer* to do it.

There has to be something here.

There's another storage bin pushed up against the machine, and this one doesn't have a padlock on it. She undoes the latch, lifts the little metal hasp, and opens the lid. A neon orange hazmat suit glares up at her, the cracked faceplate of the gas mask glinting dully.

"Huh," she says. She pulls it out, lets it drop onto the floor behind her. There's a pair of boots at the bottom of the bin, resting on top of something metal that's been bundled into a blanket. She pushes them aside, grips the bundle. Its shape doesn't make sense in her hands. She lifts it out, backs away from the bin, and sets it on the floor. She holds her breath as she takes one edge of the blanket and unrolls it.

It almost looks like a scuba rig. There's a tank and a hose, and some kind of harness that looks like it would go across a person, but instead of a mouthpiece there's a long, thin metal nozzle that ends in a little mesh ball. She looks back at the hazmat suit, wondering what the hell Rusk was spraying down into the depths of the ice, and then she picks up the tank and unscrews the top.

There's a hiss and a faint chemical odor, but nothing sprays out at her, and when she turns it upside down only a few drops of something patter out onto the floor. She does her best not to inhale directly above them, shuffling a few feet away with the tank clutched against her. She inspects the rest of it, putting her arms through the straps until it's situated on her shoulders in a way that almost makes sense. The hose doesn't have a trigger, but there's a little squeezy handle on the front of the harness, and when she closes her hand around it she sees a breath of something puff out of the mesh ball.

"Okay," she says. "Okay."

She reaches back, puts the lid on the tank, and slings the hose over her shoulder. She approaches the door to the outside at an angle, arcing across the interior of the barn. She doesn't *really* think the monster is waiting just beyond the threshold, but she's not going to just waltz into it if it is.

The snow in front of the barn is smooth, the sunlight dazzling; Riley doesn't know how much time has passed since she and Ilse climbed into the vent, but clearly the storm is over. The ice sparkles, dusted with an even layer of fresh powder. She sweeps her gaze back and forth, letting her eyes adjust, until she's sure she doesn't see anything like footprints in the space between the station and the barn. Then she steps outside.

She crosses the yard in jerky, uneven steps, her legs rebelling as her boots sink into the snow. She remembers their first night in the station, trailing Luke back from the barn, the feel of eyes on the back of her neck. If she had said anything then, would things be different? Would he still be here? Would the rest of them?

She shakes her head. *Can't go there.* Not now.

The back door is unlocked, which Riley no longer has the energy to be scared by. Either Luke left it that way when they made their second attempt at Arcturus, or Ilse opened it at some point while she and Dae were waiting for them, or it was the monster. She steps into the kitchen.

The station, once again, is almost distressingly normal. The furniture is piled in front of the fireplace where they'd left it, and there are dishes in the sink, but aside from that it looks exactly like it did when they first arrived. She doesn't *want* it to look like it's been ransacked by a creature from her nightmares, but at the same time, that might make her feel a little bit saner.

She keeps her borrowed coat on as she walks through the station, keeping an ear out for any sound. She just has to make it to the lab. She holds her breath every time she rounds a corner, sliding a foot out before she makes the turn to tempt anything out of hiding. She wraps her fingers around the little squeezy thing on the harness, worries at it quietly. She has to remember not to do that once the tank is full.

Her breath catches in her throat when she sees the door to the lab. It's almost gone, smashed beyond recognition, just a pile of splintered plastic. Larger chunks swing from the hinges. She walks toward it, pulling the big coat more tightly around her. She still doesn't know how Dae's wound got so infected, but she can't let that plastic cut her. She shuffles her feet, clearing a path through the debris on the floor, and then she ducks under the remains of the ruined door.

The fridge is tipped over, coolant and melting ice and broken sample containers everywhere. It must have opened as the creature shoved its way in. The rest of the lab is relatively untouched, and—her heart rises in her chest—Ilse's little contraption is lying on the counter.

The slide with Riley's blood on it lies next to it.

She crosses the room and lifts the little thing with shaking hands, trying to figure out how Ilse had heated it. She plugs in one of the little flat-top induction boilers and waits for the light to turn green, turning the device over and over in her hands. It reminds her of the coffee frother her mom has, a silly little thing her dad had gotten in some kind of free-swag demonstration at Costco, like a tiny immersion blender. She sinks it into her coffee mug every morning, not removing it until there's a layer of foam cresting the edge of the cup. Or—another memory surfaces, from lower down, when Riley was much younger—a doctor, cauterizing something inside her nose, long thin rod with a glowing metal pick at its tip. She used to get nosebleeds even worse than she does now. *Like a goddamn faucet*, she hears her mom saying, holding her head over the sink as she wads towels underneath her nose. *Pinch it, Ri, squeeze hard, don't let up for even a second.* They went to the hospital after she had one so bad for so long that she fainted from blood loss. *They're going to burn it,* her mother says in her memory. *It's gonna hurt for just a little bit, but when they're done you won't get nosebleeds anymore, okay, Ri? Be a big girl for me, okay?*

She shakes her head, freeing herself from the echo of her mom's voice. It had worked, the cauterization, but she just started getting nosebleeds from the other nostril instead. They weren't as severe, though, and the procedure was expensive. She learned to deal with it.

The light on the coil flips to green, and Riley considers it thoughtfully. She takes the little machine and rests its tip on the burner. As she waits for something to happen, she looks at the slide with her blood on it.

It's still there, the blood, which she thinks is a good sign. Everything the creature sheds seems to evaporate or something pretty quickly, so if she were infected, her blood would be gone, right? All the tiny creature-bits inside, cut off from their body, they would have shriveled up and died and vanished, leaving an empty slide. So she's probably fine. She doesn't need to press the white-hot wire into it, doesn't need to watch it sizzle and burn and do whatever else normal human blood does when it's exposed to heat. She doesn't need that validation.

She ignores the voice in her head that says *That's not why you're not going to do it.* She knows.

The wire coil is glowing now, edging through orange on its way to white. She slips the tank off her back and casts around the room, looking for whatever Ilse had funneled into that gallon jug that's probably still down there in the tunnel, and her gaze falls almost immediately on the drum of alcohol.

It's the preservative they would use for biological samples, if there had been any. She doesn't know how long it's been there. Greta had just sort of waved her hand at it and said, "It's there if you need it." It has a series of variously complicated plastic things on top meant to keep people from opening it unless they really, really intend to open it, and there's a handle like the one on a bike pump jutting out of it.

Alcohol is flammable. Riley doesn't know a lot, but she knows that. She sets about trying to open the drum. There are so many tiny things to unscrew, and all of them seem to have that childproof press-and-turn thing built in. She piles them on top of the drum as she removes them, and finally one comes free with the strong, sharp smell of concentrated alcohol.

There's a rustling noise from behind her. She turns slowly, hand reaching for the wire coil, feeling along the countertop as she swivels her head toward the source of the sound. She's wrapping her fingers around the base of the little gadget when she realizes.

"Oh," she says quietly. "Oh, honey."

The rat—Greta's rat, the lab rat, the one that doesn't even have a fucking name—is standing in the corner of its cage on its hind legs, front paws wrapped around the metal grid like a tiny prisoner. It stares at her, blinks its little beady eyes.

"God damn it," she says. "Ah, shit. All right."

She goes over and opens the little door. The rat runs right out onto her arm, climbs her sleeve, and nuzzles promptly into the space between the coat and her neck.

"Are you gonna stay there?" she asks it. "You're gonna have to stay there. You can't be, you know, *Ratatouille*-ing around in my shirt or wherever."

The rat curls its tail around her neck.

"God damn it," she says again, beleaguered, and she sounds so much like her dad for a second that it makes the corner of her mouth twitch into a smile.

"I know she didn't name you, and I wanna respect that," she says as she turns back to the other counter. "But apparently I'm going to be talking to you, which feels, I guess, slightly better than talking to myself, so I'm gonna call you Basil." She pronounces it the British way, *bazzle*, gives it a little oomph. "Like the Great Mouse Detective."

Basil squeaks.

"I know you're a rat, but Ratigan's the bad guy. He's got a good song, but he's the bad guy, and you're on the good-guy team, so you have to be Basil. You're the Great Rat Detective, okay?"

She's perhaps too comforted by the small soft weight of it against her skin, the prick of tiny claws grounding her in her body for the first time in days, but what's done is done. She's not going to leave a rat in a cage to burn to death.

"Now, where were we?"

She turns back to the drum. She presses the bike-pump handle down and yelps as alcohol spatters across the floor. There's a piece of plastic tubing she hasn't seen, snaking out of the side of the drum.

"Well, shit. Did I even need to open it?" She sets the tank on the floor and feeds the tube into it. "Probably I did. It's probably a, um, for air flow, or whatever. You know, like how the coffee cup has the extra tiny hole in the lid."

Basil, presumably having limited experience with disposable coffee cups, crawls farther into her coat and doesn't respond.

"Here we go," she says, and starts pumping in earnest. The tank fills quicker than she expects and more alcohol splashes onto the floor. She yanks the tube out and holds it, pointing the open end toward the ceiling like that will stop the flow. The pump handle returns slowly to its neutral position. She stands and pulls the tube up, letting the remainder of the alcohol in it flow back into the drum. She doesn't bother to put the caps back on.

"Okay," she says, screwing the lid back onto the tank. "Now for the dangerous part."

She slings the tank over her shoulder once more, picks up the metal hose, and grabs Ilse's wire thing with her other hand. She takes one last look at the drop of her blood, sitting there on the counter, and then she ducks out into the hallway.

She realizes quickly that she doesn't have enough hands for what she needs to do. The squeezy handle, the spark, the hose. She stands there for a moment, thinking. Then she turns and moves quickly down the hall toward her room.

The hot-pink claw clip is lying on the floor in the hall, where she threw it a lifetime ago. She lets go of the hose and scoops it up. Then she puts the base of the wire thing between her knees, squeezing them together and praying she doesn't set herself on fire. She grabs the hose again, adjusting it so the little mesh sprayer-ball is as far from her as possible, and points it away from her face. She opens the claw clip, holds her breath, and clamps it onto the squeezy handle.

A fine mist of alcohol blooms around the nozzle of the hose.

"Yes!" she whispers, punching the air. The wire thing slips and she lurches downward, grabbing it before it can hit the floor. She maneuvers it carefully, walking her fingers down its body until she's holding it firmly, and then she reaches out and brings the still-glowing tip to the sprayer.

A ball of flame bursts into life.

She stares at it in disbelief. It's . . . well, it's a ball. It's not *throwing* anything. The way the mesh atomizes the alcohol, the mist around the nozzle, it's just sort of keeping itself contained. It's like a deadly pom-pom.

"Fuck."

She makes a few experimental jabs with it, feinting down the empty hall. It could certainly set something on fire, but she'd have to be right up against it. Certainly within the range of those long arms.

"Fuuuuuuuuuuck."

She opens the claw clip and the flow of alcohol stops. The flame burns out a moment later. She takes the tank off and kneels on the floor to examine the hose. The little mesh thing . . . if there was a way she could snap it off, the way the tip snaps off a bottle of hair dye . . .

She puts the toe of her boot on top of the mesh ball and shifts her weight onto it with a soft *crunch*. She wiggles her fingers under the body of the hose, slides them up the nozzle until they're just a few inches from her boot, and then starts pulling. The metal is still warm, which helps; after a few fruitless seconds it starts to give and lift, folding where it's pinned underneath her. She pulls until it's almost vertical, then starts pushing it back down, trying to weaken it at the bend. The metal warps, lifting her boot with it. She growls and shoves her foot down, trying to put more weight on it, and suddenly there's a snap and her hand—with the hose in it—jerks upward, free.

She looks at the nozzle, now two inches shorter. Her weight has crushed it flat where it broke off. She puts it back under her boot, rotating it so the flat edges are perpendicular to the ground, and leans on it ever so slightly. Small hole means more pressure, she knows that from years of watering the garden, but there still needs to be a hole. She feels the slightest creak under her foot and pulls the nozzle out, bringing it to her face. The metal has given just enough to separate the two flat edges of the nozzle, bowing them outward into a hole barely bigger than the head of a pin. Fierce triumph floods through her. Without thinking she squeezes the handle and is rewarded by a jet of alcohol that just barely misses hitting her in the face. With *force*.

She puts the tank back on, patting the back of the coat to make sure the rat is still there. He's crawled into the hood, but he's there, and he pokes a claw gently into her skin at the disruption from sleep. She stands heavily, knees popping again, wondering if it's possible to completely erode cartilage by the tender age of seventeen. The wire device lies on the floor, tip gone cold. She stares at it. She could go back to the lab, heat it up again, pray that she doesn't ever need another spark for this thing, but there has to be a better way. Surely there's a lighter somewhere in here. She says another mental *Fuck you* to Rusk for the switch-operated fireplace and starts toward Nelson's room. He had the most visible vices, she reasons. He probably has a pack of weird fancy English cigarettes and a lighter stashed away among them.

The room smells like his cologne, which she hasn't realized she misses until this moment. Sadness crests again, leaving hopelessness when it recedes. All these smart, caring people, these kids who wanted to help make the world better. Kids who were still finding their way, figuring out who they wanted to be, gone. Gone because of Anton Rusk.

Her hands close into fists. She starts rifling through Nelson's stuff. He brought books, which is weirdly charming. He thought he would have time to read. Riley did, too, but she sort of assumed there would be social hours she wasn't going to attend. There's an open envelope tucked into a paperback of *Lonesome Dove*; she pulls it out and turns it over. It says *Nelson* on the front in curvy handwriting. She peeks inside the envelope, just long enough to see *Dear Son*, and puts it back. For all his issues with his mom, he brought her with him. She closes the desk drawer, and something rattles. She pulls it out again, all the way out, and a little baggie drops to the floor from underneath it.

"Nelson, you beautiful boy," she murmurs, kneeling. The baggie holds two joints and a lighter, a heavy, sleek metal thing with a flip-top. It has his initials on it. Riley's never liked weed, finds it makes her both sleepy *and* paranoid, but she loves it in this moment more than she has ever loved anything, because Nelson brought it with him, and he brought a lighter for it.

She tucks the lighter into her pocket and gets up off the floor.

"Once more with feeling," she says.

25

THE JET OF FIRE BILLOWS OUT OF THE NOZZLE WITH a force and a roar that surprises her, knocks her back on her feet. It shoots almost five feet down the hall. She watches it with satisfaction, imagining the creature at the other end of it. Her face curls into something like a smile.

"Let's go, then," she yells into the hallway. "Let's fucking *go*."

She starts down the hall, banging on the walls every few feet. It feels strange to make so much noise, to be *trying* to attract attention, but part of her relishes it. Her body hums, the aches and pains of the last few days receding in the face of her bloodlust. She wants to hurt this thing, she realizes. Really hurt it, watch it suffer. She wants it to burn slow, and she wants it to know that she's the one who killed it.

"Come on!" she howls, triggering another burst of flame. "Come out and get me! Come on!"

As the roar of the flames dies, she hears something behind her. A small, wet sound, like slow-moving liquid. She whirls around, nozzle raised.

"I'm here, motherfucker!" she yells.

Her eyes find the grate on the wall. A thin trickle of something black is making its way toward the floor, undulating in the dim light. She moves toward it, pausing after each step, waiting, and then without warning it comes.

A mass of black-red blood surges through the grate with a pulpy, gurgling *slurp*. It sticks for a moment and then drops to the ground, splattering across the hall. For a moment Riley thinks that's all it is—just blood—and then it moves. The larger clots start to quiver, pulling toward each other as if drawn by a magnet, and the smaller ones follow. The mass gathers itself at the base of the wall, and then something bubbles to its surface. It breaks through a thin membrane of viscous goo and swivels toward Riley and blinks.

An eye.

Riley doesn't flinch.

"Which one of them?" she asks it. "Who are you going to be?"

The eye rolls and sinks back into the muck, then reemerges surrounded by a face.

Ilse.

Riley's lips tremble, but she still doesn't move.

"That's a good trick," she says. "I can see why Rusk wants to keep you in a box forever."

Ilse's blood-slicked face rises, pulling the oozing mass with it, and as it does it starts to take shape. A hand emerges, bracing it on the wall. Then another hand, on the wrong side of the body, lurching forward to where it should be. It holds that hand out to her and a thin gash opens in its palm to show a row of neat white teeth.

"Riley," it says with Ilse's voice.

It starts to move toward her, condensing with every step, edges raveling inward until it's an almost-perfect copy of Ilse. Her face is wrong, like it can't remember where the bones go, and her skin is mottled inside and out with blood and black tendrils, but it tips its head to the side in a familiar way that makes something inside her clench.

"I'm so hungry," she says. The face moves, the place where

the mouth should be, rippling and bulging, but the voice is still coming from that extended hand. The teeth shift inside the hole, trying to find where they're supposed to be, and her words are mangled by the movement. "It's cold in here, and I'm so hungry."

"You're not Ilse," Riley says.

"But I am!" she cries. "Look at me. Help me."

The mouth in her hand closes, only to open again a little ways up her arm.

"Don't listen," it says. "It's not me."

A thin shard of doubt pierces Riley's heart. "Ilse?" she whispers. "Are you in there? Can you . . . remember?"

Another mouth, this time across her clavicle. "Yes." Another on her cheek. "Yes." Another on her thigh. "Yes."

They all speak, overlapping each other. "It's me," one of them says. "It's not me," says another. Mouths open across Ilse's body, tearing open and closing faster than Riley can process the sight, and all of them are talking to her, begging her, saying her name. She drops the hose and puts her hands over her ears.

"Stop it," she whispers. The mouths yawn, bristling with teeth—how are there so many *teeth*, where is it *getting* them— and grin at her.

"I'm getting stronger," it says in a hundred voices. "I can use their minds, their knowledge."

She stares at it, scrabbling for the hose and holding it to her chest. "What do you mean?"

As she watches, Ilse's form stretches upward. The shoulders broaden, the face gets craggier and squarer. The mouth appears, opens to reveal an undulating black mass.

"This is what her father looks like," it says. "Or looked like. Before she killed him."

"You can't sustain it," Riley says. "You'll fall apart."

"You have no idea what I've become," Ilse's father snarls. "You have no idea what I can do."

"I know you'll burn," Riley says, and as it lunges for her she wraps her hand around the trigger.

The first blast misses it entirely, goes arcing over its head to shatter into tiny flames that die on the floor behind it.

"Ah, fuck."

The second one catches it full in the face.

It screams and reels away from her, clawing at itself, flinging gobbets of burning flesh away from its body. It starts to change shape, collapsing onto all fours, keening and gibbering as it paws at its face. Its mouth opens and the writhing coils inside it are burning. Riley smiles and lifts the nozzle.

Something slams into her back, sending her sprawling forward into a pool of smoking viscera. She jerks her hands back, frantically wiping them on her pants as she stumbles to her feet and turns around.

It's the monster.

It's *another* monster.

It's the same monster, the rest of its body, the part that chased them into the vent. The part that has the rest of her friends. She can *see* them. It's crouched low on the floor, limbs splayed in all directions, poised like a spider. All eight of its legs end in hands. Its body—the mass at the center of it—opens with a shriek and she can see into its insides, its raw red throat, the churning mass of flesh inside it that every so often looks like a face that she knows.

She does scream, then.

Then she turns and runs.

The monster skitters after her, legs pulling it up onto the wall, propelling it past her along the ceiling. She stares, frozen in horror, as the underside of it bubbles into a human head. The head turns a hundred and eighty degrees to stare at her. It's Nelson.

"You hurt me," it says, its tone almost petulant.

"You killed my friends!" she yells up at it.

The head droops lower, stretching, until its neck puddles on the floor behind it like Silly Putty. It lifts itself off the floor, right side up now, and drifts toward her like some horrible balloon.

"You *hurt* me," it says again. "I want . . . to know . . . how."

"It's *fire*, you stupid motherfucker," she hisses, pulling the tank tighter against her. "Guess you haven't seen a lot of that out here."

"Give it to me."

"Like fuck," she says. She's raising the nozzle, aiming right between its eyes, when it lurches sideways around her and lunges forward down the hall. The rest of it follows, dropping from the ceiling with a wet smack. It pulls its legs underneath it and races past her, after its head, and she turns in time to see it collide with the rest of its body.

The spider-monster *opens*, its skin splitting along an unseen seam, and the Ilse-monster simply steps into it. Still burning, still melting from shape to shape, it climbs inside itself and the body-mouth of the spider closes around it. The body contracts with a crunch. Then it turns to Riley, already changing.

Its neck retracts, Dae's head dragging along at the end of it, narrowing into something wolfish as it goes. The extra limbs are pulled in, adding to its bulk, and it stands up on two legs and keeps standing, somehow, stretching until its back is pressed to the ceiling and its long, curving neck swings down above Riley. It's still Dae's face, but the bottom half is all teeth, his features pulled inward into a short snout. His jaws loll open, spooling black liquid onto the floor. *Christ, I wish it had fur,* she thinks wildly. Its glistening skin, the way it shifts over its morphing bones, it's obscene. It's too human.

"I remembered . . . what you said," it growls at her. The mouth it's using is no longer one that was made for human speech, and the voice that comes from it is a harsh, squealing bark, the words almost indistinct. "*Snake . . . bear.* Is this . . . how you imagined?"

"No," Riley whispers, cowering backward. "It's not even real—"

"*I am real!*" it roars, spraying her with blood-tinged spit.

"But *what are you?!*" Riley screams, lashing out in desperation. The nozzle catches it in the face and pulls its lower jaw aside, yanking it out of alignment with its skull. "Where did you come from? What do you *want?*"

Something flickers across its face, an expression she almost recognizes in Dae's eyes. Uncertainty, maybe? Fear? Its head sways, one massive arm coming up to push its jaw back into place. Before it can she squeezes the trigger, sprays a huge jet of alcohol directly into its mouth, and flicks the lighter.

She doesn't wait to see if it catches, doesn't even let go of the handle until she's already running headlong in the other direction. Behind her there's a roar and the sound of splintering plastic, and the twin thumps of front limbs hitting the floor.

It's coming, she thinks. *It's coming and you're out of time, you're out of options, what the* fuck *is the plan, Riley Jane?*

She dodges around a corner, shedding the flamethrower as she goes, needing every encumbrance gone. The rat squeals as the hood of her coat bounces against her back. The lumbering steps of the monster behind her get louder, the sound of its wet clotted breathing closer and closer. She puts her head down and runs faster, putting everything she has left into it, the faintest thread of an idea unspooling in her mind.

She knocks over every piece of furniture that's left standing in the lab, smashing bottles and jars and shoving everything into a pile on top of the downed fridge. It won't buy her much time, but it might be enough. She unlaces her boot as fast as she can, hands shaking almost too hard to function, and rips the shoelace free. She jams her foot back into it and stumbles toward the drum of alcohol. She doesn't dare think about what happens if it's not full enough, if the lace isn't long enough. If this doesn't work she is going to die, that is just a fact, and Rusk will have his monster and the world will probably end. But she will die knowing she tried.

She loops the shoelace loosely around the bike-pump handle and drops the end of it into the drum. She fumbles the lighter free of her pocket and opens it, flicks it once, twice. "Come on," she pleads, wrapping one hand around the other to steady her useless, twitching fingers. "Please, please, please—"

It catches and flares, leaping high into the air above the wick, and she gives a short, sharp sob of relief. She touches the flame to the shoelace, below the little plastic thing she *knows* she knows the name of, and if she dies trying to think of the name of the little plastic shoelace thing wouldn't that just be—

The lace catches, the flame small and hesitant.

"Come on," she says again, glancing back at the ruined doorway to the lab. "Come on, little buddy, come on, you can do it."

The flame climbs a little higher, wraps itself more fully around the lace. It flares and shakes and then it moves, just a fraction, just enough that she can see it.

The monster's hand slams onto the floor beside her. She screams and lurches sideways, twisting as she falls to protect Basil, and starts half crawling, half running toward the electrical panel. She can hear it digging through the debris behind her, dragging itself through the splintered doorway.

"Riley!" it howls, that horrible voice-of-a-thousand-voices scraping along the walls behind her.

She launches herself over the edge of the hole in the wall, only this time she's prepared, and she holds on to the lip of it and her wrist twists and something pops and she doesn't let go, not until the front of her body slams into the wall on the other side of the hole and then she lets go and drops, her ankle at last giving way completely, the snap of bone inside her unlaced boot audible. She screams, agony and fear and rage all twined into one inhuman sound, and above her in the lab the monster screams with her. She crawls toward the hole in the wall, toward the tiny, tiny tunnel she prays will protect her, and she shoves herself into it headfirst. She worms her way in, scraping her face and her knuckles against the rough ground, no longer thinking at all. She is a being made of pain and terror, hurt poured into the shape of a human. She slides deeper into the tunnel, broken ankle grating as she kicks, waiting desperately for the sound she hopes to hear.

"*RILEY!*"

She screams. It's so much closer than it should be, close enough that it bounces off the little space inside the electrical panel, and she knows she's failed. The monster is inside the lab, inside the electrical closet, and in another moment it will heave itself over the side of the wall into the hole, and it will hit the ground in a puddle of its own body, and then its long, long arm will snake out into the tunnel and wrap around her legs and drag her, screaming, to her death.

She closes her eyes. "I'm sorry, Basil," she whispers. She doesn't even know if the rat is still alive. It might be better if he isn't, she thinks. Then the monster can't have him. She wonders if it will eat her whole, or if it will leave her in the tunnel to smother, all the while infesting her slowly, eating her from the inside out. "I'm sorry, Luke. Everyone. Mom."

Her voice breaks on the last word. She had been so eager to leave, to get out of the house and onto a different continent. Her mother had said *Bye, sweet girl, I love you,* and she had gotten out of the car and slammed the door and said *I'll email you when I get there,* and she hadn't even done that. Her parents won't even know she's dead for another week when she doesn't make her flight back to the States. Tears leak from her eyes, dripping onto the metal beneath her. She wonders if they'll ever know what happened to her, if they'll find Dae's flash drive. If Rusk will ever let anyone say anything, about anything. Maybe he'll tell them she had a panic attack and killed everyone. A final insult. She sniffles.

Then the entire world shakes beneath her.

A WAVE OF HEAT ROLLS PAST HER, CHOKING AND blistering, and there's a flash of light so bright she can see it through her closed eyelids. The smell of singed hair fills the tunnel.

She opens her eyes.

It worked.

The drum of alcohol has exploded, and now—hopefully—now everything else in the lab is catching, adding fuel to the fire, surrounding the monster in flames it can't shapeshift its way out of. Spreading to the ceiling, the walls, swallowing the entire station. She thinks she's safe here, underground in the tunnel, but even if she isn't . . .

It worked. Probably. Hopefully.

She listens to the roar of flames, the crackle of melting plastic. The crunch of what she hopes is the ceiling collapsing.

Then the screaming starts. A high, unearthly keening sound, a shriek like nothing she's ever heard, one that vibrates in her bones and teeth and bounces around the inside of her skull until she thinks her eyes will burst. It's a cry of pain, but there's such *anguish* in it, such fear, that it brings tears to her eyes again. The monster is burning to death somewhere above her, and she should feel satisfaction, and she *does*, but. It's a sentient creature, something with a sense of self, and it never thought it could die. *I am real*, it had said to her, and it was, and she has killed it. She cries for it, and for her dead friends and for herself, and it doesn't make her feel any better.

The ground shakes beneath her again, only this time it feels different. It doesn't feel like it's coming from above her but below. It's a low, shifting, grinding motion, almost like—

Sliding.

"Oh shit," she murmurs, and then there's a lurch so violent it jerks her out of place and then she is, she's sliding backward out of the tunnel, because the space under the station is collapsing beneath her.

She wriggles while she's sliding, trying to speed up the process, and when she emerges into the little chamber below the electrical panel she gasps.

The whole ceiling is gone, burned away, and the rest of the room isn't far behind. She takes off her boot, the one with the shoelace, and unlaces it. She laces the other boot so tightly around her broken ankle that it makes her vision swim. Then she stands up, weight on her good foot, and jumps.

She hoists herself back into the electrical closet with a groan, letting herself drop hands-first to the floor. She drags her legs through the hole carefully, then gets to her feet. She limps out of the closet into a world of carnage.

The lab is gone, obliterated. The fridge is a charred lump on the floor and the rest of the furniture might as well have never existed. The door, the walls, the *ceiling*—all of it is gone. The light above her is the goddamn sun. She picks her way across the floor carefully, stepping into the hall on legs that shake like a newborn fawn's. She can hear the fire, and when she turns her head she can see it, shimmering along the walls. She wonders if the monster's body contained it somehow, dampened it, caused it to shunt sideways like this. The dorms are almost completely untouched. Her injured foot bumps into something and her knees buckle at the pain, and she topples into a heap on the floor next to her flamethrower. Somehow still here, somehow still intact. She pulls the tank into her lap, cradling it like a baby.

"Basil?" she asks, reaching over her shoulder. "Buddy? Are you—are you in there?"

She takes the coat off carefully, pulling it around so she can look in the hood. The rat is curled into the bottom of the pouch. He's so still.

"Oh, Basil," she says. "I'm so sorry."

She reaches out to stroke his fur, one light brush with a fingertip, to apologize, and his beady eyes blink open.

"Basil!" she yelps. "Are you—were you seriously just asleep that whole time? Are you *good?* Are you okay?"

She tucks her hand under him and he stretches, one little leg after another, and then he runs right up her arm and plops down under her hair.

"Oh my God," she murmurs, tilting her head to nuzzle him with her cheek. "You guys really are survivors."

She stands up slowly, bracing herself on the wall, and puts the coat back on. She plucks Basil off her shoulder and tucks him into an inside pocket. He looks up at her balefully.

"I know," she says. "But we're gonna be outside, and I don't know for how long, and I can't have you freezing to death after you survive a literal explosion, okay?"

He blinks. She zips the pocket shut, then unzips it just a tiny bit so he can breathe. Then she zips up the coat and hoists the flamethrower over her shoulder.

"One more thing," she says.

The stuff in her bedroom catches so easily. She has a brief, giddy moment of pure joy as the sheets go up and the flames climb the walls, and she thinks about her freshman English teacher reading *It was a pleasure to burn* off the first page of a tattered copy of *Fahrenheit 451*. It is a pleasure, strange as it seems. There's something powerful in it, and cleansing. She sweeps the flamethrower back and forth in a smooth arc as heat billows around her. The ceiling licks the fire up from the walls fast and hot, burning paint and plastic drifting free to land on her head and shoulders. She backs through the door, fire still dripping from the nozzle, and moves down the hallway to Dae's room. When she emerges again the walls are burning, the hallway a rapidly-narrowing fiery gauntlet. She does each room as the ceiling buckles overhead, as flames bite through her clothes. She has to. She can't say why, but it feels right.

She does the kitchen last. It's already starting to catch, in the back hallway where the pantry is, and she has a brief pang of regret about the Pop-Tarts, but it's too late for them. She burns it all.

She pauses by the front door, picks up her own coat, then drops it back on the floor. "This one's lucky," she says to Basil.

She steps outside just in time to watch the barn collapse in on itself, taking the last snowmobile with it. *Fucking Rusk and his fucking tunnels and his fucking drill,* she thinks. *Look at it all now.*

"At least the storm is over," she mutters. Her face is already freezing, despite the residual heat from the fire. She wonders if she should stay close, keep warm until someone comes to get her. Then the ground shakes under her feet again, sending a bolt of pain through her ankle.

Over the roar of the fire, she hears a new sound, a distant drone that resolves into a throbbing pulse that drills its way into her eardrums, and then she sees the helicopter. Her first instinct is to beckon it toward her, but then she realizes it's too soon, and too impractical, for it to be anyone but Rusk. This black dragonfly swooping toward her—this is not a rescue.

She turns away from the helicopter and grits her teeth.

She runs.

"AND YOU KNOW THE REST," SHE SAYS. "AM I GOING to get to go to a hospital at any point, or is Rusk going to have you take me back out there and shoot me?"

Good Cop flinches at that, but Bad Cop just looks at her levelly. "Is that what you think he'd do?"

"Is it not?"

They hold each other's gaze for a moment. Good Cop finally breaks in. "We can get you some more painkillers, Riley, and we will," he says placatingly. "But we can't let you go just yet. Not until we understand what happened."

"I just told you what happened," she says. She feels indignant, somewhere far away, but it's blunted by exhaustion and Vicodin or whatever it is they've given her, and she can't get her tone to reflect her emotions.

"You told us—" Bad Cop slaps her hand onto the table. "You told us some kind of, of *fairy tale* about Anton Rusk using *children* as *bait* to catch a shapeshifting *monster*—"

"You saw the hole, right?" Riley asks her. "When you flew in. You saw the crater where the station was."

"Yes," Bad Cop snaps.

"So you know I'm right about the drilling."

"I don't know that," she says. "And even if there was drilling, which again I'm not saying there was, we don't know that it was Anton Rusk who was doing it. He could have bought that station well after any kind of illegal drilling operation was taking place."

"But he didn't," Riley says.

Bad Cop sighs.

"And if I'm right about the drilling . . ." Riley lifts her hand, marveling as she does at how quickly the frostbite on her index and middle fingers is advancing now, even indoors. "Why can't I be right about the monster?"

"There's no evidence," Good Cop says. "You have to see that, Riley. There's nothing in that station that proves any of this."

"Rusk has a video of it," she says. "He found it when he was checking in on his little drilling operation. It's in the cloud."

"Even if he does," Good Cop says, "what does that prove? That there's an unidentified creature in the Antarctic that a prominent eco-tech CEO is interested in finding?"

Riley deflates a little. Then she perks back up. "There were cameras everywhere," she says. "He was watching us. The monster would be on there."

Good Cop looks almost like he's disappointed in her, and she knows this is an interview tactic, this is Good Cop 101, but it does tug at something inside her. She presses her lips shut, reaches to pet Basil.

"Can I have something else to eat?" she asks when it becomes clear they're not going to say anything more.

"I'll find something," Good Cop says, shoving his chair back and slamming out of the room. She's surprised to see him show frustration.

"He doesn't like being jerked around," Bad Cop says, reading her face.

"I'm not—"

"Look, kid. I don't care. I mean that, that's God's honest truth. I do not give a *shit*. I get paid whether or not you tell us what really happened, and I'm not the one with an arrest warrant waiting stateside."

Riley blinks. "What?"

"You *at minimum* committed arson. If we can find any of the others' bodies, then there's negligent manslaughter. Tack on your history of, mm, mental instability and paranoia, I'll bet you we can get that up to murder two if we try. And that's before we even get into the financial side of things. The property destruction, the expedition resources, the irreplaceable scientific material."

Bad Cop smiles slightly. The words are having their intended effect, cutting through the fog of numbness around Riley's thoughts like a scalpel. Her heart rate starts to kick up, her breathing gets shallower. She puts her hands in her lap and twists them around each other.

Bad Cop leans toward her. "If your story is true," she says in a low, silky voice, "why would you think we would ever let you live?"

"What?"

"If this monster is real, there's no question you're infected," Bad Cop continues. "We couldn't let you leave. We'd have to quarantine you, watch you, study you. *Sample* you."

"Did you say *leave* the first time, or—"

"Unless." Bad Cop lifts a finger. "Unless you confess. We can get you a good lawyer, get those charges down to reckless endangerment. You'd be looking at community service, nothing more."

Riley's head swims. She's suddenly too warm. "Is there more water?" she asks, licking her cracked lips.

"If you sign a nondisclosure agreement, we can make this go away," Bad Cop says, almost whispering. "If you promise to never, ever say anything about what you think happened here—"

"It happened!" Riley slams her hands onto the table, curling them into fists when she realizes how hard they're shaking. "It happened."

"No one will ever believe you," Bad Cop says.

"Why are you doing this?" Riley whispers, a tear sliding down her cheek.

"Don't you want to go home, Riley? See your parents? Have a chance to live a normal life?"

"I—"

"That can still happen. All you have to do is tell us what really happened. Tell us how you killed them. Tell us where their bodies are. We can make it go away, I promise you."

Riley bows her head. She stares at her hands, the mottled black tips of her fingers. She tries to imagine a trial, the sharp slice of the word *Guilty* across the silent courtroom. Pictures from television spill across her mind; handcuffs, jumpsuit, jail van. Hard-eyed girls waiting to get her alone in the yard. No more trips to the beach, ankle-deep in the tide pools watching the starfish undulate. No more movie theater. No more books, probably; do they let you have books in prison? No more—

Wait—

She lifts her head.

"I'm still a minor," she says triumphantly. "Even if they do put me away, I'm out at eighteen."

"That's true," Bad Cop says. "But think about the media, and how much publicity surrounds every single thing Anton Rusk ever says or does. Imagine that magnifying glass turned on you the second you get out."

She thinks about how it will look, what it will do to her parents to see her splashed across the news. *Homicidal teen blames morphing snow monster for murder! "We always knew she'd snap someday," a former friend confided. Could pharmaceuticals be to blame? Where did Mom and Dad go wrong? Why did they let her out? Click here to learn how to keep YOUR child safe from conspiracy theorist killers!*

"How do I know you won't do that anyway?" Riley asks.

"You don't," Bad Cop says. "And you never will. That shoe could drop at any time, for any reason, for the rest of your life."

"I just wanted a chance to escape." Riley's voice shakes. "Just for a little while, just to be . . . to see if I could be different. I just wanted . . . the space. To change."

She can't look up, can't bear to see the derision she knows is plain on Bad Cop's face. She's so fucking tired.

"Show me what you want me to sign," she says quietly. "But can I—can I call my parents first? So they know I'm okay?"

Bad Cop smiles like she's about to bite.

"I think we can manage that."

AS SOON AS SHE LEAVES THE ROOM RILEY STARTS
picking at the seam of her sleeve, shielding the motion from the
camera as best as she can.

Can't say Asha never taught me anything.

She slides Dae's tiny storage drive out of the hole and tucks it
into her cuff, pinned between her wrist and the fabric. When Bad
Cop comes back she's sitting calmly, hands flat on the table.
Bad Cop puts an iPhone on the table in front of her.

"It's unlocked," she says. "Make it quick."

Riley nods.

"The camera is on," Bad Cop says.

Then she leaves.

Riley coughs into her hand, surreptitiously hitting the little
sync button Dae had shown her. A small white light flashes once,
twice, then burns steadily. It's found the phone. She taps the
screen, pulls it toward her.

Daetripper wants to send you something.

Accept.

Downloading.

She taps her parents' phone number into the phone, watching
the light on the drive. It's flashing again, thinking hard as it
pours data onto the phone. She presses the round red button with
the *X* and puts the phone to her ear.

She watches the light, counting slowly. She's at ten Mississippi when the light goes solid white again.

"Hey, guys," she says. She doesn't have to fake the wobble in her voice. "It's me. Um. Some stuff happened on the trip and I'm coming home early, but I'm okay. I'll explain everything when I see you. I just . . . I just love you both so much. Okay? I just want you to know that, how much I love you. I'm sorry I didn't say it back when I got out of the car, Mom. I should have." Tears brim in her eyes and spill over, and she wishes she were actually recording this, actually leaving them with something kind to remember her with. She knows they won't let her go home, no matter what lies Bad Cop tells her.

She pulls the phone away from her face just enough to jab the email icon.

Compose.

Attach file.

Uploading . . .

"Well, I guess you're not home," she says, wiping her nose gingerly. "I wish you were. Or maybe you are, and it's night there, in which case I'm sorry I'm blathering in the kitchen while you're trying to sleep."

A quick glance. Still uploading.

"I really miss you," she whispers. "More than I thought I would. And I'm so excited to see you. Both of you. I'm gonna hug the shit out of you. The crap. Sorry. I . . . I love you. I know I said that, I just . . . feel like I should say it more. Like, all the time."

Upload complete.

"I'll see you really soon." Her voice cracks into a sob. "I love you both so much."

She pulls the phone from her ear and enters the email address Dae had scrawled in the front of his notebook. She hits Send as Bad Cop slams the door open.

"Are you done?" she demands.

Riley smiles at her through the tears as another wave of exhaustion crashes over her.

"I'm done," she says, barely above a whisper. She puts the phone on the table. "And so are you, and so is Anton Rusk."

They both look at the screen.

Sent!

So cheery. Thanks, email.

"You little bitch," Bad Cop whispers. She spins toward the door. "DONNIE!"

Good Cop bursts in a moment later, looking frazzled. "What?"

"She sent an email," Bad Cop says.

He sighs, turns the disappointed face on her like high beams. She just looks at him.

"It's fine," he says. "The other one signed."

The room tilts around Riley. All the blood rushes to her head and then away from it, shooting through her veins, waking up all the pain her body has worked too hard to put to sleep. She sways in the chair, grabbing the table to keep herself from falling.

"The what?" she asks thinly. "What?"

Good Cop looks at her, eyes flat and hard, and she knows he was never really Good Cop. They're both Bad Cop.

"The other one," he says. "The other survivor. Did we not mention him?"

"Who is it?" Riley asks, trying to push herself to her feet. She's been sitting for too long; her legs are asleep, her movements clumsy. She's caught in the chair somehow, her mind reeling as she tries to absorb this unbelievable new idea. The humming sound rises in her ears, and she raises her voice over it. "Who— Luke? Is it Luke?"

"It is indeed," he says.

Tears spill from her eyes, stinging her ravaged face. *He's alive.* Luke is alive. Relief and triumph flood her body, smoothing her movements, and she shoves the chair back from the table.

"I want to see him."

"Too late," Bad Cop says. "He's already in the chopper."

Riley's mind is tripping over itself, poring back over the hours in the interview. He'd been here the whole time. The *whole time*, and she'd never realized. Telling them the same story she'd been—

"Wait," she says. She forgets about her ankle until she stands, and it buckles and sends her crashing to the floor. She tries to push herself up, but her arms are so heavy, and her fingers are numb. She lifts her head as high as she can and looks at them. "He'd never sign that."

"And yet," Donnie Bad Cop says, sliding a folded piece of paper out of his jacket, "he did." He hands the paper to Original Bad Cop, who tucks it into her folder with a smug smile.

"He wouldn't," Riley whispers. Her head dips as she tries to hold it up. "Why would he . . ."

For me.

To protect me.

"Oh no. Oh, Luke, no."

She closes her eyes. The humming sound is so loud now, all around her. Her forehead meets the floor. She lifts her head again and dizziness washes over her. She grabs for the chair leg weakly. She has to get up. *Get up, Riley.* She grabs again, misses again. Her eyes fall on her discarded water bottle, knocked off the table when she shoved the chair back.

"What . . . did you give me?" she pants. Everything is so heavy. It's hard to breathe.

"Nothing," Donnie Bad Cop says. He crouches in front of her, looking almost confused. "Is she going into shock?"

"She's been in shock," Original Bad Cop says. "She's probably dying. I mean, we gave her enough drugs to kill someone who *wasn't* already halfway out the door."

"I thought most of those were stimulants," he mutters,

reaching out to pry one of Riley's eyelids up. "Jesus, Meg, he's not gonna like this."

"We'll just put her in the station," Original Bad Cop says dismissively, from the end of a tunnel a thousand miles away. Her voice buzzes against Riley's ears. "Burn her."

The humming sound rises, rises, drowns out the bad cops and their faraway voices until it's all she can hear, drilling into her head like an ice pick. She screams and clutches at her head, trying to block it out, writhing on the floor of the interview room. Every part of her *hurts* and she can't make it stop and she's so *tired*. She thrashes, catching the table leg with her broken ankle, and screams again. She claws at the floor, hitching brokenly toward the cops. She doesn't know what she's doing, where she's trying to go, she just wants the *pain* to *stop*, God, please, make it stop. Her vision is narrowing, drawing slowly inward. She reaches out, somehow managing to roll onto her side, and as her head turns her tunneling vision sees movement at the door.

"Luke," she gasps, and it is. It *is*. He's walking past the interview room right now, flanked by other cops, healthy and whole and looking in the other direction, and when she says his name this time it's a scream.

"LUKE!"

His head turns almost in slow motion, his gaze raking across the glass window set into the door. She can feel the moment he sees her. The humming sound stops, the pain stops, for one incredible, blissful moment she is completely outside of her body as they make eye contact, and that's when she knows.

"No," she says as he lunges for the door. Bad Cop slams her body against it as the cops in the hall start yanking Luke away. "No, wait—no, you don't understand—"

"Riley!" Luke yells. The doorknob rattles and for a moment she thinks he'll make it, burst into the room with them, and then the other cops drag him back again. He slaps a hand against the glass, fingertips scrabbling for a hold on the doorframe as he says her name, and then he's gone.

Riley starts laughing. The sound comes from far away, somewhere deep inside her, and it bubbles out of her in shrieks. She laughs until her body hurts again.

"What possibly," says Bad Cop, nudging her with the toe of her boot.

"He's . . . infected," Riley wheezes. "And you're letting him go back."

She grabs for Bad Cop's foot, or tries, but her arm won't cooperate.

"Yeah, yeah," Bad Cop says. "You had your chance."

"You're so fucking stupid," she whispers. Blackness crawls, prickly and fibrous, at the edge of what vision she has left. She stares at the ceiling. *You're letting it out,* she tries to say. *Rusk's monster. Our monster.*

"It's for the best," Original Bad Cop says. "He'll be better on TV anyway. *Isolation madness,* I think we're gonna call it. The defense, I mean. He'll be famous. Good famous. Everyone loves an acquittal."

Riley sucks in one last breath, almost convulsing with effort. "It's not him," she gasps, and then her lungs seize and hitch and stop moving altogether. The blackness swirls, lashing across her eyes in curling, seething tendrils. She tries to hold on, tries to keep the room in focus. She drags her head up off the ground, just far enough to see Basil once more. He blinks at her over the edge of the Tupperware and she feels a wash of love, a throb of it so strong it hurts her heart, for Basil and for Luke and for Ilse, Dae, Nelson, Greta, even Asha, even the fucking bad cops. She sees herself getting off the plane, her parents crying as she runs to them. She sees Luke in the desert silhouetted by the sun atop some gigantic rock formation. Nelson hugging his mom, Dae accepting a Pulitzer, Ilse and Greta unveiling some sort of ozone-renewing machine. Asha getting married. A thousand different lives unfold before her in the blink of an eye, and she can't hold on to any of them, and Luke is getting in the helicopter.

Her head drops to the floor with a hollow, final sound, and then there's only darkness.

"COME ON," ORIGINAL BAD COP SAYS. "I NEED SOME fucking coffee. We'll get the new guy, the one you hate, he can clean that up." She doesn't even glance at the girl on the floor as she says it.

"I really think Rusk is gonna be proud of us," Donnie Bad Cop says. "Obviously this is a colossal cock-up, but all things considered, I think we handled it, you know?"

"We'll have to do something about that email," Original Bad Cop says. "Find out who she sent it to, see if we can get them doxxed or SWATted or something. I mean, maybe just a drug charge. We don't have to get fancy with it."

"We'll find 'em," Donnie Bad Cop says, holding the door for her. "What kind of contacts could a seventeen-year-old have, anyway? She probably sent it to her *bestie*."

Original Bad Cop laughs. "That one didn't have any friends, remember? She probably sent it to her mommy."

"Even better. The crazed rantings of a grief-stricken mother. They'll eat her alive." A small, contented sigh. "God, I love this job."

Across the ocean, in a coffee shop, Dae's brother—the assistant editor-in-chief of one of South Korea's most prominent newspapers—receives an email from an address he doesn't recognize, blank except for an attachment with a nonsense filename. He hovers over the Mark as Spam button for a moment, then clicks.

Then it hits him, a flicker of recognition, and he drags it back out of the trash.

upload917438ht03lun11.daetripper.zip

He clicks Open.

Tingling, again, but this time it doesn't hurt. This time it's almost pleasant, a warmth instead of a burn, and it spreads like the glow of candlelight.

In the darkened interview room, on the floor, Riley's fingers twitch. They curl into a fist, whole and healthy and pink with blood.

Her eyes, when they open, are wide and clear.

And dark.

acknowledgments

HERE WE ARE AGAIN. IN THE INTEREST OF TIME, AND understanding that the generosity extended by most to reading through the acknowledgments of my first book—at that time my only book and therefore my only chance to say thank you to so many people—will probably have worn thin at this point, I will do my best here to be succinct.

Rena: You are the best agent, and a remarkable person, and I am so grateful to have you in my corner. You make everything happen.

Lauren: I have said this a lot but it needs to be said again. You are an amazing editor, one I have been blessed to work with, and it means the world and a half that you chose me on purpose this time.

Meg Baskis, Tamara Grasty, Franny Donington, Meg Palmer, Hayley Gundlach, and Mary Beth Garhart: Thank you all so much for working with me, making my dreams come true, and giving this book life. Special thanks to Julia Tyler for a truly incredible cover.

Amber McBride & Ally Malinenko: You get a dual acknowledgment because you were brought into my life as a duo, and we have become the best little hype squad, and I could not be more grateful. The two of you have a rare and precious combination of talent and empathy and it makes everything you write absolutely shine. You have both made me cry so many tears and I just respect the absolute hell out of you. You have made me a better writer, you have brought so much love and joy into my life, and I am so, so glad to call you both my friends.

Liz Parker: We started as critique buddies and now you are part of the fabric of my life, and it seems so strange that that has not always been the case. You are so smart, so incisive, so good at seeing where things need to change and grow, and it is an absolute gift that you have given me in looking at my work. I am so grateful for your friendship, and your insight, and your uncanny ability to send excellent witchy gifts that are exactly what I need. I am so, so glad that I will finally get to hold your book in my hands this year, and to shriek to the world about how good a writer you are, and to see things continue to blossom for you.

Ania Stypulkowski: This is a little bit of a joke but also it's not, at all, because you are one of my favorite people on this earth and it's almost alarming how fast that happened. You are a treasure; your practicality and levelheadedness and general competence have saved my ass more than once during the course of this book and generally in the last few years of my life, and your friendship makes my life more fun every single day. It is truly an honor to be someone you care about and I love you dearly.

Brad Steinike, Rachael Edwards, Alex Schaffner: Thank you for being the most enthusiastic early readers I have ever known, for cheerleading me and supporting me and showing up for me. Alex, thank you especially for braving the body horror (and for being the best event host I've had so far!). I appreciate you all so much.

At this point, if your name was featured in the acknowledgments for *To Break A Covenant*, please insert all of that feeling here again. It's all still true. I love you all endlessly.

Mom, Dad, Mason: I'm never going to get over those shirts. I'm really not. Your support and encouragement lights up a part of my heart that will never go out, and I can't ever say enough about how important it is to me. I love you.

Emily: This one's for you, baby girl. We joke but you are absolutely the source of inspiration in my life, no matter how you express it. You keep me sane, you keep me going, you sometimes unintentionally keep me humble. I'm so glad this book's hair is small. I love you forever.

Semi-finally, to Leelu, who still cannot read: You gigantic stripey bitch. You tried to delete 40k of this manuscript and you almost succeeded, and you still love Emily more than me. I'm so glad I saved you from a life on the streets and spend all my book money buying you crinkle toys.

Finally, most importantly, hugely importantly, and I can say this now because I know you exist: READERS. You are out there. You read my first book, and hopefully did not hate it, and in a lot of cases definitely didn't hate it and wrote reviews and made playlists and took some truly impeccable glamourshots. You showed up for me in a way I could not have dared to hope for. You are the only reason that *Covenant* was quote-unquote successful, and that success is what made this book possible. You are literally, literally making my dreams come true, and I can never thank you enough. I hope you stick around.

about the author

ALISON AMES IS THE AUTHOR OF *TO BREAK A Covenant*. She lives in Colorado with a lot of animals and her almost-wife. She loves birds and dislikes using the word "fiancée." Find her on social media @2furiosa, and if you know (or are) Harry Styles, she insists you do so.